Change of Possession

Book One of The Sheepfold

JT Dwyer

http://www.dwyerbooks.com

ISBN: 979-8-9864007-0-9

Cover Art by Ann Kuta Creative

Edited by Susan Ciancio

Produced in the United States of America

Dwyer, JT

Change of Possession, Book One of The Sheepfold

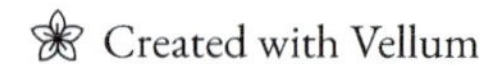

Acknowledgments

I have done a terrible disservice to the beautiful city of Asheville. To this day, you can't find a better place—a place where there is still civility and even affection between people of drastically different worldviews. Asheville is a crafty, artsy, hippie city. But it's also a redneck good-old-boy city, an entrepreneur's city, and a city of Southern Ladies and Southern Gentlemen. Everyone seems to get along. This is not particularly reflected in *Change of Possession*. In a sense, I let the broader world come and infect the city. In the process, I misappropriated the beautiful campus of UNC Asheville to Biltmore College, had Vanderbilt's architecture migrate north, plopped farms right where they couldn't be, changed the flow of rivers, moved Lake Martin from Alabama and renamed it Lake Juniper, and invented stockyards and churches and schools and put them wherever I liked. Consequently, anyone looking for the city described in the following pages will be pleasantly surprised to find the real Asheville in its place.

This work was born out of years of thought, but once begun carved courses that I never intended. In a terrifying sense, the book wrote itself. The characters took on lives and actions that I never purposed but that could not be erased without invalidating the characters themselves. Writing it was painful, joyful, and both enlivening and utterly draining.

I have, of course, many people to thank. First of all is my wife Elizabeth, who despite her love of chickens and Liane Moriarty books, bears no other resemblance to Anne Norris. Second is my friend Les, with whom I reconnected after decades. I started writing a couple of weeks after his visit, and his encouragement and wisdom as he read each draft were critical in the completion. Without him, this book never would have been written.

I also need to thank Will, who gave me essential insights into the various levels of football, which of course, I had never experienced, and to Kelley Griffin, who set a great example as a successful author and gave me excellent advice. My gratitude goes to Susan Ciancio, my editor, who abided with my grammar and awful punctuation and who helped resolve various plot and development issues.

Thanks as well to my beta readers: Erich, Greg, Warren, and Fr. Charlie.

Finally, despite the profanity and depravity that are the soul of this book, I hope that I have invested well the meager talents I have been given.

A.M.D.G.

J.T. Dwyer

The Omni Grove Park Inn
Asheville, NC
January 2022

We sit by and watch the barbarian. We tolerate him in the long stretches of peace. We are not afraid. We are tickled by his irreverence; his comic inversion of our old certitudes and our fixed creed refreshes us; we laugh. But as we laugh we are watched by large and awful faces from beyond, and on these faces there are no smiles.

– Hilaire Belloc

Prologue

The lake water—a vivid, almost unnatural shade of green—lapped the hull of the gently rocking houseboat.

The vessel showed every one of its thirty years of use, from the black oxidation on the exposed aluminum to the fading green accent paint and the scrapes and scars of many an encounter with floating debris.

Far below, in the hidden folds of the lake bottom, silt drifted silently down to the flooded homesteads and the graves of Indians and slaves and hillbillies.

Though the boat was secured both fore and aft by Davis anchors and though the cove was sheltered by high banks and thick trees, a fickle breeze still snuck through, nudging the vessel from side to side in the play of its mooring.

And as the boat swayed, so too did the forearm of Mandy Boyd, which, not yet stiffened, hung over the side of the couch. Her hand swung from the sleeve of her boyfriend's St. Ambrose High School letterman jacket, her forefinger pointing downward toward the crumpled leaves of plastic pill wrappers that littered the matted rug. The glossy curvature of one dead eye reflected both the light from the window and the bodies of the other three teenagers, their images distorted like figures in an M.C. Escher drawing.

In the corner, the space heater chugged along, keeping the cabin cozy and warm on that cool lake morning.

Part One

Interregnum

CHAPTER 1

PRESUMPTION

Anne Norris completed the Liturgy of the Hours at Lauds and rose from her kneeling posture on the prie-dieu in the sunroom of her home. The Canticle of Zechariah was fresh in her mind:

> In the tender compassion of our God
> the dawn from on high shall break upon us,
> to shine on those who dwell in darkness and the
> shadow of death,
> and to guide our feet into the way of peace.

She felt a serenity that was seldom present at other times of the day. The rest of the house was quiet. The sun was rising over the fields, and the vista opened up before her as she raised her eyes to look through the window. Patches of fog lay low in the hollows of the field, and the risen sun blazed hotly through the atmosphere. Oaks were islands in the dell, rising out of the misty blanket. The high pasture was already clear, and far away her horses—one speckled, one black, one hoary white—were grazing. The donkey that kept the coyotes at bay stood lazily munching hay instead of the fresh grass.

Anne sighed involuntarily and turned her back on the window. Stepping through the great room and into the kitchen, she took her favorite mug from the cupboard. It was a simple, small, white mug with a stylized cross centered upon five linked Escher-like doves flying in a circle and the words IUBILAEUM A.D. 2000 in a circle around the cross. The mug was her one souvenir from the advent of the new millennium, purchased while she and Dane were in Rome. She filled it with coffee from the fresh-brewed pot and mixed in a vanilla creamer. Taking her mug with her, she went through the sunroom to the back deck of the house and settled into a wrought iron chair behind a similar table to watch the sun rise.

It took only a moment before she processed the moisture that was beginning to seep through her silk pajamas, and she hastily leapt up, spilling some of her coffee. Every day she made the same mistake. *I should know better!* she chided herself. She set her mug down and pulled a dry towel from the chest that stood by the door to the deck, left there for just this purpose. Draping the towel over the chair, she took her seat again and resumed her peace.

At forty-six years old, Anne Norris was still a striking woman—tall and heavily built, but well-proportioned, though she didn't think so herself. She felt her age deeply and fought hard against its onset. She knew her body was thicker, and she watched her weight creep up and up. *Vanity of vanities, all is vanity,* she thought to herself, grappling with her pride. Her brunette hair was held back by a headband to keep it under the mantilla that she wore during the Liturgy of the Hours, as her head bobbed up and down reading through the prayers. Her deep-brown eyes, set under thick, arched eyebrows, squinted at the light of the rising sun. All in all, she had the strong, straight features that marked her Polish ancestry, and for whatever she might think about her figure, she knew she was beautiful and that it was sinful to think so.

Despite her outward calm, Anne was riven by fissures. Who could not be, who took the gospel seriously and yet who lived in peace and luxury? Her husband's fortune was un-squandered and invested—unlike so many of his NFL teammates—a fact that she took silent credit for, though without enhancing her self-opinion. She put it down to a miserly upbringing. And, in fact, she had remonstrated with herself for clinging to the growing financial accounts and arguing against any spending, until sophistry convinced her that hoarding it was a greater evil than spending it. *Easier for a camel to pass through the eye of a needle* she heard her inner voice say. And she sipped her coffee.

In a few moments, she would go out to the barn to check on the new hatchlings, warm under their incubator lamp. Her matured chickens would cluck and caw in their roost, brazenly trumpeting their production of eggs. Her thick lips turned up at the corners in a smile as she thought of Dane's mockery of her "chicken math," which had turned a half-dozen chickens (just for fresh eggs!) into a dozen, and would be more, counting this year's hatchlings.

With the growing number of chickens, the horses, the donkey, the dogs, the goats, the vegetable garden, the herb garden, the flowerbeds, a Christmas Tree field, an orchard, and all the sundry houseplants, Anne had to break down and hire a hand—a flighty, earthy young woman, probably a hippie, who arrived midmorning to help with the farm work. This, combined with the cleaning lady who came daily to pick up after her sons and husband, the trainer who worked with the horses, and the trainer who exercised with her, had made her realize that she had servants. The awareness shocked her system. *The rich young man went away sad, for he had many possessions.*

She broke out of her reverie. Her coffee was done. She had work to do before the Little Hours, and of course had to exercise, shower, and dress for the drive into Asheville for noon Mass.

She tiptoed back into the house and peeked into the kids' wing of the sprawling home. Dylan's and Janus' doors were both closed (and, she presumed, locked). Maryanne's was open, of course, for she was grown and gone and who-knows-where. Emilia's door was also open, and she slept soundly, still relishing the late mornings now that the school year was over. Turning back down to the other side of the house, past the kitchen, she tiptoed through the bedroom where Dane lay snoring, a massive bulk of a man made still more massive under piles of pillows. Only his head was exposed to the cool air. Dane kept the thermostat at 67 degrees year-round and then piled blankets on top of himself at night. He would have had it colder if he could, but he relented when seeing little Emilia shivering in the middle of summer.

Changing into jeans and her high rubber boots, she crept back out of the bedroom. The dogs, knowing her routine, wagged their tails and rose, stretching, from their dog beds at the side of the room. The Weimaraner (Buddy) and golden retriever (Jingles) were old enough now that their energy wasn't completely overwhelming, but they delighted in this morning jaunt out to the barn, and so did Anne.

Anne opened the door, and the dogs bolted out into the dew-coated grass, running this way and that, peeing periodically, then peeing where the other dog had just gone, in a sort of double-helix pattern. They wove roughly around her straight path to the tractor barn.

Inside the barn, she checked the temperature of the hatchlings, freshened their water, filled their feed tray, and checked the security of the wire cover to their incubator tank. The dogs sniffed around the barn and then followed her to the chicken coop. Retrieving this morning's eggs, she put them in her basket, and shutting the door on the complaining chickens, headed back up to the house.

Dane awoke with a start, his apnea deciding it was time for him to rise. He rolled over to realize that Anne was already up, as her side of the mattress felt cold to his touch. He swung his legs over the side of the bed, feeling every aching bone and muscle, and came to his feet. Padding into his slippers, wrapping his terrycloth robe around himself, he ventured forth into the kitchen, poured the remainder of the pot of coffee into a mug, and stepped outside to the deck.

Anne was on her way back from the barn, the dogs cavorting

around her. Her path down to the barn and the meandering paths of the dogs were dark trails through the silver-dewed grass. He watched her for a little while, smiling.

If there could be a counterpoint to Anne's acrobatic mind, it was Dane's. Self-satisfied and presumptive, Dane's mind was lethargic fat layered on the bones of a clever intellect. He was happy.

He had always been happy. A big, boisterous man who worked hard, played hard, and loved a good joke, especially at someone else's expense. Generous because he could be, and joyful because he could be, Dane had grown up with money, health, and of course, an athletic prowess that elicited envy and admiration. The only real tribulation he had known was the self-imposed discipline of football, though that was no trivial thing. If his belly was beginning to be distended, and a second (or third) chin was emerging over his bull neck, well, he could afford those things after a long career of punishing physical and psychological exertion. And he paid a constant price from the pain of old injuries and arthritic aches, numbed to some extent by a combination of pills and alcohol.

There were, of course, some emotional scars as well. Finally being cut at the end of his playing career was chief among them. To walk away from the locker rooms, after so many years of Thursday nights, Friday nights, Saturdays, and Sundays, was paralyzing (for a while). The absence of Maryanne—and his constant worry for her —sat in the recesses of his mind. But most days, it was far back, detached. And such hurts, perhaps also numbed by the pills and booze, were certainly also buried under the unrelenting tide of happiness brought by prosperity, a good wife, a sweet little girl, and fine sons who, he firmly believed, would eclipse his own success.

Dane's flat-top hair was fully grey now, although clipped so short it seemed silver instead. Crow lines had emerged at the sides of his brown eyes, made darker by a prominent forehead and bushy eyebrows that were still black, despite the greying of his hair. Clean-shaven, fist-nosed, and thin-lipped, Dane was still rugged even considering the growing softness of middle age.

He took a seat at the wrought iron table, ignoring the dew as it slowly seeped through his robe and then his flannel lounge pants, and sipped his coffee. Suddenly the dogs burst up the steps and onto the deck, rushing over to him and nuzzling his hands until he scratched them behind the ears. They took turns crowding him, pushing the other away, each demanding his full attention. As Anne surmounted the stairs, they rushed back to her and almost toppled her from the last step. She walked over to the table, placed the basketful of eggs in front of her, and sat down on her towel.

"Good morning," she said.

"Morning, honey."

"Only eleven today. I think Henrietta's not laying for some reason."

"I don't know how you tell the difference," Dane replied.

"Henrietta's eggs are blue," Anne answered, a little exasperated. She didn't understand how Dane could continue to be so obtuse with respect to the hens.

"What's the plan for today?" he asked.

"Nothing much. I was going to run into town for Mass. What are you doing?"

"I'll go with you. I can stop by campus while you're at church. Carter wants to see me about something."

"Okay. I guess the boys can watch Emilia."

Dane shrugged and returned his attention to his coffee. Anne watched him for a moment, then pulled her iPhone out of her pajama pocket.

Here comes Facebook, Dane thought to himself, as she started flipping through her news feed. They sat quietly for a few moments, the dogs settling themselves below the table, the Weimaraner's muzzle resting on the back of the golden. Then Anne gasped.

"Oh my God!" she breathed, as she put her hand to her mouth. There was something different in her tone that told Dane instantly that this wasn't just one of Anne's friends announcing a new puppy or some fresh outrage that Pope Francis had committed.

"What is it?"

"Hold on," she replied, and almost frantically touched her

phone screen and read. At last she looked up at Dane, an expression of horror on her face.

"You remember Peter Morton?"

"One of Dylan's friends?"

"They played baseball together at St. James. He's dead. And not just him. Three other kids."

"What? How?"

Anne's eyes were glued to her phone, and she kept reading as she replied.

"They found them yesterday on a houseboat. They think it was carbon monoxide poisoning."

"Terrible," Dane replied, but somewhat pacifically. Anne continued to read.

"It was on Kerry's Facebook page. She's friends with Peter's mother, Jennifer, I think. Oh how horrible! They were all in Dylan's class at St. Ambrose. They were all going to be seniors."

"Terrible," Dane repeated, and sipped his coffee.

Anne's peaceful morning slipped away as she gathered up what details were already on the Internet. The four teenagers had been found on the Morton's houseboat in a cove on Lake Juniper. The suspected cause was carbon monoxide poisoning from a space heater on the boat. Alongside Peter Morton, the NCWRA patrol had found his friend Doug Smith and their girlfriends Mandy Boyd and Sarah Hernandez—all rising seniors at St. Ambrose High.

Anne got up from the table and phoned her friend Kerry Logan, and Dane listened to a few moments of the one-sided conversation before finishing his coffee and retreating into the house. Inside the kitchen he found Emilia at the stovetop cooking scrambled eggs.

"Morning, Daddy," she said, and quickly followed her greeting with "Where's Mom?"

"Out on the deck, but give her a while. She got some bad news this morning."

"Awww," Emilia replied, unknowing, of course, the gravity of the news and responding in a simple, sympathetic way. Emilia had her mother's dark hair and big brown eyes and the spindly arms and legs of preadolescence. She was wearing faux-silk purple pajamas festooned with little cats in various troublemaking poses.

Anne came in quietly.

"Good morning, Mommy," Emilia said, scooping the scrambled eggs onto a plate. "Want some breakfast?"

"No thank you," Anne replied and turned to Dane.

"Did you tell Dylan?"

"No; I just came in."

"What happened, Mom?" Emilia asked, only slightly concerned.

"Something bad happened to one of Dylan's friends," Anne replied, then crossed over to Emilia and swept her into a smothering hug. She clung onto her for an uncomfortable moment and added, "One of his friends died in an accident."

"Oh that's terrible! Poor Dylan."

Anne broke off her hug and stood up straight. She looked purposefully toward the kids' wing of the house and walked across the sun-paneled floor of the kitchen. Reaching Dylan's door, she knocked quietly.

"Dylan?"

A muffled response came from inside. She tried the handle, and of course it was locked. She knocked again and repeated: "Dylan?"

A banging noise came from inside the room followed by heavy footsteps. The door opened, and Dylan stood there with a bare, furry torso and a navy-blue comforter wrapped around his bottom half. His eyes were sleepy slits, and his brown hair was ridiculously askew and piled up high on the side of his head that had met the pillow.

"What?" he asked, petulantly, and continued: "I don't have to be up yet. Let me sleep."

"Dylan, I need to tell you something," Anne replied, her voice full of concern. He caught the tone and rubbed his eyes with his free hand while the other held the comforter in place.

"Is this about Pete?" he asked, and seeing his mother's surprise he added, "It was going around last night. The word's all over. I know all about it."

Anne was taken aback, whether from the fact that he had known about this since last night or that he seemed unconcerned this morning, she couldn't say.

"Do you want to talk about it?" she asked.

Dylan stood there, a younger but bigger version of his father, with the same bull neck, thick eyebrows, and smashed nose. His chin was obscured by a two-week beard that was already filling out —a luxury for the weeks between SAHS' dress code (which prohibited facial hair for boys) and the start of the summer football camps, which both reinstated the rule and was additionally too hot for a beard. Dylan hulked over his mother as he stood in the doorway. Then he looked steadily at her. He was fully awake now.

"Nothing to talk about. I hadn't hung out with Pete in years. Or the other kids."

"Listen, I know this is hard," Anne replied, almost hopefully. "It's okay to be upset."

"I'm really not," he replied slowly, his deep voice steady and convincing. "I bet Pat will be tore up though. He hung out with Pete all the time. I'll text him later. Can I go back to sleep?" And without waiting for an answer, he pushed the door closed, and she heard it lock.

Just as Anne was turning away, the door on the opposite side of the hall opened, and Janus Norris emerged. Like his older brother, Janus was bare-chested, but he wore thick flannel lounge pants. Also like his brother, his hair was crazily piled on top of his head, and he blinked in the morning light.

"What's happening?" Janus asked. Walking toward his mother, he stopped and gave her a hug. Her nose involuntarily wrinkled at the stale-sweat smell coming off of him.

"Oh," Anne began, a catch in her voice, "Dylan's friend Peter died in an accident yesterday."

"Yeah, I heard about that," Janus replied. "Sucks."

Anne was less taken aback now that the third of the men in her household reacted to the horrible news with such . . . calm? Janus turned his back on her and walked toward the kitchen yelling: "Emilia! Make me breakfast!"

Emilia answered, a laugh superimposed on her voice: "Put some clothes on, Jane!" A running joke between the two of them. Emilia and Janus teased each other relentlessly, half of the time taking a real joy in the other, and the remaining half of the time baiting each other to shouting (Janus) and tears (Emilia).

Anne followed him to the kitchen, and as Janus put a pod in the Keurig coffee maker (leaving the used pod on the counter rather than throwing it away, of course), Anne took two pounds of bacon from the refrigerator and started the pre-heat cycle on the oven. Washing the eggs that she had gathered earlier, she was struck by a sudden memory of how peaceful her morning had been as she had taken the eggs out of the roosts, contrasted starkly against this sudden sadness, and had she admitted it, anxiety. Partially to escape the pressure of her own turbulent feelings, she started talking to Janus. Emilia had finished her scrambled eggs and was now rinsing the plate and fork.

"What else have you heard about the accident?" Anne asked.

"Just that they got poisoned from the heater. Pete, Doug, Mandy, and Sarah were partying on Pete's houseboat."

"What kind of *poison?*" Emilia asked, and Anne was suddenly aware that the little girl was listening.

"Carbon monoxide," Dane answered. "It's an odorless gas that comes off engines. You can't smell it, and it puts you to sleep, and you just never wake up. Not a bad way to go."

Anne shot him a brief angry glance. An expression of fear came across Emilia's face.

"Don't worry, honey," Anne said, crossing over to Emilia and putting an arm around her. "We've got carbon monoxide detectors in the house. It won't happen to us. Dane, we should really get the system monitored though."

"One of these days," her husband replied negligently.

Emilia's brows furrowed, and she crossed over to where the dogs lay basking in one of the brilliant patches of sunlight pouring through the kitchen window. She lay down next to them and put her arms around the golden retriever. Buddy the Weimaraner lifted his head up to look at her, then laid it back down again on the floor and made a deep groaning sound. Anne tore several sheets of parchment paper, placed them onto baking trays, and began laying the strips of bacon on the paper. She continued silently until all the bacon was loaded on the trays, put them in the oven, and set the timer. She stood in front of the oven for a moment, her thoughts still whirling.

"Do you want to go to Mass with me?" she asked the other three. "I think it would be good. We should all go today."

Emilia answered first: "Sure, Mommy. And we should pray a rosary for them."

"Not today," Dane replied. "I've got that meeting with Carter. I'll drive in myself if you're going to St. James."

Anne looked expectantly at Janus.

"I guess. But I've gotta get my workout in."

"You can do it after," his mother said. "You've got to take a shower, and I'd like to be there a little early so I can go to confession."

Buddy's head jerked up, and he emitted a long warning bark. Jingles leaped up, and Emilia was tossed aside in a sudden flurry of furry dogs, who rushed barking toward the front door. A second later, the doorbell rang.

"Oh! It's Lisa," Anne gasped. "I forgot she was coming today."

"I'll get it," Janus said, and hurried out of the room. Dane smiled knowingly at Anne and sidled back toward the master suite.

Moments later, Janus re-entered with a young woman in patterned leggings, sneakers, and a grey hoodie partially zipped over a red sports bra. Lisa LeBlanc, Anne's personal trainer, was thin, fit, blonde ponytailed, and clearly making an impression on Janus, who followed her into the room with his shoulders thrown back and stomach tight to show his abdominal muscles. She and Janus were circled by the dogs, who excitedly pushed their muzzles into hands and legs and did their best to trip and impede the two.

"Good morning, guys," Lisa bubbled, shifting her workout bag on her shoulder and smiling at Anne. "You ready to go?"

"I'm sorry, Lisa," Anne replied. "I should have called you. I just don't have it in me today."

"Aw, well that's why I'm here! We all have these mornings. Let's just do a quick workout. You'll feel better if you do."

"No, I'm sorry. We've had a shock this morning, and I need to go into town."

"If it's okay," Janus interrupted, tentatively, "I can do your workout, Mom. I was just saying I need to." He was distantly aware that he was transparent.

"You were going to Mass with me," his mother objected.

"Let the boy do his workout" came Dane's amused voice from the master suite.

"Yeah, I really need to get moving," Janus added, encouraged. Anne looked defeated.

"Is it okay, Lisa?" she asked.

"Sure, he can use your session. But watch out, kid. I won't take it easy on you."

"Okay, I'll get ready," Janus said quickly, and rushed back toward his room.

"And put some clothes on, Jane!" Emilia giggled.

"I'll head down to the workout room," Lisa said, smiling. "We're still on for next Tuesday, right?"

"Yes, Lisa. Everything should be okay by then."

Lisa left the room and made her way toward the stairs down to the lower level of the house. A few seconds later, Janus came through headed in the same direction, his lounge pants replaced by loose SAHS shorts and a sleeveless BC Rangers shirt covering his chest. The reek of Axe body spray followed in his wake. As he passed through the room, his father's voice called out from the master suite: "Don't get worn out, Jane. You have lifting tomorrow!"

Anne walked back into the master bedroom and asked Dane to take the bacon out when the timer went off. Then she walked into her tiled bathroom and took a long, hot shower. She carefully dried her hair, dressed in a patterned blouse and long black skirt, applied her makeup, and sat looking at herself for a while. Sliding into a comfortable pair of flat shoes, she emerged back into the kitchen to find Dane and Dylan at the breakfast table, plowing through the pile of bacon, eggs, and toaster waffles. Anne called for Emilia, who returned dressed in a lacy top and with her hair in a ponytail.

"Are you sure you don't want to go?"

"I'm sure. Have a good Mass. I'll see you this afternoon," Dane answered.

"Bye," Dylan said through a mouthful of eggs.

And Anne and Emilia strode out to her Land Rover and drove off toward Asheville.

Chapter 2

THE RANGERS

At a wide bend of State Route 401, a few miles past the bridge over the French Broad River, sat a rapidly fading relic of past times when SR401 was a two-lane road and Asheville was still far away. Rapidly fading might be too gentle a term. The Jiffy Stop was, in medical terminology, circling the drain. In two years it would be gone. The building would still be there, vacant and doomed to remain so, but the business will have vanished, the owner disposing of the inventory at the highest possible (and still dreadfully low) prices.

The Jiffy Stop was nestled precariously between 401 and a tributary of the French Broad called Stark's Creek, which for years had cut its way deeper and deeper along the route of 401 so that the north side of the highway was, in many places, only yards away from the deeply shaded banks of the creek. Before 401 went to four lanes (with a fifth turn lane down the middle), the Jiffy Stop had a generous parking lot in front. But the highway expansion had taken three quarters of that lot, and now along the face of the rambling building there was just room for the remaining gas pumps and a dozen parking spots that routinely courted disaster from the westbound traffic. Unlike many of his contemporaries, Danny Renfroe —the current owner and great-grandson of the founder—had invested in the new gas tanks mandated by environmental regulations, and thus the Jiffy Stop still served some of its original filling station purpose. Its later demise would be precipitated by yet more underground tank regulations—regulations which Renfroe could not afford—owing to the station's proximity to Stark's Creek. Without the gas, there was one less reason for people to stop there.

The original service station—Old Clyde Renfroe's first building—was still there and formed the easternmost part of the complex. The garage was the furthest right of the structure—built of brick that had been painted so many times that it looked like stucco. In the 1970s, the garage's roll-up door had been replaced with plastic, which was now so frosted and coated with grease and dust that it was completely opaque. If one were to look behind it, one would find a 1973 pea-green Chevy Impala jammed between rows of decomposing cardboard boxes and contemplated by dirty walls that still bore ranks and ranks of automotive belts, chains, exhaust pipes, and other such relics of the service days.

The garage opened onto the office of the service station, which like the garage itself was full of old boxes, a file cabinet containing sixty years of fading papers, and everywhere dust, grime, and grease.

Next door to the offices was the only currently functioning part of the Jiffy Stop—a long cinderblock building fronted with pane-glass windows and a single reinforced wire-glass door half-covered with vibrant lottery stickers and faded Chamber of Commerce seals, all brooding under the sagging flat-top shade-roof that extended from the front of the building and over the two filthy gas pumps.

The final structure was the diner—which projected to the westernmost part of the complex and had been long closed—with a dumpster crouched up against the side of the building in the brief space before the flat land dropped off into Stark's Creek. All manner of detritus crowded around the dumpster and back behind the moss-covered rear of the building, making it impassable to all but the bravest scavenger. Behind the Jiffy Stop, and across Stark's Creek, the land rose up sharply, shading the makeshift scrapyard.

The Renfroes were never ones to discard things. The environs of the buildings were time capsules of decades of roadside service. Automotive parts, construction materials, and buckets half-full of brackish water—which would belch forth mosquitos from spring to fall—compacted layers of trash, all awaiting a use that would never come and that would plague the demolition crew at some future date.

The inside of the Jiffy Stop was full of slightly more valuable inventory, which though voluminous, was artfully whittled down on Renfroe's tangible personal property report each year. But if one were performing an honest accounting, it would have to be admitted that much of the store was fully depreciated. Aside from the close-packed shelves filled with junk food, bread, baked beans, and picnic items; aside from the glass-fronted coolers of beer, soda, and bottled water; and aside from the ranks of cigarette packs, chewing tobacco, and dip, the inventory was itself a time capsule that might read as:

10 assorted T-shirts ("Don't Break My Achy Breaky Heart," "Twerk it Miley," "California Raisins," etc.)

8 souvenir baseball caps ("A Country Boy Can Survive," "Born to Fish," "Forget Hell"—with confederate flag crest and two crossed cavalry swords, —etc.)

15 Zippo lighters and Zippo rotary display cases, mostly patriotic and military themed

1 Billy Mullins—bearded, tanned, and diminutive

For if one were taking inventory on any given morning, it would have to be assumed that Billy Mullins constituted a part, fixed as he was at the end of the register counter, leaning on it with his right arm, and either eating a sausage biscuit or smoking a cigarette, as the case might be.

Billy cut a figure of remarkable appearance. He had the dimensions of a normal man, one might even say a well-built, burly man, only at scale. He was not short or thin; he was just in miniature. All parts of him, from hands to head, were very well proportioned, but small. He stood only five feet tall, but at age forty-five, with a black and bushy beard, deep lines around his eyes, and a weather-beaten face, he would never be mistaken as a child. Despite the warm weather this morning, he wore his habitual mustard-colored Carhart jacket over a gray T-shirt and dirty dark-blue jeans with a lime-green Biltmore College Rangers baseball cap over his close-cropped black hair.

This particular morning—an early summer morning in which the sun was already lighting up the often-shadowed Jiffy Stop—Billy was engaged in conversation with Tommy Hess, who stood working the register. Tommy was a tall, wiry man with a grey complexion; a craggy nose; sullen, heavy-lidded eyes; and salt-and-pepper hair. He wore three days of stubble on his cheeks. It was a slow morning, but from time to time customers would interrupt. The regular customers, Billy, and Tommy had this routine well practiced, and the conversation flowed around the disturbances.

"How do you think we're gonna end up?" Tommy asked, closing the register drawer.

Billy washed down the last of his biscuit with coffee and answered after sighing out the heat from his drink.

"Top five. No question. Maybe even two or three. Nobody's gonna beat 'Bama."

"Yeah, Tide will be one, but it'd be great to be number two."

"The way I see it," Billy replied, "the SEC is gonna have maybe eight of the top ten. You got Bama, Georgia having a great year, Auburn, Florida of course, Ole Miss, the damn Vols, the Razorbacks, and us. Clemson and OSU will be in there, but I think that's it for the Power Five, top ten anyway. If we get the Duffy kid—Ja'Quan or Ja'something-or-other—then we have to get Nolan. They're a package deal."

"They're both four-stars, right?" Tommy asked.

"Nah. Duffy's a four, but Nolan's just a three. But they've got to take him to get Duffy."

"Damn, that's great. Sure nice to be thinking about a top-ten class. Been a while. Carter's doing a great job. Course, that's what he did at TMU."

Billy freshened his coffee from the pot and stirred in some sugar.

"Yeah, you gotta give him credit, but he's lucky to have the legacy kids."

"That's what I've been saying," Tommy responded. "It's finally gonna turn around. You knew that someday the kids of our Ranger Royalty would start making a difference."

"That's what I told Hopper yesterday on the SportsBeast. You've got the legacy kids coming in a year when we've got the recruiting numbers on our side. Gonna be able to sign a big class, so there's plenty of room. You've got the number-one overall prospect committed already, so that's locked down, and plenty of kids want to play with him. You've got a new coach, you've got playing time on the table for the skill positions, solid O and D lines, so no one's gonna get banged up. Everything is comin' together."

"So how good is the Norris kid? I don't watch that Catholic team. All I hear is the hype."

"I didn't watch those fuckers either until Norris committed. Cheap assholes recruiting kids to play high school. Every year it's the same thing. It's easy to win State when half your team are the sons of NFL players."

"Yeah, but if they're getting kids to go to the Rangers it's all good."

"IF they go to the Rangers. Norris is the first five-star to come out of there and stay home. Pisses me off every time they show clips of McKenzie burning us for 350 yards. He was a St. Ambrose kid. He didn't stay home. Neither did LeQuan Thompson or Derrick Anthony, and we could've used those receivers when we had Broome as QB . . . "

Billy paused to let his anger cool, then continued: "But, yeah, anyway, I think Norris lives up to the hype."

"You think he comes in as tight end or middle linebacker?"

"Tight end, definitely. No way they waste him on defense."

The Jiffy Stop door opened, its chime ringing to announce potential business. Through the door came a well-dressed and thus atypical set of customers. Him in a V-necked pullover and designer jeans. Her in a bohemian sundress and calf-high leather boots.

Through the window, one could see their silver Audi pulled up to the pump. Occasionally, such people would come in. Usually westbound, low on gas, afraid of running out. On their way from Lake Juniper, or to Lake Juniper, or out antiquing, or trying a cut-over to the Blue Ridge Parkway. Out of place and knowing it, they told themselves the Jiffy Stop was retro, or a throwback, and talked about it later with amusement. But if they were honest with themselves, they were slightly afraid of the building and its clientele.

"Uh, do we have to pay first?" the man asked.

"Yep, card reader's down on both pumps," Tommy answered.

As the man stepped forward to the register and reached for his wallet, the woman asked: "Where's your bathroom?"

Tommy pointed toward the left, beside the register counter, where a brief and grimy hallway led into the diner wing of the Jiffy Stop. It was poorly lit, with thin fluorescent light coming from only one of the four fixtures in the yellowed and sagging drop ceiling. The woman looked in obvious disgust and went down the hallway.

The man laid a twenty on the counter.

"Twenty on pump one, premium. Rangers fan?" he commented, seeing Billy's cap.

Tommy laughed and responded: "He's THE Rangers fan."

"You've probably heard me on the SportsBeast. I go by Ranger Bill. I'm on there just about every day."

"Uh, we're just passing through. Go Rangers, though," the man replied, and pocketing his wallet, exited to pump his gas.

"Fucking hipsters," Billy muttered, and turned back to Tommy. "Well, I gotta get back to the house. Open line today."

"Give Hopper hell, Billy," was Tommy's response.

Billy dropped his empty coffee cup in the trash bin, picked up his pack of Camel cigarettes from the counter, and pushed his way through the door with a final nod at Tommy. Climbing into his battered, blue compact pickup that sported the lime-green Biltmore College "B" on the rear window, Rangers stickers on the bumper, a Rangers license plate frame surrounding a personalized "RNGR-BLL" license plate (which, to the uninitiated, evoked "Ringer Bell" instead of "Ranger Bill"), and a sun-faded Rangers car flag on the passenger-side window, Billy left the public no doubt of his allegiances. Executing the dangerous reverse onto 401, Billy spun off toward his home.

Coach Trey Carter sat behind the polished institutional desk in his paneled office in the Biltmore College athletics building. Behind him, the early-morning summer sun lit up the broad valley, and the land rolled lushly across the Botanic Gardens and up toward Sunset Mountain. His office door closed as his offensive line coach retreated from Carter's blistering dressing down.

Carter's brows were knotted directly in their center, his eyebrows' sharp lines converging on that twisted point dimpling the apex of a sharp nose. His thin lips were pulled in and almost pursed, and his face from forehead to chin was a gaudy crimson surrounding grey eyes with pupils focused to pinpoints. His right hand squeezed a stress ball in a steady cadence, and he stared straight ahead at the closed door as if it were the object of his displeasure.

On the desk before him lay a memo from the Biltmore College Compliance Director, the necessary bastard who was charged with keeping the Rangers from violating the Byzantine laws, rules, regulations, and codes of the National Collegiate Athletics Association. That memo detailed minor recruiting infractions incurred by O-line coach Roger Sampson—recruiting infractions that were unnecessary, stupid, and the product of a rapidly departing "old-school" culture of college football. With the year that he was having, Carter did not need to bend the rules. The players were falling into his lap. A legacy class was the lodestone pulling in athletes from Florida, Georgia, South Carolina, Texas, and California. Local talent was astonishingly good for a region that historically provided a meager crop. You never quit in recruiting; anything can happen, but it would take a monumental collapse to spoil this class.

Coach Sampson's violations were relatively minor. They would be self-reported by BC Compliance, and some hand slapping would probably result. But Coach Carter demanded perfection—in his players, his coaches, his staff, his entire program. His mantra was "do everything right every time." This dedication to relentless perfection was diametrically opposed to the previous BC culture, which is why Carter had been hired.

It had been almost twenty years since BC had been at the top of the SEC East, perennially competing for the SEC Championship and in the hunt for the National Championship. The Rangers never finished out of the top twenty-five, and the years that BC called "bad" were, in light of recent history, enviable. The fans, always passionate, had grown complacent with the success. Thus, the coaching staff that delivered wins, but never the National Championship, came under ever more pressure to achieve the ultimate victory. Star quarterback and Heisman candidate Ricky Taylor spent his three years at the school delivering SEC East victories and one SEC Championship, but the Rangers flamed out in their bowl games all three years. Taylor went on to the NFL early, skipping his senior year, and the fans howled that BC had wasted its chance. With a roster stacked with future NFL talent, anything short of the National Championship was failure.

Pressure increased with the resurgence of Alabama, whose uncharacteristic mediocre years were clearly behind it, and BC started losing talent to Florida, Georgia, and even, most painfully, to archrival Vanderbilt and the hated across-the-mountain foe Tennessee. With all of this pressure to succeed, the coaching staff began to take risks, and ultimately the program was crippled by NCAA sanctions for massive recruiting violations and blatant player payoffs from several boosters.

Firing the coaching staff and the athletic director was inevitable; the NCAA sanctions reduced the number of scholarships and tied the hands of the next staff with constant oversight, recruiting visit limitations, and the pall of disgrace and malaise that did as much as anything to keep the talent away from Biltmore College. Faced with this mess, BC's boosters opened their deep pockets, and after a two-year interim coach posted dismal back-to-back 2-9 records, those boosters ponied up the dough to bring Bobby Kemper back from the NFL to resurrect the program. Kemper's past NCAA success was indisputable but had not translated to the NFL. Seeing what Alabama had done under Nick Saban, after Saban flamed out with the Miami Dolphins, gave BC and its boosters the notion that imitation is the surest form of success. But Kemper had muddled along, never recruiting five-star talent, practicing an old-school "win the trenches" strategy that saw him build solid offensive and defensive lines but that never translated into success.

Moreover, his teams had a habit of losing games in the fourth quarter. Most people blamed this on the lack of depth; the starting players were worn out by the end of the game, and the second- and third-string players were just not talented enough to sustain the effort. But others saw a culture that simply gave up and that did not have the intensity or commitment to play a full game. There was a lot of truth to this. Bobby Kemper, for all his success, was tired. His coordinators were of his same vintage, and they were tired as well. Their miasma spread to their team, and the Rangers occupied the mediocre middle of the SEC East, with a trend toward the bottom. In his term as head coach, the only thing that Bobby Kemper did that would last was the creation of the Ranger Royalty program—a promise that the Rangers' great athletes of the past would always be treated like kings and queens when they came around the program. But surrounding his anemic team with emblems of past greatness only highlighted how far the Rangers had fallen.

The boosters had enough. They pressured the BC administration to dispose of the athletic director and replaced him with Mick Haynes, a lawyer-turned-executive with a reputation for viciousness and a track record of turning around smaller programs in short periods of time. Mick Haynes came in, looked around, and summarily fired Bobby Kemper, whose enormous contract buyout was again paid by the boosters. The lion-worshipping fans who had been in ecstasy at the hiring of Kemper now heaped scorn upon him, blaming him for all of the program's woes, and salivating over the next coaching hire. From the fans' point of view, every big-name coach in the country was a candidate. The prevailing arguments on the SportsBeast radio station were that BC was going to hire Saban away from Alabama or that Don Shula was going to come out of retirement to lead the Rangers. Naturally, the two camps for these unlikely options had great disdain for the other. And both camps were shocked and stunned when Mick Haynes announced that the next head coach of the mighty Biltmore College Rangers would be Trey Carter.

But no one was more shocked and stunned than the boosters who had brought Haynes in, not to take a chance on an admittedly talented up-and-comer, but to deliver immediate results whatever the cost. Letters were written. Meetings were held. But the boosters found that they had met their match with Haynes, who pursued a divide-and-conquer strategy among them, finding in their well-nurtured egos and competitiveness ample territory to set them at odds and prevent any concerted effort. In any case, the deal was done, the contract signed, and Trey Carter was the Rangers' newest head coach.

At forty-two years old, Carter was on the younger side of the Power Five Conference's head coaching spectrum. But his experience was extensive and seemed a string of unbroken successes.

Trey Carter's life was football. From pee-wee days through high school, his intellectual and social lives were dominated by the sport. Growing up near Dayton, Ohio, he went to college at the University of Toledo, where, playing as a fullback in a time when fullbacks were still major contributors, he amassed school-record rushing yards. He was solid, tough, clever, and fast. But not solid, tough, clever, or fast enough to succeed in the NFL. He made the roster for the Detroit Lions, sat on the bench for most of one year, and was cut. He bounced around on practice squads, trying to find his way back in, but eventually gave up, married his college girlfriend, and took an assistant coaching job at Toledo. After four years, he moved on to Florida State, then on to coach the University of Miami's running backs. His two children were born during the four years with the Hurricanes. Then back north to Cincinnati to coach both running backs and receivers, partly because he didn't want to raise his kids in South Florida, and Cincinnati was close to home. But his work at Cincinnati caught the attention of Virginia Tech, and he spent the next four years there as offensive coordinator. Finally, Texas Methodist gave him a head coaching job. His two years at TMU saw the program enter the top fifteen, with an overwhelming bowl win against Oregon in his first year and a secure bowl berth in the following season. TMU was ecstatic, offering him a contract extension and a raise and trying to secure him for the long term.

Then Biltmore College called. There had been a time when the BC job was one of the most coveted in the nation. It was a wealthy university with powerful resources, a rich tradition of success, and a committed fan base. The program was one of the very few that sold itself as a national brand. Kids grew up dreaming of playing for BC. And, as an SEC institution, it was the largest stage possible.

But that time had passed. The power was still there, the tradition was still there, and it was still an SEC school, but kids didn't dream of playing for the Rangers, and without a national draw, there wasn't enough local talent to fuel a perennial contender. BC was likely to have good years near the top, but an argument could be made that it would never recover its previous status. BC had simply fallen too far for too long.

But Trey and his family took the visit to Asheville anyway. They met Mick Haynes, whose intensity matched Carter's. They met the boosters (who did not take the meetings very seriously). Then Carter met the team and saw the foundation that Kemper had built there. He looked at the up-and-coming local talent, and he saw something there that perhaps others would miss.

Further, and most importantly, his wife, Jackie, fell in love with Asheville. They visited in the fall, after Kemper's firing, before the early signing period. The leaves were turning, and the mountains were alive with color. Asheville's lively but still accessible downtown, its old quaint neighborhoods and wealthy suburbs, and mostly the friendly and engaging people were inviting and comforting and warm.

Carter went back to TMU and informed the administration that he was taking the job at BC. His TMU contract extension was unsigned. He had no buyout. He was free, and the lack of a buyout meant that Haynes didn't have to beg from the boosters. Signing a three-million-dollar annual contract, guaranteed four years, Carter uprooted from an enraged TMU, left before the bowl game, and became one of the most hated men in Texas.

What he did next poured salt on the wounds. As BC's new head coach, he contacted the top players he had been recruiting for TMU and began to recruit them for the Rangers. The talent on the offensive and defensive lines that was left in place by Kemper, coupled with the top picks he had been recruiting for TMU, gave him a good shot at a solid first year. And the upcoming legacy class for the following year would give him the talent to take BC back to premier status.

That legacy class contained five players—the sons of former BC Rangers standouts and tenured NFL greats—who had five-star projections and showed sincere interest in Biltmore College. At the top of that list of legacy kids was the already-committed player from St. Ambrose High School: Dylan Norris.

Chapter 3

SLOTH

Transcript: The *Hopper & Howe Show*

Hopper: Hi, welcome back to the Hopper & Howe Show, *coming to you live from the Cox Convenience Studios. It's the eleven-o-clock hour, so let's go to the phones. We've got our old friend Ranger Bill on the line. Good morning, Ranger Bill.*

Billy Mullins: Hey there, Hopper.

Hopper: What's on your mind, Ranger Bill?

Billy Mullins: Did you hear about those kids from St. Ambrose . . .

.

Howe: [Interrupting] Yeah, just tragic. Our thoughts and prayers go out to the whole St. Ambrose High School community. What a tragic loss.

Hopper: Yeah, what a terrible, terrible accident. You just feel so bad for their parents. I can't even imagine it. And really for that whole school community—to lose four kids from that upcoming senior class. It's just tragic. So what are your thoughts, Ranger Bill?

Billy Mullins: Well, maybe you all know this better than I do, 'cause I don't follow St. Ambrose that close. You know I'm a Madison County booster . . .

Hopper: [Interrupting] Yeah, we know that, Ranger Bill. The whole listening audience knows that . . .

Billy Mullins: [Interrupting] but what I wanted to know was whether these kids dying is gonna do anything for the Norris kid as far as his recruitment.

[Brief dead air]

Howe: I just don't see how that has anything to do with it.

Billy Mullins: Well, were they friends with Norris? I mean, that might mess the kid up, right?

Hopper: Yeah, I don't know, but I think that whole community is thinking about more important things than football right now. Thanks for the call, Ranger Bill. Let's go to our next caller, Dave. Dave, you're on the line.

Billy hung up the receiver on his yellowing Bell landline and sank back into the fraying maroon stuffed chair. The fabric of the arms was glossy from years of friction and greasy hands, and the chair squeaked on its springs and hinges as his weight shifted the seat cushion backward. Billy reached over to the table next to the chair, which was crowded by the telephone, an overflowing ashtray, three empty and one half-full Camel hardpacks, empty cans of Natural Lite beer, various remote controls, an eyeglass case, smudged reading glasses with the nose cushions missing, a cube of Kleenex, and underneath it all a stack of grocery-store magazines covering the SEC in general and BC Rangers football in particular.

The rest of the living room was cramped. His chair and table took up a full quarter of the room, which was floored with worn carpeting over which an oval pattern rug had been placed to hide the bare spots. The walls were a dark paneling, which in many cases had warped as the ground beneath the trailer settled over its forty years of labored existence. In a few places, the paneling had separated enough for popcorn insulation to spill out. Billy fought an occasional battle against the pellets of insulation, light pink and made of some probably toxic material. But his vacuum had given up the ghost, and now small piles of the insulation lay at the corner of the walls and carpet next to various articles of clothing that were awaiting laundry day. Each year the trailer got a little colder, and the pile of dust, lint, and refuse outside the trailer got a little higher as Billy had scooped out the vacuum bags for re-use.

Aside from his chair and table, the rest of the room was occupied by an LED TV that was much too large for both the room and for the old, black-painted cabinet that it sat upon. The doors of the cabinet were open so that the remotes would work on the VCR, DVD player, and Satellite receiver. The TV was clearly Billy's shrine and perhaps the only thing in the room that was dusted and clean. On one side of the TV was a bookcase crowded with paperbacks and more magazines. On the other side of the TV was a tripod with a High-8 camcorder atop. Red, white, and yellow RCA cables ran from the camcorder to the VCR. Billy would use this occasionally to watch the tapes he had made of himself and his first wife, himself and his second wife, and himself and the other women he had lured to his trailer after his last divorce.

Another armchair (this one in pea-green corduroy but equally derelict) sat beside a simple table on which was crowded a yellowing Compaq tower computer next to a small flat-screen monitor, with the keyboard and mouse sitting on a board that had been nailed to the top of the table to provide space for the mouse. A TV table and three folded bag chairs filled out the room.

In various places about the walls hung framed BC Rangers pictures: An aerial photo of Seely Stadium from the day that BC beat Notre Dame, hand-drawn pictures of BC football players in various action photos, a framed ticket stub from one of the few games that Billy had attended, and a portrait of Coach Young in a crested blazer and fedora. On every surface there were little BC Rangers mementos: a set of nesting dolls with players from the '07 season, bobbleheads, a signed football from Coach Kemper (which Billy had almost thrown away in disgust), and a few miniature footballs in BC green with SEC East Championship seasons memorialized in game dates and scores. And in between these mementos were stacked beer cans and one or two Mad Dog 20/20 bottles.

Grime and filth covered everything but the television. The living room had big windows that looked out over the property, but these were frosted and made the trees outside look like misty ghosts. The louvers were partially open now, letting in cool, fresh air and mosquitos. A single storm door, fitting its frame badly, hung partially open and led out to what remained of Billy's party deck and the stairs out of the trailer. Beside the door was a short-barreled Mossberg shotgun, loaded with alternating slugs and scattershot. One open passage on the west side of the trailer led to Billy's bedroom. On the other side, the living room segued into the kitchen, with a rounded Formica countertop marking the two rooms as distinct. Worn wooden cabinets, their white paint fully chipped away around the stainless-steel door pulls, hung desolately on the kitchen walls above a grimy vinyl floor that still retained its yellow and white stylized flower pattern. The kitchen counters were crowded with an air fryer, toaster oven, toaster, Mr. Coffee, potato chip bags, used plastic cups, a quarter-full whiskey bottle, and cereal boxes. The sink was piled with used dishes—none of which matched—and silverware of various assortments. Dirty pots and pans resided on the stove top, and a lonely, padded stool sat next to one relatively clear area of the counter where Billy ate most of his meals.

A single door led from the kitchen into the bathroom, where a stand-up shower with a black-moldy curtain stood across from the filthy toilet. Brown cardboard toilet paper rolls littered the floor around the bowl, overflowing from a small dustbin. An ashtray sat on top of the commode tank. Tan wallpaper stuck stubbornly to the walls, stained yellowish-brown up to just below the height of Billy's waist. The louvers of an opaque window were open, letting in air, but not enough to free the room of its urine stench. The outside of the window was covered with moss.

The covering over the outside of the window was just a vanguard of the army of moss slowly encroaching from the north-facing side of the trailer, which was heavily shaded by the trees and brush and the rising hill behind it. The parts of the trailer that weren't mossy were covered in long streaks of mildew and dirt. The fiberglass sides of the trailer clung stubbornly together in a display of integrity that was disconsonant with the rest of the structure. The rusty trailer forks thrust out from below the bathroom window into a V shape that had long since lost its hitch—the trailer having sat in place since it was towed in many years ago. A blackberry bush grew up through the trailer forks. Dingy grey latticework covered the bottom of the trailer, falling away and revealing the cinderblocks upon which the trailer was perched.

On the downhill side of the trailer, wooden stairs led up to a small landing that had been constructed years ago. Billy had added his "Party Porch"—a deck that at one time had extended the rest of the length of the trailer—to the side of that landing. But it was not well built, and within a couple of years, the far corner post had begun to sink, and then the entire deck pulled away from the trailer and slanted toward the corner. A card table, rotted bag chairs, and a cooler had slid down to that depression and were still there, piled with leaves and pooling stagnant water. The railing was warped and had separated in places and split in others. The deck had become a death trap for anyone foolish enough to attempt to step on it.

The Party Porch was Billy's last real attempt to improve his home. He had added it in the year following his second divorce, after receiving a small bequest from the dissolution of his elder brother's "estate." At that same time, Billy had become the sole heir of his family's property, which consisted of the entirety of Mullins Hill outside of the small lot on which his trailer sat. This, in turn, was a previous bequest from his uncle. A scruffy pile of rock, trees, and brush, Mullins Hill rose steeply on all sides. The original family cabin was up toward the top, near the spring that flowed from the cabin site down past his brother's trailer and finally past Billy's, only to dump out in a tributary stream near the road. The cabin had long since collapsed and was now a pile of rotting boards and shingles perched atop a natural stone foundation, with one dark door leading below it into a cellar that was now home to copperheads and spiders.

The Mullins family debris still littered the site: old refrigerators, washtubs, broken furniture, the rusting hulk of a Packard, and tires, tires, and more tires filled with stagnant mosquito-breeding pools. Billy's brother's trailer, once nicer than Billy's, had been converted by the heir into a storage room and then neglected. With the electricity long since cut and a window broken open to the elements, it was now uninhabitable. Two of his brother's trucks still sat—flat-tired and immovable—in the driveway outside the trailer. A sapling grew through the open engine compartment of one.

The same dirt road that traveled past his brother's trailer also wound its way down to Billy's. It was deeply rutted on the uphill side. From Billy's trailer down to the road, it was less so. One of his cousins would come over with a box blade from time to time and level the drive. Billy could not afford to have new gravel put down, so he would go two or three times a week to an electrical substation nearby and steal gravel by the bucketload. This rearguard action kept the drive from being completely washed out, but it was a painstaking (and constant) process that kept it passable. Billy's Ford Ranger struggled up and down the drive but always made it.

Mullins Hill had been home to his family for time immemorial, but only Billy and his cousins knew it by that moniker. Now it was just a pile of unwanted land on the side of a seldom-traveled road, though home to the World's Greatest Rangers Fan. The county assessors would come every three years, and invariably Billy's property taxes—his only fixed expense besides electricity—would creep upward. He was now several years in arrears, a condition that threatened his only real asset. But he was optimistic in his ownership of the three hundred acres of Mullins Hill. In his mind, the continued spread of yuppies from Asheville would result in a sale of the land, and he would someday become a millionaire and have a luxury box at Seely Stadium.

Those three hundred acres, however, could be described as one hundred fifty acres straight up and one hundred fifty acres back down. Other than the cabin site, his brother's trailer, and Billy's lot, there were no good places to build. The trees that covered the hill were scraggly and useless for timber. For whatever reason, the hill was sparse of wildlife. Even squirrels were rare. Coyotes came to call from time to time, but there was little good to hunt on those three hundred acres. There was nothing of value on the property, unless the world were to run out of gravel and someone could find a way to reduce the hill into sellable rubble.

Even the view from Mullins Hill, which might otherwise have appealed to the cabin-building rich folk from Asheville, was uninspiring. The hill was nestled closely in a rough bowl of nearby taller hills, obscuring the distant mountain views and the sun setting and rising. It was a hill within a hollow, damp and dreary.

Dylan Norris finished his breakfast and had gone back to his room to change. Unintentionally he put on the same uniform as his brother—gold St. Ambrose Saints shorts and a sleeveless lime-green BC Rangers shirt. He laced up his Nike running shoes and sat on the edge of his bed, flipping through his iPhone.

Dylan's bedroom was on the east side of the house, and light streamed through the plantation shutters across his mahogany-framed king bed. The floor was carpeted and currently covered by a day's worth of apparel: his workout clothes from yesterday, lounge pants from last night, a couple pairs of boxers, socks, jeans, and a hoodie. Rosa would be in to pick them up later. He almost never used the black wicker hamper along his wall, for what was the point if Rosa had to pick them up anyway? Rather, his clothes lay where he shed them. A 55" TV was mounted to the wall above his bureau—all of the drawers of which were partially opened with folded and semi-folded clothes popping out. Another disorder that Rosa would put right later in the day. A glass display case held his trophies—and there were many—from football, baseball, and basketball. On the walls hung some nondescript landscapes selected by the interior designer to match the dark green textured paint on the walls. There were two deer heads mounted, one on each side of the TV, their black glass eyes looking out aimlessly on the room above indignant nostrils. His two best hunts.

Dylan's phone was blowing up with texts and DMs from his friends, but none from Pat. He connected his earbud headphones, triggered his running playlist, and slipped the phone into his runner's armband, exiting the room to a screaming heavy metal/rap fusion.

He padded back through the kitchen, past the breakfast table where his and his father's dishes sat, past the granite countertops and distressed-white cabinets, out into the entry hall with its high ceiling, chandelier, tiled floor, and a great round walnut table that served no purpose but to take up space in the center of the room. The hub of the table was occupied by a crystal vase filled with a variety of leafless sticks and a mass of string lights whose batteries were currently drained.

He turned left and proceeded down the stairs to the lower level of the house, emerging into the great recreation room with its wet bar (all custom woodwork with the BC Rangers logo inlaid), pool table (with lime-green Rangers felt), leather couches, his father's trophy cases, BC Rangers and KC Chiefs photos and paintings, and TVs mounted on all of the walls. One side of the room was dominated by paned windows and French doors that opened up onto the flagstoned outdoor kitchen beneath the deck. The sun was already high enough that the patio was shaded, and the landscape beyond it was almost painfully bright in comparison.

He walked toward the wing of the basement beneath the kids' rooms above, passing the gym where Janus was being punished by his mother's trainer. Dylan's lip curled in a smirk as he heard her yelling at him. *That little pussy*, he thought, walking by the glass door of the gym. He passed the bathrooms and the sauna and arrived at the end of the hall where the door opened into the video game room—a room dimly lit, with two black leather gaming chairs facing a massive screen and a cabinet crammed with different video game systems. Dylan discontinued his playlist, punched himself down, and logged in.

He digested his breakfast while he shot, stabbed, exploded, strangled, kicked, punched, and slaughtered his way through a virtual landscape. He had been trying a speed run through the game, which had long ago been beaten, but his heart wasn't really in it, and when he began to lose the sense of fullness in his stomach, he logged out and walked out of the room. The gym was empty. Poor Janus was probably upstairs jerking off to memories of Lisa LeBlanc, he thought, grinning. He grabbed a Powerade from the fridge and walked out through the French doors and across the patio to begin his run around the property.

Behind him rose the Norris mansion—a sprawling pile of grey fieldstone punctuated by bright windows with real shutters that could be (but never had been) closed in the event of a storm. The house was topped by a hunter-green metal roof that was marred by solar panels that were still not connected to the electrical system. Like the carbon monoxide detectors, the security system, and the voice-controllable window shades, the house was full of technology that was both first-rate and underused.

Over the master suite, and accessible by a spiral staircase, was a ridiculous octagonal tower with a tall spire that culminated in a rooster weather vane. If someone were ever to mount that tower, they would read the name "NORRIS" cast onto both sides of the rooster.

The house was built into a low rise in the ground, with its upper floor even with the level of a circular drive, and the back of the house—with deck, patio, and outdoor kitchen—looking over a rectangular infinity pool. The water spilled over the edge facing the pastures, down a fieldstone retaining wall, and back up into the pumps. Chaise lounges and deck chairs circled the pool, with lime-green umbrellas (currently closed) jutting upward here and there.

Dylan took the steps down to the pool, passed beside the pool house (likewise fieldstoned and green-roofed), and out through the gate in the low cast-iron fence. The jogging trail picked up here, a packed fine-graveled path that ambled through a rough one-mile loop through the property. Dylan began jogging along the trail, first parallel to the house, then back behind the motor barn where boats were stored off-season. He passed his black Yukon Denali SUV beside the barn, ran past the tractor barn with its chirping chicks, past the stables, and up along one of the fence lines. Music blared in his ears. The morning cool was fading, and the dew was evaporating from the grass. Horses nickered in the pasture. Birds alighted as he ran. For a little while he was accompanied by purple martins, clearing his path of disturbed insects.

He jogged past the "wilding" field, where the old chimney and tumbled foundations of an old settler homestead squatted amidst the wildflowers. From time to time, archeology students from Biltmore College or UNC Asheville would arrive and dig about in the dirt, inevitably turning up arrowheads or musket balls. Most recently they had found an old iron ax-head and some brass buttons.

Dylan circled back toward the house, up and around the bonfire pit and past the garages, to enter the gate on the other side of the pool. He was tempted to do another lap but instead went back inside, discarded his Powerade, drank another, and entered the basement wing under the master suite. Passing the home theater, he opened the door to the garages and looked inside. His mother's Land Rover was gone, as was his father's Mercedes coupe. The rarely used Porsche 928, two Harley-Davidson motorcycles, and his dad's Ford Dually took up three of the six bays of the garage.

Dylan let the door swing closed and went back upstairs. His brother's door was closed (*damn that's a long jerk off*, he thought). Dylan went into his own room, closed and locked the door, shed his clothes, and stepped into his bathroom. Bright milky tiles surrounded him. He resisted the urge to sit in the jacuzzi tub and instead walked into the shower, shampooing, soaping, brushing his teeth, pissing, and finally masturbating.

Cooled down and relaxed, he toweled off and dressed in yet another pair of loose SAHS shorts and a black Mastadon concert T. Running his hands through his wet hair, he sat back down on the bed and pried his iPhone from the sleeve of the armband. There was a missed call from Pat.

Dylan's thick fingers punched his phone and texted:

How you doing bro?

...

...

I was supposed to be there

WTF?

Supposed to smoke out with Pete. Cancelled.

Ok man

I keep thinking it wouldn't have happened. If I hung out with Pete he wouldn't have gone on the boat.

No way. You don't know that. Maybe you'd be dead now.

Maybe Pete wouldn't be dead or the others . . . if I was there then he wouldn't have had Mandy there. . . it was just guys supposed to be there. We wouldn't have been cold and made him turn on the heater.

Bro, that's crazy. You should feel lucky you weren't there. Its just an accident.

I know

Bro, let's hang out. I'll pick you up.

Cool.

Dylan pocketed his phone, grabbed his wallet and keys, and walked out of his room, leaving the door open. Rosa was hard at work in the kitchen, already clearing the dishes from breakfast. Janus' door was still closed. Dylan pounded on it and yelled "Wake up bro!"

"Fuck you!" came the muffled reply. Dylan chuckled and walked down to the motor barn. He hit the remote and unlocked the Yukon. The door opened to a reek of sweat, leather, air freshener, and underneath it all a persistent stench of marijuana. Dylan couldn't smell it, but he was paranoid enough to start parking by the barn instead of in the garage. He didn't think his mother would recognize the smell, naïve and ignorant as she was, but he bet his dad would, and after everything that happened with Maryanne, the last thing he wanted was for his father to think that his prize football boy was risking a career by smoking pot.

Climbing in, then reversing out and up the gravel drive to the main driveway, Dylan glided away from the Norris estate, with the leather seat heated and massaging, and the subwoofer punching away at the small of his back.

Ranger Bill came bouncing down over the ruts in his driveway and out onto Brown Hollow Road. He passed the faded "Land for Sale" sign that had graced the front of Mullins Hill since he had first begun to dream of selling his property. A red-letter sign that yelled "Acreage!" was nailed to the bottom of the plywood signboard. The idea that the word "acreage" was some sort of yuppie translation of the word "land" had popped into Billy's head, and he had stolen the sign rider from a lot that he passed on the way to the Jiffy Stop.

Down shaded roads and out onto SR401 and into the parking lot of his favorite haunt, Billy drove and smoked, and then the door chime rang to announce that the Rangers-fan-in-residence was back at his post. Tommy Hess was behind the counter, and next to the register stood Kenny Watkins, wearing his tan deputy sheriff's uniform, Styrofoam cup of coffee in his hand. Kenny had a brown buzz haircut, a head that was noticeably larger at the neck than at the crown, multiple chins rolling over his black necktie, a prodigious waistline, and thick sausage fingers.

"Ranger Bill!" Kenny announced.

"Tommy. Kenny," Billy said simply, as he moved to his familiar spot against the counter. Kenny moved back away to give him space, ceding the territory.

"Did you hear me this morning?" he continued.

"Yeah, I did. Hopper didn't give you much airtime," Tommy replied.

"Couldn't let me say anything bad about his Catholic team," Billy sneered. "They coddle those boys. It was a legit question, I thought. Bound to mess kids up. What do you know about it?" Billy finished, looking at Kenny.

"Well, I was out there all right. I was just telling Tommy."

Billy looked expectantly at the deputy.

"There were drugs all over," he began. "The kid whose dad owns the boat was sitting in a chair, looked like he was sleeping. One of the girls was on the couch and then the other kid and his girl were under a sleeping bag on the floor. They had a big ol' bong and a ton of pot and pills. Probably ecstasy. You know these kids. Found 'em in the morning, probably been dead a few hours. Space heater was chuggin' along."

"Damn. Big ol' houseboat?" Billy asked.

"Yep. Course goes to show that money don't buy sense. Damn kid killed himself and his friends through not knowin' what he was doin'."

"Parents shouldn't of let 'em be out there," Tommy said.

"Yeah, givin' kids houseboats and cars is just askin' for this sort of thing to happen," Kenny replied. "Every summer it's the same thing. Course it's usually drownin'. Got to be careful on the water. They think it's just for fun, out on their damn wake boats. I am sick and tired of being damn-near rocked out of my boat when they come flyin' by. Oughta be 'no wake' signs up all over the lake. Course the money people wouldn't like that."

Kenny paused and sipped his coffee.

"Well, as long as it don't fuck up the Norris kid. He's the anchor for Carter's class." And Ranger Bill returned his attention to the three-stars, the four-stars, the early-signing period, and the trolls on the message boards who "never knew nothin' and oughta keep their mouths shut."

Chapter 4

SEEDS

Anne's British-racing-green Land Rover pulled up through the porte cochère in front of St. James School, where the children were being released from their second day of Vacation Bible School. She rolled her passenger-side window down as a wide-waisted woman in a white blouse approached.

"Hi Anne!" the woman said, and then into a walkie-talkie said "Norris." Behind her, the door opened, and she saw Emilia walking slowly toward her.

"Emilia's just a joy. Just a joy," said Hannah Fletcher, leaning slightly in the window.

"We're blessed," Anne replied, as Hannah moved away to let Emilia open the passenger door and climb in. "Bye Hannah," Anne said, waving her fingers through the window in front of Emilia's face. As they pulled away, Emilia rolled the window up.

Anne noticed immediately that something was bothering the little girl.

"How was it today?"

"Fine," Emilia said, sullenly.

"You had fun at VBS yesterday, what's wrong?"

"Nothing, I'm just hungry," Emilia answered.

They drove on a little way in silence. Anne had been listening to

EWTN radio but had turned it down when Emilia got in the car. You could still hear the voices over the road noise, but indistinctly.

"Do you want some chicken fries?"

"Yeah, I guess."

"Okay. We'll stop. How about a milkshake?"

"No thanks. I'm dieting."

"That's ridiculous, Emilia. You don't need to diet. If anything, you need to be eating more."

"Well, I just don't want a milkshake."

"Okay," Anne answered, and then resumed her prodding. "Why won't you tell me what's wrong?"

"I just don't want to talk about it."

"Honey, if something is bothering you, you should talk about it. Did one of your friends do something?"

"Yeah. Stupid Maci." And then the words tumbled out in a torrent. "I just can't stand her. She's always like 'you're such a little girl,' and she acts like she knows everything, but everybody thinks that she's so cool and popular. Ugh!" Emilia folded her arms across her chest and kicked the floorboard with one foot.

"And that bothers you because you don't feel cool and popular?" Anne asked.

"No! It bothers me because she's a jerk."

"Well, you don't always have to get along with everyone. Maybe there's something bothering her and she's just taking it out on you."

"No! She's always like that! I just can't stand her!" Emilia was leaning out of her seat now, pushing against the seatbelt, and then slammed herself back into the seat as she finished talking.

The girl hugged her arms even tighter and glared out the front window. Anne decided to let her sulk, as she knew from experience that pushing her daughter to calm down would only make her more upset.

They made the turn onto Interstate 26 and drove north toward their farm. At the exit before theirs, she planned to stop at Burger King for the snack.

Suddenly, Emilia asked: "Mom, what's a pansexual?"

Anne was stunned. The question had come from nowhere, but it triggered her instinctual reply: "Is that what's got you so upset?"

"Maci said she's a pansexual and made fun of me when I asked her what it was."

Anne was silent, then honestly replied: "Honey, I don't know what a pansexual is. How did this come up?"

"Well, Maci told me that I can't call Fiona a girl anymore and I have to use boy pronouns when I talk about her because Fiona wants to be a boy. Maci said I was *a little girl and I didn't know what pansexual or nonbinary are.*" Emilia emphasized these last words with a mocking imitation of Maci's voice.

Anne sat in shock. Of all of the things she had expected to hear from an eleven-year-old girl after Vacation Bible School, this was perhaps the very last. She didn't know what pansexual meant, but she certainly had heard enough of the term "nonbinary," and it was pretty clear in context of the gender-pronoun issue that pansexual must have something to do with it.

As they drove on silently, the lush green hills and madly growing trees of early June rushed by the windows. Anne was barely conscious of the drive, her mind spinning the rolodex of possible responses, sorting through what little she knew of all the gender craziness that she couldn't help hearing about. *At St. James!* She thought, disbelieving. *Not at St. James!* It was as if an enemy had just breached the walls of her fortress. Her mind spun quickly to blame. *I know Maci's parents. This is not a surprise. I'd expect this kind of thing from them. Filling their daughter's head with nonsense. She's a little girl! I'm calling them when I get home. I don't care what they say in their own home, but when they bring my child into it, then they have to stop. Why do they even send Maci to VBS? She's like a virus. She'll infect everyone.*

Anne was surprised at her rage, and calming, suddenly realized that Emilia was looking at her, the expression of sullenness had been replaced by a questioning and concerned look.

"Is that what Maryanne is?" Emilia asked, softly.

A great sob almost burst out of Anne's mouth, but in an instant she stopped it.

"No. I don't know what a pansexual is, but I don't think Maryanne is one. Maryanne has . . . other issues."

"I wish she'd come home," Emilia said.

"So do I, honey," Anne replied, and then she asked herself whether that was truly honest.

Coach Carter's door opened, and Professor Monty Sanders entered, closing the door behind him. Carter looked up, stood, walked around the desk, and extended his hand.

"Professor," he said, as Sanders took his hand in an almost feminine manner, quickly disengaging. The coach gestured to two distressed leather chairs in the corner of the office, as opposed to the "dressing down" chair in front of his desk, saying "Please, sit" and then strode over to one of the chairs.

Monty Sanders was neatly dressed. In fact, Carter got the impression that he would be wearing a turtleneck if not for the oppressive heat of the early North Carolina summer. Instead, he was dressed in a slate-grey Oxford shirt, open at the neck, over yet-darker grey slacks leading down to polished black shoes. His hair was closely cropped on the sides but long and loose atop his forehead with a tendril or two always escaping to hang roguishly over his brow. Around his ears, the hair up to his temples was a distinguished grey—adding to his erudite appearance—and carefully dyed by Sanders to give just this effect. His sharp features were undeniably attractive, and his blue puppy-dog eyes inspired openness and trust. Only faint pockmarking from an unfortunate adolescence marred his cheeks. He had the body of a swimmer (which he had been)—broad shouldered, thin waisted. His entire body seemed to come to a point somewhere below the floor.

"Lovely," Sanders said, surveying the chair. "I believe these are the same as at the Grove Park. Stickley, I think. Very nice. Very expensive." His voice carried a hint of a New England accent and was almost pained and exasperated. He had the timbre of a diluted William F. Buckley—a fact he would have found abhorrent if he had been aware.

"Yes, well, the chairs were here when I arrived," Carter returned, a little sour. The professor took the other seat and folded his hands in his lap.

"Thank you for seeing me, Coach Carter," he began. "I know your time is very valuable." And with a downward glance at the arm of the leather chair, he seemed to be stressing its decadence again. "I'll get right to the point. I wanted to warn you that I will not brook any attempt at interfering with my honest evaluation and grading of any of your football players in my course. I take academic integrity very seriously, and attempting to bring pressure upon me to alter grades will not only fail but will result in my bringing every effort to bear to expose such an attempt."

"Professor, if you have knowledge of any such attempt, you should let me know right now."

Sanders smirked and continued.

"Yes. Of course. Let me say that this is a preemptive warning. Your starting center is in a very bad way already in the summer term, which, as I'm sure you know, is required for his academic suspension to be lifted. Frankly, based on his past performance and the lack of enthusiasm he shows for both attendance and attention, I do not believe that he is able to rally. I have experience with such matters, and in that experience it is inevitable that the *athletic importance* of the *football player* is respected to a higher degree than keeping inviolable the fair and judicious grading process."

"Thank you for bringing this to my attention, Professor Sanders. You can be assured that no effort will be brought to bear to encourage you to alter any grades or change any standards for my player. However, I can also tell you that we will use all means at our disposal to ensure that he rises to those standards and passes your class."

"Of course, of course. It is certainly my hope that your athlete is able to turn things around. But I would hate for him to be under the impression that his special status would excuse him from putting in the necessary effort, and I'm sure you feel the same."

"Of course. Are there any other issues you would like to bring to my attention?"

"No, that was the sole cause for this meeting."

"Okay then," Carter said, standing. Sanders did the same, offering his hand.

"Coach Carter."

"Professor."

As Monty Sanders exited the room, the cherry-paneled door closing behind him, Coach Carter returned to his desk chair and sat in it heavily. The interview had gone as well as could be expected. Carter had been warned of Sanders and knew something of his history. The sociology professor had been at the center of an academic cheating scandal at Maryland University, which had ballooned into a series of NCAA violations and show-cause penalties against both the football coach and the basketball coach. The NCAA had been less concerned with the academic cheating and pressure brought on the professors of that institution than they had been with the recruiting violations churned up in the ensuing investigation. In the end, Maryland U. had fired both coaches, given up scholarships, and seen its promising football team struggling at the bottom of their conference. The basketball team had fared better, but then it hadn't been much to begin with.

Monty Sanders had emerged as both a hero and pariah—hero to his fellow academics and villain to the football fans, boosters, and prominent alumni. His tenure seemed to have been put on hold, although there was nothing "official" in that regard, and he had limped along at Maryland U. for a few more years until his wife had been offered a position at Biltmore College, and Monty went along in tow, eventually joining the sociology department as an associate professor. Such a job was clearly beneath his capabilities and reputation, and it was not long before he became a full professor. Almost immediately, he formed an independent Academic Integrity Committee, of which he was chair.

Despite the concerns of Carter's predecessor, Sanders hadn't caused any serious trouble for the athletics department at Biltmore College. He had taught, fired shots across the bow of anyone he thought was interfering with his teaching, and gathered the confidence and accolades of his fellow professors. A quiet push began for tenure, but Biltmore, like most institutions, became ever more reluctant to grant this. Tenure, a tool for maintaining a university's valuable personnel assets, was a two-edged sword, for once granted, it could not be rescinded other than for flagrant cause. When it was granted, the institution lost considerable leverage over those personnel assets. In an increasingly tribal world, tenured professors could be loose cannons. The primacy of academic pursuits and free inquiry butted up against social media and instant journalism. So, despite the pressure from his colleagues, Sanders found himself again waiting for that elusive prize.

Now, as Coach Carter sat in his paneled and gilded athletic department office, Professor Sanders walked along the sunlit paths of the park-like campus, back to the old buildings. He enjoyed the walk and particularly enjoyed reaching those parts of the campus that reminded him of what a college should look like: brick buildings with imposing cast-concrete scrollwork above the entryways, long curving paths and well-kept lawns, benches and alcoves, and little gardens where the free exchange of ideas could (and did!) take place. It was his milieu.

He reached the humanities building where he had his office, entering a very different world than the glistening athletic department. Up a flight of steps to the front entrance (past the disabled-persons ramp), into painted cinderblock hallways, narrow and festooned every few feet with bulletin boards, he strode purposefully, nodding here and there to a colleague or a recognized student. He was very aware of the contrast between Coach Carter's building and his. He honestly preferred this building, but also honestly resented the difference: money.

He had heard all the arguments before. Athletics, and football in particular, brought in millions of dollars, whereas humanities did nothing but educate students. Which was the purpose of the university? To raise funds to build ever more glamorous accommodations? To entertain the mass of local populace that had never attended and never would attend Biltmore College? No matter how one arranged facts, the purpose of the institution was to take in students, teach them to think, and to instill in them the virtues that they had most often been denied in their youthful education at the hands of ignorant parents and feeble schools. The purpose of the university was to create an army of enlightened warriors, to turn back the hordes of barbarians, and to advance civilization.

In such an idiom, athletics was a poorly grafted appendage that sucked the vitality from the university, preoccupied the administration, and corrupted the academic process every chance that it had. To Professor Sanders, the ultimate outrage that encapsulated this topsy-turvy world was this: As a professor, he had to pay for parking on campus. But on Saturdays in football season, he was not allowed to park in his own space, it being reserved for game-day attendance. This trivial thing galled him and was never far from his mind whenever he heard mention of the Biltmore College Rangers.

Coach Carter's secretary knocked on his door, leaned in, and said "Dane Norris." Carter gestured for her to send him in. Shortly after, Dane's bulk filled the doorway, and he walked stiff jointed into the office, going right to the "dressing down" chair in front of the desk. Carter half-rose to greet him and then sat back down.

The two were dressed almost identically: glossy BC Rangers pullovers—inappropriately long-sleeved despite the June weather—over khakis whose hems floated above tennis shoes. Seeing the two together, one might have supposed that Carter was a more evolutionary-advanced version of the more troglodytic Norris:

Exhibit A: The "Football Player." Known by his muscular

physique and intimidating bulk, the Football Player can eat up to eight cheeseburgers a day and has surprising speed in a sprint.

Exhibit B: The "Football Coach." Inhabiting the demesnes in which football occurs, the Football Coach can be identified by his small size, relative to the Football Player, and by the greater intelligence which is often indicated by a high forehead and receding hairline.

Carter began without preamble.

"Thanks for coming in Mr. Norris . . . "

"Dane," he interrupted.

"Sure, and call me Trey. Anyway, I'm sorry our appointment last week was canceled . . . "

"No problem," Dane interrupted again.

"What I wanted to see you about was our kickoff game against Carolina Central. As you know, we're going to spend this season honoring our Ranger Royalty, and I was hoping you'd be our first honoree this year."

"Sure. Proud to do it."

"Great! We'll put you in then."

"What does it involve? Going on the field at the half, I guess?"

"Well, we're going to be a bit more elaborate than that," Carter responded. "This year, we'd actually like some of our Royalty to be in the Ranger Ride, so you and a few of the non-football Royalty would ride in during the pregame parade."

"Oooo . . . you might want to rethink that," Dane said, laughing. "The last time I was on a horse the damn thing could barely move, and the whole ride it just grunted like it was going to die."

Carter chuckled and replied: "Trust me, we've already thought about the size of the horses. You're in pretty good shape compared to some other Royalty. I'll just say that the linemen in particular were of concern."

"Okay," Dane laughed, "that's fine. Anything else?"

"After the Ranger Ride, you'll have seats in one of the Cox luxury boxes, then come down at halftime for the on-field recognition. There will be a reception after the game as well, in the Ranger Royalty lounge."

"Okay, sounds great! Thanks. It's an honor. I just assumed you had invited me down here to talk about Dylan."

"Well, I hope there's nothing to talk about there. We're very excited that he's joining the program, and graduating early will give him the chance to get a head start for his freshman campaign. He's still graduating early, right?"

"Yep. He already got credits from a couple of years of summer school, so he doesn't even have to take classes this summer. He just has to finish up the first semester of his senior year. Dylan's dedicated."

"That's one of the things we're excited about. I'm looking forward to seeing him in action in the Ambrose opener. I'll be there with some of the other coaches."

"Sure is different from when we were playing, right?" Dane asked, and Carter nodded his head. Dane continued: "I don't envy your job, but I envy these kids even less. Dylan had made up his mind about BC pretty early, and for the most part that's kept other schools away. But some of these kids in the recruiting battles . . . they must think they're gods."

"You don't know the half of it," Carter said. "It's the haves and have-nots. The five-star kids have so much sunshine blown up their asses that it's pretty hard to get their attention. Schools are flying helicopters into high school campuses now, photoshopping the kids onto *Sports Illustrated* covers, doing crazy shit, and it all goes to the kids' heads. The four-stars are getting just as bad, and before you know it the three-stars will be the same way. The competition is just too intense, and there are more programs than ever that can afford these stunts. On the other hand, you've got those two-stars that are just desperate to get a scholarship. Those kids don't think they're gods. It's pretty sad when you have to sit across from them in their shanty, with their family sitting around, and listen to them pitch themselves."

"I'd imagine you don't have too many of those kids on your schedule."

"No, I still do. You never know where you're going to find those special kids, so I try not to get too focused on the premier players."

"Good for you," Dane nodded, but they both knew the valuable commodity of the head coach's time was only going to be rarely diverted to such noble endeavors.

"Okay, well, if that's it I'm just going to walk around campus a bit," Dane said, rising from his chair.

"Good to see you, Dane," Coach Carter said, rising as well.

"You too, Trey."

Wilford Memorial Home was a long, white-brick building with a faux-copper roof, black shutters, and a long-sloped parking lot that caused driver-side doors to swing open heavily if one were not careful. There were many a dent, ding, and then the obligatory note left on the windshield of damaged cars, which were seldom replied to. Perhaps people were more forgiving of accidents occurring in the parking lot of a funeral home than those at a grocery store.

A long line stretched outside the building as the Norris family arrived in their separate vehicles: Dylan driving his Yukon alone, and Dane, Emilia, Janus, and Anne in Anne's Land Rover. They were running late, and the parking lot was almost completely full. Dylan pulled in next to Anne on the uphill side (and managed to avoid cracking the side of his mother's SUV as the door of his own vehicle flew open). The rest of the family climbed out of the Land Rover and stood for a moment in the late-day cool breeze, their black clothes and suits crisp. Janus had grown significantly since he last wore his, and his arms stuck far out of his jacket sleeves, giving him a comical appearance. He had been unable to button the top of his dress shirt, and his tie clumsily attempted to cover this up.

Pete Morton's receiving line had pulled in a huge crowd of mourners. The first of three such events (the two dead girls would be mourned together), it had occasioned a shortage of black dresses in

Asheville's department stores. Aside from the Morton family, their friends, and coworkers, almost the entirety of St. Ambrose High School's student body had turned out, along with many of their parents and family. As the Norrises walked toward the end of the line, more vehicles turned into the treacherous lot, more mourners joined the crowd, and the funeral director's assistants pattered up and down the line, expertly dispensing advice and asking "Whom are you here for?" There was another service occurring simultaneously: an elderly woman who had passed away at a hospital. Her remembrance was overshadowed by that of the teenage boy, and it was only rarely that someone would answer "Collins" and be whisked out of the line and taken inside to the second and smaller receiving room.

The Norrises had arrived fifteen minutes after the opening of the receiving line, and now they slowly moved forward, towering above their neighbors, and inching their way along with the queue to Wilford's open, black double doors.

By 6:45, the Norris family had finally entered the funeral home and saw that the line continued on before them, winding to the right through a large hallway, past a lectern upon which the visitors' register lay open and nearing fullness, where only two or three "Good Shepherd" prayer cards remained, and into the large room from which the murmur of subdued voices drifted out.

The funeral director himself made an appearance, walking down the line and quietly saying "Please pay your respects to the family quickly, as there are many people waiting to do so." This advice seemed to be unheeded by whomever was currently paying their respects, as the line paused in place for a full ten minutes.

At 7:10, the Norrises entered the great room and saw that the line still stretched before them. The Morton family had been reduced to the father and two older sisters. Mrs. Morton now sat, exhausted, in a pew with the family matriarchs. The funeral director appeared again and began making his way down the line and repeating his admonition to be quick. The cloying scent of attar of roses filled the room, mixing with perfume, cologne, and body spray. It was uncomfortably hot. Dane loosened his tie.

Finally, close to 7:30, the family stepped up to the Mortons.

Dylan was first: “I’m real sorry. Pete was a great kid.”

Mr. Morton shook his hand, and Dylan moved forward to express the identical sentiment to Pete’s sisters.

Then Janus: “So sorry for you.”

Dane: “Our condolences. Stay strong.”

Emilia: “We’re so sad. But we know Peter is in heaven.” Mr. Morton smiled at the little girl and said “I’m sure he is. Thank you.”

Finally, Anne, who hugged the father and said, “We’re so sorry. I can’t imagine. Give our love to your wife. We’ll be praying for Peter.”

Behind the Morton family, Peter was displayed in an open casket. His black hair neatly combed, the sides of his face waxy, and his cheeks hollow. A kneeler sat in front of the coffin. Dylan waited for it to be vacated, then quickly kneeled, crossed himself even more quickly, waited a few seconds, and stood up. He glanced down at Pete’s body and then placed one hand on the side of the casket in a farewell gesture, but a second later, he jerked his hand away. Despite the mugginess of the room, the surface of the casket was cool and oily. Dylan felt the heat of his hand being sucked into the wood, and he had the illusion that his life was being sucked along as well. He stood bemused for a second or two, rubbing his hands together, then he moved off, looking out over the crowded room until he spotted some friends. Without a word, he left his family and joined them.

Janus, Emilia, Dane, and Anne took their turns at the kneeler and then found a seat near the front of the room. The Mortons were ushered to the front pews. The receiving line was cut off. And Fr. Kelly was making his way forward, continuously detained as he did so.

Knowing the rosary was coming, most of the mourners made their exit, but the room was still crowded. Dylan found his way to a seat in the back pews, along with a crowd of SAHS rising seniors. As he sat down, Wendy Taylor took the place next to him.

Wendy wore a tight black dress that surely had not been

purchased for a funeral; it was low cut across her small breasts, and the hem was well above her knees. She wore black stockings and black high-heeled shoes, carried a shiny black clutch, had a necklace of black beads, a mop of unruly black hair, black eyeliner, black fingernails, and black dangling earrings which featured little black dreamcatchers and descending black studs. She wore no lipstick, which seemed odd, since she could certainly have found it in black. She put her hand on Dylan's leg and looked up at him.

Dylan towered over her. He looked down and grinned, and then, thinking better of it, tried to attain a mournful expression but achieved only a kind of grimace. He bowed his head but looked sideways at Wendy a couple of times.

Fr. Kelly was now standing in front of Pete's casket. The room was quieting as conversations became hushed, leaving the final whisperers as rude little islands who, once realizing their error, were suddenly silenced.

Fr. Kelly was dressed in his ebony priest's tunic and collar over similarly colored slacks and shoes but wore a grey Irish cardigan as a sort of trademark. One generation removed from the Emerald Isle, Kelly had a strange way of speaking, with some words almost slurred into a brogue and others stiffly overpronounced. He had reassuring gray hair, reassuring thick grey eyebrows, and reassuring blue eyes set in a thin and acerbic face. He exuded, along with that reassurance, a sort of foggy or blurry presence and seemed a charismatic spirit speaking out of the center of a cloud of mist.

"We gather here tonight to remember our brother Peter, who was taken from us too soon. In the coming days we will remember not only Peter but also our friends Doug, Mandy, and Sarah. They will forever be joined together in our memory as they were joined together departing this world. But we must remember also that it is our hope that they go before us to the Father's house. In our time of great sorrow, we must also remember that joy. The depth of our loss here on earth will be overcome by our elation at seeing the Father. An elation that Peter feels today. And so we pray that comfort may come to the family and to the friends as we pray for Peter tonight.

"Today, Friday, we commemorate in the prayer of the rosary the Sorrowful Mysteries."

As Fr. Kelly said this, there was a rustling from the many people in the room, as pockets and handbags disgorged their beads. Anne saw Emilia take her ivory First Communion rosary from her little handbag, and seeing Janus and Dane patting their pockets, she pulled extra rosaries—cheap plastic ones sealed in little bags—from her purse. Janus and Dane took them and loudly tore the bags open as Anne withdrew her own rosary made of ornate jade beads and a silver crucifix from a little pouch.

In the back of the room, Dylan, like the other young men in the pew, pulled out his iPhone. Wendy reached for neither rosary nor phone, but bowed her head along with the others.

"I believe in God the Father almighty, Creator of heaven and earth . . . " Fr. Kelly began, and prayed aloud the Apostle's Creed, the Our Father, three Hail Marys, and finished: "Glory be to the Father, and to the Son, and to the Holy Spirit. As it was in the beginning, is now, and ever shall be, world without end. Amen."

He continued:

"The first Sorrowful Mystery: The Agony in the Garden. Here we sit in our own agony. The agony of loss. The agony of fear. The agony of despair. A young life taken from us, leaving behind an empty place that should have been full of hope, a bright future of possibility. Jesus, too, felt the agony of fear, and His disciples would soon know that same agony of loss. Their king, their Messiah—whom they trusted and who would deliver them and redeem the kingdom of Israel—would be gone in a few short hours. A thing that they could not foresee, even though Jesus Himself warned them what was to come. But through that loss would come the redemption. There was no other way. They could not understand it. To them it seemed that bright hopes and dreams were snuffed out on the edge of victory. To us also, we cannot understand. Let us remember that God's victory is not the one we foresee. His ways are not our ways. Let us trust in Him that His plan leads to glory. And so we pray: Our Father . . . "

Kelly continued, his unusual voice carrying throughout the room. He recited the meditations on the second mystery, and the third mystery, dwelling long upon the Crowning with Thorns, the shame, embarrassment, and mockery, and continued: "Our Father, who art in heaven . . . "

In the back of the room, Wendy slid her hand over Dylan's leg and between them. Dylan felt an electric thrill run up his spine, and with head still down, looked over. Wendy was in the same posture—head down with black hair concealing her face. Dylan looked back toward his left hand, in which his iPhone glowed. Then with his elbow, he nudged Randy Thompson, the big offensive lineman. Randy looked over, and Dylan motioned with his eyes down to his lap, where Wendy's hand rested. A big toothy smile broke over Randy's ruddy face, and he suppressed a laugh.

The congregation's prayers continued:

Hail Mary, full of Grace, the Lord is with thee; blessed art thou amongst women and blessed is the fruit of thy womb, Jesus. Holy Mary, mother of God, pray for us sinners, now and at the hour of our death. Amen.

Hail Mary, full of Grace, the Lord is with thee; blessed art thou amongst women and blessed is the fruit of thy womb, Jesus. Holy Mary, mother of God, pray for us sinners, now and at the hour of our death. Amen.

Hail Mary, full of Grace, the Lord is with thee; blessed art thou amongst women and blessed is the fruit of thy womb, Jesus. Holy Mary, mother of God, pray for us sinners, now and at the hour of our death. Amen.

The fourth mystery, then the fifth and final mystery. Fr. Kelly spent a long time on the crucifixion and death, looking softly at Mrs. Morton as he described Mary's sorrow at the foot of the cross. A row of SAHS freshmen girls sobbed in front of Dylan.

Wendy began to move her hand up and down, rubbing Dylan's penis through the cloth of his pants.

Fr. Kelly finished praying the Hail Holy Queen, the mourners made the sign of the cross, and as heads lifted and rosaries were pocketed or pursed, Wendy pulled her hand away. Dylan, aroused and unfulfilled, pushed his iPhone into his pocket and buttoned his suit coat over his lap, then stood as his schoolmates did likewise. Randy grinned at him and jokingly punched his shoulder. Behind him, Wendy moved away toward the opposite end of the pew, exiting behind some of the girls of her class, but wordlessly and aloof.

The mourners made their way out of the funeral home to congregate in small groups outside. Some headed for their cars, some lingered. Inside, the Morton family was taking their last look at Peter before the casket was closed. Fr. Kelly sat in a pew next to the matriarchs, waving off their effusive praise of his rosary prayers. Floral splash displays and potted plants were being removed, Kleenexes picked up from pews and the floor.

The sun crept down behind the mountains, and the shadows lengthened. Anne found Dylan in a small group of his teammates. Ties had been removed and stuffed away. Suit coats were open, and hands were in pockets.

"Hello boys. It's so terrible that you have to go through this."

"Hi, Mrs. Norris," said one. The greeting was echoed by the others.

"Dylan, are you coming home with us?"

"No," he said, almost sharply. "A bunch of us are getting together to remember Pete. I'll be home before too late."

"Okay," Anne responded. "Goodnight boys."

"Goodnight, Mrs. Norris" came the chorus of deep bass voices.

As she walked away, Randy turned to Dylan and asked: "You goin' with us?"

"Nah, just waiting for her to go so that I can meet up with Wendy."

"Alright!" Randy grinned and laughed. Dylan watched his family pile into the Land Rover and drive away. Then he said his goodbyes and walked to the Yukon, where Wendy waited by the passenger door.

Chapter 5

WORMS

As Dylan drove away from Wilford's, he turned briefly to Wendy.

"Damn! I can't believe you did that."

"You could have stopped me," she replied, calmly.

"Girl, you are hardcore."

"So where are we going?"

"Party Field?" Dylan asked, hopefully.

"Cool. Can we stop and get something to eat? I'm starving."

"Sure. Where?"

"I don't care. Not Taco Bell."

They merged onto Interstate 26 and drove north. The night was descending, but a full moon was already on the rise, edging up over the mountains. Headlights and taillights and streetlights stretched out before them. Billboards and signs streaked by. They spoke very little. Wendy reached over and changed the satellite radio, flipping through until she found an EDM channel. Dylan used his steering wheel controls to change the radio back to metal. Wendy changed it again. They laughed, and he finally let her have her way.

"I hate this shit," Dylan said.

"I like it."

Wendy's small, thin body was nestled in the Yukon's passenger seat, her legs drawn up and her shoes on the leather. With her right hand, she fiddled with the lumbar control, moving it up and down and in and out.

"Why do you always have it so cold in here?"

"I like it," Dylan laughed. "There's a hoodie in the back." Wendy unbuckled and leaned over the center console, rummaging through the pile of clothes and empty bottles in the back before sitting again in her seat with an odorous grey hooded sweatshirt, which she draped around herself.

They pulled off an exit and went through the drive-through at a Roosterz, a chicken sandwich for her, triple cheeseburger and fries for him, and a couple of Cokes. Back on the interstate, Dylan wolfed down the burger in three bites and ate fries by the handful. At the next exit, they pulled over again as Dylan ran into a convenience store for bottled water and a bag of chips.

They continued on SR 401; there was very little traffic this far out of town. About a mile past the Jiffy Stop, Dylan made a left-hand turn onto a gravel road. The headlights lit the trees and bushes that crowded the drive, brushing against the side of the Yukon until the gravel faded into the Party Field.

Surrounding the city of Asheville was an ever-shifting cluster of sites where the students of SAHS and other schools spent their unsupervised time. Party Field, off of State Route 401, was one of a number of clandestine meeting places, along with Party Cove, Rutsville, the New Lots, and the Pavilion. There was a constant cat-and-mouse game between the sheriffs, the Asheville Police Department, and the teenagers, in which the authorities identified a location being used by the teens, staked it out, made an occasional arrest, and then figured out which location was next. Party Field was currently *de rigueur* (although empty tonight), but within a few weeks, the Madison County sheriffs would likely begin posting a cruiser in the Jiffy Stop parking lot, looking for increased traffic among late-model vehicles headed up toward the gravel road.

Dylan opened the sunroof and cracked the windows. The crickets, disturbed by the passing of the vehicle, resumed their chirping.

All else was quiet but for the EDM beat thumping. The two were lit up by the dazzling array of dashboard lights, little buttons with glowing symbols for seat warmers, rear hatch, air conditioning, and traction control. Glancing at Wendy, he saw her produce the missing tube of black lipstick from her bag and apply it generously. The headlights shone out onto the emptiness of the field, just barely illuminating the concrete picnic table, desolate in the open.

Dylan reached down with his left hand and unbuckled his belt, unbuttoned his waist, and unzipped his fly. Then he reached over and put his right hand behind Wendy's head, pulled her across the console, and pushed her down. She pushed back, knowing that he liked it. So he pushed harder until her head was in his lap, and then locking his huge hand around the back of her head, moved it up and down until he finally fell back against the headrest and let go of her hair.

Wendy stayed lowered for a moment and then rose up. Dylan panted beside her, his eyes closed. She unscrewed a water bottle and took a long drink and said, "So you have weed."

A smile came to Dylan's face as he answered, his eyes still closed and his head back.

"Of course I have weed. I always have weed. Hell, that's probably what you were feeling for in my pants."

"Didn't find it, did I?"

Dylan reached across her and opened the glovebox. Taking out a medicine bottle, he opened the cap and took out one of the joints, then handed it to Wendy. She pulled a lighter from her clutch and lit the joint, taking little puffs and then a big drag, which she held in before coughing it back out, handing the joint to Dylan.

It was a scene that they had acted out perhaps a half-dozen times over the last two-and-a-half years.

Dylan Norris' first sexual experience took place in the St. James Youth Group. He had gotten a hand job from Theresa McGinnis in the middle of a crowd of teenagers in sleeping bags while one of the *Thor* movies played on a projector screen on the stage of the gym. This experience had kindled a brief period of faithful attendance at SJYG events, where Dylan found a fertile field of his classmates whose sexuality was emerging. He endured the drama of teenage dating, with love regularly declared and just as regularly disavowed, and needy girls easily pulled into and thrust out of his orbit. Amidst all of the felt banner making, hand clapping, hugging, and worship songs, Dylan fed his ego and his appetites. Then he got his driver's license and the big black Yukon Denali that came with it.

The youth group was comprised of three distinct sets of kids. The first was the group of queers—the Christ-motivated boys who were obviously gay but wittingly or not buried that within the vocabulary of the young Catholics. These boys were beloved of the second group, which were the true-believer girls—by far the largest core of the youth group. The gay boys sang and clapped and hugged along with the girls, plumbed the depths of their feelings in peer ministry exercises, and were transported into ecstasies at youth conferences and summer camps. The third group consisted of kids whose parents were making them attend, and that generally included kids like Dylan who fed upon the activities and drew out as much as they could while waiting for better and less-restricted times.

Around these three primary groups there were a few satellites: the hard-core gays who embraced their sexuality and, like Dylan, were only there for the target-rich environment; the bad girls who sneered and withdrew and formed a little hateful corps of rejection; and the little kids who were slow in maturing physically or mentally and who still took pleasure in the elementary school mentality of games and clean humor. This last group constituted the only real outcasts, kids left behind in the wake of their adolescent superiors.

In this environment, Wendy and Dylan orbited each other without coming together. Wendy was firmly in the bad-girl camp. Sullen and moody and rejecting social compliance. Dylan Norris was the despised "jock" and "popular" kid.

But Dylan's driver's license ultimately changed all that. One night in early summer, Dylan had stopped by the Youth House near the St. James campus to see one of his teammates who was still trapped in obeisance to the SJYG, and Wendy had struck up a conversation. Thirty minutes later, she snuck away with Dylan, and he drove the Yukon behind the gym to a disused parking lot. Dylan folded the rear seats back and they climbed into the cargo compartment. He pulled down her jeans and panties and popped her cherry on the beige carpet, while the seat-back dug painfully into her side and the smell of sweat and body spray assaulted her nostrils. Feeling the blood flowing between her legs as Dylan lifted himself off of her, she grabbed a shirt from the floor next to her and wiped herself.

The next afternoon Wendy left school with her upperclassman friend Amber to purchase levonorgestrel. Wendy sat silently in the passenger seat of Amber's Audi, while Amber prattled on about how Plan B wasn't really abortion.

That same afternoon, Dylan found his white SAHS practice jersey wadded up in the back of the Yukon, streaked with Wendy's blood. He wore it to practice anyway. Inquiries from the coaches were met by claims of a bloody nose. Inquiries from teammates were met with the truth, and with both disbelief and admiration. Wendy, the freaky little emo girl, found herself the sudden object of attention and could pick and choose among suitors, provided she was willing to sustain her reputation.

Dylan drifted from one girl to the next, his own reputation growing among the SAHS girls for his crudity. From time to time he would find himself with Wendy again, but Dylan found that his taste for her had to be coupled with exercising power, and until she learned the trick of feigned resistance, he found himself disappointed and lusting instead after some unconquered territory. But most of the time he found himself partying with teammates and watching them peel off one by one into their adolescent boyfriend/girlfriend theatrics. None of the eligible girls really wanted to spend time with Dylan, nor he with them.

Marijuana rolled easily into his life, as natural a thing as shaving or driving a car. Pot was ubiquitous among his friends. THC in a vape, edibles, one-hitters, and joints, hip-hop and metal, vodka and hard lemonade, late-night runs for Krystal hamburgers and Taco Bell. This was the atmosphere that Dylan breathed when he wasn't breathing football.

For Dylan, driving and weed went hand-in-hand. They were wrapped up together with the bourgeoning sense of his independence, and both were sparks that had been ignited by Maryanne.

Maryanne was Dylan's cool older sister, his childhood playmate. When he got his learner's permit at fifteen, it was Maryanne who first took him to a parking lot and let him drive her BMW around. From then on, instead of his father and mother, it was his sister who rode with him all over Asheville. As Maryanne was under twenty-one, this arrangement was illegal, but Dane and Anne either forgot about this or remained willfully ignorant, caught up in their own concerns and more than happy to let their daughter take on this minor burden.

Impervious to fear and to the law, Maryanne would task the unready Dylan to drive on backroads and interstates, in the afternoons and the early nights of winter. After a little while, she began using Dylan's driving as an excuse to get out at night, and Dylan would find himself shuttling her from the farm to basement parties, dropping her off at the cove and waiting in the car until she returned, and taking the blame when they were home late.

One night in early spring, as Dylan sat outside of a house in Asheville's Dewey Heights neighborhood, Maryanne's boyfriend Trent came out to the car and invited him in. Dylan found himself on a couch in an RV parked beside the house. His sister was nowhere to be seen. Trent packed the bowl of a bong and showed Dylan how to hit it. When Maryanne finally came through the door of the RV, Dylan was as high as a kite. She and Trent laughed and laughed, while Dylan sat smiling in a haze.

From time to time they would make Dylan part of their fun, and he found himself a sort of mascot to Maryanne and her friends.

He tagged along at concerts and parties and tasted the edge of her increasingly wild life.

Then Maryanne finally began crossing the line—staying out until the next morning, locking herself in her room, letting her grades slip, skipping school. Anne became suddenly aware of her oldest child's lifestyle, and the war began. Her mother took her car keys, so Maryanne's friends would drive her after school. Anne showed up at SAHS to pick her up. Maryanne would sneak out a different exit. The school counselors, then private counselors were involved. Priests and confession were invoked, everything short of an exorcism. Maryanne snuck out her window, so Anne had her window replaced with one that didn't open. Maryanne snuck out her bedroom door, so Anne slept across the threshold. Maryanne carefully cut the drywall from her closet that shared a wall with Dylan's closet, then snuck out his window. She got away with this for about a month, and when it was discovered, Dylan feigned ignorance.

Every night was screaming and crying. Dylan heard his sister and mother at war and definitively sided with Maryanne. His early attempts to intercede on her behalf, however, were shut down harshly by his father, who, it seemed, could tolerate Maryanne's profanity and aggression toward his wife but could not tolerate the same from his son. Dylan, cowed, took his resentment and directed it toward his mother.

The war lasted until Maryanne turned eighteen. Having failed to graduate SAHS, she packed her bags and left while her mother was at Mass and her father was golfing. Dylan remembered it vividly. He stood in her doorway while she hastily stuffed a duffel bag, saying nothing. A car honked in the driveway, and Maryanne brushed by him, then turned and said: "Good luck living with HER."

She didn't wait to say goodbye to Emilia or Janus.

The morning of Peter Morton's funeral was overcast and humid. St. Francis Church sat at the center of a vast parking lot. A big, round building in yellow brick, with a conical roof that was pitched with crenellated peaks around its edge, each peak undermined by stained glass windows, the church was reminiscent of a circus tent that had been hardened and solidified.

The Norris family shuffled through the glass doors into the church's vestibule and joined the other black-clad mourners dipping their fingers into a holy water pool, then sidled to the end of one long, arced, and cushioned pew on the side of the church. A stylized St. Michael, all sharp angles and severity, lurked to their right, dull in the subdued light from outside, his sword raised high and his foot upon the head of the writhing Enemy. Green banners of wheat and grapes hung tautly against the bright drywall, the gold-chasing of the tapestries shining in the array of LED track lighting. Behind the simple wooden altar there was no crucifix but rather a big stained glass window featuring Jesus extending His arms for a big hug. Rather than some Latin inscription or scripture, the text along the bottom of the window said: "I Love You This Much."

Dylan, tired and foggy headed, sat with his head bent. Janus looked around as his future SAHS classmates filed in. Then silence as all stood. Peter Morton's casket was rolled into the center aisle outside of the vestibule by the pallbearers—all from the SAHS baseball team: John Hubert, Pat Ryan, Danny O'Brien, Skylar Evans, Marcus Parmaley, and Patrick Howell. Altar servers processed in, the crucifix held high, followed by St. Francis' two deacons, the pastor Fr. Kelly, the SAHS chaplain Fr. Dixon, and four other diocesan priests. The Morton family—father, mother, sisters, aunts, uncles, cousins, and matriarchs—followed behind them to stand in the aisle in front of the casket. Incense wafted over the congregation.

"The grace and peace of God our Father, who raised Jesus from the dead, be always with you," Fr. Kelly intoned, his voice robbed of resonance by the banners and acoustic-tile ceiling.

"And with your spirit," the congregation answered.

Fr. Kelly waved a fern soaked in holy water over the coffin, and then he and Fr. Dixon slowly unfolded the pall until the casket was draped. The priests passed by the coffin as the entrance hymn sounded, and the family made their way to the reserved pews at the front of the church. The pallbearers wheeled the casket to the end of the aisle, in front of the altar, and took their seats.

Dane Norris fingered his collar and loosened his tie.

Opening prayers, then all sat for the readings as Morton cousins came forward. Coughs and sniffles in the pews. Standing again for the gospel. Seated for Fr. Kelly's homily (an extended discursion of his comments during the rosary). Standing again for prayers, then seated once more. Bread and wine brought forward, casket incensed.

A guitar was strummed. Dane began well, but his mind immediately wandered.

Holy, Holy, Holy

Lord God of Hosts

Heaven and earth was the coop open this morning?

I thought I had that lock fixed. If those chickens are out again . . . that hawk was back yesterday circling . . . green metal roof on the barn leaves from last fall still choking the gutters need to get Janus down there to clean them out.

Maybe I'll just hire someone. Who was that guy we hired last year?

Kneeling, standing. The Lord's Prayer. Everyone at St. Francis holding hands. Anne refusing to do so, clasping her hands as the deacons did. The arms of the congregation raised high in the orans position. Anne clasping her fingers at her breast. Hands released, going back to pews or pockets. Then the sign of peace. Hugging, crying, hands shaken, Kleenexes wadded and dropped to the pew cushions.

Kneeling again, and then the ushers walked from the back of the church, releasing the mourners a pew at a time to come forward for Communion. Dane rose stiffly from the pew and shuffled forward, followed by his family, completing the arc of a great circle with the

Eucharist at its summit, and then back to the pew to kneel again. His mind went immediately back to his farm, thinking this time of getting the Jet Skis out of the barn for their annual drive to the lake house.

Anne kneeled, her mantilla around her face, with Emilia beside her and between her and her husband. She recited: "What has passed our lips as food, O Lord, may we possess in purity of heart, that what is given to us in time, be our healing for eternity . . . " and as she prayed the words by rote, her mind also wandered in two directions. Along with the words, her inner eyes were drawn upward into what she perceived as a great shining mist. But beside her, spreading out in a plane in all directions, was a crowd of faces. Her mother, father, grandparents, Dane's father. Saints and souls who had passed away, almost like fluttering wings beside her. She felt a crowded sea of spirits that mingled in her person with a singular and dominating presence that stretched from the depths of the earth into the ether.

Shuffling. The congregation stood. A sob from Mrs. Morton. Fr. Kelly praying: "Into your hands, O Lord, we humbly entrust our brother Peter. In this life you embraced him with your tender love; deliver him now from every evil and bid him enter eternal rest. The old order has passed away. Welcome him then into paradise, where there will be no sorrow, no weeping or pain, but the fullness of peace and joy with your Son and the Holy Spirit forever and ever."

"Amen," answered the mourners.

"Eternal rest grant unto him, O Lord," Fr. Dixon intoned.

"And let perpetual light shine upon him," came the murmured reply from the older members of the congregation.

"May he rest in peace."

"Amen."

"May his soul and the souls of all the faithful departed, through the mercy of God, rest in peace."

"Amen."

Fr. Kelly finished: "May the love of God and the peace of the Lord Jesus Christ bless and console us and gently wipe every tear from our eyes. In the name of the Father, and of the Son, and of the Holy Spirit."

"Amen."

The cantor raised her arms and said: "Our departing hymn is number six-fifty-two in the blue hymnal: 'Eagle's Wings.'"

The guitar player picked his arpeggio, and the cantor led the congregation. The SAHS schoolgirls sobbed. The SAHS schoolboys bowed their heads. The altar emptied, and the Mortons followed the casket of their son out of the church to the waiting hearse.

As at the funeral home, little groups of people formed in the parking lot. A queue of cars lined up behind the hearse, and the funeral director stood handing out tiny purple flags on magnets to be stuck on the hoods of the procession.

Anne Norris tried to get Dylan's attention, but he seemed engrossed in conversation with a small knot of his teammates. Dane had been unable to prevail upon her to skip the interment, and now he, Janus, and Emilia waited by the Land Rover. Anne regretfully left Dylan alone and headed toward the rest of her family. She walked past a half-dozen SAHS girls in their black dresses. They were crushed together while one of them took a selfie of the group.

Dylan watched his mother out of the corner of his eye, afraid that she would come over to him as she had done the night before. When her Land Rover circled through the lot to get into the procession line and was given its little purple flag, Dylan turned back to find Amari Hanson grinning at him.

"She gonna make you go to the burial?" Amari asked, chuckling.

"No way, bro. The bitch can do what she wants, but I ain't goin'."

"Aw man, you call your momma a bitch! Damn! That woman's a saint!"

"You don't know her like I do, bro."

"Damn, I ain't never call my momma a bitch."

"Well maybe your momma ain't a bitch," Dylan answered.

Randy Thompson came up to the group and pushed his way into the circle.

"Hey, keep it on the DL, but Micky's got a nitrous tank. We're gonna hang out at Bryce's tonight."

"Cool," Dylan responded. "Count me in. One of you try'n get Pat there? Get his mind off it."

"I've already texted him," Randy responded. "He's gotta go to the burial, but he'll try to meet up with us later. They're all going back to the Mortons after, so it'll be a while."

"Hey bro didga hear that Morton's getting sued by Doug's dad?"

"No way!"

"Yeah, blames him for them dying. Wrongful death."

"Shit. I bet he'll regret it when he finds out Doug's the one that brought the pills."

"I already got my folks lookin' over my shoulder all the time. Shit just needs to settle down for a while."

"Alright," Dylan said, pulling himself back from distraction. "Bryce's. What time?"

"Around seven."

"See you there," Dylan said, and moved away from the group. He climbed into his Yukon, navigated the parking lot, and headed back north toward the farm.

Chapter 6

IN HEATHENESSE

Dylan arrived home, parked his Yukon by the barn, and walked back along the jogging trail to the house. Rosa's blue Honda was absent from the driveway, so she must have finished up and gone back to wherever she lived. The patio doors under the deck were unlocked. Dylan pushed through into the silent house, hearing the dogs barking from their kennels as he entered, and the alarm system began its warning tone. Dylan punched the code into the keypad and made his way upstairs.

Getting to his room, he stripped off his suit and left it on the floor, changed into his running gear, then trotted back downstairs to grab a Powerade for his jog along the packed-pebble path. As he passed the tractor-barn, he felt a sudden cramp in his hamstring and pulled up short. The humidity was really coming on now, and the overcast morning was giving way to a bright day. Dylan limped over to the barn, into the shade. From inside he could hear the peeps of the hatchlings, and on an impulse went into the barn to look at them.

He walked over to the stock tank and leaned his thick hands on the rim, looking down. Below him, the chicks were disconcerted and made little shallow hops toward each other before settling into incessant peeping, ineffectual and indecipherable. Not one looked up. Aware, obviously, of Dylan's presence, and yet unable or unwilling to see him.

If he had been asked in that moment what he felt, and if he would have answered honestly, he would have said godlike. Able to reach down, pick a chick up, and set it on a new course. He lifted the wire cover on the stock tank and reached in, grabbing one of the chicks. He held it up and looked at it. The hatchling's head darted this way and that. He squeezed. The other chicks below him sensed something, and the frequency and volume of their peeping became frantic, but the chick in his hand made no sound. Dylan lowered it back into the stock tank where it stood in the pile of wood shavings. The other chicks clustered under the incubator lamp.

He let the wire cover fall back into place with a clang, set the Powerade bottle down, and then reached back and massaged his hamstring.

Dane Norris sat in the passenger seat of the Land Rover as Anne drove it north along the interstate. Peter Morton was in his place in the ground. The mourners were going their separate ways. Janus and Emilia were teasing each other in the back seat, and Dane was looking forward to the long-delayed start to his weekend.

EWTN radio played on the car stereo, but Dane tuned it out. There was a certain amount of religion that he could handle, and between the receiving of friends, the rosary, the funeral, and the anticipation of Sunday Mass the next morning, he was about at his limit. Further, he knew that in the coming week there would be two more receiving lines and three more funerals. He felt for the parents, but not in a personal way. The deaths of the four kids were tragic but remote. It might have touched him more closely if Dylan had been affected, but his oldest son went about his business as if nothing had happened, and at some level, Dane thought that was good enough for him too.

He wasn't resentful toward Anne for making the family attend the memorials. Rather, he admired her and the open heart that she had. He wasn't envious of her either; it was part of her character that she could feel sorrow and remorse when she didn't have skin in the game. She had always been compassionate, and he understood the turn she had taken toward a life that was constantly imbued with prayer and devotion. But he couldn't share it.

Dane Norris was Catholic in a sort of ethnic and family manner. There was a deep sense of identity in his Catholicism that was rooted in ancestral pride. Dane's great-great-grandfather William had come over from England in 1889 as a sort of hanger-on to Richard Morris Hunt, the architect retained by George W. Vanderbilt for the design and construction of the Biltmore estate. The members of the Norris family were die-hards in England, one of those old families of aristocracy who had maintained their Catholicism in spite of exclusion from public life, having skirted both royal oaths and papal injunctions by a sort of shape-shifting adherence to both. William Norris was a seventh son, a tame adventurer who flitted about Europe enjoying the life of a young gentleman, and in the process acquired a diverse skill set that consisted of two primary elements: knowing people and getting things done. During the construction of Biltmore, he made himself useful in diverse ways to both Hunt and to G.W. Vanderbilt, and over the six years of the Biltmore's construction, he went from being "that papist fellow" to "Hunt's man" to finally just "Willie."

William Norris never aspired to move in the rarified circles of the Vanderbilts, or even the Hunts, though for a brief time he had a fascination for Hunt's daughter Esther. Rather, Willie was consigned to the edges of the socialite circle. He became a pillar of Asheville's embattled Catholic community, and to the disdain of his family in England, settled into life in North Carolina, married and had a son, whom he politically named George after his Vanderbilt patron, and began accumulating money.

Norris had his hand in everything. For a while he was de facto manager of Biltmore Village. He arranged for the commissioning of the stained glass at the Cathedral of All Souls, then led the campaign to raise funds, plan, and finally construct the Catholic Basilica of St. Lawrence. When Edwin Grove began the purchase of lands for his great hotel, Willie Norris was there to help clear off the TB sanitoriums that stood in the way and then held the whip and the pocketbook as the Grove Park Inn was raised on the side of Sunset Mountain. His son George entered service with the Vanderbilts at Biltmore Village, and their family led the mourning among Asheville's small Catholic community for G.W. Vanderbilt after his untimely death in 1914.

Across the ocean, the ancestral Norris family that he had left behind slouched toward decrepitude. The Great War came, and the scions of the Norrises were killed, to a man, in the trenches of Europe. The family of old Catholic stalwarts simply faded away. Their estate, bequeathed to the city of High Wycombe, would later serve briefly as a home to officers of the RAF Bomber Command before being demolished. Only Norris Green, the estate's old park, remained to mark their Catholic intransigence.

But in the backwoods of the United States, by the time of his death in 1926, William Norris had accumulated a modest fortune, which enabled him to build his own estate at the base of Sunset Mountain for himself, his son, and daughters. The estate was lost in the depression, but George Norris, like his father, was a useful man who rebuilt the family wealth, rose to the rank of colonel under Mark Clark in World War II, reclaimed the property, and finally left the estate to his heir Roger in 1961.

Roger Norris' life marked the end of the multi-talented "useful men." Rather, Roger dedicated his life to the practice of law, and by the time of his father's death he was a circuit court judge. He presided over the court during the turbulence of the 1960s and gained a reputation for unpredictability that frustrated his allies and emboldened his enemies.

His son, Roger Norris Jr., followed in his father's footsteps and opened a law practice, which thrived, though he never advanced to the judiciary. The papist label was long gone, and though residual elements of anti-Catholicism lurked beneath Asheville's social circles, Norris found himself part of the "Old Money Set" and settled into an easy life of country clubs and patronage. He took his own son, Roger Norris III, into his law practice and would have done the same for his younger son, George "Dane" Norris, had the latter not impractically taken to football.

When Dane spurned an offer from Notre Dame and against his father's wishes stayed home at Biltmore College, Roger Norris II good-naturedly embraced BC and became a minor booster as a sort of low-brow appendage to his other philanthropic work. He lived to a gentile old age, watching one son take over the thriving law practice serving Asheville's Old Money and the other son go on to NFL stardom. He was there for weddings and baptisms at St. Lawrence, regally occupying the same pew each week at the ten-thirty Mass, watching his grandchildren grow. He died at seventy-four, his body broken but his mind still intact, surrounded by family and the comforts of both Church and wealth.

Roger Norris III found himself the patriarch of the family, but it was clear that the Norrises had reached a divide, and what had been an unbroken family line of diluted English gentlemen now split into the Old Money Norris family and the New Money Norris family, founded by Dane. During Dane's fifteen years living in Kansas City, Roger went about continuing the dynasty, raising three children (and forbearing to curse his eldest with the moniker "Roger IV"), and settling into the grand but antiquated Norris estate at the base of Sunset Mountain.

But Dane, eight years Roger's junior, embarked on a different adventure. Drafted in the first round by Kansas City, just as free agency supercharged the salaries in the NFL, Dane lived the life of a football star. Soon after his contract was signed, he proposed to his college sweetheart, Anne Kowalski. They were married in her hometown of Gary, Indiana, under the stern and unforgiving eye of Anne's mother rather than in Asheville at St. Lawrence. This mildly bothered his father and mother (who saw him slipping out of the Norris dynasty's orbit). He built a modest McMansion, and for five years Dane and Anne lived a life of football, travel, and indolence.

Then Maryanne was born, and Dane saw his wife turn her attention to their daughter. He was at the peak of his playing career, and he didn't really mind the loss of attention. His focus was football. When his body could no longer take the abuse, he found himself slipping, and the easy dominance passed away along with the balls thrown his way. Finally Kansas City cut him from the roster, and though he briefly considered moving on to another team, he, and the NFL, knew he was done.

Dylan was born the same year his playing career ended. For a while Dane tried to stay home and reclaim the lost years of family, but he just wasn't suited to chauffeuring Maryanne to and from preschool and changing Dylan's diapers. He hired on to the football operations department for the Kansas City Chiefs and spent a few years as a sort of faded fixture while his family grew with the birth of Janus, but his heart wasn't in the new career. Football call-in shows, the meaningless job, autographs, and accolades could not make up for the loss of locker-room camaraderie and the sense of purpose that drove his discipline. That discipline broke down, and Dane found himself at home more often than not. Drinking in his pool float in summer, drinking and watching television in winter, drinking on the golf course, drinking by himself at night, getting fatter and stiffer.

By the time Emilia was born, both Anne and Dane knew something would have to change. It was as if Anne suddenly looked up from her devotion to her children to see what her husband was becoming. During a Christmas visit to Asheville, rare because they usually traveled to Indiana to spend a cheerless holiday with her family, Anne saw her children being taken in turn by their much older cousins, saw Dane's easy relationship with his brother and parents, and felt the old familiar charms of her North Carolina college town. She decided that this was home, and within a year, they had uprooted from Kansas City and moved their family back to Asheville.

The move was immediately good for Dane, for while he was still somewhat purposeless, the proximity of family and a re-engagement with the Biltmore College Rangers—then oblivious to the depths of the program's decline—lightened his mood and tempered his drinking. But the move was devastating to Maryanne. She had left behind her school and all of her friends just as she was entering adolescence. Her nearest cousin was eight years her senior, and despite the doting of her grandfather Roger, she was lonely and angry.

Anne conceived the idea of the farm. As a little girl, she had always wanted a horse. She superimposed this desire on Maryanne, and with this sudden inspiration she finally let go of the purse strings and encouraged Dane to erect his own estate. And so they built the farm. Finding twenty acres of old pastureland on the north side of Asheville, they planned it out and then used Dane's football millions to construct their fantasy. As the property grew, Anne noticed that her own devotion to the farm was not shared by her oldest daughter. Maryanne was disinterested by the horses, never romped in the field or picked wildflowers, and seldom swam in the pool.

So, while Dane discovered that eight-year-old Dylan was interested in football, and while Dane learned how to operate a tractor and all of the endless implements that could be purchased for it, and while Dane golfed and lived amidst fame and respect as a Biltmore College legend, Anne poured herself into Maryanne and her school. She was room mother, assistant Girl Scout leader, and volleyball coach at St. James School. She hosted parties at the farm for Maryanne's class, and before long, things seemed to be going better.

Then her mother died.

Anne's Land Rover rolled past the circular drive at the front door and around to the garage. She pulled into her bay, and she and her family got out. Emilia and Janus raced out of the car, Janus pushing the little girl behind him just before they reached the door. "Janus!" Emilia shrieked, and tore after him.

Anne and Dane moved more slowly. When they reached the rec

room, Dane went behind the bar, and picking up remote controls, started turning on all the televisions. Anne took a seat at one of the bar stools, while Dane thumbed through channels, picking among various baseball games until he found the desired mix.

"You're staying in today?" she asked.

"I was planning on it."

"I thought we might go to dinner tonight."

"Sounds good," he answered, distracted.

"I thought you were taking the Jet Skis up to the lake today."

"I'll do that next weekend when we go up."

"Oh good. Janus wants to bring a friend up, and Emilia's jealous. I was thinking of seeing if the Fletchers would come up. They can bring Emma."

"Whatever you want."

"I wanted to make sure it was okay with you. The last time we saw them you said you didn't like him."

"Who?" Dane replied, looking away from the TV screen at his wife.

"Tim Fletcher."

"Oh yeah. He's a peckerhead, but whatever. I'll need a spotter if Janus is going out on the wakeboard."

"Emilia will be so excited. I'll call Hannah now." Anne got up from the bar stool and headed up the stairs as Dane pulled a bottle of Four Roses from the shelf. He let a couple of ice cubes drop into an etched-glass BC tumbler and poured the bourbon over the ice. He drained the glass at one pull, then filled it again. Taking off his suit coat and draping it over a bar stool, he stood silently for a moment before walking over to the humidor, prodding around amongst the cigars, and selecting a fat Ghurka. Pocketing his cutter and a lighter, he took his bourbon out to the patio.

The sun was lighting the fields. The hippy girl's jeep was out at the horse barn. Dylan's Yukon was nowhere to be seen. A redtail hawk glided in circles high above the chicken coop.

Dane went behind the outside bar, opened a drawer, pulled out a remote, and found the Atlanta Braves game. An ashtray with yesterday's cigar butts was on the glass-top table. Rosa had missed it, but he didn't care. He knew that would drive Anne crazy, though, so he dumped it into the rubbish bin under the sink before returning the ashtray to the table and commencing the little cigar ritual: sliding the cigar out of its glass tube, removing the thin cedar sheath of wood and splitting off a few splinters, cutting the cigar, toasting its end with the lighter, then using the lighter to set one of the cedar splinters on fire and taking quick puffs while he rolled the cigar around until it was lit to his satisfaction. Then he leaned back, taking little sips of bourbon and savoring the smoke.

He heard the door open upstairs on the deck and feet treading around. There was an explosion of rapid clicking as the dogs burst out onto the deck, their claws tapping on the wood as they cavorted around. Emilia's voice rang out: "I can smell your cigar, Daddy. Yuck!"

"It's just to keep the bugs away," he joked.

A few moments later, the dogs came hurtling down the stairs. Jingles saw him and rushed over, followed by Buddy. Dane set his tumbler down and scratched the golden retriever behind the ears until Buddy pushed her head out of the way and Dane started scratching him. Then Jingles body-slammed the Weimaraner and staked her claim, followed by the same tactic from Buddy. The two dogs wagged and nuzzled and pushed chairs out of the way until Anne and Emilia descended the stairs, and then both dogs galloped away with them. Dane's wife and daughter passed along the flag-stoned patio, in jeans and boots and bright T-shirts. Emilia carried the little egg basket, and the two went out the gate to cut across the field toward the barn. Dane set his cigar down in the ashtray then went inside and got the bottle of Four Roses and a glassful of ice. It was a good day for a drink.

Anne and Emilia re-emerged from the field, the dogs playing herald and rushing over to Dane once the gate was opened. As Anne came over and turned on the ceiling fans over the patio then sat down across from Dane, Emilia made her way up the stairs to the deck with her basket of eggs.

"Something wrong?" he asked.

"One of the hatchlings—one of the new Easter Eggers. It's just sitting in the corner. It's the one Emilia calls 'Hen-mione.'"

"Well, you always lose one or two. Probably shouldn't let Emilia name them until they're in the coop," Dane answered.

"I suppose so. I wish you wouldn't smoke during the day."

"Well, I won't have one later," Dane answered.

"Can I get you a club soda?"

"Nope. I'm fine with the whiskey."

They sat in silence for a few moments, Dane looking past her at the TV screen.

"Okay, well . . . I'll be inside."

"Okay."

The afternoon bloomed into a beautiful sky with great white clouds floating across a brilliant blue background. The vivid green of the pasture rose toward ranks of darker green trees and then climbed off into the violet mountain ridge. A humid haze exaggerated the distances and brought an air of majesty to the scene. Outside on the patio Dane switched over to beer and lit a second cigar. Inside, Janus was engrossed in the game room, Emilia was glued to YouTube, and Anne reclined on the sofa, browsing deck furniture online for the lake house.

Around four o'clock Anne called down from the upstairs deck: "I'm going into town for confession. Do you need anything?"

"Nope, I'm good," Dane answered.

"Do you want to come along?"

"Nope."

On her way to the garage, Anne stepped out onto the patio.

"Okay, I'm not staying for Mass. I'll be back around six. I thought we'd try that new place on Biltmore. The tapas place."

"Sounds good," Dane grunted. Anne let the door swing shut and made her way to the garage. A minute or two later she was driving out through the rows of Bradford pears.

St. James Catholic Church was a stone-gray castle standing defiantly on a street of red-brick and white-columned Protestant churches. Everything about St. James spoke to intransigence, from the inviolable Mass times carved in stone on the exterior, to the pre-war swastikas set into the tile floor, to the rigid faces of the parishioners. If St. Lawrence was the mother-church of western North Carolina, then St. James was the mother-in-law church. There was a story that made its way around the deanery that St. James was only built because the Irish railroad workers who had founded and funded St. Lawrence were "run off" by a wave of Italian immigrants. Another tale claimed that St. James was named in defiance of the Lutheran church across the street, as a salvo against Luther's condemnation of St. James' "epistle of straw." But whatever the truth of these stories, it was certainly the case that in the wake of Vatican II, St. James was the last parish to abandon the Tridentine Latin Mass and the first to take it up again after Pope Benedict's *moto proprio*. It was also undeniable that, carved into the lintel above St. James' polished wooden doors was the inscription: "FIDES SINE OPERIBUS MORTUA EST."

At St. James, one found a curious mix of aged parishioners and younger "radical traditionalists"—the women and girls wearing mantillas and the men and boys in suits. The interior of the church was dark, solemn, and cool. Ushers wore forest-green sport coats with gold-colored name tags. Parishioners were guided to dark-stained pews under imposing stained glass windows depicting saints and apostles. Instead of the ubiquitous banners of Asheville's other Catholic churches, there was instead a profusion of statuary, which were, indeed, mostly saints beloved by the Irish.

Anne Norris stood in line by the north transept of the church, near a brooding confessional of carved and knotted wood. In line in front of her was a nun in a blue and white habit. There were another three parishioners behind her. The muffled voices of another nun and the priest came from within the confessional, and though everyone in the line stood a respectful distance back, Anne always wondered how much of her own confession was audible to prying ears.

Then a little green light came on above the confessional door as it opened. The nun exited and made her way toward the side altar, while one of her sisters entered. The little light changed to red, and the muffled voices commenced again.

Anne looked down at her watch. 5:35. She fidgeted. The nun who had just finished had spent a good fifteen minutes in the confessional. The priest would promptly exit at 5:45 to prepare for Mass. There were still three people behind her. *What on earth could a nun have to confess for fifteen minutes?* Anne wondered, not for the first time. It was her usual practice to arrive early, knowing as she did that there was limited time and having stood in line behind the nuns before. She fingered her rosary beads and silently prayed for patience. The clock ticked. Her watch said 5:40. She was just reconciling herself to missing the sacrament when the little light changed to green, and the door opened.

Anne hurried in and closed the door behind her. Kneeling in front of the little screen, she crossed herself, saying: "In the name of the Father, and of the Son, and of the Holy Spirit. Bless me Father, for I have sinned. It has been two weeks since my last confession. I'm going to try to go fast because there are people waiting behind me."

"Take your time," came the voice from behind the screen. It was Fr. Dixon.

"Thank you, Father. In the last two weeks I have been angry with my husband and my children. I have lost patience with them. I have used profane language on two occasions when I was stuck in traffic. I have been angry at other parents at the school for things their children have said to my daughter. There have been times when I have been slothful, and I wonder about whether I am greedy. We have so much, and I know that I have not been charitable enough. I have not contributed my time and talent as much as I should. I have missed my devotions in the Liturgy of the Hours on four occasions. And I have not been merciful in thinking about those poor children who died—instead focusing on my own fear for my children growing up in this world. Also, I was angry at the two nuns who took so much time in their confessions."

Anne paused.

"Is that everything you have on your mind today?" Fr. Dixon asked.

"Yes, Father, that is all I am aware of that weighs on my conscience."

"Okay. Well, first, the Liturgy of the Hours. You must know it is not an obligation. That you are attempting to keep this devotion is admirable, but God knows you are trying. It is difficult to keep that up with everything else going on. As to the profanity in traffic, was this blasphemous?"

"No, it was more . . . uh, crude."

"Well, while I certainly don't encourage profanity, just try to do better. As to the other things, sloth and greed, it is indeed a struggle amidst our abundance to understand how much to give to God and our neighbors and how much we are rightly to use for our own families. If your conscience is telling you that you should do more, then do it. I'm not going to encourage you to financial martyrdom, and you have a family to think of. That's where your time and talent should go first. But listen to your conscience, and if there is room in your life, then there are many ways that you can help your neighbors. Perhaps you could use some of that energy that you are putting into the Liturgy of the Hours and use that time in some charitable work instead."

Anne was a little taken aback by this but tucked it away to be considered later.

"Finally, what I am hearing is that you are angry with your family. Are you feeling resentful toward them for not sharing your overt faith? I ask this because of your anger toward that other family."

"Partly, Father. My husband seems to just want to lie around, and he lets the kids do whatever they want. He's not engaged with them except in our sons' sports. I'm afraid our children are becoming little monsters, except for my youngest. My sons just want to lock themselves in their rooms and play video games, and they don't want to spend any time at home."

"It sounds like you are trying to justify your anger . . . "

"I'm sorry, Father. Maybe I am."

"Well, this sacrament is not about them; it is between you and God. Anger is natural and can motivate us, but we have to let it go. If you can let it go and not let it turn into resentment, then you are doing well. You have to accept that others must be free to make their own choices. *You* are responsible for your own. Let God's grace work in your life and trust that He will always be trying to call everyone to Himself. I know this can be very hard, especially in families. What tremendous courage it takes to join your life to a spouse and to take on the challenge of being a parent."

"I'm very afraid for them. I'm not courageous."

"So that fear for them makes you angry and then turns into resentment when they won't listen to your attempts to protect them. Take the good of that as well as the bad. If you are motivated by fear for people you love, then love them all the more. Jesus warns us to enter the narrow gate, for the wide gate leads to destruction, but He also says that His yoke is easy and His burden is light. Remember that He is the good shepherd, who leaves the many to seek out the lost one. He is always seeking them. Keep yourself on the narrow way, and don't make His yoke heavier than He has made it. For your penance, I would ask you to say one Our Father and to recite the Prayer for the Virtue of Patience, which you can find at the back of the missalette. The Act of Contrition?"

Anne whispered: "O my God, I am heartily sorry for having offended Thee, and I detest all my sins because of Thy just punishments, but most of all because they offend Thee, my God, who is all good and worthy of all my love. I firmly resolve, with the help of Your grace, to sin no more, and to avoid all occasion of sin. Amen."

Fr. Dixon rapidly intoned: "God the Father of mercies through the death and resurrection of His Son has reconciled the world to Himself and sent the Holy Spirit among us for the forgiveness of sins; through the ministry of the Church may God give you pardon and peace, and I absolve you from your sins in the name of the Father, and of the Son, and of the Holy Spirit."

"Amen. Thank you, Father," Anne responded, and rose and exited the confessional. Above the door, the little red light turned to green.

Chapter 7

CONTRITION

Anne negotiated I-26 toward home, practicing the virtue of patience. She felt a calm that she knew would fade once she walked through the door of her home, but she enjoyed the moment. Traffic streamed into the city as suburban residents made their way to downtown Asheville. She hoped that by the time she and Dane returned for dinner, some of the restaurant crowds would have dissipated.

Be not anxious for tomorrow, for tomorrow will be anxious for itself. Each day's own evil is sufficient.

Anne began a rosary, praying along with the ridges along the backside of the steering wheel. Her Land Rover had a smooth, leather-wrapped wheel, but Dane had found her a steering wheel cover made specifically for praying the rosary while driving. One large stud on the back of the left-hand side marked the beginning of the decade, then ten smaller studs along the arc of the wheel for the Hail Marys, and finally one large stud on the right-hand side for the Glory Be. Little white crosses marked the front side of the steering wheel corresponding with the location of each stud. It had come with a disclaimer about distracted driving and could no longer be purchased, as the company that made it had been sued by an accident victim.

Along with her absolution, Anne made her resolutions. *Forgive us our trespasses as we forgive those who trespass against us.* She would be more understanding of her boys and their growing need to distance from her. She would be more understanding of Dane and try to help him channel his abilities into something rewarding. She would be patient with Emilia and would not make the same mistakes she had made with Maryanne. She would spend more time doing good works and concentrate only on Lauds and let the rest of the hours go where they may.

As she pulled into the driveway, she tried to feel grace working in her, but instead the text of Matthew 12 sprang to mind and left her disquieted:

When the unclean spirit comes out of a person, it passes through waterless places seeking rest, and not finding any, it then says, "I will return to my house from which I came." And when it comes, it finds it swept and put in order. Then it goes and brings along seven other spirits more evil than itself, and they come and live there; and the last condition of that person becomes worse than the first.

Downtown Asheville was alive, and Biltmore Avenue was crowded with people making their way along the sidewalks. Both lanes were lined with cars trying to negotiate turns onto the narrow side streets, circling and looking for parking. Anne had found a garage and tucked her Land Rover in between two enormous SUVs. She had to let Dane out before she parked and then sidled out her own door to where he stood in the garage lights. His concession to a night out on the town was to wear a collared shirt, this one a nondescript beige with a subtle diamond pattern that was stretched unattractively by his large belly. Although he wore Rangers and Chiefs gear almost all the time at home, when he went out in public he tried to avoid notice. Anne, by contrast, wore flowing, high-waisted orange slacks over heels that made her almost as tall as her husband, with a white blouse and a long, knit sweater. She carried a black and tan Burberry purse, wore her dark hair braided into a long tail, and finished the ensemble with layered, thin gold necklaces. She crossed to where Dane stood with his hands in his pockets and put one arm through his.

"What time's our rezzy?"

"We don't have one," Dane answered.

"What?"

"I called. They don't take reservations."

"We'll never get a table tonight!" Anne looked annoyed as the two walked up the stairs and on to the street.

Under a low portico and past a tiled entryway bearing the insignia "Archer Drug"—for a pharmacy that had last occupied the premises decades before—Dane opened the door of Malaga Tapas and let Anne walk in. The benches in the small foyer were all full, and the black-clad hostess glanced up from her podium with a look of petulant annoyance.

"Can I help you?" she asked, her face lit by the glowing screen below her.

"Table for two," Dane said.

"It's gonna be about a one-hour wait," the hostess answered.

Anne and Dane looked at each other.

"Your call," Dane said.

"I'm starving. Do you want to wait? It'll probably be the same everywhere."

"Should I put your name in?" the hostess asked.

"No thanks," Dane said, and the two exited back to the street. They stopped under the portico.

"Let's just go to Tres Fontaine," Dane said. "I can always get a table there."

"Fine," Anne said, disappointed. "I was really hoping for tapas."

"We'll tell them to make us Italian tapas," Dane replied, grinning. They made a left, walked along the street back past the garage, and turned into the doorway of a familiar streetside restaurant. The four tables outside were all occupied. At two of them, dogs sat leashed underneath, looking up expectantly at the owners. Table-top candles were lit against the coming twilight. The low buzz of conversation competed with the rumble of passing cars and the loud voices of pedestrians.

Dane held the door for Anne, and they entered. The small foyer of this restaurant, too, held waiting customers. String lights glinted from overhead; little glass spheres descended from the black-painted exposed girders above. Tres Fontaine had just recently been transformed from a dark-paneled, red-checkered tablecloth, straw-Chianti bottle parody into a slick, modern, hipster-magnet, but the ownership was the same. Richard Ferrera's daughter had driven the changes, and she stood beside her father at the hostess podium dressed in the ubiquitous black, but Ferrara himself was still the maître d', host, master of the house, and ever-present proprietor. As he looked up from the glowing screen and saw Dane, his concerned face transformed into a big smile.

"Mr. Norris!" he said, walking around the podium. "We'll have your table in a moment." He shook Dane's hand and turned to Anne.

"Welcome back, welcome back." Then he returned to the podium for a hushed conference with his daughter, whose displeasure at this disruption to her schedule was apparent.

"It'll be just a moment," Ferrara said, hurrying off. Anne stood awkwardly, uncomfortable at the little charade that they had been expected. After a moment, one of the waiting customers—a man in his sixties with a gray, balding head—got up from his seat.

"I just wanted to shake your hand," the man said, as he pushed it forward to Dane. "I was there when you caught that game-winner against Georgia. Never seen anything like it."

"Thanks," Dane said, a big, sincere smile on his face. "What's your name?"

"Hicks, David Hicks," the man answered, delighted to be asked. "This is my wife Donna," he continued, gesturing toward a heavyset woman who remained seated, but who smiled, waved, and said "Hello."

"My wife Anne," Dane said, and she greeted the stranger.

"Heard your boy is gonna be playing at BC next year. Think he'll break any of your records?"

Dane continued smiling warmly.

"I hope so, I hope so. He's got a way to go, though."

"Well," Hicks responded, suddenly a little awkward, "just wanted to say hello. Thanks for all you've done for Rangers football."

"My pleasure, David, I'm just proud to be part of the program. Good things are ahead."

The man smiled and sat back down with his wife, as Ferrara returned.

"Your table is all ready," and he led them to a little two-top table by one of the front picture windows of the restaurant. The gauze curtains were open, and they looked out over the little sidewalk tables and the stream of traffic as they sat down.

"Hi, I'm Jade," said a small blonde girl in a white blouse, placing menus before them and filling their water glasses. "I'll be serving you tonight. Can I get you started with a cocktail while you look over the menu?"

"Yeah, great," Dane answered. "I'll have a Maker's on the rocks."

"A glass of prosecco," Anne added.

"Absolutely," the girl answered, and walked back toward the bar, stopping to check at a couple of other tables.

Anne reached across the table and took Dane's hand.

"Honey, I just wanted to say thanks for taking me out to dinner tonight. I know you haven't liked getting dragged around the last couple of days and you would have rather settled in at the house."

"It's okay," Dane lied. "It was important that we go to the funeral to support the kids. I love going out with you. Rare enough that we get a chance."

"Life's been crazy lately, but I promise this summer we'll take more time to spend together. Dylan's not taking classes and he can drive Jane to practices, so I really just have to worry about getting Emilia to her camps."

"I've been looking forward to opening the lake house," Dane replied.

"Me too. I promise we'll go next weekend."

"Water's still cool but we can get out on the pontoon."

"Hold on, let me show you these new cushions I found for the decks. You're gonna love them!"

Anne rummaged in her purse and pulled out her phone, saw a missed call from Emilia, and called her back just as Jade returned with their drinks.

"Can you check back in a second?" Dane asked her in a low voice, as Anne held one finger to her opposing ear to hear above the low buzz of conversation.

"Absolutely," Jade answered, placing the drinks down, backing away, and making her rounds of tables.

The hushed conversation with Emilia ended.

"Everything okay?" Dane asked.

"Yes, Emilia just wanted to know if she could watch a movie with Jane. Oh, I was going to show you the cushions," and Anne thumbed through her apps until she found what she wanted and held the phone up to show Dane a teal and gold cushion with a ship's wheel on it.

"Looks great," he said, disinterestedly.

Anne put the phone back in her purse and continued: "I could have gotten them on sale . . . " before Jade returned to the table and interrupted.

"Have you had time to decide?"

Dane looked over at Anne, who rapidly picked up her menu.

"I think we'll have the bruschetta as an appetizer," Dane said.

"Absolutely, and for your main?"

"Veal parmesan."

"Absolutely. And what can we get you?" she asked Anne.

"Can you tell me about the orecchiette?"

"The orecchiette Bolognese? Oh, it's fantastic! It's orecchiette pasta with a minced veal Bolognese sauce. Chef just added it to the menu last week, but it's one of our most popular dishes. Is that what you'd like?"

"Yes, I'll try that."

"Absolutely."

"And we'll have the Pio Cesare dolcetto with dinner," Dane added.

"Absolutely."

As Jade turned and walked away, Dane broke into a huge grin.

"That was like five."

"Five what?"

"Five absolutelys. You didn't notice?"

"Dane, you're horrible," Anne said, smiling. Then continued: "There's something else I wanted to talk to you about. I started feeling bad today about pressuring you into going to the Knights meeting. I know you don't want to go, and I'm sorry for committing you. If you don't want to go, it's alright."

"No, it's okay," Dane answered, surprised. He wasn't sure what had gotten into Anne, suddenly backing off of the pressure she had recently been applying, but he was also aware of how deep a rut he had fallen into and knew that she was trying to gently get him back out.

"It's okay," he continued. "I haven't been to a meeting in quite a while. It'll be good to see Roger and George too."

"Oh good, you should invite them up to the lake."

"Later this summer maybe. Got the Fletchers coming this weekend, remember?"

"So you're going to the meeting?"

"Sure."

Anne smiled at him and took his hand again. She continued to ride the sense of peace that she had maintained since the drive back from St. James.

Their dinner came and went, as did the bottle of dolcetto, a bottle of Montepulciano, and glasses of chilled limoncello. By the time Dane and Anne exited the restaurant, they both had a warm glow of contentment.

“Let’s walk a bit,” Anne said, and the two made their way back up Biltmore Ave. Dane stopped outside the Franklin Theater, below the glowing marquis that displayed the name “Drumbelly Jones – June 26” in black letters.

“Never noticed this before,” he said, pointing at a bronze plaque on the brick wall of the theater front.

Asheville Historical Society

The historic Franklin Theater, 1925
Site of the Danville/Hawkins debate, 1943
Earl Tubman’s last performance, 1959
Johnny Cash arrested for profanity, 1965
Renovated, 1988

“What the hell is a Drumbelly Jones?” Dane asked, looking back up at the marquee, as the two walked away into the languid evening.

The Bishop Lowe Council #763 of the Knights of Columbus had its meeting hall on the second floor of a Biltmore Avenue shop that, over the many years since the Knights had taken up residence, had been inhabited by a shoe store, a pawn shop, an antique dealer, and now a comic book and collectible store. By the street-front door that led up to the Council Hall, there was a little bronze plaque with the Knights of Columbus emblem, and below that was another little plaque with a prayer for the end of abortion. The lower plaque was currently defaced with the spray-painted word “choice.”

Dane had parked his Mercedes in the same garage that he and Anne had used on the weekend night, now mostly empty on this Monday evening. He had considered parking at St. Lawrence and walking down, but his knees were bothering him again, and there was a slight drizzle of rain. As he approached the door to the council hall, he saw vaguely familiar faces entering ahead of him, and he stiffly followed them up the stairs.

The room at the top was occupied on one side by a small bar with six black half-barrel stools and on the other by an enclosed kitchen. The bar was poorly stocked, with a few name-brand bottles such as Jack Daniels, Bacardi, and Smirnoff, a little hand-lettered sign that said "$5/drink," a non-functional beer tap with a Schlitz emblem, a refrigerator with another sign that read "$3/beer," and an array of little dusty trophies featuring miniature golfers and nondescript bronze cups. The door to the crowded galley kitchen stood open, revealing the inner workings of the spaghetti dinners and pancake breakfasts. A worn black faux-leather couch sat below the windows. The paneled walls were replete with gray photographs of past Grand Knights.

The bar stools were currently occupied by overweight, middle-aged men, two of whom sported shiny K of C jackets in navy blue with gold trim, the backs of which featured "Bishop Lowe Council 763" spelled out in red letters around the logo. Another similarly clad, similarly overweight, and diminutive Knight sat on the couch next to a Hispanic man in a tan security guard uniform, engaged in conversation. Dane knew the first man—an insufferable prick named Jimmy Oakley, who was reputed to have been reprimanded for impersonating a priest at various K of C events.

The door in between the kitchen and bar opened up into the council chamber itself, which consisted of a long, beige, tiled floor, inset in the middle with the K of C logo, leading to a slightly elevated dais where the officer's table stood, a podium in the center, and US, Vatican, and K of C flags to the sides. Old plastic and steel stackable chairs were arrayed in rows. Various Brother Knights sat in the chairs in a motley array of costume. T-shirts, oxford and tie, blue jeans and slacks, dress shoes and boots, long hair and short (and all mostly gray). As he entered, a deep voice bellowed:

"Dane!"

Roger Norris approached. He was, of course, one of the shirt-and-tie specimens in the room. Perhaps in his character as attorney, and perhaps in his character as scion of aristocracy, Roger was rarely without shirt, tie, or suit. He shared the same prominent brow and bushy eyebrows as Dane, but his hair was neatly cut, and he sported a grey goatee that helped conceal his own growing collection of chins. He reached out a hand to his brother as he approached.

"Thanks for coming."

"Good to see you, Rog. How've you been?"

"Blessed."

The word made Dane uncomfortable. For some reason, it smacked of a too-wholesome enthusiasm that befitted Roger's continued progression into a sort of satellite of the parish. The last times that they had been at Mass together, on the holidays that propelled Dane back to St. Lawrence to join the extended family, Roger had taken to mumbling additional prayers at odd times during the Mass. Very unlike his own wife's turn toward traditionalism, Roger was displaying a sort of Pentecostal Catholicism that Dane understood even less.

People began filing into the hall from the anteroom and taking seats. Dane sat next to Roger's chair.

"Is George coming?" Dane asked.

"No, he can't make it tonight. Out of town with the kids. The traveling team takes a lot of his time, but he loves it."

The officers were now seated, and the Grand Knight took his place behind the podium. He rapped his gavel and said: "Brothers, we are foregoing our usual business meeting tonight with a special speaker, Council 763's own Dane Norris, but before we begin, let us invoke the divine blessing by saying together a decade of the holy rosary. Clete will lead us tonight." He banged his gavel again, and some of the assembled Knights took to their knees. Dane, and many of the other less-flexible brothers, remained seated.

As he pulled his rosary from his pocket, Dane inwardly gave thanks that the chaplain was absent and the duty to lead the rosary had fallen to Clete.

"Clete" James was a grizzled old specimen of Madison County who was barely mentally competent to live outside of a home, but he was adopted by the K of C council, who ensured that he got a ride to every meeting and event. The rosary was his specialty, and some of the Knights said that he had "a direct line to Mary" and that whatever you asked him to pray for, you would receive. He had a chain of sturdy rosewood beads from which he had long worn the original dark stain and whose formerly rough texture was now shiny with use. The little metal Marian icon at the heart of the rosary chain was now worn to a flat disk with barely any features still visible. Clete certainly prayed enough, but he felt immense joy when he was asked to lead the rosary. And for some of the less patient members of the council, it was also a treat because Clete could pray the rosary in nothing flat. His Hail Mary was a jumbled together pile of words that resembled the actual prayer only in cadence:

Hammaryfoogracedalowiswiddee. Blessedadowmungwimanblessdfroo-ah-dwoomJeez. Homarry murrgodd prayfersussinners nowanathowerfdeth.

In the silence of the room, Clete began:

Innanamadafarrandasonandahospirit...

The decade of the rosary complete, the gavel rapped, and the council stood for the Pledge of Allegiance. Then, as hands lowered from hearts, the Grand Knight gestured for Dane to take the podium.

Dane walked stiffly up to the dais and looked out across the gathered men.

"It's great to see you again, I apologize that I don't attend more meetings, but I promise that I pay my dues, and I do have a current membership card if any of you would like to inspect it. [*thin laughter*] My brother, Roger, who is a far better Knight than I am, invited me to speak to you on the topic of Catholic fatherhood. I have to admit that Roger is also a better father than me and would be a much better speaker on that topic, but well, here I am.

"As you know, Roger and I come from a long line of Catholics here in Asheville. Our great-great-grandfather William Norris helped build St. Lawrence, and our family line includes priests and nuns who served in North Carolina, if not in Asheville itself. So you can imagine the shock when one of the Norris boys decided that, instead of pursuing a gentlemanly path, he was going to play football, although having grown up with St. Lawrence, ending up on the gridiron shouldn't be a surprise. *[brief and muted laughs from those who recognized the manner of the saint's death]* In any case, you can imagine the further shock for my good Catholic father when that Norris boy passed up Notre Dame and stayed home to play at Biltmore.

"But my father, rather than encourage me to a different path, honored my choice and supported it. I think it worked out. [*laughter*] Let me tell you a little about how that went."

Dane launched into his stock "story-of-my-life" speech, which he had given a hundred other times at booster clubs and civic organizations. It was a speech remarkably devoid of relevance to the topic of Catholic fatherhood but that nonetheless held his audience's rapt attention. He tried to finish on an appropriate note.

"So now here I am, back in Asheville with my sons playing at St. Ambrose. I hope that I have been a model to them that you can have a life devoted to playing a game and never forget that it is just a game, but still be a good Catholic. True, football at the pro level is a very tough environment, and the temptations are many. But that's true of everything in life. There's no place in this world where our kids aren't going to be challenged by people who want to tear them down. I don't have a solution for that, but I remember how my father trusted me, and his example and that of my brother were an inspiration to me during some times when it would have been a lot easier to go down the roads that my teammates were going down. Hopefully my kids will have that same inspiration when they get out into the world. And I think that's the best I can hope for."

Dane stopped and there was a moment of silence, and then his brother said: "Vivat Jesus!"

"Vivat Jesus!" came the reply from the rest, and there was applause as Dane stepped down and sat beside his brother.

"I forgot about the 'Vivat Jesus' thing," he whispered, as the Grand Knight stepped back up to the podium.

"Thank you, Brother Norris, for your inspirational words. Brothers, that concludes our meeting tonight. Clete, will you lead us in the Prayer for Vocations?" He rapped the gavel again and those who could, took a knee.

"*Hevnlyfarblessyrchuchwidanabundcepreestsdeansbrosists . . .* "

Catholic gentlemen rose from their seats, a number of whom made their way over to speak to Dane in person. The first among these was Jimmy Oakley, who thrust his hand out to Dane, interrupting his conversation with Roger. Dane took his hand.

"Great talk, Dane. Great talk. Really inspirational. How's your daughter Maryanne?"

Dane stared hard at the little, fat man in his shiny blue jacket; his hand, still holding Jimmy's, squeezed it until the little man winced.

"She's good." Then he pushed past him and made his way to the bar. A barstool freed up for him, and he sat down heavily. Roger went behind the bar, poured some Jack Daniels over ice, and handed it to Dane.

Then it was football talk. Rangers, Chiefs, Ambrose Saints. Recruiting prospects for the coming year. That catch against Georgia. All-purpose yards against Denver. Pro-bowl in Hawaii. Dane shook away the scowl that Jimmy Oakley had left him with, and smiled, shook hands, and drank his whiskey.

Dylan Norris hit the bong, and before exhaling, passed it to Amari. Then he coughed out a big cloud of smoke and sat back on the dilapidated couch. The air was hazy and thick. The inside of the trailer was hot and uncomfortable, the music too loud.

Freshman camp would start in the morning, and Dylan had to be there to help the little kids walk through the drills. He was in the last few "free" days of summer before practices began for real.

He grinned and laughed and ate handfuls of potato chips and joked and hit the bong and laughed again.

Principal Hubert Rollins, Fr. Dixon, and Coach Willy Williams stood on the side of the practice field in the drizzle of rain as little knots of the incoming freshmen pushed blocking dummies, walked through passing plays, and stood listening to the assistant coaches. The field was thinly populated for a camp day, as very few of the upperclassmen were present.

"I wish you would reconsider," Rollins said, still looking at the field and not at the coach. Rollins was a short, stocky, sandy-haired man with a thin-cropped beard holding a black umbrella to keep the rain off of his gold SAHS polo shirt. Beside him, Fr. Dixon stood rigid in his black cassock and biretta, protected by his own umbrella.

"It's not that I wouldn't like to accommodate you," Williams answered. "But delaying the freshman camp just wasn't an option. If I moved this camp to next week, then I would have to move conditioning a week out, then I'd have to move walk throughs, shells, and we'd get stacked up on two-a-days. The whole schedule would have to change. Some of the upperclassmen have college camps to go to, and they've already made their plans around our practice schedule."

"Coach," Fr. Dixon interjected, "can't you at least give them tomorrow off? There are two funerals for their classmates. I can't see that one day would hurt them that much."

"Father, with all due respect, there is a cadence to these practices that you probably don't understand. It's taken me fifty years to develop this routine. I know what works and what doesn't. Besides, we've told all the freshmen that they can opt out of practice tomorrow if they want to go to the funeral, and the upperclassmen got to opt out of the whole camp if they wanted. As you can see, most of them did."

"Coach, it's the optics of the whole thing, you see?" rejoined Principal Rollins. "I'm getting angry calls from parents wondering why we're still practicing football when these kids are dealing with a tragedy."

"I bet you'd be getting angry calls from parents and boosters if we had canceled the camp."

"Possibly, but maybe I should forward my calls to you. You can explain how it's so important."

"Happy to do so," Williams answered. "Send 'em my way. Besides, I know how tragic this whole thing is. Hell, I tried to poach the Morton kid from Coach Schnauffmann. I knew the kid, and the others too. It's an awful thing. But you've done the whole counselor thing at the school, and from my experience, it's probably better for the kids if they're together with their classmates instead of off on their own. Besides, the freshmen that are here were never in school with the kids who died."

"You forget how small our Catholic community is," Fr. Dixon responded. "The freshmen may not have been in high school with the rising seniors, but many of them were in the same elementary and middle schools. And the children who passed away have brothers and sisters who are in the same grades. I appreciate the point about the benefit of having the children together instead of isolated, but I still believe that we should at least cancel tomorrow's practice."

"We're going to have to agree to disagree on that, Father. But I'll remind them again that attendance tomorrow is optional if they want to go to the funerals."

"Okay then," Principal Rollins answered, "but I'm serious about sending those angry calls your way."

"I'm serious about taking those calls. I'm happy to explain things to 'em. Again, I feel awful for those kids who died, but our football program is really important to the kids who are still with us, and to be successful in the fall, we've got to work hard in the spring and summer. We have a good chance to take State this year. Now, I get that doesn't seem too important when you're talking about life and death, but it's gonna feel pretty darn important when the playoffs roll around."

"Okay, Coach," Rollins replied, nodding to Williams as he and Fr. Dixon strode away.

Coach Willard "Willy" Williams was seventy-five years old and looked every day of it. Thin, wrinkled, and of decreasing height, he was almost comical in his perpetually oversized SAHS Saints gear and tennis shoes, with an absurd golden whistle that hung around his neck on a white lanyard. Williams was a relic of a bygone era. He had never played football himself. Rather, he had hired on as gym teacher and coach in the 1960s when the nuns who taught at SAHS decided they needed a layperson to better handle athletics. In those long-past days, Williams had coached every sport, managed all the equipment, maintained the gym, and driven the bus to away games, all under the watchful eyes of the Augustinian Sisters. A proud and churchgoing Southern Baptist, Williams had nevertheless become a fixture at SAHS.

Historically, not much was expected from SAHS' athletic programs. They would be occasionally competitive in basketball, only intermittently had a good baseball team, and were notoriously poor in football. Once in a while, a very gifted student would bring home trophies in track and field or nudge one of the team sports up above .500 for the season. But all that was okay. Parents weren't paying for their kids to go to SAHS for the sports, and no one ever thought of replacing Williams.

But in the 1980s, things began to change. Two things happened at the same time: Dane Norris arrived at SAHS, and booster money started arriving as well. Norris, of course, was a prodigy. So much better than everyone he played against, particularly in the Saints' lowly division, that he could disrupt every play. St. Ambrose suddenly started winning in football and basketball, and parents whose athletically gifted children would otherwise have stayed in the public school system began to reconsider. With wealthier parents and sports success came money. The SAHS campus was in awful condition. Newer sports facilities were followed by renovations of classrooms and payroll for additional teachers who could share the coaching duties. As the Augustinian Sisters died off and retracted from their teaching mission, laypersons were hired with an eye to what they could teach and what they could coach.

Around him, as sports became better funded and more competitive, coaches of Williams' vintage were edged out after a couple of losing seasons. But Williams had a great advantage in that he continued to win, even after Dane Norris' graduation. Given his long experience, his tactical brilliance, and a sufficient pool of talent, it became inconceivable that the school could do better than Coach Willy, and instead the parents and boosters worried about what they would do when he finally got too old.

Williams just chugged along, now relegating more and more of the interactions with players to his assistant coaches. He could still spot and develop talent, but he was losing touch with the kids. He was repelled by their music, appalled by their language, offended by their conduct, and never really plumbed the depths at which his players had changed.

Wednesday morning at the Norris farm found the sun shining brightly and beginning to dry the damp ground. It had rained all the preceding evening, which had left those in line outside of the funeral home huddled under umbrellas until they could pay their respects to Doug Smith's family. There was hushed talk of the lawsuit that the Smiths had filed against the Morton family, who had not been in attendance. After the rosary, Dylan had gone off with friends, and the rest of his family went home so that Janus could rest for freshman camp. That night, Dane turned in early, but Anne had stayed up late, unable to put aside the images of the grieving Smith family and the waxy face of Doug Smith in his casket.

Anne had been slow to awaken, but she managed to arise in time for Lauds. Now she walked, foggy headed, from her prie-dieu with the words of the psalm in her mind:

They have neither knowledge nor understanding,
They walk about in darkness;
All the foundations of the earth are shaken.

I say "You are gods,
Sons of the Most High, all of you;
Nevertheless, you shall die like men,
And fall like any prince.
Arise, O God, judge the earth;
For to thee belong all the nations!"

Somber, she thought, but for the Feast of St. John the Baptist, it was what she expected. She had always been disturbed by that story, the wild man of the desert beheaded at the request of a girl. In her mind, Anne always saw John as he had been played in the 1970's miniseries—with unkempt hair and spittle flying from his mouth.

"Good morning, Mommy!" Emilia said brightly.

"Good morning. Can you get the eggs today?"

"Okay," Emilia said, and grabbed the basket. Hearing Emilia open the door to the deck, the dogs burst forth, and the little girl laughed as they rushed past her and cantered on the flagstones below.

Anne pulled her mug from the cupboard and poured her coffee then sat down on a stool by the kitchen island and browsed through her phone.

A few minutes later, Emilia came back in, clutching the basket of eggs. There were a full dozen. All of the chickens were laying regularly now.

"Want some breakfast, Mommy?"

"Sure, Emilia." Anne smiled as her daughter made her way over to the stove and started banging away among the pots and pans. Anne heard Dane stirring as the noise disturbed him. Distracted by her phone and the clashing and banging of her daughter making scrambled eggs, it was a few moments before Anne heard the distant sound of the chickens.

"Emilia, where are the dogs?"

"Oh gosh!" Emilia said, dropping the spatula and looking around.

Anne jumped up and ran to the window.

"Dane! Dane!" she yelled, and bolted out the back door, Emilia racing after her.

As she ran toward the chicken coop, she saw Jingles madly dashing after one of the hens, its wings flapping wildly. Buddy was sitting with his paws on another chicken. Feathers floated through the air.

"No! No! Bad dog!" Anne screamed as she ran barefooted across the field.

"Stop! Stop!" Emilia shrieked.

Jingles pounced on the hen and up went a shower of feathers. She shook the bird back and forth.

Buddy saw Anne running toward him, and he ran forward with a chicken in his mouth.

"Drop it!" Anne yelled, but Buddy, thinking it was a game, bounced away from her and ran. Anne rushed over to where Jingles was mauling the bird and hit the dog hard on the hindquarters. Jingles jumped up and ran a few feet away, turning and looking back, her tail between her legs. Emilia chased Buddy around, madly trying to get the hen from him.

Dane came jogging across the field bare chested and with the legs of his lounge pants soaked with dew. Buddy ran toward him, and Dane yelled a commanding "SIT!" The Weimaraner sat, tail wagging, and dropped the bird between his paws.

The damage had been done. The loud clucking from inside the coop told Anne that at least some of the chickens were alive, but outside the coop there were five piles of feathery carcasses.

"I'm sorry! I'm sorry!" Emilia sobbed, standing and staring at where the coop's nest door hung open. It only took a moment to realize what must have happened. Unlatched, the nest door had dropped open, and the chickens must have hopped out of the coop that way. Then the dogs, left out by Emilia, had set upon them and rushed from one flapping bird to the next. Two of the chickens had made it to the barn. Anne could see them poking their heads out from behind the feed bins and could hear their clucking.

Emilia rushed over to Buddy and yelled "BAD DOG!" and

swatted him on the hindquarters. Buddy yelped and jumped away as Dane snatched up the carcass.

"Oh no!" Anne said, and sat down in the wet grass.

"I'm sorry, Mommy," Emilia said. Anne looked from the tear-streaked face of her daughter to the hopeful faces of her dogs, tongues rolled out of their mouths and panting from their exertion. They wagged as she looked at them.

"It's not your fault, Emilia," Dane said. "I should have fixed that latch. It's my fault."

"It's not your fault, honey," Anne said, holding out her arms. Emilia rushed to hug her mother and cried onto her shoulder.

"I'll clean up the birds," Dane said quietly. "You take the dogs back to the house."

Emilia and Anne grabbed the dogs' collars and headed back across the field; Dane went to the barn for a wheelbarrow. As he walked back to the coop, the two chickens who had hidden in the barn came rushing back and walked beside him. They went to the side of the coop door and clucked to be let in. The chickens inside set up a ruckus in response. Dane closed the nest door and clipped the perfectly good latch that he had replaced the day before. Then he opened the coop door, and the hens rushed in with a flutter of their wings, darting up the ladder into the enclosed part of the coop. He shut and latched the door and gathered up the chicken carcasses into the wheelbarrow. As he did, he tried to remember the ridiculous names that his wife and daughter had given them: Henrietta, Eggs Benedict, Omelette, Huevos Verde, Chick Korea. He couldn't really recall which was which.

He pushed the wheelbarrow back to the barn, grabbed a rake, and tried his best to gather up the myriad feathers, but with limited success. For the next few months, feathers would stubbornly remain in the grass, reminding the Norrises, and perhaps the chickens, of what happens when hens leave the coop.

Chapter 8

THEY KNOW NOT WHAT THEY DO

Billy Mullins was just thirteen years old the summer of the Hardwell family reunion at Brushy Fork State Park. He was dressed in dirty jeans and a striped T-shirt. His spindly arms and legs awaited a growth spurt that would never come. Hamburgers and hot dogs were cooking on grease-encrusted charcoal grills. Dixie cups full of lemonade were guzzled by the kids. The air was awash with yelling, games of tag, and flying Nerf footballs. Billy was exploring the maintenance barn, looking at the tractor, when his cousin Ernie came up behind him. Ernie reached around and started to fondle Billy's crotch.

Billy pushed away from him and yelled "You fucking faggot!" and then quicker than he could have believed, his cousin's fist struck out and hit his eye. Billy was knocked to the ground, and his cousin was on top of him, hitting him again and again, and then he found himself rolled over on his stomach, his cousin sitting on his back.

"No! No!" Billy yelled as he thrashed.

"Shut up!" Ernie said, and Billy saw him removing his belt. Then Ernie's hands yanked down Billy's pants. In shock and horror, Billy kept yelling "No!"

Then his cousin's belt lashed down on his exposed buttocks,

and stinging pain erupted. Billy winced as his cousin strapped him again and again. Panting, he lay still as Ernie got up off of his back and slowly put his belt back on. Despite the pain, Billy gasped in relief as he realized that his worst fear had been displaced by the violence of the lashing.

"You keep your mouth shut, Billy," his cousin said. "You tell anybody, and I'll fucking kill you."

Billy reached back and pulled his pants up over the screaming flesh of his buttocks. Tears welled in his eyes as he heard his cousin walking away. Finally he came to all fours, then up on his knees. He sat there sobbing, hearing the distant sounds of playing children and the country music blaring from a boom box.

When he was as composed as possible, he staggered back toward the riverside and found the picnic table where his father, uncles, and brother were sitting—the men with beer cans and cigarettes, his brother with a can of Coke. His father looked at him as he approached.

"What happened to you?" he asked.

"Got in a scrap," Billy answered, his voice soft and low.

"Damn, boy," his father continued. "I oughta whoop you agin for getting yourself so beat up."

And then his uncles and brother laughed, and his father joined in.

Billy stood there sullenly, his hands in his pockets and his head down low. The conversation resumed as if nothing had happened, and Billy sidled off, making his way toward a picnic shelter where his mother sat with aunts and cousins. Diminutive like him and his father, his mother sat in a folding strap-chair, her head turned away. As he walked toward her, he saw Ernie come up with a Dixie cup of lemonade and hand it to his mother. Ernie winked at him, and Billy tacked away, looking for a place to hide.

Six years later, Ernie was dead. Shot during a meth deal gone bad. He had been in and out of prison, and by the end of his life was an emaciated, grey-skinned, and foul-toothed wreck.

The Hardwells gathered at the mountain cemetery, Ernie's mother sobbing, Ernie's father stone-faced, and Ernie's brothers doing their best impressions of corpses, advanced as they were along the path Ernie had blazed for them. Billy stood with the little knot of the Mullins family as the pastor read from the Good Book, and then one by one the mourners took flowers from a tin tub, processed by the casket, and placed the flowers on the wood covering Ernie's mortal remains.

As they paraded away behind the minister, Billy lingered, finding a shaded chair under the big funeral home tent. The gravediggers came and uncovered the frame around the casket. One attached a crank to the gear mechanism on the side and began turning it. With a jarring noise, the straps under the casket began to loosen, and Ernie was slowly lowered into the ground. When the crank stopped, Billy stepped up onto the plastic turf cover that surrounded the hole in the ground, unzipped his fly, and began pissing on the casket.

The gravediggers stared at him. One, a thin, grizzled-faced man with an ugly cast set of eyes, looked at him and said "You ain't right, boy," and then he chuckled, waited for Billy to quit pissing, and began dismantling the equipment.

A few years later, Billy volunteered to take over maintenance of the family cemetery. The Hardwells took up a collection and began to pay him for this service. He raked, mowed, and trimmed around the graves. And pissed on Ernie's headstone every time.

The cemetery work that Billy performed provided not only this satisfaction but the fifty dollars that was not an inconsiderable part of his income. Billy received eight hundred dollars a month in partial disability (based on the dubious recommendation of a pill-mill doctor) and another five hundred as part-time janitor of Hilltop Elementary School. He supplemented this regular income by collecting scrap, and it was well known in the area that if a valuable chunk of metal disappeared, there was a good chance that Billy Mullins had something to do with it. He collected everything—

cans, bottles, bald tires, anything that might have value. What he could sell, he sold. And if something couldn't be sold or needed to "cool down" for a while, he tucked it away in his brother's old trailer. The only thing he wouldn't touch was the scrap heap around the Jiffy Stop. "Don't shit where you eat," was Billy's justification for this forbearance.

So by conniving and scraping, Billy afforded his cigarettes, his cheap beer and cheaper whiskey, his electricity and his gasoline, and his Madison County High season tickets.

The deaths of the four Catholic teenagers had created an awkward scheduling conflict among the parishes and parents of the dead, and between the Smith, Boyd, and Hernandez families an unusual schedule had been devised in an attempt to accommodate the grieving community. The two girls would share a receiving but would have separate funerals the following day, while Doug would wait in his casket to be buried on Friday.

Thus Wednesday night arrived with two caskets at the funeral home and two families at the end of the receiving line. Mandy Boyd and Sarah Hernandez, eyes closed in repose, seemed more lifelike than Peter Morton had. Perhaps the makeup on their dead faces was more natural than that on the boy.

Sarah's large Hispanic family gravitated toward one side of the room. Sobbing St. Ambrose girls, Fr. Kelly in his sweater, Fr. Dixon in his cassock, and Fr. Oakes—who ministered to the Hispanic community—gathered on the other. The guest book was signed, prayer cards were pocketed, handshakes given, and hugs and crumpled tissues discarded. Dylan sat beside Patrick Ryan, looking around hopefully for Wendy, and was surprised when Patrick took out a rosary. Embarrassed, Dylan left his phone in his pocket, bowed his head, and mumbled the prayers, but his mind was elsewhere.

After the final "Amen," Dylan stayed close to Patrick as they filed out of the big double doors.

"You alright, bro?" Dylan asked him as they separated from the crowd.

"It's fucked up, Dylan. It's fucked up."

Patrick was tall, lean, and redheaded as befit his Irish name. His usually sparkling eyes were dead, and there was a sort of twitch at the side of his mouth that give him a crooked look. His suit was rumpled and seemed slightly too big, as if he had shrunk within it. There was a yellowish stain around the inside of his collar.

"You gonna be at camp tomorrow?" Dylan asked.

"Nah. Got two funerals to go to," Patrick replied with a note of sarcasm. Dylan noticed and made his excuses.

"I gotta be at camp. It's Janus' first year. My mother wanted us to go but my dad put his foot down and said that Janus couldn't miss freshman camp. I'm gonna go to Doug's funeral on Friday."

They stood there silently for a minute before Dylan continued: "I went to Pete's funeral."

"Good for you," Pat said flatly.

"Listen, once camp starts, we'll be too busy to think about it, and you'll feel better."

"You don't get it, Dylan. Pete and I played baseball every summer until I quit for football. I can't believe he's gone. He was always there."

"I do get it, bro. It's fucked up. Come out with me tonight and we'll get your mind off it. You can't sit around thinking about it all the time."

They were joined by more of their friends, and as Dylan chatted and joked with them, Pat stared away over his shoulder and remained silent. When the group broke up, Pat said: "Okay. Where are we going?"

"We were going to Party Cove tonight."

"No way man. That's right by where it happened. Next cove over."

"Okay, cool. Let's just cruise then."

"Okay."

Dylan looked around for Wendy once more and saw her with her little group of goth losers. She met his eyes but turned back to her friends dismissively. *No BJ tonight*, Dylan thought. *Better hang out with Pat anyway.*

The St. Ambrose Saints practice field was even more thinly populated on the day of the funerals. A few of the freshmen were absent and almost all of the upperclassmen. Coach Williams stood with his offensive coordinator, Thonie, and watched the little groups of players struggle through drills.

"How's that younger Norris kid coming along?" Williams asked.

"Pretty good, pretty good," responded Thonie in a deep baritone. Walter Thonie was a large black man who towered above his head coach. With a thick moustache and an afro, Thonie reminded Coach Williams of the players his team had lost to in the 1970s. Walter had been a local standout and a two-year starter on the offensive line at Biltmore College but had gone undrafted and had turned to coaching. He related well to the team and was a clever coordinator, both in games and in player development. This freed up Coach Williams to concentrate on the defense.

"Funny he wants to play QB. He's got a similar build to his brother, so I just assumed he'd go for the tight-end job like his family," Williams commented.

"Where you gonna play him on D?" Thonie asked.

"Linebacker or safety. We'll see how he develops. How's the McDowell kid coming?"

"Phenomenal, Coach. The Norris kid has got skills, but Jimmy is the real deal. Wouldn't surprise me if he challenges Ryan for playing time, and I think he's already ahead of Mitchum."

"He's got some growing to do."

"That he does, Coach."

Anne's Land Rover was left behind so that the whole family could ride along in her old Cadillac ESV. The Jet Skis were towed along behind on their double-trailer. Dylan and Janus took the second-row passenger seats, while Emilia sat in the third row, crowded by Jingles and Buddy. All the Norris children sat quietly with their heads looking down on glowing screens. Dylan had insisted on driving separately, but his father had put his foot down. He knew perfectly well that Dylan would use every possible excuse to leave during the weekend, and Dane wasn't having it. His older son's attitude had gotten worse, and Dane could see how much his wife was hurt by the growing distance. The whole family needed some time together, and as Janus' classmate Ben had been unable to make it, Janus would need company since Emilia would have a friend to spend time with.

They drove along SR 401 toward Lake Juniper. Janus suddenly snorted and said: "Oh my God. . . . That's hilarious! Ha!"

Dylan looked up from his own phone as Janus passed his over.

"Press play. Oh my God! I can't believe it."

Dylan stared at the phone, and then his mouth dropped open, and he said: "Oh my God! Damn, bro! Where was this?"

Emilia tried to look over the seat at the screen, but Dylan held it to his chest and said: "You can't see this. It's for grown-ups."

"Lemme see! Lemme see!" she laughed.

"It was at the Franklin last night," Janus said.

"What was at the Franklin?" Anne asked him.

"Just this video we're watching. It's hilarious. I can't believe it."

"What is it?"

"Uh . . . I don't wanna say."

"Give me the phone," Dane demanded. Janus tried to grab for it but Dylan, laughing, passed it up to his father.

Dane was quiet for a moment as he punched the "play" icon. Then: "Oh my God. And this was at the Franklin?"

"Would somebody please tell me what's going on?" Anne asked.

"Uh . . . Emilia, put your headphones on."

"Aw, Dad . . . "

"Just do it." He looked over his shoulder to see that she complied, then selected "DVD" from the car's touch screen, pressed play, and looked over his shoulder again.

"You remember that band, Drumbilly Jones, that we saw on the Franklin's sign?"

"Yeah," Anne replied.

"Well, this video is of the singer peeing on someone in the audience."

"Oh! That's horrible! I hope he was arrested."

"It was a she. She's on video peeing on this guy's head."

"What?"

"Yeah, she's got him lying down on stage and just pees on him. Was she arrested, Jane?"

"I don't know. I just saw the video."

"What's this world coming to?" Anne lamented.

"Drumbilly Jones . . . " Dane mused. "Strange name for a girl."

Janus clarified, "It's not the singer, it's the band name, Dad. And it's DrumBELLY, not DrumBILLY."

"Probably a rap band."

"That's racist, Mom."

"Well, am I right?"

"Actually, no. They're like a bluegrass-metal band."

"You know this group?" Anne asked.

"Yeah, everybody knows them. I mean, everybody our age."

"Well now everybody else is gonna know 'em too," Dylan laughed.

"HEADPHONES, EMILIA!" yelled Dane, seeing his daughter sneakily lifting one side of the cordless headphones away from her ear.

Several miles up SR 401 the divided highway began to split off into the old country roads that surrounded Lake Juniper. Until the mid-1930s, the area had just been a motley collection of hollows peppered around various tributaries of the French Broad River. Residents of North Carolina looked across the mountains, however, where FDR's Tennessee Valley Authority was damming rivers and generating both power and jobs. A coalition of local businessmen, along with Howard Tyler, president of North Carolina Power and Light, met to discuss financing for a dam project near Asheville. The plan ran afoul of Nebraska senator George Norris, a virulent opponent of privately held utilities who, having stymied the great Henry Ford's attempts to build a private dam, had no trouble defeating the little North Carolina coalition.

The idea, though, wouldn't go away, and after the war, it was resurrected by another group of businessmen led by Clyde Cox Sr. Cox had come across the idea while building his chain of groceries, and thanks to the moonshine distribution network he had run during prohibition, he knew the area well. He quietly went about acquiring land around the proposed site of the dam, and when he was confident enough, he formed the Tyler Dam Committee. Many of the obstacles to such large construction projects had been cleared by the defeat of legal challenges to TVA, and though it was a partially private venture, both FDR and Senator Norris were in their graves, and there was only limited federal opposition. Construction was completed in 1948, displacing a fair share of old homesteads and drowning the sites of the moonshine stills that had provided Clyde Cox's early fortune. The resultant lake was named Juniper after Cox's mother. North Carolina Power & Light got the hydroelectric utility, and Cox and his cronies got the new shoreline. Cox formed a company called Cox Land & Lake, and instead of selling his shoreline parcels, leased them out—a measure that gave him control and ensured a continuing revenue stream. But also a measure that limited development of the shoreline. Cox's attention was diverted by his growing grocery empire, and for many years the shores of the lake were dotted only with small "Cox cabins" that

Asheville's middle class would inhabit in the summers. But when Cox split up his empire among his three sons in the late 1980s, only his oldest son, Clyde Jr., maintained the "leased land" concept. The younger sons, Claude and Henry, began selling their parcels to developers, and the monied class began moving in with significant numbers, building larger and larger lake houses, which were followed by restaurants, marinas, and a yacht club.

There was still plenty of land around the lake, but the Norris family had acquired one of the last of Henry Cox's really desirable lots—the end of a peninsula that jutted into the lake and that met the water with a long, gently sloping descent. The steep drop-off of the edge of the shore allowed year-round access to the docks.

The house itself was prominent with its three levels of gray-shingled siding, each level with a large, covered deck overlooking the lake, trimmed in gleaming white and with a blue metal roof. The house straddled the slope down to the lake, the main floor level even with the driveway, the lower level about twenty feet above the dock, which stuck out from the rocky shore toward a covered boat slip whose upper story was a railed deck and waterslide. A third floor, which comprised the master suite, rose above them with large picture windows on every side with front and back decks that could be screened in during mosquito season.

Anne drove her Cadillac down the gravel road until it met their driveway, then pulled in front of the house. Janus' door opened and the dogs leaped out, sniffing around the bushes and peeing every few feet. Her overnight bag on her shoulder and her iPad in her hand, Emilia climbed out over the top of Janus, before he could exit.

"Stay in the car, boys," Dane said, as he walked around to the driver's side. We've gotta get the Jet Skis in the water. "I'll be back in about thirty minutes," he added to Anne.

"Don't get in the water," his wife said to her sons, "it's probably still cold."

"Sure thing, Mom," Janus responded.

"I mean it. No screwing around. Just come right back to the dock."

"They'll be fine," Dane assured her. He helped Anne unload their bags from the back of the Cadillac. They traveled light, as Rosa had already been up to get the house ready and make sure that they were well supplied. Pantry, fridges, bar, and humidor were all stocked and ready for the weekend. Firewood awaited lighting in the fire pit. Wood pellets and propane for the grills. Gasoline for the boats. The boys from the marina had already been out to de-winterize the wake boat and the pontoon. The only thing that had been missing was the Norris family itself.

As Anne and Emilia entered the code to unlock the front door, Dane and the boys drove off toward the public launch a few miles away.

An hour later, Anne was beginning to get worried, until Dane called and let her know that they'd had trouble getting the Jet Skis started but that Janus and Dylan were on their way, and he himself would be there shortly. As she hung up her phone, the dogs began barking at the front door, and she saw the Fletcher's Honda Pilot pulling into the driveway in front of the house.

"Emma!" Emilia yelled, yanking open the front door and running over to her friend, who had bolted out of the car as soon as it had stopped. Tim and Hannah got out after her, Tim going to the back hatch to get bags, while Hannah came forward and gave Anne a hug. Jingles and Buddy pranced around wagging and sniffing. Tim had to push Buddy's muzzle away from his crotch. "Down! Down!" he said, commandingly, but Buddy just circled around him, wagging and half-jumping before abandoning him to give attention to Hannah, who said: "We're so excited! This is our first time up here. It's beautiful!"

"Thank you! How are you guys?"

"Hell of a drive up here," Tim said, closing the hatch and coming forward saddled with their overnight bags.

"I haven't seen you since VBS," Hannah said. "Emma is just so excited to see Emilia." The two girls had already vanished back into the house, the dogs galloping after them.

"Where's Great Dane?" Tim asked.

"He and the boys put the Jet Skis in. He'll be back soon. Come on in!"

Anne gave the Fletchers the house tour, showing them the main level with the gleaming white kitchen, living room of sandy-fabric couches and chairs and teal accents everywhere, glass-topped dining room table with white-clothed chairs, and then the bedrooms on the ground floor, radiating out from the tile-floored rec room with its big wall-mounted televisions, inevitable bar, and tables for pool, cards, and foosball. Everything teal, white, and beige, and thus amplifying the bright summer sun.

As they made their way up the stairs, Dane entered.

"Great Dane!" Tim yelled in an affected deep voice, going forward to take his hand. Dane shook it saying, "Sorry about that. Had a little trouble getting the Jet Skis going. Are the boys back yet?"

Anne walked over and opened the door to the deck, looked down toward the dock, and answered, "Not yet."

Out on the lake a mild wind kicked up a billion points of light from the dark-green waters. Up and down the lake went the wakes of pontoon boats, fishing boats, ski boats, and even a sailboat. On the opposite shore, little kayaks were paddled along. The lake was alive with the Saturday recreational boaters. Engines roared, and "thump thump thump" went the bass notes of some assholes in a wake boat, blaring their music back at the wakeboarder behind them, and everyone else for that matter.

"What can I get you to drink?" Dane asked, walking toward the stairs down to the bar.

"I'll come with you," Tim said, following.

"Prosecco?" Anne asked, and Hannah nodded.

The boys and the Jet Skis finally arrived. The Fletchers and Norrises had changed into bathing suits, with T-shirts for the men and kaftans for the women. The two pairs of adults were oddly matched. Dane with his big belly and thick neck, with Hannah who was pudgy and obviously self-conscious in her bathing suit, opposed by the shapely Anne Norris and Tim Fletcher, slim and athletic. Tim had a boyish face that contrasted with small, sharp eyes and a mouth always half-cocked toward a sneer. His wife's visage was truly beautiful, framed by short blonde hair, but below her neck she had ballooned, and her body seemed incongruous with her head.

Jet Ski instructions were given, so Tim and Dylan took off down the lake, the former being thrown from his ski when he tried to jump the first wake he came across. Before long, Tim was back at the dock to give up his Jet Ski to Janus. The wake boat was lowered to the water, a big float tied to the back of it, then the two couples rode out on the lake with Emilia and Emma squealing with delight as Dane turned the boat and slingshot the float from side to side until the girls were launched into the air with flailing arms and splashes. Back to the dock to drop off the girls and load up Dylan and Janus who took turns wakeboarding. Janus was the better of the two, to his delight and to the despair of his competitive older brother. Then swapping out the wake boat for the pontoon, the adults took a twilight cruise as the sun glimmered painfully off of the water and the cool night air descended.

Throughout the day, from the back of the Jet Ski to the wake boat to the pontoon, again and again came Tim Fletcher's "Great Dane!" in an absurdly low voice. It had indeed, and inevitably, been Dane's nickname during his college days, but the way that Fletcher intoned it was needless and mocking.

So as the two couples sat down on the middle deck after changing clothes, Dane in a Rangers polo and shorts, Tim in linen pants and a gauzy button-up shirt, and the two women in slacks and knit sweaters, Dane felt relief that the evening was coming to an end. Now that he was off the boat, he could really start drinking, and he was four bourbons into the night already. Tim drank a beer from the bottle, while the ladies finished a bottle of chardonnay. The boys were downstairs playing video games, and the girls were back on Emilia's bed looking at their tablet screens.

"So, I didn't tell you this," Anne said, reaching out and touching Hannah's knee, and interrupting the conversation. "Emilia asked me the other day about what a pansexual is."

"What!" Hannah said, in a slightly inebriated voice.

"What in the world is a pansexual?" Tim asked.

"I had to look it up. It's someone who is sexually attracted to both men and women."

"I thought that was bisexual."

"No, it's not the same. It's someone who is attracted to men and women whether they're really men and women or they're transgendered."

"Jesus Christ!" Tim said. "That's the craziest thing I've ever heard. How about 'not sexual' since she's an eleven-year-old girl!"

"Where did she hear it from? YouTube or something?" Hannah asked.

"Okay, get this. She heard it from Maci at VBS."

Hannah gasped: "No!"

"Yes. Maci said that Fiona was identifying as a boy and yelled at Emilia for not using the right pronouns."

"Maci Johnson?" Tim asked. "Figures. Her parents are leftist nutjobs. Pisses me off that they're filling their kid's head with this shit and then she brings it to VBS of all places. It's like a virus. Now our kids are infected. All this nonbinary shit is too much. These liberals are becoming caricatures of themselves. You never know what batshit crazy stuff they'll come up with next."

As Fletcher ranted away, Dane tuned him out. He had no stomach for politics. He had never voted and didn't watch the news. The Norris family had been staunch Southern Democrats until the hard left-turn under Bill Clinton toward "Don't-ask-don't-tell" and the purging of the party of all anti-abortion voices had left them without a political home. His brother Roger had gone over to the Republicans and tried on occasion to bring Dane along with him, but Dane just smiled and nodded and ignored him. People could live their own lives, Dane thought, and he would live his. If they raised his taxes, well . . . he had more than enough. If they wanted to say they were men or women or Napoleon, it was no skin off of his back.

". . . the culture is just rotten," Tim continued, happy to have an audience and to air his grievances. "It just gets worse and worse all the time, and now it's affecting our kids. I tell you what they ought to do, they ought to kick the Johnson kid out of St. James and the other one too. What was her name?"

"Fiona," his wife answered.

"Her too. If there's one place we don't need that crap, it's St. James."

"What did you do?" Hannah asked Anne.

"Nothing. Do you think I should do something?"

"You ought to at least talk to Principal Strickland. He needs to know that this is going on."

"I thought about the school counselor," Anne replied. "But I looked at her Facebook page, and she has a rainbow LGBT frame around her profile picture."

"The fucking school counselor! In a Catholic school!?" Tim was incredulous. "She oughta be fired!"

"Tell them about the video," Dane said, taking a puff of his cigar and then trying, unsuccessfully, to exhale the smoke away from the other three.

"Oh the video! Hannah, you won't believe this. Janus found a video online from a band at the Franklin last night. What was their name, honey?"

"Drumbeat Jones, or something like that."

"Yeah, Drumbeat Jones. They're some kind of folk-metal band. Anyway, in the video, the lead singer, a woman, gets a guy up on stage and pees on his head!"

"No!" Hannah replied, shocked.

"Did they arrest her?" Tim asked.

"That's what I asked. You know that's the same theater where they arrested Johnny Cash for profanity. Now there are people peeing on stage."

"And the guy who got peed on, what happened to him?"

"Well, in the video it looks like he liked it," Dane answered.

"Do a lot of men like being peed on?" Hannah asked.

"Honey, I've been meaning to talk to you about that," her husband replied, and Dane, in the midst of a sip, snorted bourbon up his nose as Anne's and Hannah's faces turned red.

"Fletcher, you're alright," Dane said, when he regained his composure.

Sunday morning. The sun came up over the ridge behind them, sneaking across the surface of the lake. Dylan heard movement upstairs—his parents up, getting their coffee, and preparing to drive back into town. *Can't miss Mass!* Dylan thought, annoyed. It would have been much better to stay at the lake and run the wake boat around. But, on the other hand, that would mean spending more time with his parents.

His phone buzzed on the nightstand next to him, and Dylan rolled over and looked at it. The text message popped up on the lock screen:

Randy Thompson: Call me!

Dylan set the phone down and stretched, then sat up in his bed. He pulled a pair of lounge pants over his boxer shorts and padded out to the refrigerator, grabbed a water bottle, drank half, and went back to the bathroom to relieve himself. Then he picked up his phone and hit the icon by Randy's name.

"What's up, bro?"

"You better sit down, man."

"What's up? I'm sitting," he said, as he lowered himself back onto his bed.

"It's Pat. They found him yesterday; he hung himself."

"Bullshit. Not funny dude."

"I'm serious, Dylan. I just found out."

"Fuck you. I'm calling him."

Dylan hung up on Randy, pulled up his contacts and punched Pat Ryan's number. The phone rang, and rang, and went to voicemail: "Hey, it's Pat. Leave a message."

Dylan hung up. *What the fuck!?*

Chapter 9

REDOUBT

Deputy Sheriff Kenny Watkins sat on a ripped, hunter-green vinyl stool in front of the evidence bench in a damp, mildewy room made with painted cinder block walls. On the table at his left was a pile of bags collected the night before and a gray plastic tray with the items to be processed, and to his right were the bags he had already completed. It had been a late night outside working under halogen lamps, searching among the leaves and scrub for anything that might be evidence.

Which was ridiculous, Watkins thought. Clearly a suicide. The kid had climbed up and tied the rope around a big branch, tied the noose around his neck, and jumped off. There was no clean break of his neck; he had been asphyxiated. His fingernails were torn off, and the rope around his neck was bloody where he had tried at the end to reverse his fatal decision. There he swung in the tree, while the deputies looked for signs of foul play. Eerie, to have that kid swaying there behind him while he nosed around uselessly in the dirt.

Finally they had cut him down and bagged him. The loose end of the rope got its own little bag. The leaves directly below the kid's body were collected. Various bits of trash that had washed up from the cove—bottle caps, a rotten hair scrunchy, and a pair of men's jockey shorts flattened to a hard fossilized platter—were all deposited into little plastic sleeves.

And now Kenny was stuck at the sheriff's station with an unwanted Sunday morning chore—bagging and tagging the belongings that the coroner had removed from the body: urine-soaked Nike tennis shoes, urine-soaked low-profile socks, urine-soaked jeans, urine-soaked boxer shorts, canvas belt, nondescript T-shirt with a few streaks of blood from the kid's fingers, leather wallet, key ring with various keys, cell phone.

As Deputy Watkins picked up the cell phone, the screen lit. There was a picture of a football field with the sun rising (or setting). The time and date were superimposed at the top of the screen. And there was a grey bubble with text inside it. A small icon of a bearded face beside the name "Dylan Norris" and a phone number. Instinctively, Kenny reached into his own pocket, pulled out his own phone, and snapped a picture of the screen then slid his phone back into his pocket.

The Fletchers had departed quickly, embarrassed to be in the mixture of people when tragedy had come so close. Dylan stayed in his room until the family was ready to go, listening as his father ordered Janus around, covering the pontoon, raising the wake boat, making sure the Jet Skis were secure. His mother had come to check on him a few times, but Dylan left the door closed and mumbled "go away."

It was unreal. If it was true, it made no sense. The two of them had driven all over Asheville on Wednesday, just cruising. Pat had been pretty quiet, but after they'd both stuffed their faces full of burgers and fries, made crude jokes, and finally kicked back and watched the streams of cars moving below them on the interstate, Pat had seemed like he was back to his old self. Camp was coming up, and Pat was full of bravado on how he was going to stay ahead of Mitchum, and there was no way he was going to lose his starting

QB job to a freshman, no matter how good this McDowell kid was. And he wasn't worried in the least about Dylan's younger brother. He'd end up getting moved off to running back or something when he flamed out at QB.

Just four nights before. They were making plans for football camp, dreading the workouts, plotting their hazing of the freshmen. And now they say Pat Ryan is dead.

Dylan shook his head. It was not believable. He'd get back into town and someone would admit that it was a joke. Or he'd wake up.

"We're ready," came a voice and a tapping at his bedroom door.

Dylan got up, grabbed his overnight bag, and opened the door. His mother stood there, expectantly, tears welling in her eyes.

"I don't want to talk about it," Dylan said. His face was set like stone, and not a tear had crossed his cheeks. He brushed past his mother and made his way up to the waiting Escalade.

"Thanks for coming on such short notice," Principal Rollins said from the head of the conference room table. The side chairs were occupied by Fr. Dixon; Willy Williams; Dana Groen, the diocesan counselor; Angela Barstowe, the vice principal of SAHS; and Sr. Mary Michael, the last Augustinian sister still serving, a sort of trustee of the school. Other staff that would normally have been at such a meeting were absent on vacation, so it was a skeleton crew that met to discuss the aftermath of Patrick Ryan's death.

"Father, will you open with a prayer, please?"

"Certainly," answered Fr. Dixon. "In the name of the Father, and of the Son, and of the Holy Spirit."

"Amen."

"Heavenly Father, look upon us as we gather here tonight and help us guide your flock through this tragic time. Give us the wisdom to make good decisions for the boys and girls of St. Ambrose, and grant that we may do Your will. In Jesus' name, we ask this in the name of the Father, and the Son, and the Holy Spirit."

"Amen."

Rollins breathed a heavy sigh.

"Well. Here we are again. The main reason I called you here is to decide what actions we need to take as a school in the wake of Pat Ryan's death. I think the eight-hundred-pound gorilla in the room is the football practice." Saying this, he looked over at Coach Williams, who looked down at the mottled grey-and-white print of the conference room table.

"If I may interrupt?" Dana Groen asked. Dana was a heavyset woman who wore a blue and black tartan around massive hips, a ruffled white blouse, and maroon lipstick that matched her bobbed maroon hair. Her pasty makeup gave her skin a flaccid, dead appearance, livened only by the blue eyeshadow that wafted menacingly to the sides of her eyelashes. Seeing Principal Rollins nodding for her to continue, she did so: "I'll obviously be available for counseling, but I want to point out how different this situation is than when the others died."

"God rest their souls," intoned Sr. Mary Michael, crossing herself.

"Well," Dana continued, giving the nun a side-eyed glance, "in the case of suicides, there is a high incidence of copycat behavior, and I think we really need to get ahead of this."

"We're presuming it's a suicide at this point," Principal Rollins said, "but we should step cautiously. We need to be conscious of the privacy of the family. I don't think we should be advertising that it was a suicide."

"I'm sure the whole school already knows," Dana responded. "But we don't have to be . . . *official* about it. There's a whole suite of resources that we can deploy. Studies show that when anti-bullying and affirmation techniques are used in the wake of a teen suicide, the risk of copycat behavior can be reduced by seventy-five percent."

"Of course, of course," Rollins replied. "You know your business there. Do you need any help?"

"Why, yes. I'll need some assistance from other counselors. I think we can expect modest attendance from the school. After the last four kids died, we had about forty percent of the students take advantage of our counseling. This time I think we would expect about twenty percent or less."

"Less? Why less?" Rollins asked.

"Two factors," the counselor answered. "First, the proximity to the deaths of the other students. I think you'll find that there's a certain novelty effect to sudden death amongst children. Secondly, the nature of the student's death. There is a strong desire to view suicide differently than an accidental death. After all, it's not that long since the Church was burying suicide victims in unmarked graves at the village crossroads."

"An objective view of history, Ms. Groen, will show that it has in fact been a rather long time since any such practices," came the quiet rebuttal of Fr. Dixon.

"No offense, Father," she went on. "I only meant to say that people view the suicide as being responsible for his own death, unlike in an accident, so there is a diminution of empathy. Now this plays to the good and bad for our benefit. The good is that in the absence of a sort of spectacle of sympathy, there is less likelihood for the would-be copycat to become envious of the attention. But the bad part is that such kids are also more isolated because there is less social support from the community.

"Now, we have one big advantage," Groen finished.

"And what is that?" asked the principal.

"You have football practice going on."

At this, Coach Williams looked up from the table and commented: "No, no. I've already agreed. Can't expect the boys to practice under these conditions. Ryan was too much a part of the team to just go on with practice. Got to take at least a week off."

"I think that's a mistake, Coach," Groen replied. "We can take the first day of your practice for counseling. At least since you have your football team in one place at one time, we can make sure that one hundred percent of those kids get access to a counselor and our anti-copycat programs."

"But, Dana, the optics of it all . . . " Rollins interjected.

"Listen, we'll do our counseling on the first day, and then Fr. Dixon can do a religious thing on the second day, some sort of retreat or something, and instead of it being practice it's a community healing event."

"I think she's got something there," Williams pivoted, as the principal still appeared uncertain. "The same thing I said about the other kids dying. It's a benefit for the boys to be together now, and practicing will get their minds off of it. We don't need to go rushing into it. But if Ms. Groen and Father can do some sort of program the first couple days, then I'll get the boys back into the practice cycle by Wednesday."

The meeting continued on with logistics and budgetary discussions. After it was over, and a closing prayer was said, Fr. Dixon found himself sitting at the conference room table alone with Sr. Mary Michael. The shrunken old nun was wearing the black and white habit of her order, out of which her lined and wrinkled face hung suspended. She had distant, pale blue eyes, horrendous teeth, and a perpetual smile.

"I can't help but feel that we are somewhat ancillary to this process, Sister," Fr. Dixon commented, his brows furrowed.

"Of course not, Father. We have the most important job here."

"And what is that?"

"Praying, of course."

Fr. Dixon smiled at the old nun as the two rose from their seats.

The Augustinian sisters had come to Asheville in the early 1920s with the express mission of starting a parochial school for Asheville's small Catholic community. It was a dismal two-year drought while they taught in the basement of St. Lawrence and in private homes, but the nuns trudged along relentlessly, and in 1925, when Asheville's stockyards moved out of the city, the site was acquired for the purposes of the school, and the sisters threw up a small convent on the bilious mud flat.

A year later, the first schoolhouse was opened—a three-story anachronism that would have looked at home in a wild-west shootout, with wraparound porches and balconies and brooding shuttered windows.

Off the nuns would trudge to the market, taking along the biggest of the schoolboys to keep the local urchins from trying to lift the nuns' skirts, looking for the tails that the "Romans" were rumored to have. Back the nuns would trudge to cook, clean, and teach. Like any good missionaries, these daughters of France, Ireland, and Italy lived amongst the natives, spending a few years in Asheville before escaping to more familiar climes. St. Lawrence School stood in the midst of its stinking stockyard fields, surrounded by the growing city, opening its doors to the trudging children of the Irish railroad workers, then the Italian immigrants, and finally to the settled North Carolinian Catholics.

Edith Shaughnessy entered the doors of the old St. Lawrence schoolhouse, and in a sense, never left. A pleasant, plain, and simple girl, Edith admired the sisters, and when she graduated from St. Lawrence, she took the train to the Augustinian convent as a matter of course and emerged Sister Mary Michael. Assigned by her order to St. Lawrence, she arrived just in time to see the elementary and middle schools absorbed by the new St. James across town and the old schoolhouse torn down and replaced by a modern building of asbestos, cinderblock, and sloped mid-century architecture. The new high school was rechristened St. Ambrose after the patron of Augustine, and the parishioners of St. Lawrence had to be content to wait until high school to reclaim their children from the upstart St. James.

There in the glistening new school, the meek and mild Sr. Mary Michael plodded along through the turbulence of Vatican II, the new vernacular Mass, the tearing down of tabernacles, and the slow subduction of the organ in favor of the guitar.

Sr. Mary Michael smiled and took up the banjo, playing it (not well) to the amusement of her "children" at SAHS. When Asheville's local rowdies broke into the school, smashed statues, and spray-painted their bigoted messages on the school walls, Sr. Mary Michael was there with a paintbrush for the walls and glue for the statues.

And she was the number-one cheerleader for SAHS' awful athletic teams. Riding the bus with Willy Williams to away games, cleaning the girls' locker rooms, and waving a little gold and white pom-pom in the stands as the SAHS Saints went down in defeat in track and field, went down in ruin in basketball, went down in embarrassment in baseball, and went down ingloriously in softball or in football.

Sr. Mary Michael was firmly in middle age, and suddenly her world was transformed. In the same year that Dane Norris arrived, the year that would ultimately bring athletic success for her beloved Saints and booster money for her beloved SAHS, Pope John Paul II was shot. Years later, when the third secret of Fatima was revealed, and John Paul interpreted it as his own attempted assassination, it made perfect sense to Sr. Mary Michael. In the mind of the nun, the blood that poured out of the pope was like the blood of Christ and washed away great sins, and the blood of the pope seemed to mark a dramatic transformation in the environment around the nun. Certainly, within her little world there was transformation. The old cook, clean, and teach days were long gone. Her school was thriving, and if every year there was one less Augustinian sister, well, every year there were also more students. The bawdy, bigoted anti-Catholicism of the 1970s vanished overnight, as the Reagan/Vatican axis broke the Godless Soviets. Suddenly Catholics in the south were American. Even the briefly resurgent Ku Klux Klan—for years the most vicious antagonists of the Romans—seemed to decide not to dilute its racial hatred by bothering about their old papist enemies.

Triumphal, year by year, Sr. Mary Michael's smile got wider, her eyes grew paler, the convent grew quieter, and her love for her students grew deeper. Cook and clean and teach had become simply "teach," and finally even that was gone. But Sister strode the halls and was loved in return, and that was enough.

Polar opposite to Sister Mary Michael, within the orb of SAHS, was Fr. Thomas Dixon. Young where she was old, sharp features and "Father-What-A-Waste" beauty against her wrinkled and round face, grey eyes against her blue, black cassock against the white habit, tall and perfectly formed against the old and shriveled body, dour face against beaming smile, Fr. Dixon moved through the halls of SAHS in a concrete reality that seemed to defy the nun's effusive presence. And if for the nun the world was tending ever toward the better, inhabited by the smiling faces of youth, for Fr. Dixon the halls of the school were a thin façade over corruption. Where Sister saw happy, giggling children, singing and clapping and loving God, Father saw a school ever more secularized, competing against Parkdale in ACT scores and college placement rates, against Biltmore Forest and Buncombe County in athletics, and increasingly populated by rich kids, jocks, and the non-Catholic faithful. Indeed, SAHS could count among its student body devout Episcopalians, devout Muslims, devout Hindus (including a single Brahmin), and devout atheists. What seemed to be lacking, to Fr. Dixon, was devout Catholics.

At seventeen years old, as a student at St. Ambrose, Thomas Dixon had watched Pope John Paul II open the great Jubilee Doors at St. Peter's, ushering in the third millennium *anno domini*. Thomas had felt the first stirrings of a vocation, a martial impulse to join the army of black-clad men fighting the devil. Before graduating high school, he presented himself as a candidate to his pastor and then to the vocations director of the diocese. Thomas attended the retreats, filled out the forms, underwent physical exams, was fingerprinted, background-checked, wrote his essays and autobiography, and was interviewed, interviewed, interviewed. And he was stunned when he was not recommended to the bishop as a candidate.

Gently encouraged to give college a try, he did so, enrolling at Christendom College in Virginia. There, surrounded by the like-minded—by young men and women who were serious about their faith—Thomas pursued his classical liberal arts studies with stern intensity. He made good, but never close, friends. He watched the little circles of society form and disperse, serious young Catholic boys and girls flung from the swirling mass or pulled into it from their forays into the wider world.

As Thomas prepared for his final exams and wrote his thesis and term papers, Pope John Paul II lay dying in Rome. That great, towering figure who stood atop the institution that Thomas was striving to serve was suddenly gone. But then, *miraculum miraculorum*, Cardinal Ratzinger was elevated to the papal office and became Pope Benedict XVI. There could have been no greater salve for Thomas Dixon than to see the brilliant and reserved "*Panzerkardinal*" as pope. More determined than ever, he emerged from Christendom otherwise no different from when he entered: serious, aloof, and still feeling called.

Home with his philosophy degree and an ally on the throne of Peter, he marched off to the diocesan chancery and presented himself to the vocations director. How have you changed in the last four years? I have studied and I have learned. Yes, but how have YOU changed?

He didn't have the right answer for that question, though he should have anticipated it. All the forms were followed, the interviews and essays and retreats. But in the end, the result was the same: Perhaps you should give graduate school a try?

Back to Christendom he went, floating on his parents' largesse, his disappointment and regret over the rejection being quickly lost in the warm comfort of Augustine, Aquinas, and Kierkegaard. His small circle of friends tried to pull him into their larger world, but

Thomas stubbornly resisted being suborned. If this, then, were the test, why surely he could pass it. All it took was discipline and constancy. So, slowly the small circle of friends became even smaller until, most often, Dixon was alone with his dead philosophers and his God.

With his master's degree in hand, he approached his diocese for the third time. Knock and it shall be opened. Seek and ye shall find. With hesitancy, the vocations committee recommended him to the bishop, and Thomas found himself, at last, accepted as a candidate.

Thomas Dixon was thus part of the first wave of "Benedict priests" who rolled into the American seminary system to disturb and disrupt it. Still in pain from the stinging rebukes of Pope John Paul II's inspections, reprimands, and reforms, the masters of the seminaries nursed a resentment and disdain for this wave of serious young men. Thomas found himself, along with many others, battling against the stigma of "excessive devotion," "rigidity," "over-scrupulosity," and "lack of pastoral attachment." He was constantly presented with the twin temptations of laicism or monasticism, his spiritual formation director nudging him either out the front door to the world or into the cloistered world of prayer, but never offering him a place among the ranks of God's soldiers.

But Thomas wanted to go where the fight was, and that was not in the monastery. He wanted to do more than pray. He wanted to confront the devil at the sheepfold gate.

Before he could be ordained, he was told, he must take a pastoral year, and he found himself assigned, still as a seminarian, to St. Francis Parish in Asheville, under the nebulous eye of Fr. John Kelly. This year, away from studies, away from compatriots, and instead ensconced in the guitar-Mass, felt-banner world of St. Francis was a sore trial to both Thomas and Fr. Kelly. Thomas routinely witnessed what he felt were serious liturgical abuses, but to whom could he go? Fr. Kelly was beloved by the diocese and by his congregation. A sort of cult existed around him. The bishop had left him at St. Francis much longer than was usual for a parish priest, but now he was almost impossible to move. He and the parish were fused into one. And, to Thomas' critical perspective, this made Fr. Kelly a sort of diocese of his own.

So he spent that year, demeaned and berated by Fr. Kelly, subtly disliked by the parishioners, tending to non-sacramental tasks, and embraced by the strictures of "pastoral formation." In the end, though, even St. Francis Parish was not enough to end his vocation, and with his return to the seminary, his directors finally let him proceed to graduation. Ordained a deacon, he spent a blessed year at St. Lawrence, where the parishioners smiled in amusement at his obscure homilies and his stiff position by the door of the basilica, hands clasped behind his back, freshly ironed cassock, a tall, stiff figure nodding gravely at greetings and farewells.

Then the glorious day in June when Thomas prostrated himself in front of the altar, the Litany of Saints echoing around him, the stole and chasuble laid upon him, the chrism oil on his hands, then he and his fellow priests . . . fellow priests! . . . gathered around the altar importuning their God to become manifest in the bread and wine. A constant rushing in his ears, flickering candles, and brilliant lights. The perfume of incense and then enfolded in the priestly community, absorbed in poverty, obedience, celibacy, and simplicity.

For the diocese, there was only one thing to be done with the young man: Send him to St. James. A rarity for a young priest to be first assigned to the parish where he grew up, but the bishop may have been making amends for that awful year at St. Francis. This unexpected and welcome assignment was followed by a cataclysmic shock. Fr. Kelly, long the chaplain of St. Ambrose High School, was suddenly removed from that post. Rumors abounded. Parishioners and parents watched closely for any disciplinary action. A brigade went forth to the chancery in protest. But no explanation was forthcoming, and Fr. Thomas Dixon found himself striding into his alma mater, a stern, black-clad, Tridentine challenge to the students.

"Who's next?" Dana Groen asked, walking into the common room between the offices. She was holding court in the administrative wing of SAHS, along with some of her compatriots from the public school system, recruited to help with the mass-counseling sessions.

"Norris. Dylan Norris," Coach Thonie answered, standing by the glass door. A line of young men stood with their backs to the wall in the hallway, hands in pockets, in conversation or not, looking generally bored.

"He's the older of the Norris boys," Thonie continued. "Better watch this one; he was good friends with the Ryan kid."

"Ok, thanks." Dana strode up and opened the glass door and called out "Norris? Dylan Norris?"

There he was, the first kid in line. Huge. Muscles bulging from his SAHS Saints T-shirt, bull-necked and with a five-o-clock shadow. He said nothing as he walked past Groen and Thonie. Dana took a dozen short little steps to get ahead of him and escort him into the office. She motioned for him to take a seat, while she sat in a matching easy chair across from him. Behind her, the light shone through the slats of a venetian blind and onto shelves filled with books and knickknacks that reflected the light almost painfully.

"This is a safe space, Dylan. I know you must be hurting. I just want you to feel that you can say anything you need here."

"How long do I have to stay in here?" he asked, his voice deep and angry.

"Don't worry about that," Dana replied. "You can take as long as you like."

"So I can go now?" he asked, beginning to rise.

"Please, sit. Give me a few minutes before you decide to go."

He sat wordlessly and looked at her.

"Did you know Pat Ryan well?"

"Yep."

"How long had you known him."

"Years."

"You played football with him for a long time?"

"Since pee-wee days."

"How are you handling it?"

"Listen, I'm fine. Coach said I had to come talk to you, so I'm here."

"It's okay. You don't have to be defensive. If you don't want to talk, you don't have to, but I really wish you would."

"Can I ask you a question?"

"Certainly. You can ask me anything."

"When Peter and Doug and the girls died, there was a counseling thing like this, right?"

"Yes. I take it you didn't come to it."

"Nope. But Pat did. You were the counselor, right?" Seeing her nod, he continued, "Bet you feel like shit now that he's dead. Didn't help him much, did you?"

"It's normal to be angry, Dylan . . . " she began.

"I'm not angry. I just don't want to end up like him. Maybe if I spend a half-hour in here with you, I'll leave wanting to kill myself too."

She was silent, trying to find some appropriate response and coming up blank. Classic deflection. Transferring his anger to her. Coping with the unacceptable by creating an enemy. Oh, but it stung.

"Can I go?" the young man asked, rising from his seat, and without waiting for an answer, he opened the door and walked out.

Sweat. Sweat creeping into the corner of the eye. Stinging. Sweat soaking into the pads of the helmet. Saturating. Sweat beading up in the hair. Sweat rolling down the small of the back. Sweat streaming, constant from the brow, from the nose. Sweat pooling on the vinyl bench pads. Sweat rolling down the powder-coated legs to puddle underneath the bench. Sweat replaced by Powerade, Gatorade, water, water, water. The body a vast factory taking in trays of carbohydrates and protein and producing sweat, sweat, sweat, sweat, sweat.

A fish-eyed view of a cleat-print in the ground. Sweat, sweat, sweat dripping down to bounce off springy blades of grass in the one moment of rest. Thin, beaten grass, abused by sun and step, ground into mud, seeded, springing to life then clinging to life. In little bare patches, the fossilized remnants of cleat prints in all directions.

But only a moment to observe it, though there have been a dozen years of moments just like it stretching back to earliest memory.

A dingy closet room at the Y. Every kid scrambling to get a helmet and looking for that one helmet with a sticker of their favorite team instead of the one that fit.

Strapping on the mouthguard, told it "tastes like grape."

"You're playing safety."

"What's safety? I know what quarterback is."

Little kids running, with great, bulbous helmets on top, vainly chasing after the guy with the ball.

Then growing awareness. Growing prowess, and everything suddenly easy. The jargon of Pop Warner coaches. The jargon of middle-school coaches. The jargon of camps. Commitment. Work ethic. You've got to want it.

Pummel, pound, pound, pound, give it a hundred percent, leave it all on the field, hit it again again again again again again.

First, aching muscles and exhilaration. Then later, aching muscles, exhilaration, and pain. Constant pain, always something injured. Tape and braces and BENGAY ointment and protective cups and mouthguards—all the streaming pennons inevitably accompanying power and dominance.

Coach Williams' summer program was tough, and the worst of it was invariably the first week. But Dylan welcomed it. Welcomed the chance to swim again in the waters that he knew so well, welcomed the chance to become again the predator.

On the offensive side of the ball, Dylan lined up most often as tight end. But Coach Thonie would play him at times at running back or lineman, lining him up in the wildcat to run or pass. On defense, Coach Williams most often left him as middle linebacker but again would put him on the line or in the secondary. As the most dominant player on the field, Dylan knew the key was in denying the opponent the chance to game-plan away from him, and in some games, the only position that Norris did not play was kicker.

All of this versatility meant that Dylan spent his time with the blocking dummies, in the seven-on-seven skill drills, in the film room, in the weight room, and running laps. His practices were, in a sense, tailored to him. But ultimately he was most a part of the "skills team"—the players who would handle the ball.

The first thing he noticed about the camp, as unwilling as he was to recognize it, was the novelty of Pat Ryan's absence and junior Jeff Mitchum taking the "first team snaps." But that was all. From the moment of this realization, Dylan walled it off and concentrated on the walk-throughs, the drills, the treatment, and the film. And he breathed a spiritual sigh of relief as the rhythm of camp took hold and life returned to normal. Free of dead friends. Free of family. Free of everything but football.

"Shit, Billy. You ain't gonna believe this."

"Ain't gonna believe what?" Billy asked. Kenny had caught him outside the Jiffy Stop as Billy was getting into the old Ford Ranger. Dirt and road debris crunched under his boots as he walked over, and a couple of cars turned the corner, saw Kenny's sheriff's cruiser, and slowed as they passed the gas station.

"Check this out," Kenny said, stepping closer and pulling out his phone. He toggled the lock screen, thumbed over to his photos app, and opened the picture of Pat Ryan's screen.

A big smile came over Billy's face as he took the phone from the deputy.

"Dylan Norris! Damn! He was callin' the dead kid?"

"Yep," Kenny answered, reaching for his phone. Billy hesitated a moment before handing it back.

"Thought you'd like to see that. He called on Sunday morning. Must have gotten the news and tried to reach his buddy."

Billy's face turned to a frown.

"Aw, shit. I bet this fucks him up good. Just our luck. Finally get a good class coming in, and then this kind of shit's gotta happen. Bet you dollars to donuts that the Norris kid sucks this fall. On top of them other kids, I bet the Saints get stomped every game. Shit, they're gonna miss a whole summer of practices."

"I heard they're having practice anyway."

"No shit? Fucking Catholics. You see what's important to them. Football. Half the damn class could be dead and they'd still be practicing football. Course I suppose they couldn't recruit kids to go there if they let their program have a bad year."

"Well, maybe Mad County'll whoop 'em this year."

"Yeah, there's that, I suppose."

"Well, see ya around, Billy," the deputy said, walking toward the door of the Jiffy Stop.

"See ya," Billy said, and in his mind he repeated four-oh-six-seven, four-oh-six-seven. Dylan Norris' area code and the first three digits were the same as Billy's mobile number. All he had to do was remember the last four. Billy didn't know why he was so satisfied to have the football player's number, unless it was just another piece of information that rightly belonged to the World's Greatest Rangers Fan.

The receiving for Patrick Ryan had been delayed for almost two weeks so that the older Ryan boys and one Ryan girl could arrange leave from the military to attend their brother's funeral. The two-week gap also gave the medical examiner time to receive the toxicology report, which came back showing no recent drug use, but evidence from a sample of his hair indicated he had marijuana in his system at some point in the preceding months. This information was shared by the authorities only to Patrick's parents, who, needless to say, kept it to themselves.

Patrick's coffin was closed, a big splash of white carnations on top. Displayed by the side of the casket was a picture of Pat in his Ambrose Saints uniform depicting him kneeling on one knee, his hand on the top of his golden helmet. A little die-cast Scooby Doo Mystery Machine sat in front of the picture. Fanning out to the right, the parents, aunts, and eight siblings of the deceased. Two older brothers and one older sister stood crisp in their Marine Corps Dress Blues. Five younger siblings slouched about. The youngest, Bridgette, was the same age as Emilia Norris but attended St. Francis School south of Asheville.

Dana Groen's prediction about lower attendance at the counseling sessions also seemed to hold true for the receiving. While the Ryan's extended family, coworkers, and friends were there, a much smaller contingent of the SAHS students made their way through the receiving line. The football team was there, of course, along with the coaches, trainer, and equipment managers. Principal Rollins, Vice Principal Barstowe, Coach Schnauffmann of the baseball team, and several teachers. But the misery-choir of weeping freshmen girls was not to be found on this night.

Dylan, flanked by his parents, shuffled forward in the line. The last two weeks had been awful. Outside of football, his parents had left him no freedom. His mother painfully hovered near him. She begged him to unlock his door, and when he did not, he heard the little click as she pressed a pin into the lock from outside; he would keep his eyes closed as the door inched open and his mother looked in to make sure he was okay. On Friday of the first week of practice, the whole family had bundled into the Escalade and gone back to the lake for the July 4th weekend, where Dylan was kept continuously busy by Janus, Emilia, and his father. On Sunday morning, Anne and Emilia had driven into Asheville for Mass, while Dane took the boys out fishing. Monday they had sat on the porch watching the fireworks rise up from a distant barge, and then early Tuesday they had driven back into town and deposited Janus and Dylan safely in the hands of the Saints coaching staff.

Anne had begun to calm down a little in the following days, but the upcoming receiving of friends and funeral reawakened her terror. She kept prying and prodding, trying to understand why Dylan wasn't breaking down. Looking for some sign that he was moving past a sort of stunned apathy. Finally it had come to a head on Thursday night, as she insisted that he attend the receiving on the next evening.

"Fuck Pat Ryan!" he had yelled, letting his anger out.

His mother's mouth dropped open, and she started to say something, but he hurried on, saying aloud what had been echoing in his mind the prior two weeks.

"No. I'm serious. Fuck him. The little prick . . . the SELFISH little prick. Who fucking does that to their team? To their friends? To their family? How could that little fucker sit around wallowing in Pete's death and then do the same fucking thing to his own TEAM?"

There was silence. Dylan's parents looked at him. Dylan's brother and sister looked at him. He stood in the kitchen by the granite-topped island like a piece of granite himself. His fists were balled up, his face was red, but his breathing was slow and steady. He was, Coach Willy would have said, "ready to make a football move."

And after that explosion, Anne seemed to relax. Dylan apathetic in the face of his friend's death she could not grasp. Dylan enraged by his friend's suicide, she could.

"I understand," Dane said, breaking the silence. "But you're going to the receiving. Not for Pat, but for his family."

So there Dylan walked, shuffling along. Shaking hands with Pat's brothers and sisters, receiving a huge, wet, uncomfortable hug from Pat's mother, and coming to Pat's father, who looked up at Dylan. His eyes were red but somehow twinkling as if he and Dylan were sharing a private joke. Mr. Ryan reached out and took Dylan's hand then placed a second hand over the top in a strange grip.

Dylan, who had said nothing at all to the brothers, aunts, and mother of his friend, was suddenly compelled to say *something*, anything.

"Uh . . . Mr. Ryan, I uh . . . I'm gonna miss Pat a lot. He was a good guy."

"He still is a good guy, Dylan," Pat's father said, releasing Dylan's hands, gently but abruptly dismissing him, and turning his attention to the next in line.

Dylan stood confused for a moment then followed along to the kneeler, waiting until Janus got up and crossed himself. Dylan strode over, knelt heavily, and saw the little Mystery Machine Matchbox car beside the coffin.

What the fuck is that all about? he thought. Then he counted to thirty in his head, and figuring that was a reasonable amount of time, got up from the kneeler and walked away.

Chapter 10

PURCHASED GLORY

Coach Trey Carter stood on the riser platform and looked down at the field. There was movement everywhere, as two hundred young men ran through drills, sprinted, jumped, threw, caught, blocked, or walked through plays. His assistant coaches wandered about, their lime-green shirts standing out amidst the motley colors below. Around each assistant coach was another little orbit of managers, student assistants, practice-squad players, and other hangers-on.

It was the opening day of the Rangers' camp week, and those two hundred hopeful student athletes had paid fifty dollars each for the chance to show off their skills to the Rangers' staff. The rising seniors weren't of a lot of interest to Carter; they were mostly two- or three-star players who were shopping themselves around to as many teams as possible. Every kid on the field knew that the Rangers' recruiting class was just about full and that the team was only looking for four- and five-star players to fill out the scholarship slots. But coaches came and went, and in the mid-tier recruiting game, it paid to show off your skills and your name to as many potential recruiters as possible.

Every year over a million high school students played football, and only about six percent ever went on to play at the college level.

In Division I football, about five thousand scholarships were handed out each year, so only about two percent of high school football's graduating seniors filled those Division I scholarship slots. Indeed, of all levels of NCAA college football—from the elite Division I FBS, to the junior college "JUCO" programs—there were only about twenty thousand slots for new players each year, including the many non-scholarship players. Beyond that, only about two percent of NCAA athletes would go on to the NFL. So of the roughly quarter-million graduating seniors, only four one-hundredths of a percent would go on to play in the NFL. The dream of playing pro was just that: a dream.

But it was a dream that powered legitimate camps like the Rangers' and for-profit camps that could take in up to $4,000 per athlete. NFL veterans had their camps, colleges had their camps, and everywhere there were hopeful kids lined up to pay for a chance to be seen. With travel and lodging and registration fees, parents spent thousands of dollars trying to get their sons into a program. And of course, the parents who couldn't afford such expenses had to go without or scrape together enough for their kid to go to a local camp.

And then there were players like Dylan Norris who simply didn't need to attend the camp. Dylan had considered going to some other D1 camps just to see what they were like, but he knew that in doing so, it would be interpreted that he had "opened up" his recruiting, and the next thing he knew he would be getting all of the unwelcome attention of coaches competing to pry him away from Biltmore College. But Coach Carter had asked him to come by the camp anyway, so here he was, striding beside the O-line coach, Sampson, clanging up the stairs to the observation platform. Despite the fact that he was the same age as many of those on the field, Dylan felt that he belonged on the deck with Coach Sampson and Carter rather than down on the field with the kids.

"Dylan! Glad you could make it," Carter said, walking forward and holding out his hand.

"Thanks for the invite, Coach," Dylan replied, taking his hand for a quick shake.

"Wish you could have made one of the camps this week," Sampson said. "Helps the other kids know what they're up against in D1."

"Would have loved to, Coach, but with missed practices earlier in the summer, I've got to get as much time as I can with the Saints. We have a shot at State this year."

"Yeah, sorry to hear about your QB. Really tragic. How are you and the other players doing?" Carter asked.

"We're doing alright. They had counselors and stuff. It's good to be back prepping for the fall."

"Well, I'm looking forward to seeing y'all play," Sampson interjected. "Me and some of the other coaches will be there at your season opener."

"That's great. Thanks," Dylan replied flatly.

"So, Dylan," Coach Carter spoke up, "there are another couple of players here that just came to observe the camp. You probably know the Biltmore campus better than they do. If you see them just kind of hanging around, it sure would be good if you could maybe show them around a bit? Nothing official of course, and only if you feel like it."

"Sure thing, Coach. Anybody in particular?"

"You see Richardson down there watching the linemen at work?"

"Yeah. I see him. Hard not to, the guy's huge."

"Well, go on down and say hi to him," Sampson said.

"Sure thing, Coach," Dylan nodded, and descended from the platform. There was nothing in the NCAA rulebook about a couple of high school students bumping into each other on campus, provided, of course, that the meeting was neither facilitated nor attended by any of the program's staff. Carter and Sampson watched as Dylan approached the big Madison County lineman, Dylan Norris' white Saints T-shirt gleaming in the sun, as Taevon Richardson's maroon Mad County shirt made his dark skin look even darker. Carter watched the two sizing each other up, making brief exchanges, and pointing to the struggling kids out on the field. Moments later, Norris and Richardson were joined by a couple other prospects who were there just to observe, and within minutes the group was laughing and wandering away from the practice field toward the campus.

As they pushed open the chain link gate that led out of the practice field, some words came drifting up from the four young men.

". . . Norris? Where's Biltmore keep their pussy at?"

[laughter]

"Come on, I'll show you," Dylan said.

Carter turned to Sampson.

"Have one of the managers keep an eye on them, from a distance. Let's make sure they don't get in any trouble."

"Sure, Coach," Sampson replied, and hurried off to dispatch a skinny young man in a Rangers polo and golf cart to tag along at a distance.

The Biltmore College campus was a gem set into four hundred acres on the north side of Asheville, occupying the center of a shallow valley between the French Broad River and Sunset Mountain. To the south were the Botanic Gardens, to the north rose Nut Hill, and in between was an eclectic mix of buildings representing the many benefactors of the private college.

When the old Commodore gave his one million dollars to fund Vanderbilt University in Nashville, Tennessee, it was almost inevitable that one of his descendants would try to one-up him. For a long time, it looked like that honor would fall to Cornelius' son William, who doubled his father's fortune and became the richest man in the world. But William was content with contributions to his father's university and to Columbia in New York. Three of William's four sons spread their fortunes around liberally, but it was the grandson of the Commodore, George Washington Vanderbilt

II, who conceived the idea of a school that would rival his grandfather's Vanderbilt University.

A progressive thinker, G.W. Vanderbilt sought not only to build a self-sustaining estate at Biltmore and a model community in Biltmore Village, but to also transform the sleepy little hill town of Asheville. He acquired the land for his college in much the same way that E.W. Grove would later acquire land for his Grove Park Inn, that is, by both legitimate and nefarious means. When he had the land, he asked his architect Richard Morris Hunt to throw off the first building, and thus "Old School Hall" was designed, looking a little too much like The Breakers of Rhode Island, but with a copper roof whose green patina would later give Biltmore College the lime green for the Rangers.

Rafael Guastavino added a Spanish Baroque dormitory a half-dozen years later, before the art-deco movement of the '20s coincided with the influx of funds from philanthropists outside of the Vanderbilts themselves. Grove, Fred Seely, and rayon production company American Enka all contributed to a campus and school that were fulfilling G.W. Vanderbilt's dream. Through the depression, the school struggled along, emerging in the aftermath of World War I with an influx of research money (particularly in woven plastics) and students. New dormitories and lecture halls of mid-century architecture rose. The college survived a brief attempt at integration into the North Carolina University system, clinging to its private status just like the rival Vanderbilt University across the mountain.

Indeed, Biltmore College was continuously motivated and inspired by that rivalry, and in often unusual ways. As Vanderbilt University struggled with integration and racial issues in the 1960s, Biltmore College easily opened its campus to black students and civil rights activists. As Vanderbilt Football limped into the 1970s, struggling for one or two wins a year, Biltmore College was becoming a powerhouse. And as Vanderbilt University was recruiting Nobel Laureates and leaning into scientific and medical research, Biltmore College was using its own legacy in a city of writers as diverse as the Fitzgeralds and Thomas Wolfe to build its liberal arts reputation.

By the new millennium, either the old Commodore or G.W. Vanderbilt could have claimed victory. Their legacy schools had gone different directions, but each was still private, still proud, and still powerful.

But only one could claim that pride in football.

Until their collapse in the first decade of the new century, the Biltmore College Rangers were as feared as any team in the SEC. Save for the elusive National Championship, the Rangers had achieved all that could be asked from a small private school in the Appalachian Mountains, far from the old plantation lands that, year after year, produced the best new football players of any race, creed, or color. Whatever BC's shortcomings in local talent, football success had brought money from a national fan base, which leveraged into having one of the largest on-campus football stadiums in the nation. Gleaming luxury boxes, high-tech training rooms, athletic dorms like little palaces, cafeterias like food courts at a mall: All were trappings of a rags-to-riches life that awed recruits and incited envy from the other wing of Biltmore—the academicians.

Professor Monty Sanders watched from his office window as four big football players strolled along, ogling the summer-session coeds shamelessly. Sanders recognized the Saints logo on the big white kid. After all, St. Ambrose was the school that his only child attended. But the other team logos were obscure—probably local high schools where the less affluent went. The boys had chosen their route well, for ogling at least. Outside Sanders' window was one of the main paths between the dormitories, sorority house row, and the lecture halls.

Sanders had positioned his desk with his back to the window but would leave the blinds open and observe the reaction of anyone seated across from him. It amused him to see his students attempt to concentrate as the parade of scantily clad girls walked behind him. It amused him even more to see the same reaction from fellow professors. Before long, summer would pass into fall, and the coeds would cover themselves up for the winter, emerging from it much heavier and less willing to expose themselves. It was a cycle that Professor Sanders had seen repeated throughout his academic life, the only real difference being the increasing polarity: skimpier clothing in the summer and fall, greater obesity in the winter and spring. He expected that someday the females of the campus would fall into two classes: fake-tan stick figures wearing thong bikinis or massive spheres of flesh waddling on haunches of jiggling cellulite.

"Alright bro, meet me in the lobby," Dylan said into his phone. He stood with the three young black men in the entrance of the athletic dorm. A great glass rotunda towered before him, at the center of which was the information/resident assistant's desk. Two tanned students—a boy and a girl—sat behind the desk looking at consoles hidden by the faux-marble countertop. Leather couches were dotted around the room, little end tables here and there. There were three exits from the rotunda—one straight ahead to the cafeteria and study halls, one to the left to the women's dormitories, and one to the right to the men's.

While much of the campus was sparsely populated for the summer, the athletic dorms were fuller, with students packing in summer credits to graduate early, staying on campus for practices or training, or in many cases making up classes or trying to boost their GPAs to stay eligible to play.

Dylan stood near the entrance, hands in pockets and relaxed. His three companions shifted from foot-to-foot somewhat nervously, looking around at every detail. After a few moments, from the corridor to the men's dorms a heavyset ginger-haired young man emerged, walked over to Dylan, and high-fived him.

"Johnny Campfield," Dylan introduced him, and then turned

to his three companions. "This is Taevon Richardson, Mad County line, and Ty Beal and Anthony Flowers of Shelby."

"Hey," Johnny said, as he gave each of them a fist bump.

"So you wanna check out the dorms?"

"Yeah! We're not on an official visit or anything. Just looking at the campus."

"Cool. Cool," Campfield said. "We can check out my room and then look around a bit, and then if you want I can show you some of the other dorms." As he finished, he gave Dylan a sort of inquisitive look. Dylan shrugged.

All five strode back toward the men's dorm and crowded into a wood-paneled elevator. Up they went to Johnny's room—part of a suite with a living room, large bathrooms, twin beds, and maple desks. Johnny's suitemates were out, and he was disinterested in showing them the room, but Taevon, Ty, and Anthony couldn't get enough.

"Shit! Check out this shower!" Ty said. Anthony stretched out on the sofa in the living room. "Sure got it nice! Ima take a nap."

"Come on," Johnny said, opening the door, and gesturing out into the hall. Back into the elevator they went, emerging into the hallway. They entered the gleaming rotunda again, then walked through the cafeteria. Most of the food stations were empty, but there were still white-clad workers at the grill and a rack of sandwiches and salads in an open-faced cooler.

"It's open twenty-four hours," Johnny said. But just the grill and Cokes and stuff. If you want other stuff you have to be here on time. Good breakfast here. Flapjacks are fucking awesome."

"What the fuck's a flapjack?" Ty laughed.

"Same as a pancake," Johnny answered, unamused.

"So with the meal plan, you basically get all-you-can-eat during the meal hours, and then you get like, one or two snacks afterward. You gotta buy your own Cokes unless you use the fountain. And you can bring one guest a day, but only during the meal times."

"Damn," Anthony said.

Dylan bought them Powerades, and they exited the cafeteria to take a quick tour of the dormitory exercise room.

"The real workout rooms are at the gym and at the practice facility. This is just for the dorm," he said, pushing open the lime-green door, which opened into a massive room with a gleaming floor, rank after rank of exercise machinery, mirrors and benches, and free-weight racks. Everything sparkling and new and antiseptic. Shelves of clean white towels with the Rangers "B" logo. A couple of students picking up discarded towels, wiping down equipment.

"Shit man. And this ain't even the real stuff?"

"No. Wait till you get your walk-through on your official visit. They'll show you the real shit then," Johnny answered.

Dylan strode along, bored. He had, of course, hung out at the athletic dorm, eaten in its cafeteria, and seen every inch of practice facility and stadium. Ty and Anthony bounced around, in awe, but Taevon walked, like Dylan, slowly, and took it all in.

Finally, the five stood outside the dorm and Johnny asked: "You wanna go check out one of the other dorms? Got a buddy I was gonna drop in on. Usually a good time."

The three black men looked at each other and then at Dylan.

"Nah, I ain't into that today," Dylan said, getting a read from Taevon that he was uncomfortable.

"Gonna head back to the practice field," Richardson said, walking over closer to Dylan.

"Athletic dorm is okay, but if you wanna get into something cool it's a lot easier in some of the other dorms."

"Easy to score here?" Ty asked.

"Yeah. Real easy. Gotta keep it on the DL. Not so bad as in high school."

"Alright, bro," Dylan said, fist bumping Johnny, "gonna head back too. See you later."

With that, the four high school students headed back toward the practice field, trailed at a distance by the lime-green golf cart, as Johnny Campfield made his way toward the "cooler" dorm.

Monty Sanders missed their return trip, engaged as he was in grading an essay, head down over his desk and red pen fiercely wielded. Monty could not or would not grade using the computer. He would run the essay through the plagiarism checker, then print it out for his ruthless analysis. A stack of essays to his left, unmarked, showed that he had his work cut out for him.

The sun was sinking as Dylan, Taevon, Ty, and Anthony arrived back at the practice field. Coach Sampson came over to say hello, but for the most part, the Rangers staff very carefully avoided contact with the four.

"Aight, man, nice meeting you," Ty said, shaking hands with Dylan, and Anthony followed suit.

"Y'all staying in town tonight?" Dylan asked.

"Yeah, with my cousin. He'll be here to pick us up in a few."

"Gotta be going too," Taevon said, starting to walk toward the practice field gate.

"Where you goin'?" Dylan asked.

"Got a bus to catch."

"Shit man, lemme give you a ride."

"Nah, it's cool. Rode down here on a bus. I can ride back."

"Fuck that. I'll give you a ride. I'm just leaving too. Where you goin'?"

"Bentonville. Up 26."

"Cool. My car's this way," he said, gesturing toward the parking garage.

Dylan opened the passenger door of the Yukon and threw the contents of the seat into the back, then walked around to the driver's side as Taevon climbed in. Dylan presumptively flipped through his satellite radio favorites to a rap channel. They backed out of the parking space and wound their way down to the garage entrance, taking corners slowly to negotiate the big SUV around the bends, tires squeaking loudly. Finally they came to the turnstile. Dylan waved his dad's "Ranger Royalty" prox card, and the gate opened, then they were out on the road making their way toward I-26.

"So where you taking your officials?" Dylan asked.

"Definitely gonna do 'Bama, Georgia, UNC, Clemson."

"So your fifth? Thinking about BC?"

"Thinkin' about it."

"What's your reservation? I mean, why not BC?"

"Shit man, program still down. Plus Ima play D-line. Did you see Coach Holloway come over? Disrespect."

"Shit, you know they gotta watch out for contact on an unofficial."

"Yeah but they had Sampson out there."

"That's why, bro. Trust me. You got all the respect. Carter wants you bad."

"Yeah, we'll see. But e'en so, I got to think about my development. Yeah I get playin' time at BC 'cause the line's gettin' old, but Holloway ain't half the coach as Beaty."

"So you're leanin' Georgia?"

"Man, you don't have to be no spy. I know you here to try'n recruit me and that's cool, but Ima make my own decision."

"Peace, bro, I get it. You know why I'm going to BC. I got my own reasons, right. It's cool you got yours."

After a moment or two of silence, Dylan turned the topic back toward high school.

"So, how's Mad County gonna be this year?"

At that, Taevon's face was split in half by a huge grin.

"Gonna tear you boys up. You just wait."

"Yeah, well don't get your hopes up," Dylan said, laughing. Then a couple moments later: "So how come you didn't want to smoke back on campus? I could see you weren't into it."

"Don't smoke."

"Everybody smokes. It's cool."

"Cool for you maybe. You get caught smokin' and it's no big deal. I get caught, and folks'll say I gotta problem. Just another black kid on weed. I ain't takin' that chance."

Up I-26 they went to the Bentonville exit, then Dylan drove west down a poorly paved two-lane road. They cruised through the downtown of Bentonville, brick buildings with bars over the windows, most of them closed. Parking lots full of derelict semi-trailers. A disreputable Cox Convenience store with four gas pumps. One traffic light blinking orange. Bentonville Elementary up on a hill, its red-brick, dirty windows, and desultory playground ringed by a sagging chain-link fence.

And then they were through the little downtown. Taevon called out the turns, and Dylan negotiated smaller and smaller roads up through a neighborhood of clapboard houses that clung to the sides of the hills. Broken down cars on the street, piles of accumulated leaves and trash between them. Hostile looks from porches as the blacked-out SUV rolled down the street. A raised Chevy Impala with shining thirty-inch rims rolled slowly by, bass notes lingering in the air. Finally Taevon stopped him and said, "This is my place," and as Dylan put the Yukon in park, Taevon opened the door and got out.

The house behind him had a steep driveway that leveled off briefly in front of a single-car garage that had to be built right into the hillside. The door of the garage was stuck open, and the interior was filled with broken furniture and boxes. A pathway led to dangerous-looking wooden steps up to a little porch, all in faded red paint, its rails draped with threadbare towels drying in the sun. A plastic kiddie pool in one of the few flat spots in the front yard explained the towels. The siding of the house was splotched with mildew and had long stains running down from the eaves where gutters had failed and years of water had begun rotting the walls. Rising from near the center of the roof, a brick chimney sat wrapped with a blue tarp tied with row after row of bungee cords.

Taevon pushed the door closed, and Dylan rolled down the window.

"See you bro. You want my number in case you want to talk about BC?" Dylan asked.

"Nah, it's cool. If I wanna talk I'm sure someone'll gimme your number."

"Alright then. See you in the fall."

"Hey Norris," Taevon said, coming back to the open window.

"Yeah."

"Just drive the fuck outta this neighborhood, got me? You outta place here."

"Got it," Dylan said, unconcerned, rolling the window up and driving away.

Thirty miles to the east, near a spur of the Pisgah National Forest, was the Edwin's Gulch State Recreational Area. There were still a few hours of sun left, but near the trailhead a row of pickup trucks with their trailers was surrounded by teenage boys loading up their ATVs and UTVs. Polaris, Honda, Suzuki, fluorescent green, bright blues, and reds. Mud splattered everywhere after a day of riding. Boisterous shouts, helmets removed, sweat-soaked racing jerseys getting pulled off of bare shoulders and replaced by T-shirts. Coolers loaded, straps tightened, and some of the trucks pulling out of the lot and heading down the mountain.

John Hubert started to steer his Honda toward the trailer, but he heard a rattle and felt a shudder.

"Did you hear that?" he asked Danny O'Brien, who had just lowered the trailer ramp.

"What?"

"Did you hear that noise?" he asked again. "As I was driving up?"

"Didn't hear anything. Back up and try it again."

Hubert backed the UTV away and started toward the ramp. This time there was no rattle or shudder. He stopped short of the ramp and said: "I'm gonna take it up the Bucktrail, just to make sure."

"Hold on, I'll come," Danny said, jumping in and tightening the restraints around himself. John drove back out of the parking lot toward the Bucktrail entrance.

"Where y'all going?" Skylar Evans called out.

"Just checking out the suspension," John yelled, and then flew up the trail.

More trucks pulled out of the lot, and the sun sank lower. Amber Krieger, Skylar's girlfriend, was impatient, but Skylar hung on, waiting to see his friends emerge back into the lot. When thirty minutes had passed, and Skylar's Dodge Ram was the only truck left besides John Hubert's big Ford, Skylar tried calling John's cell phone. Service was notoriously bad up here, so he wasn't surprised when he didn't get an answer. Amber pressed him again to leave, and he hesitated, walking toward his truck door and then suddenly turning and lowering the ramp on the back of his trailer.

"What are you doing?"

"I gotta see if I can find them. It's weird that they're not back."

"So you just want me to wait here?" Amber whined, crossing her arms across her stomach and, intentionally or unintentionally, pushing up her breasts in the process.

Skylar fished around in the back of his truck and handed Amber a walkie-talkie.

"I'm going to run the loop. It should take about ten minutes. I'll call you on the walkie if I need you. I'll be right back. They've probably got a flat tire or something. Promise I won't be long."

"Well hurry up! Creeps me out up here by myself."

"Then get in the fucking truck and lock the doors!" Skylar snapped, exasperated.

Amber saw this as good advice and climbed in, locking the

doors and looking petulantly at Skylar as she waved the truck keys at him.

"I swear," he muttered under his breath, "she can be such a bitch." He swung his body into the seat of his Polaris, neglected his helmet, strapped in over his white T-shirt and jeans, then drove off toward the Buckhead Trail. Fifteen minutes later he emerged again, having completed the loop. He had seen no sign of his friends.

He unstrapped and jumped out of the UTV, startling Amber, who was sitting in the cab of the truck swaying her head to music.

"Roll down the window," he yelled, and she did so.

"Drive down the mountain until you get a signal and then call 911!"

"What?"

"Just do it."

"I don't like to drive with the trailer . . . " she began.

"JUST FUCKING DO IT! Call 911 and tell them we're up here and they're missing."

Comprehension started to show in Amber's dull blue eyes. She nodded and started the truck.

"Where are you going?" she yelled, as Skylar got back into the Polaris.

"To fucking look for them!" he yelled. "I'll call you on the walkie if I find them."

And then he drove back up the trail, yelling for his friends as he went.

"Nah, there were fucking ruts all over the place. Couldn't see where it left the trail at all," Sheriff's Deputy Watkins explained to Billy Mullins and Tommy Hess.

"Damn fools runnin' around up there. Mountains are dangerous enough without tryin' to race on 'em," the clerk opined.

"So how long before y'all found 'em?" Billy asked, smacking his pack of cigarettes against his palm.

"They went over the edge sometime on Wednesday night. Finally found 'em the next afternoon, and that was just luck. One of their cellphones was still working, and they picked it up and tri-ang-u-lated. Never would've found 'em otherwise. They were right off the trail but down at the bottom of this crevice. Must've been flyin' round the corner and just launched over the edge. Not a damn sign that they'd gone over there. No snapped branches, nothing. And like I said, the trail is so rutted up you couldn't see no tracks. Some friend of theirs had been drivin' round and round yellin' for em until we got up there. I mean, rangers and whatnot. Had a damn helicopter and a big light . . . "

"Thought I saw that up there," Billy interrupted.

"Didn't do no good though. Couldn't see 'em at the bottom of that ravine."

"Killed right away, I guess?"

"One of 'em definitely. The driver. He hit pretty hard, and he was smashed up pretty good. The other one though, he might've lived awhile. He was hung upside down, had a compound fracture in one arm. That's where the bone comes through. Probably bled out. But the cell phone was by his other hand, so he might've been alive long enough to try'n call for help."

"Fuck."

"Anyway, it was probably about three o'clock yesterday afternoon when they found 'em. So they were out there, what . . . not quite twenty-four hours."

"Get 'em out yet?"

"They got the bodies out last night. Ain't no point in gettin' that ATV outta there. Probably be there until it rots."

"Shit," Tommy said.

"Damn. That's seven of them Catholic kids dead, and the summer ain't halfway over yet," Billy observed.

The mothers and fathers of St. Ambrose's students sent their children into a complete lockdown after the latest two deaths. The summer was out for blood, and there was no indication of when it would stop. Certainly the death of Pat Ryan was related to the accident on Peter Morton's houseboat, and so mothers and fathers could tell themselves that, barring any copycat suicides, with perhaps a little more oversight, their kids would be safe. But somehow the UTV deaths, while no less an accident than the houseboat deaths—and totally unrelated—still gave the impression that something was hunting their children.

Party Cove was silent. Jet Skis and wake boats remained docked. Party Field was dominated by crickets and a cicada brood and saw none of the late-night headlights and discarded solo cups. Around Asheville as the sun went down, teenagers made their way back home, and not just the children of beleaguered St. Ambrose but teenagers from good Protestant homes, good Jewish homes, and good agnostic homes.

The SAHS baseball team, already hurt by the absence of Peter Morton, slid into irrelevancy with the loss of rising seniors John Hubert and Danny O'Brien and with the distraction and depression of the rest of the team, who went about practice half-heartedly. Dana Groen and Coach Schnauffmann had their conferences, and little counseling rooms were set up in the gym. Fr. Dixon said his prayers, and Fr. Kelly said his rosaries and Masses. The brigade of sobbing freshman girls descended on the funeral home, managed adroitly by the now-experienced funeral director and assistants. The lawsuit between the Smith family and the Morton family was settled, the Smiths perhaps seeing that it was the tide of blood, rather than the Mortons, that took their son. A rumor went around that Danny O'Brien had recorded a video on his cell phone while he hung dying in the wrecked UTV. But there was no proof of this, and such a video never surfaced.

Skylar Evans was watched like a hawk by his friends and his father. Skylar's mother had run off when he was eleven and did not reappear now to console her son. Amber Krieger, who secretly wished she had broken up before the accident, found herself bound to Skylar and encouraged in the role of devotion by her family, her friends, and her own nagging conscience. Night after night she lay with open arms and open legs as Skylar pumped his sorrow and pain into her.

Day after day, Dylan and his team pounded the St. Ambrose practice field—the old stockyard field with over a hundred years of dried manure patted down and manicured into turf. Each weekend the Norris family retreated to Lake Juniper—the flooded graveyard of a hundred homes—to vigilantly watch Dylan and Janus and Emilia. Asheville's parents waited with collective suspended breath for the next child to die, and then, at last, they breathed a great sigh when school finally began. The terrible, terrible summer was over.

Part Two

Heathenesse

Chapter 11

TIDE

The lobby of St. Ambrose High School was an enormous A-Frame, the front windows of which were a herringbone pattern of rectangular panes randomly colored in yellow, red, and green. Suspended from the eaves was a large wooden plank with the aluminum letters S A H S, along with a cross formed of two arcs, which somehow managed to look like it was surfing.

Anne pulled into the large circular driveway in front of the lobby, waiting her turn to drop off Janus for his first day of high school. Her son sat beside her in the passenger seat of the Land Rover, khaki trousers, white tennis shoes, white Oxford shirt with SAHS embroidered in gold thread over the shirt pocket. Unruly hair that was just a bit shorter than the required cut, but over a face that held sparkling eyes and a big smile. The August sun shone down on him, lighting up his white shirt and casting his shadow back toward the school entrance.

Janus had, of course, been practicing with the SAHS Saints all summer, so he knew plenty of the upperclassmen in addition to all the St. James kids who were moving up with him. This first day was just the freshmen, so the student parking lots were mostly empty. The line of vehicles ahead of her disgorged uniformed students with brightly colored backpacks. Windows rolled down and hands waved, and kids ignored them as they strode past Principal Rollins, who smiled and tried to shake all their hands. Next to him stood Sister Mary Michaels, handing out little peppermint sticks with hand-tied gold ribbons from a basket that hung from her elbow, and hugging students whenever she got a chance.

Windows rolled up, and BMWs, Audis, and Mercedes rolled out of the drive to make way for the Jaguars, Cadillacs, and Porsches advancing for their turns. Finally Anne reached the drop-off spot, and Janus was out the door as soon as she could put the SUV in park. Like all the other parents, she rolled the window and waved at Janus, saying: "Have a great day!"

Unlike most of the other kids, Janus turned around, squinted against the morning sun, grinned, and waved back.

"Thanks Mom," then "Hi, Principal Rollins!" shaking his hand and walking backward toward the doors at the base of the A-frame, waving as his mother drove away.

Anne's heart was full as she negotiated the narrow and crowded streets around the SAHS campus on her way to St. James to help get ready for their first day. The Land Rover twisted and turned through side streets and neighborhoods, cutting the back route that had evolved through the last seven years of driving between campuses. Finally there was the grey tower of the church, and Anne pulled into the parking lot beside the school.

St. James' School huddled inharmoniously next to the church. Another mid-century marvel, the school was comprised of four wings radiating out from the corners of a long rectangular central building. It was the roof that caught one's eye when approaching from the side of the school, for rather than being pitched in the middle, the roof was lowest at its center and then raised up at a shallow angle toward the wide eaves. This meant the rainwater flowed downward to the center of the roof, where it was gathered into wide troughs that were supposed to direct it outward through drains. A terrible design, the result of which was that the roof had leaked since its first installation, regularly flooding interior walls. Every year the school considered proposals to alter the roof, and every year administration determined that they would rather make more substantial changes to increase enrollment, and their fundraising went toward a new gym, new technology rooms, and of course to enhanced security. And they went on unplugging the drains, patching the troughs, and enduring the floods.

The walls of the school were taken up by enormous glass windows, which were likely the inspiration for the reverse-pitched roof. However, security concerns over the years had resulted in the interior of the windows being painted, so now the natural light was diffused and any elegant appeal the building might have had was spoiled.

Anne exited the Land Rover, walked to the porte-cochere and to the main doors, where she pressed a little button to ring for entry. The door buzzed and clicked, and she opened it and walked into the central lobby area.

"Hi, Anne!"

"Good morning, Mrs. Norris!"

"Hello, Anne!"

Voices and smiles as she made her way to the sixth-grade classroom in the middle-school wing. Anne was a little saddened; this was her last child at St. James. Sixth grade was also when Maryanne had started at the school when they had moved back to Asheville. She remembered those many days walking these halls to the middle-school classrooms where she had been a fixture as room parent, hosting parties, helping prepare for plays and assemblies, and all the days looking at childish art while waiting for parent-teacher meetings outside elementary and kindergarten classrooms.

Anne would walk into the school in the morning, Maryanne rushing off down the corridor toward the middle school while Anne walked along holding little Janus' hand, and Dylan strode beside her. She could see the faces of her little boys now, so different. Janus had always had a sort of look of wonder about him. Dylan, though, from a young age would yank his hand away if his mother tried to hold it. He had always wanted to do things for himself, and those early parental victories when he first walked or said his first words were quickly swept away into the rush to grow up and a sense that he was missing his childhood. Anne thought back to one day in the school hallway when, on impulse, she had knelt down and hugged him, and he hadn't pushed her away. The memory was bright, clear, and precious because it was so rare.

The classroom door was open. She stepped inside and saw Ms. Jordan, the homeroom teacher, standing on a chair and trying to hold a bright yellow strip of paper to the wall while tearing pieces of Scotch tape from a roll held in her mouth.

"Let me help!" Anne said, rushing over. Anne was a good foot taller than Ms. Jordan, and the work went much quicker with Anne holding the paper while Ms. Jordan applied the tape. Even the simple, yellow decoration made Anne a little sad. Ms. Jordan had just moved up to middle school, and she had been famous at St. James for having a Star Wars themed classroom every year. She evidently thought that was beneath the dignity of the middle schoolers and was decorating her room with simple colors instead. There was a sense of lost innocence in the gesture.

"What next?" Anne asked, as they finished hanging the paper border.

"We've got to wipe down all the desks and chairs, make sure the lockers are clean, and move those cabinets to the other corner. We'll wait on those until there's more help here. They're heavy."

Anne went to the supply room and came back with tubes of antiseptic wipes and started working on the desks and chairs. After about fifteen minutes, Tim Fletcher came into the room with Emma in his wake. Anne was surprised for a moment; Hannah Fletcher had been a room-parent fixture forever, and Tim was only at the school for plays and occasional awards presentations. But then she remembered that he had lost his job at Cox Carpet, and Hannah had gone full time at a medical claims company. Tim certainly looked unhappier than the last time she had seen him; his boyish face had a sad expression, and the perpetual sneer on his lips had been toned down.

"Hi Tim! Hi Emma!" Anne said cheerfully. "Oh, Emma, I

would have brought Emilia if I knew you would be here. How's Hannah?"

"Good, good," Tim replied. "So what do they need us to do?"

"Emma, if you can help wipe down these desks and chairs, your dad and I can move those cabinets."

They were big, heavy wooden cabinets that had stood in their place for years, but Anne was a strong woman, and between her and Fletcher, they managed to move them to the new corner, leaving the stained rectangles on the tile floor marking where they had stood.

For the next hour, Anne, Tim, Emma, and Ms. Jordan shuffled about the classroom, prodding it into shape for the next morning's invasion of students, and then Anne was off to Mass while Fletcher took his daughter to enjoy her last afternoon of freedom.

The next morning, while Anne dropped off Emilia at St. James, Dylan drove Janus to SAHS for the first full day of school. If Janus noticed the SUV's marijuana reek under the sweat and perfume, he didn't say anything about it. He knew his big brother's activities and had been around the football practices long enough to understand the game that was played between the coaches, staff, and the players. Indeed, throughout the summer, Janus had half expected to be initiated into that world, but Dylan, for whatever inscrutable reasons of his own, wasn't extending to his little brother the same corruption he had experienced at the hands of his older sister. Whether he knew, deep down, the wrongness of it, or whether he wanted to treasure it for himself, he could not have said, even if he had thought about it.

The SUV rolled into the senior parking lot by a back entrance away from the A-frame. Janus hopped out excitedly and half-ran toward the school, while Dylan waited for some friends who were just pulling in.

Crowd and bustle as the freshmen merged into the mass of students. Black and gold tartan skirts and ties, white shirts and blouses, khakis and tennis shoes, SAHS hairbows and ribbons for the freshmen girls. Mad chaos by lockers and then the ringing of bells, the closing of doors, and the school year was officially underway. A morning announcement from Principal Rollins welcoming them. A morning prayer led by Sister Mary Michael.

For Janus, it was a day of "establishing expectations," syllabus rundowns, heavy textbooks, playful shoves in the hallways from the upperclassmen football players, and relegation to sitting in the lobby for lunch along with the other freshmen after being left the scraps of the food court by the same upperclassmen.

For his older brother, it was a day of striding through the halls as a senior, teachers that he knew and who knew him. Intimidating the little freshmen kids, getting his way at the lunch line, taking up two seats on the bench in the small cafeteria, and letting his mind wander during the easy classes with which he had packed his last semester. Everything he was taking during these last four months of high school was a "fluff" class, with the exception of Fr. Dixon's Faith and Reason, which had a reputation for difficulty, but which he had been unable to escape. But that didn't matter, as long as he passed. His grades and ACT score were well over the threshold for Biltmore College, and a C or even a D in Fr. Dixon's class couldn't harm his future in any way. Only failing the class would keep him from graduating and moving on to BC.

Chaos and order, cycling back and forth until the bell rang again at the end of the day, Sister Mary Michael led the school in prayer, and then as students fled the building toward their cars, or gathered in classrooms for clubs, or the band room for practice, or stood in the A-frame waiting for parents, Janus and Dylan headed off for the football facilities. Only seven more practices before the first game. Coach Willy was bearing down hard; there was no way the Saints would be denied their championship season.

Anne awoke on Thursday morning confusedly feeling a dampness between her legs. She was snatching at a dream that faded immediately, and for a moment thought that she was menstruating before realizing with a sort of horror that she was, instead, aroused, and with her hand down the front of her pajamas.

Anne was in the midst of perimenopausal turmoil. Her periods were coming sporadically, and her emotions, as tightly controlled and disciplined as she was, burst forth in unexpected ways. The rhythm of her life since adolescence was suddenly changing and becoming unpredictable. And, in the tortured knot of Anne's feelings about sex and procreation, and the guilt and hurt over the dead bedroom that she occupied with Dane, the infertility was somehow welcome.

But the realization that, perhaps, menopause could reawaken lust was staggering.

"Whore!" came her mother's voice in her mind.

The city of Gary, Indiana, was founded just a few years after Biltmore College, a new metropolis built on the back of United States Steel, and indeed, named for the founding chairman of that firm. In the prior creation of US Steel, the Vanderbilts' old crony and nemesis J.P. Morgan had merged Federal Steel, National Steel, and Andrew Carnegie's steel companies into a modern behemoth. Besides the railroads that the Vanderbilts had dominated, nothing spoke of industrial power as obviously as the steel industry, with great mills, belching smokestacks, and hordes of workers.

The city of Gary grew out of the Gary Works, and like other Rust Belt cities, had its days of glory, its industrialist mansions, and its great public buildings. And it had its immigrants. By the 1920s, sixty percent of the residents of Gary were either foreign born or had at least one foreign-born parent. Most of these immigrants came from eastern Europe, and the largest block of these came from Poland.

Zbigniew Kowalski was among the Poles who arrived in the 1920s to make a new life in America. As a teenager, he formed one of the long lines of wool-capped laborers shuffling into the Gary Works in the early morning and shuffling back out in the evening. He settled into Gary's Polish neighborhood on the lower west side, in one of the little "Mill Houses" poured out of concrete for the minions toiling away for US Steel. He married late to Joanna Nowicki, in St. Stanislaw's Parish, and sired eight children before dying at the age of thirty-four, just after the end of World War II. His youngest son, Janus, was only two at the time, but those who knew both men said that Janus had inherited his father's gentle disposition, strong back, and work ethic.

Gary Indiana's postwar fortunes rose, and so did the remnants of the Kowalski family, the older children working, St. Stanislaw's Parish aiding, and Joanna slaving away to ensure that her children were educated. But when Janus Kowalski graduated from high school, he immediately entered his father's profession, taking the bus to the great steel mills in the morning and back again at night. Unlike his father, Janus had his weekends off, which he spent in the little orbit around St. Stanislaw, and where he finally won the hand of Maria Zawadski.

Maria's family, unlike Janus Kowalski's, had risen within the ranks of US Steel management and attained a level of prosperity that made them among the pillars of St. Stanislaw Parish. They occupied a large home on one of Gary's upper-middle class neighborhoods, from which they would drive each Sunday to their parish in a parade of their two shiny teal Cadillacs. They were thoroughly opposed to a union of their daughter with Janus Kowalski. Indeed, within the parish there was general amazement that the tall, beautiful, and stern Maria would deign to look favorably on the suit of the working-class Janus. But over time, Janus won over the Zawadski family with his good nature, his humility, and his piety. Fr. Piotrowski, the pastor of St. Stanislaw, was finally pried away from his firm opposition to the union and agreed to marry the two. So, as war raged in Vietnam, as Karol Wojtyla was made a Polish cardinal, as Newark rioted, and as Detroit burned, Janus and Maria were wedded in the glory of the Polish rite.

Gary, though avoiding the riots, entered a decline—one not immediately obvious. By 1970, US Steel employed thirty thousand people in the city, and Janus, now a shift supervisor at a young age, had just seen his second daughter, Anne, born. The Zawadski family moved out of its big house, and Janus and Maria moved in. The Polish neighborhoods frayed at the edges, as the immigrant city slowly became a black city. As Anne grew older, she was joined by another three sisters. On Sundays the family would cram into an ocher Pontiac and head dutifully to St. Stanislaw. Janus survived layoff after layoff and rose in rank among the fewer and fewer employees of US Steel.

The Poles of Gary, Indiana, celebrated as the unthinkable happened and Cardinal Karol Wojtyla became Pope John Paul II. Anne stood at the little St. Stanislaw school and sang the old Polish anthems, as around her in Gary the "Pollock Jokes" began their five-year run.

Anne and her sisters prayed around the clock as John Paul II lay in his hospital bed after being shot, and they wept when he finally appeared again on the loggia of St. Peter's.

By the time Anne graduated from St. Stanislaw and entered Bishop Graves High School, Gary Indiana's decline was unmistakable. US Steel was down to six thousand employees. White flight had begun and then accelerated. The old Polish neighborhood was gone. St. Stanislaw lost its pastor and was reduced to one Mass a week. This was a heavy, heavy blow for Maria and perhaps heavier for Janus. But the family stubbornly clung to the little parish orbit.

As Anne entered high school, she was her mother's creature, though doted on by her father. But Anne lived and breathed her Catholicism in a severe and uncompromising way. And yet the cracks in the façade were visible even then and began with the volleyball team. Anne entered high school as a tall, gangly girl and was immediately set upon by the basketball and volleyball coaches. Her speed and skill made her good in both sports, but she shied away from the relative violence of basketball, finding a camaraderie on the volleyball team that, for the first time, gave her an affirmation beyond that of simple holiness and devotion. But Anne wore her faith around her like armor, and as her body matured, and her beauty began to manifest, she spurned boys and devoted herself more and more to prayer.

Marie Kowalski was content. Her oldest daughter preceded Anne in graduation from high school by a year and promptly went off to discern a vocation with the Dominican Sisters. Marie looked at Anne's piety and saw a similar path for her. Perhaps it was residing in the crumbling city. The world that she had grown up in was gone; there were only a few straggling remnants of the Polish enclave stubbornly clinging to the city. Where another mother might have dreamed of grandchildren, Marie dreamed only of the end times. Her glory, she thought, would be in providing for the Church, in the legacy of prayers and good works. Her husband Janus, a simpler man, had long ago bent his will to that of his wife, and though reveling in his children, meekly went along with their formation into future nuns.

That is, until the far ripples of Title IX reached Anne. Though passed in 1972, the prohibition against sex-based discrimination in education had for many years been limited to federally funded institutions. But in the late 1980s, Congress explicitly extended the law's provisions to any institution that received government funding, directly or indirectly. The most obvious implication of the law was on athletics, and suddenly colleges and universities were challenged to ensure equal numbers of scholarships to men and women. Coping with football teams with over a hundred players, there were few options for colleges but to add women's sports to increase scholarships and to balance the increase in such programs with reductions in men's athletics. Just as Anne was graduating high school, colleges were scouring the country for women to fill their new programs, and Anne, the star player of her volleyball team, received multiple scholarship offers.

Had Notre Dame been among those schools, Anne's life would

have been very different, but among those offers she received, in the glossy flyers stuffed in manila envelopes that arrived in her parents' mailbox, something about Biltmore College caught her eye.

Her mother was adamant: She was not to go off to college. Especially not to the distant south, to a secular school in the heathen Appalachian Mountains. And then, suddenly, Janus stood up to his wife. He saw around him the vanished world and saw Anne being given a path out. He saw his favorite daughter going on to a bright future far from decaying buildings, rot, crime, and murder. His wife conceded this one defeat, but a bitterness toward Janus and Anne began—one that would never fade. With her father sitting in the driver's seat of yet another old Pontiac ready to drive her south, Anne wept and hugged her mother, who, dry-eyed, simply said: "Remember who you are, and don't get mixed up with boys. You're going to college to get an education, but I know what happens at those places. Keep your legs together and say your prayers."

Armed with her upbringing, a fear of the unknown, and these parting words, Anne arrived at the Biltmore College campus and checked into one of the old brick dorms on a floor full of female athletes. She was roomed, as she had requested on her preference form, with another Catholic girl. Elizabeth Boatner and Anne bonded immediately, their shared northern experience helping the two navigate the new climate. Together they decorated their room, found corners of the library to study in, and attended Mass at the little Catholic Center. Anne found this southern Catholicism a tremendous, jarring change from the old dying St. Stanislaw. There was no ornate altar, no altar rails, no dark-stained pews, no statuary, no great racks of devotional candles. Rather, there were carpet and fluorescent lights and stackable chairs. There were guitars and folksy hymns and a great deal of hugging. There was the homey Fr. Lowe and clay goblets instead of chalices. Anne found herself taking the bus to St. Lawrence Basilica on Sundays, where at least the architecture made her feel more at home. But, as her freshman volleyball season became more intense and demanding, Anne returned once more to the Catholic Center and pocketed the time she would have spent on the bus.

Anne returned to Asheville after a torturous Christmas break, during which she endured first her mother's glares, then the tumultuous announcement that her older sister was leaving the novitiate, with ensuing tears, recrimination, and blame cast on Anne for having set a bad example. Asheville's mild winter was underway. The Rangers' football team played and won their bowl game. The Rangers' volleyball team ended the season ranked third. And now Anne found herself with more time to devote to her studies. She had chosen architecture as a major; it seemed a good choice as Anne was always artistic but also clever with math and science. Her first semester courses had not been particularly challenging, having focused more on the engineering fundamentals. The new semester, though, was proving more difficult, and she was glad to have time away from the demands of volleyball.

Then, one Sunday, she sat in a plastic chair at the Catholic Center and saw, across the room, a tall, handsome man that she knew was Dane Norris.

In all her time going to the Catholic Center, Anne had never seen Dane attend Mass there, but everyone on campus knew the junior—the Rangers' star tight end. Mass was about to begin. He was there, at ease, towering above the kids around him, smiling and laughing as if he were the pillar of this community too. Anne stared at him a moment too long; he felt her eyes upon him, looked evenly at her, and smiled. She turned her head back toward the makeshift tabernacle, bowed her head, and prayed until Mass began.

After the recessional hymn, she stood up quickly from her seat, genuflected toward the tabernacle, and went quickly toward the exit. But then there he was in front of her.

"Hi, I'm Dane," he said, and stuck out his hand.

She was nonplussed. Now used to the informality of the Catholic Center, where the room with its tabernacle had a double use for meetings, and there was no sacred space, Anne still was unprepared for this brazen greeting from a stranger, there where the

Eucharist had been elevated. Dane seemed to sense this, and said: "Hey, let's talk outside." He turned and went out into the little lobby area, which arced away to the left to more meeting rooms used by the Jewish, Muslim, and Hindu religious of BC's student body. Anne followed him, feeling almost commanded to do so. In any case, it didn't occur to her to demur.

"I haven't seen you here before," he said, casually.

"That's because you haven't been here before," Anne answered.

"Not true. Okay, well maybe this year. I usually go to St. Lawrence with my family. When I go to Mass that is. I mean, I guess I should be honest and say that I don't always go."

"Well, you should," Anne said. She knew how casual most of her fellow Catholics on campus were. At the beginning of the year, the little room was packed, and at least half of the congregants were freshmen. But as the year went on, more and more dropped away.

"Yeah, I guess so," he answered, with a big grin. "Tell you what, let's go get lunch, and we can talk about it."

"No thank you," Anne said. "I don't really know you."

"We can fix that," he said, and now his confidence was coming across as arrogance.

"No thank you," Anne said again. "Goodbye," she stated, as she pushed past him and out into the Asheville cold.

But the next Sunday, there he was again, sitting in the same place he had been before. He saw Anne come in and smiled at her but remained sitting. Anne was distracted, and her mind wandered during Mass, several times finding herself looking over at him. After Mass, he cut her off again as she made her exit.

"Two weeks in a row! A new record for me. How about that lunch?"

"Well, good for you," Anne answered. "But no thanks."

The following week she ran into him on campus twice, which was unusual since she had only seen him on a handful of occasions previously. Each time they met, he asked her to lunch, and she declined.

The next Sunday, there he was again, and after Mass, as she was leaving, he said: "Listen, I'll make a deal with you. I'll come to Mass every Sunday for the rest of the semester if you'll have lunch with me today. Look at it like this: You're winning my soul back for the Church."

"That's not really funny, you know. You shouldn't take that lightly."

"I'm not. I'm serious. You don't have to have lunch with me again, but I'll keep my end of the deal. I should have been coming to Mass regularly anyway; I just get out of the habit during football season."

Anne equivocated, but finally agreed, saying: "Okay. So, just going to the cafeteria?"

He grinned again and said, "If you don't mind, I've got another place we should go. It's off campus. Do you care?"

"Okay," she said.

Anne found herself thankful that she hadn't gotten into the habit, as many of the other students did, of attending Mass in sweatpants. She sat beside Dane in his BMW as they turned into the front entrance of the Grove Park Inn. She looked around amazed at the towering pile of stone and the improbable red hobbit roof as Dane drove up to the valets by the entrance.

"Been here yet?" he asked, as they got out of the car, and he exchanged his keys for a claim check.

"I've seen it, of course, but not up close."

"Well, until you've seen the brunch buffet, you haven't seen anything." And he gestured past the rocking chairs into the huge lobby. Anne walked beside him as he strode into the hotel and made his way toward one of the new jarringly featureless wings that struck forward from the old stone pile of the original building. A few minutes later they were at the hostess stand, and Dane said: "Reservation for Norris."

Anne looked at him suspiciously, asking: "You have standing reservations? Do you bring all your girls here?"

"Ouch!" he said, grinning. "Actually, I've only made reservations here twice, and I had to cancel the other one last week."

She had to smile at that, and as they sat beside the big pane windows, overlooking the long grass slope, golf course, and out past the Biltmore campus, Anne smiled more and more often and finally laughed along with Dane as he heaped his plate with bacon and pancakes and biscuits. He laughed in return when she discovered a cheese blintz that left her speechless. Finally, as the plates were taken away, Dane said: "So, I'll see you at Mass next week. That is, unless YOU start skipping. My question is, should I make reservations here again? I hate cancelling."

"That would be nice," Anne said. "But don't feel like you have to do this again. I can't imagine what this cost."

Dane grinned from ear to ear. On their way out, he stopped at the hostess stand, saying: "Please make a reservation for next week, same time. Norris."

The following Friday night, Anne went to her first big college party. While plastic cups went back and forth to the keg, dance music blared from tinny speakers, and the heat in the off-campus house became unbearable, Dane and Anne sat on a couch in the corner, shouting above the music. Dane nursed a beer. Anne refused at first, but later accepted a cup, sipping from time to time but not enjoying it. Then later, walking back to campus, saying goodnight in front of her dorm, Anne was afraid he was going to try to kiss her and turned away quickly saying "Goodnight," then almost skipped up to the doors.

Another week, this time dinner out at a restaurant. Everywhere there were sparkling lights. The newness of the experience, sitting next to this man in his car, underage but still drinking a glass of wine at dinner, the waitress not even thinking that Dane Norris, already known throughout Asheville, might be there with a freshman girl. In the campus parking lot, Dane leaned in to kiss her, and she did not pull away. It was awkward and strange, but he must have known how inexperienced she was and did not press further.

"I'm sorry," she said, as he sat back in his seat, "I just . . . I'm just not ready."

"It's cool. Let's walk," and they made their way back to her dorm. Signs of an early spring abounded on campus, and while the night was cool, there was something new and hopeful in the air. They arrived at last in front of her residence hall, and rather than leaning in for a kiss, Dane took her hand and held it gently.

"See you at Mass tomorrow!" he said, the same silly grin on his face.

That night she related the events of the evening to Elizabeth, as she had after each previous date, and her roommate started concocting a plan. While Elizabeth and Anne may have started out very similar in outlook and experience, the former had quite quickly found college life far too enticing to be ignored. Within the first month, she had found a boyfriend, and now she spent most of her weekend nights at his off-campus house. She knew that the prudish Anne disapproved, but the two still shared a bond, and Elizabeth knew better than to go into details.

But the one thing missing in all of her fun was Anne. And when Dane Norris came along, Elizabeth hoped that it would open Anne's eyes to the broader world of Biltmore College, and finally she decided to take matters into her own hands. Over the next few weeks, as it drew toward spring, Elizabeth ingratiated herself with Dane and his circle of friends, double dated with Anne and Dane, eased Anne into going out with the girls, and finally, when the time was right, before Dane and Anne could say goodnight one evening, she said: "Dane, you've never seen our dorm room. Why don't you come up?"

Dane looked at Anne for approval. She didn't say no.

"Okay," Dane said, and the three went past the empty reception desk, up the elevator, and down the corridor to the room. Elizabeth keyed the lock and opened the door, nudged Dane inside, then Anne, and closed the door on the two of them.

Inside, the room was decorated with string lights. A bottle of champagne and two glasses were on one of the end tables, moved to the center of the room and draped with a sheet. A little candle stood ready to light.

Butterflies in her stomach, champagne in her head, the little lights twinkling in the small dorm room, Anne looked at this man whom she had fallen in love with, saw it returned in his eyes, and inhibitions sliding away, opened herself to Dane.

As if the repressed feelings of all her teenage years were a coiled spring, Anne's sexuality raged like an inferno. Terrified after that first night when she was late by a few days and the immensity of a possible pregnancy weighed on her, all the old lessons about the evils of contraception were cast aside, and she asked Dane to buy condoms. And from then on, she could not keep her hands off of him. The two were inseparable. Dane's teammates joked that his football career was over now that Anne was fucking the life out of him. Anne's friends rallied around her and rejoiced as she became one of the crowd. Anne met Dane's family and went to Mass with them at St. Lawrence. They were delighted in the tall, beautiful girl, and suddenly there she was at birthday parties and family dinners. As summer approached, both Dane and Anne dreaded their separation, until Dane stumbled upon the expedient of asking his dad to give Anne a summer job at his law firm. This being done, Anne told her disappointed father that she was staying in Asheville for the summer, and he needn't come to pick her up at the end of the term.

She moved her things to a little apartment that she shared with another girl from the volleyball team, but most nights she spent with Dane.

The first morning that they slept in and missed Sunday Mass, she hardly noticed.

The fall came, and she moved back to campus. The Rangers' volleyball team had a great season, and this year Anne made the traveling squad, moving all over the south to play on different SEC campuses. Dane and his Rangers team had a tremendous season as well. Every chance she could, she was there in the student section. Her father watched her on TV as the Rangers and the students celebrated the win over Georgia, and Dane, his hair matted with sweat and his helmet in one hand, kissed Janus' daughter in the end zone of the stadium. Janus said nothing to his wife.

Anne returned home for Christmas, briefly, catching a ride toward Chicago with Elizabeth and meeting her father at a rest stop before the Gary exits. Christmas was tense. Maria could sense the change in Anne. She questioned and pried, trying to catch Anne in an admission. Janus smiled and nodded and enjoyed having all his girls home again.

Back on campus, back to her studies and back to parties. Back to nights spent in Dane's arms. Then springtime, and Anne sat beside Dane in his family's living room at the old Norris estate. A camera crew was crowded into a corner and a satellite truck was in the driveway. Everyone but Dane looked nervously at the phone, which sat on a little green marble table by the sofa. The phone rang. Dane nodded and said: "Yes, sir. Yes. I'm honored. It's going to be great." Anne sat aside while Dane and his father had a huddled conversation with Dane's agent. A big smile stretched from ear to ear. He sat back down on the couch and took her hand.

"With the seventeenth pick in the draft, the Kansas City Chiefs have traded with the Phoenix Cardinals and select Dane Norris of Biltmore College."

Cheers erupted. Dane and Anne embraced, then he stood and shook hands, hugged his mom, and high-fived his brother. He was now a pro.

At graduation, Dane walked across the stage, received his BA in marketing, met Anne and his family afterward, and was off to the

Grove Park for a celebration. Anne lingered after the rest of the family departed and stayed with Dane that night in the old hotel, the little windows cranked open and the Asheville spring air cooling their naked bodies.

The unendurable separation, Dane off at training camp, unavailable from six in the morning until ten at night. Exhausted and quiet on the phone. Anne entered her junior year, distracted and lonely. She buried herself in volleyball and in her design studio coursework, which was getting progressively more challenging. When she could, on weekends, she watched the Chiefs games with the Norris family. Dane flew her out to Kansas City to see them play the L.A. Raiders —a game the Chiefs barely won and in which Dane played little to no part. But afterward, when he emerged from the stadium to meet her, he wore his ear-to-ear grin. They drove back to his apartment in his new BMW, changed for dinner, and at a table at the Stockyard restaurant, he got down on one knee and opened the little case. Anne's heart grew hot, tears sprang to her eyes. She got down on both knees and put her arms around him, then nodded through her tears, took the ring, and slid it on her finger. Polite applause from the other diners and the staff, wives smiling at husbands, and Anne was engaged.

The next afternoon, she dialed her parents' telephone number. Her father picked up the phone.

"Daddy," Anne said, "I've got wonderful news. I'm engaged!"

Her father was silent for a moment and then: "That's . . . wonderful, Anne. Who is he?"

"He's a wonderful man, Daddy. I can't wait for you to meet him. I would have said something before, but I didn't want to until I knew it was serious. He's a football player. He plays for Kansas City. I'm so happy!" Tears were sliding down her cheeks again.

"Hold on a second, your mother is here." A moment of silence and she could hear, muffled: "It's Anne. She's got great news. Here she is . . . "

"Hello?" came Maria's voice.

"Hi Mom. I just called to give you the wonderful news. I'm engaged to be married!"

"Where are you?" her mother asked, sounding confused and with her voice slurred.

"I'm in Kansas City," she said, without thinking. "He plays football here for the Chiefs."

"You're calling to tell me that you are in Kansas City with a football player and you're getting married. I knew you'd turn out to be a little whore. Are you pregnant?"

Anne was stunned and heard her father trying to take the phone away. Moments later there was a click. Dane walked into the room and saw her standing there in her nightgown.

"What's wrong!?" he gasped.

They spent the weekend at the lake house, thinking it was most likely the last weekend to do so before it became time to take the boats out and close up for the winter. Anne had talked to Hannah, who was worried about how morose her husband had become, so they invited the Fletchers to come along. Dylan was coerced into going, again to keep Janus company while Emilia played with Emma.

Tim Fletcher spent the opening of the weekend in a sulk, from which he emerged to make jealous quips about the Norris' wealth. Hannah confided in Anne that they were having financial problems and that she was worried about Tim.

But as the weekend wore on, Fletcher seemed to come back somewhat to his usual irritating but less acerbic self, and by Saturday night the annoying "Great Dane!" was sounding again. The wine and bourbon and cigars and beer flowed. Dylan surreptitiously smoked a couple of joints downwind of the house. Dogs cavorted and giggles were heard from the girls' room, and the glorious late-summer sun shone down.

Friday night, snare drums and bass drums and horns. Gold and white in the student section, with crazily painted faces and shirtless boys with S A I N T S painted on their chests. In the middle of the bleachers sat Anne and Emilia with gold and white pom-poms. Dane down on the field, where chairs had been pulled up for him, Coach Carter, and other luminaries of the BC Rangers program. The Saints running out through a big paper screen as fog machines blurred the cheerleaders and a starting gun blasted away. Air horns and cheers as the players milled about the sidelines.

Opening possession: The Saints drive down the field, and Dylan Norris torches a safety, stiff-arms a cornerback, and high-steps into the end zone. The Eagles are stuffed on their first series, and the Saints roar back to score again. Halftime concessions: popcorn, hot dogs, and soda. Emilia now sitting with a friend, Anne sits on a stadium seat and watches her husband joking with the BC coaching staff. Interrupted time and again by fellow SAHS parents passing by, leaning over the chain-link fence to pat him on the back. End of the half, and Janus is on the field. Not bad, but he gets beaten for a long completion and is back on the bench in the next series. The Saints pour it on. Up by five touchdowns, they go for it on fourth down instead of kicking a field goal, and the Eagles' fans rain a chorus of boos. But the Saints go up by six touchdowns. Dylan is up and down the field, catching, running, blocking, tackling, and scoring. This is what it was all for—the long summer of practices, the bench presses and squats, the laps and sprints and mankillers. This is what it was all for.

Skylar Evans pulled his Dodge Ram up next to the smaller BMW SUV, driver's window facing driver's window, in the back corner of the Cox Foods parking lot. The noon sun blazed in a brilliant blue sky above. The BMW window rolled down, and a ruddy, round face under tussled blonde hair looked out.

"Quentin," Skylar said.

"Hey," the other teen replied. Skylar reached out and shook his hand, and at the same time, passed him a folded hundred-dollar bill. Quentin looked down at it in his lap as he unfolded it.

"Cool," he said, sticking his hand out, and Skylar eased the little bindle of cocaine from his palm.

Chapter 12

TIME

"Bless me, Father, for I have sinned. It has been about a month since my last confession. In that time I have failed in my intentions for daily devotions on two occasions. Worse, I chose to stay at our lake house on the Feast of the Assumption rather than to make the drive back into town. I am also troubled because . . . " Anne paused, uncomfortable, and then rushed on, "I have had impure thoughts about a man other than my husband on one and maybe two occasions . . . and . . . I have been angry with my husband because he doesn't show interest in me. I have also laughed at licentious and lewd jokes."

There was a pause, then Fr. MacMahon, the pastor of St. James, said: "Is that all? Is there anything else you have to confess?"

"That's all that I can think of, Father."

Fr. MacMahon, a short, heavyset, and bespectacled man with a precise and nasally voice, drew a breath as if he were about to launch into a long discourse, but breathed it out just as quickly and responded: "Keep working on those devotions. The intention is important, but so is the act. As you should know, when the Feast of the Assumption falls on a Saturday, the obligation is removed, so there's no need to worry about missing Mass this year. As for your other concerns, we are sexual beings. As long as you do not indulge in these, you said *impure thoughts*, then I wouldn't worry too much about it. I would worry a little more about it if you didn't have such thoughts from time to time. You know that the devil has you when he stops needing to tempt you. That's when you should worry. As for your husband, has it been a long time that he hasn't been . . . responding to you?"

"Yes, a very long time. It's . . . not entirely his fault. A number of years ago I began struggling with my feelings . . . and I may have shut him out a bit. And then he stopped trying."

"Have you confessed all this before?" the priest asked.

"Yes, Father, a number of times."

"Well, it's obviously still weighing on your conscience, or the ongoing issue is. But you must understand that there is no need to confess again. If you are feeling hurt by your husband's lack of attention, then I would suggest you go to a counselor. I suspect he feels as neglected in this regard as you."

"He doesn't seem to."

"Here's a trick that I use sometimes. When you feel hurt or bad about something someone else is doing in a relationship, just imagine that you are doing the same thing to them. Think about how they would feel. Quite often we are blind to our own failings but very observant of others' failings."

Anne was silent as she considered this.

"For your penance, I want you to say four Our Fathers, and I want you to do something nice for your husband. Make him a nice dinner or give him a back rub. You know, of course, your Act of Contrition?"

Skylar Evans rolled off of his girlfriend and lay in bed looking up at the ceiling fan. His breathing was rapid, and it took a few moments for it to slow. Amber, who had been a more passive participant, sat up, straightened her T-shirt, rolled her legs off the side of the bed, picked up her shorts and underwear, then walked into the bathroom and used the toilet. When she came back in, Skylar was sitting up against the headboard and unwrapping the little bindle.

"Sure you won't try it?"

"Skylar, I don't want to. I'm scared of it, and I'd rather just sleep. I hear it keeps you up and gives you energy, and that's the last thing I want right now. I would think that's the last thing you'd want too. Let's just lie here, baby."

"Okay, okay," he said, setting the little folded paper down on the end table. Amber came back and lay down in the bed. Skylar turned on his side and rested his head on her breasts. She stroked the back of his hair, and slowly their breathing synchronized, their chests rising and falling.

Then she snapped awake. A heavy thud had jolted her out of sleep. Skylar wasn't next to her. She glanced over at the nightstand, where the lamp shone down on the open packet, a rolled-up dollar bill, and some white powder.

"Skylar?" she said, annoyed. *He had gone ahead and done it.*

"Skylar?" there was no response. She sat up and looked around, then leaned over.

Her boyfriend was on the floor, lips blue and eyes wide open but with tiny pupils. His back was arched and his hands had formed claws as he sucked his breath in short, ragged gasps. Amber screamed.

A sea of people in lime green milled in every direction outside of the high walls of Seely Stadium. Anne drove her Land Rover slowly, the only vehicle on the road in front of the colossal building. The crowd parted way, slowly, universally giving her dirty looks. A few, recognizing Dane in the passenger seat, changed their scowls to smiles and waved thumbs-up instead of middle fingers. Shirtless young men with lime-green overalls staggered by, plastic cups full of beer gripped in their hands. Young women in lime-green bikini tops sauntered past with plastic cups full of hard lemonade or vodka. Fat middle-aged men in lime-green polo shirts plodded by, trailed by pudgy middle-aged women in pastel-green blouses with bright lime-green scarves. Little boys wearing lime-green jerseys dashed after little girls in lime-green cheerleader outfits. And the crowd with all this movement parted in front of the Land Rover and closed back in its wake.

Anne hated it when Dane was invited to the games because they invariably gave him a parking pass in the lot right by the stadium. It became almost inaccessible in the hours before game time, as fans made their way to the tailgate tents or lined up early to see the Ranger Ride.

Dane sat calmly and with a contented smile while Anne craned her neck and inched forward through the crowd. Janus and Emilia looked excitedly about. Dylan had managed to beg off for the day, but the spectacle had caught the imagination of his brother and sister, and they looked forward to seeing their father honored by his alma mater.

Anne finally negotiated the turn into the lot. A Biltmore College security guard raised the gate as she flashed the parking pass. She pulled the Land Rover into a space facing away from the stadium, downhill of a field packed with tents where the sponsored tailgates were in full swing. Anne, Dane, Janus, and Emilia opened their doors and got out carefully, squeezing between the SUVs on either side of the Land Rover. Anne's white capri pants and lime-green top showed not only her support of the team, but along with her broad-brimmed hat did it with flair. Dane wore a Biltmore College polo shirt over khaki pants, while Janus and Emilia wore BC jerseys with their dad's old number: eighty-eight.

"Do we have to go to the tailgate too?" Anne asked, annoyed in advance. She did not care for Clyde Cox Jr.

"You don't have to go," Dane answered, as he walked toward the BC security guard. "If you want to watch, this is as good a place as any."

"I'm hungry, Mom."

"Me too!"

"There will be plenty of food in the luxury box," Anne said. "You can wait until then. We'll go in right after your dad goes past."

"Dane Norris," her husband said to the security guard. "Please have them send a cart."

"Okay, Mr. Norris," the guard answered, a big smile wrinkling his dark, leathery face. Then he opened a walkie-talkie channel and made his request.

"Once the ride is done, I'll take the elevator to the club level and meet you there. You can go ahead and go in the box if you want. You've got the passes?"

Anne pointed to the tickets, which were pressed up against the side of her transparent purse.

A four-seater UTV came down toward the stadium, its horn beeping and an orange light flashing on top. The driver turned it around facing back uphill. Almost immediately a girl in a tank top and tight leather pants tried to get in.

"Hey, hey, HEY!" the security guard said, moving toward her, and she laughed and walked back to her little group of friends.

Dane walked around the gate and got in the passenger seat. The UTV sank to the ground as his weight tested its suspension.

"Good luck, honey!" Anne said, waving, and she could see her husband laughing as he was driven away.

Anne remembered that she still had bag chairs in the back of her SUV, so she opened the hatch remotely and sent Janus back to get them.

"Okay if we sit here?" she asked the guard.

"Sure thing, ma'am, just have to move outta the way if a car's comin' through the gate."

Anne and the kids sat and watched the parade of people go by. After about fifteen minutes, BC police started clearing the roads, and people crowded to the sidewalks, mostly behind those who had been standing for the last hour to get a good view. They tried to line up in front of the gate, but the security guard motioned them away saying: "Got to keep the gate clear, folks."

Anne was embarrassed to be sitting right behind the gate, but the security guard just winked at her.

Another few minutes went by and then from the top of the hill, she heard the band coming. First the deep drumbeats, and then the horns and the snare drums, and then she could see the tubas above the heads of the waiting crowd, and the big lime-green flag with its single "B" came waving. Batons were thrown in the air and caught, and then, behind the band, came Dane and two other Ranger Royalty riding on massive quarter horses led by green-jacketed members of the Biltmore College Equestrian Team. Dane smiled and waved, as did the tall black woman beside him and the gray-haired older black man beside her. Emilia jumped up and down, and Dane saw her and winked. The Rangers' mascot—a young man wearing buckskins and a green ten-gallon hat—followed the Royalty, and he in turn was followed by other members of the Equestrian Team in tight riding pants and green jackets. Then the horses were all past, trailed by another group of cheerleaders, and then Coach Carter and the football team processed by. The parade wound its way to one of the stadium entrances, the BC police rolled by and moved off of the side roads, and the lime-green crowd filled the void in a rush, moving in waves toward the various gates into the stadium.

The tailgate tents began to pour their occupants down the grass slope into the parking lot, where Janus returned the bag chairs to the SUV, joined his mother and sister, and the three made their way to the club-level entrance. They walked past the long lines, past a staggering, vacant-eyed drunk being held upright by two obese women, his mouth hanging open and his face elongated like an El Greco figure. They reached their gate as another UTV pulled up and disgorged passengers. Anne and her children walked behind them, showing their tickets, and into a small lobby decorated with floor-to-ceiling pictures of Ranger greats. Then to the club level elevator where a thin, gray-haired woman checked their tickets again before pushing the club level button.

Up they rode, and the elevator doors opened on the club floor.

Gleaming white tile inset with the Biltmore "B," round stadium columns with mounted LED screens, tan leather couches and glass-topped tables, and well-dressed men and women and children lounging about. On the stadium side, a series of doors opened into the club boxes themselves, each with the "owner's" name or company logo by the door. Anne walked down the hall with her kids trailing until she saw "Cox, Inc." right at the 50-yard line at the middle of the hall. Rather than go in, she took Janus and Emilia and found a free couch, then sat and waited for her husband.

Finally, there was Dane, walking stiffly down the hall, stopping every few feet to shake hands or fist bump. Anne and the kids got up and rushed toward him. From past experience, she knew that he could move quicker through well-wishers and admirers if they saw his family with him, and indeed, their pace picked up once Anne joined him. He paused outside the Cox, Inc. box.

"Are you ready?" he asked.

Anne nodded, and in they went.

Just inside the door was a large room with a private restroom on each end, a small kitchenette, wine cooler, stocked bar, couches, padded chairs, and a table in the middle of the room piled with cheese trays, sliders, roll-ups, sushi and sashimi, chicken wings, chicken nuggets, pulled pork and brisket, rolls, bread, salad, and all other manner of appetizers arrayed about steaming trays of more refined fare: ratatouille, tenderloin, roast chicken, salmon, red potatoes, and the like. Around the table moved thin, big-breasted, and tanned coeds in tight Rangers polos and khaki shorts, followed by broad-shouldered, square-jawed, and clean-shaven young men in equally tight shirts but with khaki shorts that showed much less leg. They rearranged the piles of food, wiped away crumbs, replenished ice buckets, emptied trash, and asked their guests if they could do anything else.

Opposite the door was a low wall of windowpanes, and beyond that, rows of seats stepped down to a wall of glass looking over the field below. And in every available corner, LED screens showed the live broadcast of the game. Anne looked at the great bowl of the stadium, all the seats filled with people pointed down at the field. She had the impression of a strangely focused humanity—almost four thousand people in the stands for each player on the gridiron. A surreal concentration.

Janus and Emilia rushed to the food table and grabbed plates, while Dane and Anne looked around for Clyde Cox Jr. They heard him before they saw him, laughing from the front row of seats, and then he stood up, slapping the man next to him on the back, and started up the stairs.

Clyde Cox Sr. had gifted his three sons with drive, ambition, and competitiveness. And he had cursed his three sons with drive, ambition, and competitiveness. "Old Man Cox" had been born in a log cabin with no electricity and into a family that was scratching out an existence near the Pisgah National Forest. Cox's lifelong motto "Whole Hog" was, in fact, a lesson he had learned as a child, when his family indeed used every part of the hog but the smell.

His fortune had begun as a teenager, distilling and selling his own moonshine, and then he slyly took the risk on himself as a distributor for others' products. He had hoarded his profits, and when Prohibition ended, had started a little roadside station much like the Jiffy Stop. Only Cox had something that Old Renfroe didn't: Cox went Whole Hog. He parlayed his roadside station into a chain, then opened a grocery, then another. While still in his twenties, he re-formed the Tyler Dam Committee and started Cox Land & Lake. He met and married a mountain woman who reminded him of his mother, then fathered three boys and a daughter. Growing increasingly bored as his grocery empire grew, Cox bought a theater in downtown Asheville and started a variety show, which he hosted and televised through the early 1960s. Inspired by George Wallace, he ran for governor of North Carolina but found his flame grew dimmer the closer he went to the coast, and he lost decisively. Retracting back to Asheville, he redirected his energy into local politics, satisfying himself with being a public clown and a backroom kingmaker. Cox planned, directed, and acted in all his own commercials, creating ever more ridiculous stunts to get attention for his stores. And it worked. Cox Markets prospered and spread across the state, then across the mountains into Tennessee and Virginia. Cox Land & Lake reaped its annual profits. Cox Convenience stores sprung up as the interstate system grew greater and greater, and Cox neatly snatched up parcels of land by the exits.

A short, thin, leather-skinned man, balding with wispy grey hair, perpetually squinting eyes, and an ovular head on a thin neck, he radiated energy and seemed invincible, until a sudden stroke at the age of sixty-two left him in a wheelchair and with the left side of his face paralyzed. Without his charisma and without his smooth talk, Cox lost his confidence and drive, and he immediately broke up his empire among his sons. His daughter, having eloped and moved to Florida, was not considered and was not even found in his will when he died eight years later.

The bulk of the empire passed to Clyde Cox Jr., who took over as president and CEO of Cox, Inc., the parent company of Cox Markets, Cox Convenience, and Cox Land & Lake. Claude and Henry took their inheritances, began selling off their Lake Juniper properties, and invested in their own ventures. Claude expanded his own Cox Furniture into carpeting and acquired the mills in Canton, North Carolina, renaming them Asheville Furniture. Claude then followed his father's footsteps and expanded across the Southeast. The youngest son, Henry Cox, put his money into trucking, and soon the lime-green Cox Transportation trailers were on the roads nationwide.

The brothers were clever, hardworking, and despised each other. Their competitiveness was seen nowhere as strongly as within their family, as they all vied to build the greatest empire. Both Claude and Henry looked down on Clyde Jr.'s fortune as having been made by their father, but they were always chasing it. Clyde Jr. was the first to become a billionaire. By the time Claude reached that mark, Clyde had doubled it, with Henry trailing far behind at a paltry six hundred million.

All three had inherited their father's Whole Hog approach, but as their wealth reached levels of absurdity, they began competing not only for the biggest pile of money but for the biggest influence at Biltmore College. Not one of them had attended BC, but they had grown up in its shadow, and their father had loved taking them to the games. Now, suddenly, the three began to haunt the BC campus, endowing chairs, donating buildings, naming scholarships, and pumping money into the football program. Clyde Jr. displaced the three great boosters of the 1990s: the financier Ronald Phillips, banker Lee Adams, and Jennifer Salisbury—a Biltmore College graduate who had founded an early digital media company and sold it for 1.5 billion dollars. Each of these boosters relished his/her influence at BC, and each resented the Cox brothers' mad one-upmanship. But their choices were to slide to the back of the pack or to pour more money into chasing the Coxes, so they sat on their resentment.

Clyde Cox Jr.—the Rangers' wealthiest booster—got the fifty-yard-line luxury box on the home side of the field, while Claude was relegated to the fifty-yard-line box on the visitors' side, and poor Henry was stuck taking a box in the north end zone, choosing the visitors' side to be as far from his oldest brother as possible.

And, of course, the luxury boxes themselves became a source of competition, and at each Rangers' game the Cox brothers tried to outdo each other with their guests. As a former BC standout, Dane Norris received at least one invitation from each brother every year. The invitation to the first game got earlier and earlier, but it was always Clyde Jr. who extended it.

Now here was the man himself, coming up the stairs. Red-faced with a bulbous nose, balding and with his father's wispy hair, great shaggy eyebrows and a white, trimmed goatee, Clyde Jr., unlike his younger brothers, had inherited his mother's heavy build, but in his mid-sixties still exuded power and energy.

"Dane! Great to see you! Glad you could make it!" He mounted the top step and extended his hand. "Can't wait to see your boy playing out here next year." Then without waiting for an answer, he turned and said: "Anne! Looking beautiful as ever!" and he leaned in and hugged her. Anne half returned it with a quick touch on his back before dropping her arms. Clyde Jr. held on a moment too long before disengaging, ensuring that it felt awkward. Taking a step back, he saw Janus and Emilia sitting on one of the couches, devouring their food. Clyde chuckled and looked back at Dane.

"You're a bourbon man, right Dane?" and seeing him nod, he snapped his fingers to get the attention of one of the coeds. "Honey, get this man a Pappy. You like it on the rocks, Dane? Okay, on the rocks honey, but not too much. One of those big square ice cubes. Okay? And a club soda for me."

He turned back to Dane and Anne.

"Heard about that kid who OD'd on fentanyl. Damn shame. How many is that from St. Ambrose? Eight or nine? Something like that? Hell, if I had kids there, I'd pull 'em straight out. Not that you should, Dane, chances of winning State this year and all. Course Parkdale's likely to take State in their division. Oughta have a good team with all the money I give 'em. Just wait until Parkdale's up in six-A, then we'll see if they can take down your Ambrose boys. Great you could join us. I've got to go piss, but when I get back I want to talk to you about your boy. Gonna break all your records, right! Ha!" and he ambled off toward one of the restrooms.

Anne gave Dane a side-eyed look, and he shrugged his shoulders. The two of them turned back to the table and made themselves plates of food. Then down into the seats, the coed bringing them drinks. Clyde returned but went to sit in the front row with some other guests. More people wandered in, Clyde's children, their spouses, their kids. By opening kickoff, the box seats were full. All stood for the National Anthem, then fireworks went off as the stadium announcer roared "It's BILTMORE COLLEGE KICK-OFF!!!!!" and the ball sailed through the air. The Central Carolina Jaguars—the opening-day sacrificial opponent—had chosen to receive, and as the Rangers defense held them to a three-and-out, the guests in the Cox, Inc. box resumed conversations and got up and went for snacks, while the pretty young men and pretty young women glided about serving them.

"Yes! YES! GO GO GO GO GO! RUN YOU MOTHERFUCKER! RUN!!!"

Billy Mullins jumped off his chair and stuck his hands straight up into the air. The bag of tortilla chips fell off of his lap and onto the floor, and his hand knocked the little bowl full of microwaved nacho cheese over, the cheese spreading out in a blob on the stained carpet. On the big LED panel, a Rangers receiver danced into the end zone, and the referee's arms went up, just like Billy's, as TOUCHDOWN scrolled in red across the bottom of the screen. Billy sat back down in his threadbare chair, lit up a Camel, drained his beer can, crumpled it, dropped it next to the congealing cheese, and smiled. The Rangers tacked on the extra point and trotted off the field. Up 42-3, now the backups would get their chance to play. Billy started mentally composing his posts for the GoRangers message boards, which he would later distill into his comments for the *Hopper & Howe Show.*

Good game.

The lines looked tight.

Game plan was vanilla.

Don't want to show too much in a throwaway game against Central Carolina.

Real test will be next week. Syracuse looks good this year.

Coach Love's gotta be happy with how his receivers played today.

Dixon's out there throwing frozen ropes.

Coach Carter thumbed the remote, and the lights of his Lincoln SUV flashed and the horn tooted once, echoing in the garage under the stadium. He was worn out, as he always was after a game, and he looked forward to a shower and sleep.

But he couldn't turn his mind off. He never could.

"Great game, Coach," said the security guard as he raised the gate for Carter. Carter smiled, waved at him, and drove out of the stadium. A few fans still lingered, but across campus, tents were being lowered, clean-up crews were hard at work, and traffic moved universally away.

Carter slipped into a line of cars exiting campus and drove mechanically back home. *Dixon had made some good throws, but he was too hot and would have had more drops if his receivers hadn't bailed him out. Same with the O-line. The backs had made their own holes. Glad they didn't get exposed, but Syracuse would pick that up pretty quickly, and they were a lot faster than the Jaguars. Gotta talk to Quincy about that. If Sampson can't get more push, then they were going to get stuffed. No way they could get around the ends against speed.*

Transcript: SAHS @ MCHS

Hopper: Welcome back to our listening audience. We're coming to you live from Parker Field in Madison County, where the St. Ambrose Saints lead the Madison County Bulldogs by a score of twenty-eight to ten. There's four-fourteen left on the clock, and it's been a game full of surprises. What do you think, Mark?

Howe: You're right about that, Jason. Coming into the game, I think we all expected to see a great matchup between the Bulldog secondary and the Saints passing game. Obviously losing Terrance Gould early in the first quarter has really hurt the Bulldogs, and St. Ambrose has taken advantage of that. But probably the biggest surprise of the night for me is that Madison County's big man Taevon Richardson hasn't been able to get any pressure on the Saints' quarterback. McDowell's been able to pick them apart all night.

Hopper: Well, with four-fourteen left, there's not much time for the Bulldogs to get things going. The Saints have the ball at their own thirty-five-yard line. Let's see if they can get a stop here. McDowell's under center. He checks the line. There's the snap. He's standing in the pocket. He's got all day to throw. Streaking down the right sideline is Amari Hanson, he's covered deep. The ball is away, and Hanson has it at the forty-two AND NOW HE'S PITCHED IT TO NORRIS! NORRIS IS AT THE FIFTY, THE FORTY, THE THIRTY, and he's in untouched for another Saints touchdown.

Howe [laughing]: A hook and lateral! I haven't seen that play in years!

Hopper: Wow! Just when you think Willy Williams has exhausted his bag of tricks, you get an explosive play like that.

Howe: Norris better watch out or he'll get a flag for celebrating . . . and there it is. That dance will cost the Saints ten yards on the kickoff.

Hopper: At this point, Mark, the Bulldogs will take everything they can get. They just haven't been able to move the ball all night.

Howe: Coach Williams is giving Norris a piece of his mind on the sidelines.

Hopper: The kicking team is lined up for the extra point. There's the snap, the kick is up and away, and it's good. And St. Ambrose leads Madison County by a score of thirty-five to ten. Well, if there's any good news for the Bulldogs, it's that the Saints' drive took just fifteen seconds off the clock. The Bulldogs will get the ball back with just under four minutes to go. Let's take a moment to recognize our sponsor for tonight's game: Asheville Furniture. Asheville Furniture: locally owned since 1984. From the mountains to the coast, Asheville Furniture is your home for fine home furnishings and decorations. Make Asheville Furniture your first-down play. Back to the action. St. Ambrose is lined up for the kick, and it's away and it's a doozy.

Howe: That ten-yard penalty isn't helping the Bulldogs at all.

Hopper: Evans takes the ball at the fifteen, and he's hit right away. Terrible field position for the Bulldogs.

Howe: They've gotta get something going here. They're not gonna win the game, but they need to come away with something to get a little momentum going into next week's Buncombe County matchup.

Hopper: Jacobs is under center. His big running back Tyler Smith is lined up behind him on his right. There's the snap. Pitch to Smith. And he's stood up at the line and dropped by a whole gang of Saints players.

Howe: Tackle by committee. Not much there. He might have gained a yard or two when he fell. The Bulldogs have gotta stop running that play. It hasn't worked all night.

Hopper: Three-fifteen left in the game. Jacobs is back under center. He steps back into the shotgun. There's the snap. Jacobs looks left . . . and fires one through the hands of his intended receiver. There's a flag on the play.

Howe: That's in the area of pass interference. Let's see how they call it.

Hopper: Waiting for the call. And it is pass interference. The Bulldogs will have the first down at their own thirty-five. Spot of the foul. And the Bulldogs get a much-needed first down and some breathing room.

Howe: Breathing room is right. It seems like they've been in the shadow of their own goalposts all night long.

Hopper: The clock has stopped with the first down. There's just over three minutes left in the game. The Bulldogs line up at the thirty-five-yard line. Jacobs under center. There's the snap. Pitch to Smith, and he's met at the line again, this time by Dylan Norris.

Howe: Norris just sniffed that one out, but I don't know how many different ways to say this, Madison County has got to stop running that play. It hasn't worked all night.

Hopper: Jacobs back under center. Clock is running. Two minutes thirty seconds. There's the snap; it's a handoff up the middle. There's a hole but it closes up immediately. Smith might have gotten three yards on the carry. Met again by Norris who comes in and closes the gap. And he just took Smith to the woodshed on that one.

Howe: Textbook tackle. Got low. Wrapped him up and took him down. That's what the middle linebacker has got to do.

Hopper: Third down. Jacobs is in the shotgun. There's the snap. It's an end-around, no it's a reverse. Smith has the ball and is just hammered by Norris as he crosses the line of scrimmage AND THE BALL'S OUT! There's a pile. Let's see who comes up with it. . . . It will be the Saints' ball at the Madison County thirty-two-yard line!

Howe: Well just when you think that things can't get any worse for the Bulldogs. Norris just gets in there and lays the wood to Smith, and the ball just popped out.

Hopper: Smith is still down.

Howe: And you hate to see that. Smith is down and Norris is standing over him. He's gonna get a taunting penalty . . . and there it is.

Hopper: Fourth foul of the night on Norris. And now his teammates have pulled him away, and Smith is still not moving. Trainers are coming onto the field. You just hate to see this, particularly at the end of the game. There's silence on the field as they attend to Smith. The Saints' players all take a knee. The Bulldogs are gathered around Smith.

Howe: I didn't see what happened there. He was sort of bent backward when Norris hit him, and he went to the turf pretty hard.

Hopper: St. Ambrose leading thirty-five to ten with two minutes left in the game. Tyler Smith is still down. The Saints' coach Williams comes out on the field and over to where the Bulldogs are huddled around Smith. The players are breaking up and there's Smith sitting up. There's applause from the stands.

Howe: That's great. Looks like he just got his bell rung.

Hopper: Tyler Smith is helped off the field. While we wait for play to resume, let's take a moment for station identification.

VOICE: You're listening to ninety-nine point seven, the Sports-Beast, WBCT radio, Asheville, North Carolina.

Hopper: Waiting for play to resume. St. Ambrose leads Madison County by the score of thirty-five to ten. The Saints have the ball at the thirty-two-yard line with two minutes left on the clock.

Howe: Looks like Dylan Norris' night is over. They come out with a vanilla package, no tight end. Looks like they're going to run the clock out.

Hopper: There's the whistle, and McDowell takes a knee.

Howe: Victory formation. I think they just took all the fight out of the Bulldogs.

Hopper: Madison County has two timeouts left, but it looks like they're content to just ride this one out.

Howe: Ambrose is too. It would be a fifty-yard field goal from here. They're not trying to get into field-goal range.

Hopper: Well it looks like both teams are content to let the clock run. Ball is snapped, and McDowell takes a knee. Clock runs. Thirty seconds left in the game. There's the whistle, and McDowell takes a knee to end the game. And there you have it. The St. Ambrose Saints have knocked off the Madison County Bulldogs by a final score of thirty-five to ten. The Saints remain undefeated and move to four and 0 on the season, while the Bulldogs drop to three and one.

If there were any place, besides the Jiffy Stop, that the World's Greatest Rangers Fan held court, it was in the back left corner of the Madison County bleachers. Although, for pecuniary reasons and despite his devotion, he had only attended a few Rangers games, no such financial barrier existed for the Madison County games. Season passes could be had for fifty bucks, and Billy was a proud member of the Bulldog Boosters Club, which came from his regular disbursements of donations he could ill afford. But the dollar went further in Madison County. He was an alum of that venerable institution, as were most of his family and all of his friends. One might say that Billy's entire life could be described in a Venn diagram of just two circles: Madison County Football and Biltmore College Football. And the place that they overlapped was recruiting.

The night was warm, clear, and held almost no humidity. Billy sat clad in his maroon and grey Madison County Football jacket. Purchased secondhand, it was an actual letterman jacket that some athlete had parted with. It was too big for Billy, but he wore it anyway. He had removed the letter patches, as he honorably did not want to give the impression that he had participated in Madison County football. He had played no sports in high school at all, as MCHS lacked a smoking team, and thus his one avenue of distinguishment was denied him. In fact, while in high school, Billy had looked with disdain on the jocks who played sports and had never attended a game of any sort, avoiding such activities with the same diligence with which he avoided going to classes.

In the corner of the stands, "high up" in the bleachers, Billy looked with disgust at the scene below as players straggled off the field, team managers cleared the equipment benches, a local reporter interviewed Madison's Coach Fieldmann, and little kids ran around on the track, screeching and giggling. Billy adjusted his BC Rangers cap, its lime green clashing with the maroon and gray jacket, and fished in his pockets for his pack of cigarettes. The stadium lights shone down from above him, bugs crowding around the bulbs. Everything was soaked in the thin artificial light.

There, in the center of the intersection of his Venn diagram, were both Taevon Richardson and Dylan Norris. The former, a five-star defensive line prospect ranked third in the country by AllSports, recruited by every top program, a Madison County boy but uncommitted and thus of questionable Ranger loyalty. The latter, the number-one tight end prospect in the nation, five-star in all of the ranking services, committed to the Rangers from day one, helping in recruiting and anchoring a top-ten class. But a St. Ambrose High School Saint and a player who had just dominated and humiliated the Madison County Bulldogs.

Billy's hopes for this evening were that Taevon would sack the Saints' QB so much that Norris would never get the ball, that MCHS would win the game, and that the Norris kid would respect the Bulldogs so much afterward that his praise would lock Taevon Richardson into a BC commitment. But, of course, no such thing had happened. Dylan Norris had put up 250 yards receiving, three touchdowns, two touchdowns called back, three sacks of his own, eight tackles, and four penalties—two personal fouls and two taunting. Taevon Richardson had been stymied and had the most ineffectual game of his career. Two of the Bulldogs' best players had left the game injured, and MCHS had been slaughtered.

But within that Venn intersection, Billy's mind grasped for the good. That Norris kid was the real deal, and next year it was the rest of the SEC that better watch out.

Dylan sat on the locker room bench, his gold trousers and pads still on, but bare-chested and with his hair damp and mopped on his forehead. He leaned forward with his forearms on his legs.

"It's bullshit," he said.

"So what, bro. Out for the final series of the game. You'll be lucky if that's all that happens," Randy said from the bench next to him.

"It's still bullshit. It was a good hit."

"You got the flag for standing on top of the kid, Dylan."

"For like, a second. How was I to know he was hurt?"

"Listen bro, you keep getting those cheap-ass flags and Coach will have to do something."

"Bullshit. There's no way he'll bench me."

"Whatever, man." Randy got up and headed for the shower. The Madison County visitors' locker room was derelict compared to the new facilities at SAHS and most of the other places that they played. Old, dingy grey tile, with maroon accents, fluorescent lighting fixtures with dead, dry bugs blocking some of the light, pewter-colored hooks on the wall and worn wooden-slat benches. Grime in the corners, and the smell of mildew, sweat, and BENGAY.

Dylan stripped off the rest of his uniform and threw his pants, pads, and jockstrap into a bin as he made his way to the showers. There he took a place under a showerhead next to Amari Hanson.

"Man, that hook and lateral was sick," Amari said, as Dylan took his place under the stream of hot water. "Course I coulda run that in myself. You got to pad your stats."

"Whatever," Dylan responded. "Hey man, I was looking for Quentin in the stands. You see him?"

"Aw man, didn't you hear? Quentin got busted."

"What?"

"Yeah. He was the one that sold that coke to Evans. Somebody narc'd on him."

"Shit." Dylan was silent for a second, then said: "I was looking to score. You got any?"

"No man, I'm cashed."

"Shit," Dylan replied.

"We gonna have to go to someone else," Amari offered.

"Got any ideas?"

"I hear that Sanders kid deals."

"Sanders? The atheist kid?"

"Yeah. He don't have the stuff like Quentin did, but he can hook you up with some herb."

"Probably good anyway," Dylan responded. "If Quentin was getting shit with fentanyl. You think Sanders' shit is clean?"

"Fuck if I know. Shit, you never know what you getting nowdays."

"So it was Quentin's shit that killed Evans. That fucker."

"Shit, man, he probably didn't even know. You think he'd sell that shit if he knew? They gonna bust him good now."

"Hey, as long as shit don't dry up. You got Sanders' number?"

"Yeah man. I'll DM you."

Chapter 13

CORRUPTION

Mid-September glory, and the leaves had begun to turn yellow. The humidity was sucked away from the air, and the evenings began to cool. It was Saturday night, and Dylan's Yukon rolled into the Cox Foods parking lot. The arc lights shined down. The SUV glided past the gleaming front of the store, stopping for late shoppers wheeling their loaded carts.

Dylan drove to a corner of the lot, where a silver Honda sat in a row of unoccupied cars. He pulled the Yukon into a spot nearby, threw it in park, and flashed his high beams. The door of the Honda opened, and Brad Sanders got out, pulled a small backpack from the passenger seat, and let the door swing closed. As he walked toward Dylan, he thumbed the remote, and the Honda's signal lights flashed once. Brad was wearing a grey hoodie, jeans, and ponderous black boots, and his face was white in the arc lights as he opened the SUV door and climbed in.

"Hey," Dylan said, as he shifted to drive and began making his way out of the lot.

"Hey," Brad replied, buckling his seat belt.

After a few moments in silence, Brad asked, "So what's the plan?"

"You tell me. Quentin just used to sell me the stuff."

"Okay, cool. You wanted a quarter, right?"

"Yeah."

"I brought a surprise as well. You ever done X?"

"Ecstasy?" Dylan replied. "No way, bro. Not interested."

"Okay, cool. Just drive somewhere where we can smoke out then."

"Party field?"

"Isn't that up off of 401?"

"Yeah, it's a drive, but nobody's going there anymore, so it's pretty safe."

"Cool. Do you mind changing the music? I hate metal."

"Whatever bro."

They drove in silence for a little while longer before Dylan spoke.

"So what's your deal anyway?"

"What do you mean?"

"You just like fucking with teachers? You are the most argumentative fucker I've ever seen."

"Oh," Brad replied, chuckling, "you mean Fr. Dixon. Yeah, that's fun."

"Dude, I just zone out when you start into your shit."

"Dixon enjoys it."

"Why the fuck you go to Ambrose anyway? Why aren't you at Parkdale?"

Brad shrugged and answered: "My dad says St. Ambrose is a better school. He went to a Catholic school and says they give you the best education, and I'm doing the shared credits with Biltmore where he teaches. Parkdale does their shared credits with UNCA."

Silence, then Brad flipped through channels until he found the EDM station.

"I hate this shit," Dylan grunted.

"You taking any credit classes?" Brad asked.

"Nope. I don't have time."

"Yeah . . . *football*," Brad sneered.

"Yeah, football. But I'm graduating early, so I'll be at Biltmore while you're still arguing with Fr. Dixon."

"What was it, summer school?"

"Yeah, I went my sophomore and junior summers and got all my creds. Just have to ride out this semester, and I'm done."

"What are you majoring in?"

"I don't know. Sports management or something like that. Not gonna have a ton of time, so I can't do anything too hard."

"So you're just there to play football, huh? Think you're going pro?"

"Fuck yeah I'm going pro."

"Don't take this the wrong way, I'm just wondering. Is football something you love, or are you just doing it because your dad was a pro?"

"Dude, I'll tell you one thing that sucks about being Dane Norris' son. Everybody thinks they know your business. I don't know jack shit about you or your family. Same thing with everybody . . . "

"I wasn't trying to piss you off," Brad interrupted.

"Yeah, I know. I've been going to school with the St. Ambrose kids for a long time, so most everybody leaves me alone about it. You're new. I get it. Lemme ask you this. Is there anything that you're really good at—anything where you are totally the best?"

"Pissing off Fr. Dixon," Brad laughed. Dylan grinned in response and continued: "I love football. I fucking love it. Yeah, a lot of it is a pain in the ass. Spring practice, two-a-days, that shit sucks. But I was made for it."

"And you get to make millions of dollars."

"Yeah, well that part isn't gonna suck."

"Of course, you're already rich . . . "

"My *dad* is rich. He made his own, and I'm gonna make my own."

"So then why Biltmore College?"

"What do you mean?"

"It looks like you're following in his footsteps. Why go to Biltmore College instead of somewhere else? I don't watch a lot of football, but I don't think they're very good."

Dylan laughed, "They're not good yet. But they're gonna be. By the time I leave they will be. We've got a great class coming in."

"So you want to *save* them?"

"Nah, it's nothing like that. Listen, I grew up with Rangers stuff all around the house. Yeah, my dad went there. But so did my uncle and my cousins and my grandparents. It's a family thing. I'd probably be kicked out if I went anywhere else . . . "

Dylan paused, and the road hummed outside of the Yukon. The beat had slowed for the inevitable mid-song break. Dylan began speaking again as the bass resumed thumping.

". . . and Coach Carter, he's pretty cool. He's developed some good tight ends. Coach Love, Coach Quincy, pretty cool. Listen, I wouldn't mind getting away from home. I know everybody thinks it's great and sometimes it is. The one thing I thought about was getting away so I wouldn't have people looking over my shoulder all the time."

"You've got a brother, right? Jane?"

Dylan laughed, "I can call him Jane. You call him Jane, and he'll kick the shit out of you. You call him Janus. But, yeah, I guess I'd miss the little fucker. He's a pain in the ass. And I have one sister at home but my other one is out in Oregon."

"So . . . it's mommy issues," Brad said.

"What the fuck?" Dylan responded, his voice rising.

"No man, it's cool. I'm in the same situation. You seem pretty cool with your dad, but you want to get away. I guess you don't get along with your mother. I can totally relate. My mom's an overbearing bitch, never happy with anything I do. Guess I'm a big disappointment to her. Rides my ass all the time."

"Yeah, I got that. My mom's a holy roller. She prays like five times a day, always going to Mass. She should try praying to not be a bitch. Disappointed that I'm not gonna be a priest, I guess."

"You don't seem like the priest type," Brad offered.

Dylan took the SR401 exit. Before long they were driving

between the dark forested hills. As the lights of the Jiffy Stop spilled their weak pools across the road, Dylan suggested they get munchies and swung into the lot. He pulled his wallet out and handed a couple of twenties to Brad. "You go in."

"You're not coming?" Brad asked, a little suspiciously.

"Yeah, I get recognized. It's cooler if you go."

Brad shrugged and climbed out of the Yukon. He was back a few minutes later with a paper bag.

"I got chips, Reese's, and water."

"Cool."

Dylan pulled back out onto 401 and drove on until he reached the turnoff for Party Field. There was no oncoming traffic. The Yukon made the left onto the gravel and proceeded up the hill. Reaching the empty field, Dylan cut the lights and turned the SUV around so they could see the headlights of any cars that might come up toward them. Seatbelts came off, and Brad's backpack opened up. He took out a Ziploc bag and a small glass pipe, packed some marijuana into the bowl, and handed it to Dylan.

"Gotta see me smoke first, huh? You got trust issues."

"Fine," Brad replied, "you gotta see me smoke first to know it isn't laced?"

"Don't want to end up like Evans," Dylan replied, watching Brad light and hit the pipe. The lighter's flame and glow of the burning weed lit up Brad's face before going dark as he handed the pipe and lighter back to Dylan, then coughed out the smoke.

Dylan held the lighter to the bowl and took his own hit.

Minutes later the two were laughing. The EDM beat was pulsing as the stereo panel made its cycle through pink, blue, green, yellow, red, and back to pink. The interior lights of the SUV glinted and winked at them.

"So in comes Lisa LeBlanc," Dylan giggled, continuing his story, "and Jane gets up and stands at attention by the bench, and I couldn't help it, I just yanked his shorts down, and he's got the biggest boner you've ever seen . . . "

The two broke into uncontrolled belly laughs and coughing fits.

Dylan's eyes watered, and he struggled to get a breath. Finally he sat up and leaned back in his seat.

"This is good shit."

"I know," Brad replied. "I sell it," and it struck them as funny, and off they went into another spasm of laughter.

When it had died down, Brad said, "Second thoughts on the molly?"

That sobered Dylan. A little.

"I don't know, bro. I've never taken that shit before. After what happened to Evans . . . "

"No, this is clean. I took some last weekend, and it's good."

Dylan was still hesitant.

"I can't get busted. We get a few days warning before they test us."

"It's out of your system in two or three days," Brad replied.

"What does it do to you?" Dylan asked.

"It's cool. You're high but you're not really tripping. It makes colors brighter and music better. It's just . . . it's cool."

"I don't know. I don't wanna be up here all night."

"Well, it's two or three hours. The first hour is the best, and after that you just feel good as you come down."

"So this shit's clean?"

"Yeah; you in?"

"Yeah, okay."

Brad rummaged in his backpack again and found a little ball of cellophane. He carefully unwrapped it until he found a tiny pill with a monkey printed on it. He handed it to Dylan, unwrapped another one, and popped it in his mouth, chasing it down with water from his water bottle.

Dylan looked at the pill for a moment then tossed it into his mouth and swallowed.

The stereo thumped away, piano and bass and bizarre muffled voices sampled from some 1930's movie. Dylan waited and didn't feel anything different. Brad tapped his fingers on the leather surface of the console.

Sips of water. All of the Reese's. A handful of chips. Dance music courtesy of a succession of artists all named Nora. Then Brad took in a deep breath, and a wide grin stretched across his face.

"I'm rolling," he said, settling back into his seat. His head moved slowly from side to side, taking everything in, and the big grin got bigger.

Dylan felt nothing unusual. He watched Brad, bemused. Watched as his fingers went from tapping the console to gently touching it, one finger after another. Brad's right hand caressed the power-window button, and his head nodded slowly.

"Are you rolling?" Brad asked.

"Nothing," Dylan replied. He was feeling slightly annoyed, when all of a sudden the world lit up in front of him. The first thing he noticed was the wave-like grid on the stereo LED, in its pink phase. He had never seen a color so intense. He turned his gaze, and as he did the little lights in the SUV turned into diamonds. A tide swept through him making all his senses alive like never before. His mouth formed into a round "O."

"Oh man. Oh bro. Oh wow."

"You're rolling."

"Oh man. Oh man."

The stereo LED seemed to have stopped on pink. The music was playing, but every beat lasted an eternity. Dylan rode up and down on the frequency of the music, savoring it. At last, time began to move again, and the pink began to change to purple. Dylan tried to hold on to the color, but the violet wave pulled him up onto its crest, and surrendering to it, he was transported to an even greater height—a great purple cushioning cloud. His head swayed slowly atop his thick neck.

He could not say how long this went on, pulled from color to color. The intensity faded but was replaced by a calm sense of euphoria. Now he felt every nerve in his body, and they all felt just right. The ever-present soreness in his muscles was there, and the pain in his shoulder, but that too was right. Pain didn't hurt. His awareness traveled up and down his body, marveling.

Then he turned his head and saw Brad. Brad's eyes were closed, his hands still moving softly on the console and armrest.

Dylan's right arm reached out, and he found his hand on the back of Brad's head.

Brad's eyes opened and he looked directly at Dylan, his pupils wide, looking through him.

Dylan pushed Brad's head down toward his crotch, as he had done so many times with Wendy. But there was no resistance, and this time, it was better that way.

"He's still not answering!" Anne said to her husband, a frantic note in her voice.

"He's okay. Don't worry," Dane replied, without raising his head from the pillow.

"How can you just lie there and say that?"

Dane rolled over and sat up in the bed, staring evenly at his wife, and answered.

"If there had been an accident, the police would have called. It's a Saturday night, he's a senior in high school. He's a young man with a good head on his shoulders. I get that you didn't have the same experience."

"What's that supposed to mean?" Anne asked angrily.

"Oh come on, it's not an insult. It's just that when you were in high school, I bet your mother never let you stay out past six."

"Leave my mother out of this. She has nothing to do with it."

"She has everything to do with it. You can't keep them locked in cages. At some point they've got to get out there and start making their own decisions."

"But, Dane, he still just a kid."

"He knows better than to get into any serious trouble."

"You think that the Mortons thought that? Or the Boyds or the Evans or the Ryans?"

"Dylan's not suicidal . . . " Dane began, but Anne interrupted.

"I didn't say that he was, but what happened to the kids on that houseboat, or the boys at Deerstone . . . "

"Those were accidents."

"Skylar Evans wasn't an accident."

"The hell it wasn't. You think that kid meant to OD?"

"And Peter Morton and Doug Smith had drugs with them too. What if Dylan has gotten mixed up in that?"

"Dylan has more sense than to get into drugs. He has his football career on the line."

"Those other kids played baseball."

"It's not the same. Dylan can go pro. It's his whole life and what he wants to do. He knows that drugs can ruin that for him. And besides, they test the kids all the time."

That gave Anne pause, and Dane pressed his advantage, "Listen, honey, I get that you're concerned. Who wouldn't be after the summer that we had? But as tragic as things have been, we can't go assuming that our kids are next just because there has been a string of accidents. You can't live like that, and if you try to make our kids live like that, you'll just push them away."

Anne was stung. She remained silent for a moment and then replied, "Dane, I just wish you'd help set some boundaries. We can't just let them run wild."

"When Dylan gets home, I'll talk to him about checking in and maybe I'll make him turn on the location tracker on his phone. It's not fair to you to leave you worrying like this. But it's also not fair to Dylan to keep him on a leash because some bad shit happened to other kids."

"I hope you're right. It's our children's lives."

"I'm right."

Sunday morning, and the door of the Jiffy Stop swung open, its bell ringing to announce Billy Mullins.

"Mornin' Billy," said Tommy Hess, cheerfully, "you oughta be in a good mood."

"You got that right," Billy said with a grin. "Hell of a game. Rangers just stomped 'em! Just stomped 'em."

"Didn't see that one comin'; figured Missouri would win at home."

"Nope. Our lines were just too much for 'em. Like I always say, gotta control the trenches. Then your skill players can open it up."

Billy walked over to the coffee machine and poured himself a cup, then took his place at the counter and pulled out his pack of cigarettes.

"Gotta stop you there, Billy."

"What?"

"Renfroe don't want people smokin' in here no more."

"You're kiddin' me."

"Wish I was. Says you can dip all you want but no smokin'."

Billy put the cigarette pack back in his jacket pocket.

"What's this fuckin' world comin' to, Tommy?"

"Beats the shit out of me. Just when you think it can't get any worse, it does."

"Gimme one of them sausage biscuits," Billy said, and Tommy handed him a foil-wrapped puck. Billy handed him a couple of crumpled dollars. "I'd say keep the change, but I wouldn't give old Renfroe the pleasure." Tommy returned a couple of coins, and Billy pocketed them.

"Baer sure made Missouri's D look bad," Billy said through a mouthful of biscuit. Pieces dropped from his mouth and lodged in his beard before he brushed them away.

"Sure did," Tommy said, looking out through the windows at a car pulling up to the pump.

"That was a breakout game for Thompson. I knew they oughta move him to right tackle. Shit, he was openin' holes a truck could drive through."

Outside, the car's driver stepped out, and seeing the out-of-order sign on the pump's card reader, got back in and drove off. Tommy looked back at Billy.

"They sure poured it on 'em in the fourth," Tommy said.

"So what if they did. Hell, that's half the problem with the Rangers the last few years. Ain't no lead ever been safe. These boys don't have quit in 'em. Carter's given' 'em the winning edge. That's what's been missing."

The first thing that Dylan noticed was the pillowcase, which was soaked with sweat. The AC was on, as it always was at a Norris household, and when he turned his head, his cheek settled into the cold damp.

Confusion. He opened his eyes and saw that he was in his room at the lake house. He was lightheaded, with a dull pain behind his eyes. The sun shone down on the deck outside, and the reflected light filled the room. Dylan looked through the French doors out onto the deck for a moment. He stirred, stretched his legs, and sat up. There was someone in the bed next to him.

Dylan jumped out of bed and turned. Lying half under a blanket, a bare back, black hair. He was dizzy, and the night began to come back to him.

Fuck, fuck FUCK! he thought.

Fuck, fuck, fuck oh no oh no oh no.

Dylan's hands went to his hair. He saw his boxer shorts on the ground by the bed amidst a pile of clothes, grabbed them, and almost ran. Confusion still reigning, he ran from room to room, making sure there was nobody else there. He ran upstairs into the great room on the main level. All was still. He stood there in the center of the living room, the events of Saturday night crashing in on him, and for some reason he could not take his eyes off of the decorations. "Life is better at the lake," two crossed oars, a ship's wheel, pictures of sailboats, a life-preserver with "Norris Lake House" stenciled on it, everywhere little touches of his mother's tastes, all in teal and blue.

He walked into the kitchen and leaned on the white-granite

countertop. His mind probed his memory and found the sore spots, retreated, and then tested again. A rushing and unfamiliar anxiety filled him, pulsing from his brain. Again and again he raised his hands to lock behind his head and paced around.

Fuck, fuck fuck fuck fuck.

After a while, his hands fumbling, he loaded a Keurig pod, and when the mug was full, drained a cup of black coffee. He opened the refrigerator and grabbed a water bottle, drained that as well, then another. He was about to make a second cup of coffee when he heard movement behind him. There at the top of the stairs was Brad Sanders, dressed in his dark clothes, the gray hoodie zipped halfway.

"You fucking tell anybody about this, and I'll fucking kill you. You understand?" Dylan seethed.

Brad stood looking at him silently for a moment and then said: "Can I get some of that coffee?"

Sanders walked calmly toward him, around him, and went to the Keurig, his back to Dylan.

"Of course I'm not gonna say anything," he said, without turning around.

"You fucking did this to me," Dylan said. His fists balled up. He wanted nothing more than to swing at the back of Brad's head. The arrogant back of Brad's head. The traitorous arrogant mother-fucking back of Brad's head. But he didn't. Something restrained him.

Brad did not turn around, waiting as the machine grunted and steamed and poured the coffee into a "Lake Life" mug. But he felt the anger behind him and stood there, tense, waiting for the blow. When it didn't come, and the mug was full, he picked it up and slowly turned to look at Dylan.

"You knew this would happen," Dylan accused.

"I didn't," Brad retorted. "That's never happened to me before on X."

"Bullshit. You talked me into it. Faggot."

"Let's get this straight," Brad answered, calmly. "I'm gay. I thought you knew that. But the last thing I would have expected was to hook up with you."

"Oh fuck oh fuck oh fuck," Dylan moaned, turning away and locking his hands behind his head again as another wave of anxiety coursed through him.

"What the fuck do I do now? What the fuck do I do now?"

For a moment Brad thought about putting a comforting hand on Dylan's back, but he knew better. Dylan was like a coiled spring ready to release its energy. Brad spoke softly.

"It's not a big deal."

"The fuck it isn't!"

"No, seriously. It's not a big deal. It happens."

"I thought you said it didn't happen. What the fuck you mean it happens?"

"I said it'd never happened to me on X. But guys, straight guys, well . . . sometimes they get with other guys. It's not a big deal."

"It is to me!"

"Listen," Brad rejoined, as Dylan turned to face him, "it doesn't mean you're gay. It doesn't mean anything at all. We can both forget about it."

A ray of hope shone in Dylan's mind. *Forget about it. Forget about it.* The path opened in front of him, and his anxiety eased slightly. *Forget about it. It never happened.* But as part of his mind sought to enter more deeply into this comfort, another part of his mind began poking and prodding the painful memories of the night before. The intense release in the front of the SUV, the insane laughter afterwards, the minutes or hours of brilliant colors and pulsing music. The blurred drive to the lake house, the tumble into bed and the wrapped and tangled arms and legs.

His head swimming, Dylan leaned forward on the cool white granite.

"You got your shit together?"

"Yep."

"I'll be back in a few minutes."

Dylan went back downstairs to the bedroom, leaving Brad sipping his coffee. *It never happened. Forget about it.*

He gathered up his pile of clothes and tossed them into the bathroom. Then he yanked the sheets off of the bed and shoved them into a hamper in the room. He stripped and showered, standing under the hot water, trying to wash everything away. Waves of panic came and went before he finally exited, toweled dry, and tossed the towel in the hamper. He dressed in his clothes from the night before and inundated himself and his clothes with body spray. He took a look around the room for anything else, anything that might give substance to his memories of the night before. When he was convinced that the room was empty of evidence, he took the hamper to the laundry room.

Dylan had never washed his own clothes before, let alone sheets. But he was clever enough to select "bulky items" and stuff the sheets and towels into the washer, find the detergent, find the reservoir, fill it to the "max" line, and start the machine going.

When he came back upstairs, Brad was sitting on the couch, looking relaxed. Dylan was both angered and reassured by this. Wordlessly, he picked up Brad's mug and then gathered up his own, washed them in the sink, dried off one of the mugs and put it back in the cupboard, and threw the Keurig pods in the trash.

"You ready?" he asked.

"Sure," Brad replied, and they made their way out to the front of the house. The Yukon was in the driveway, parked directly in front of the door. The two climbed in. Dylan started the car and immediately EDM music poured from the speakers. Dylan almost punched the stereo as he turned it off. Brad looked at him side eyed as they drove away.

About a hundred yards up the driveway, the paving ended, and the drive joined the gravel road that ran along the ridge of the peninsula. As they moved upward, Brad nodded toward one of the many side-drives that departed from the road and said: "My parents have a place down there. Not as nice as yours. Funny that we're on the same lake."

Dylan didn't respond. He was silent as they made their way back down SR401 and joined the interstate. Silent as they pulled into the Cox parking lot. Silent as Brad opened his backpack, pulled out a Ziploc, and said "here's your quarter." Silent as he pulled bills from his wallet and handed them to Brad. Silent as he watched Brad's Honda pull out of the parking lot.

He sat looking out the window as the noon sun shone down on the yellowing leaves. Then he looked at the cupholder where his phone was lodged and picked it up. Five missed calls from his mother. One missed call from his father. A dozen text messages from friends and family.

Amari Hanson: Brad set you up?

Randy Thompson: Amari said your good. Give me a call.

Randy Thompson: Get the news about Richardson?

Jane: Bro, you better call home. Mom is pissed.

Jane: WTF. You better call.

Jimmy McDowell: You hear about Richardson?

Dad: Your mother's worried. Call when you get this text.

Jane: Better call. Now Dad's pissed.

674589: Low cost health insurance now available in your area. Text "IN" to 756-899-4565 to find out how you can save.

Randy Thompson: Richardsons committing to BC!

Jane: Your gonna be in deep shit [emoji with Xs for eyes]

Mom: Where are you?

Mom: Dylan, I hope you're OK. We spent the whole night worried about you. I pray that you're OK and that you're reading this message and I just want you to know that we love you and please call when you get this.

Dylan tapped a quick response to both parents:

Dylan: Sorry you were worried. Needed to be alone so I went to the lake. Evans, Pat, Johnny, Danny just got to me. Should have called. Sorry. Headed home now.

He put the phone back in the cupholder, opened the glovebox, pushed the Ziploc full of weed to the back, put the Yukon in drive, and made his way back toward the farm.

Chapter 14

HOLLOW

Fr. Dixon was as animated as he ever got, running with quick steps from one whiteboard to another and occasionally hiking up his cassock to do so. On one big panel he had drawn a table with "Chance" on one side and "Creator" on the other. Below it, he had listed out attributes of each, then expounded. He was attempting to demonstrate that belief in "Chance" rather than a "Creator" was no less an act of faith.

Brad Sanders raised his hand again, and a groan went up from the nearby students. Dylan, across the room, tried to ignore him.

"But Fr. Dixon," Brad began, petulance in his voice, "surely the assumption of a creator entity is a violation of Ockham's Razor you keep bringing up. Isn't it a matter of, in one case you have purely natural processes, and in the other, you have to invent a supernatural being? You don't have to have faith in natural processes. We see them all around us. And it is pretty irrefutable that there is mutation—*random mutation*—happening all the time. It's observed. Whereas your God is not."

"So you have seen random mutation, Mr. Sanders? What did it look like?"

There was a murmur of chuckles from the students, who were always on Fr. Dixon's side in these exchanges.

"Very funny, Father. You know what I mean. We see the effect of random mutations, and I know, I know you're going to say that we also see the effect of God. But here's my point. If you acknowledge that evolution occurs and that God didn't just create the earth in seven days—which I know you don't believe, Father—and that mutation and natural selection can explain life, then what is the purpose of God? He's just superfluous."

"But, Mr. Sanders, while I do not deny the natural processes we observe and call evolution, they are insufficient to explain how we got here."

"It's Dawkins' small steps, Father. With a billion-billion planets, even a one-in-a-billion chance that we'd evolve this way would mean that there are a billion other planets with life like ours."

"To be fair to Dawkins, that's not exactly what he said. But even taking life at its simplest form, his billion-to-one odds are still absurdly wrong. Let's consider the old monkeys on typewriters analogy. The old joke says that a million monkeys typing on a million typewriters for an infinite amount of time would eventually produce the works of Shakespeare."

"Okay. Sure."

"So, the odds of a monkey typing the first letter of the first word of the first sentence of the first work of Shakespeare is one in twenty-six. The second letter is one in twenty-seven, to allow for the possibility that the letter is instead a space between letters. The odds of having typed the first letter and the second character correctly are one in seven hundred or so. To get the first three letters right, the odds are one in nineteen thousand. Skipping ahead a bit, presuming that the first word of Shakespeare's works is "ACT I," the odds of a monkey typing that would be about fourteen million to one, and by the time you get to the first character after "ACT I" the odds are over ten billion to one. There your million monkeys go, typing all sorts of random absurdity, and every time you get excited that they get beyond ACT I, they screw it up and type some nonsense and you're back to ground zero. Because there's nothing directing it, no one taking the page out of the typewriter and saying okay, this is good, now type page two."

"I get it. It sounds daunting. But, as you've reminded us, infinity is not finite, so your monkeys have forever to get it right."

"But they don't have forever, Mr. Sanders. They only have the age of the earth, about four billion years, for their little chemical typewriters to plunk out the DNA that we can call life. That's one of the problems with the 'little steps' of your Dawkins. There's just not enough time for them, let alone the other issues."

"Okay, okay. I should have known better than to bring Dawkins in as an expert in theology," Brad laughed.

"That's just it, Mr. Sanders. I'm not objecting to Dawkins' theology. I am objecting to his mathematics."

"Oooooo!" the point was scored by several students, and Brad's brow furrowed. He opened his mouth to retort and would have done so had the bell not rung, ending the class period. As students rose, gathered their books and packs, and as Fr. Dixon returned to the whiteboard to erase his many scribblings, Dylan and Brad found themselves exiting at the same time.

"Hey."

"Hey."

"I, uh . . . you got time to talk sometime?" Dylan asked, walking a little behind Brad and lowering his voice.

"Sure. Text me a good time," Brad said, turning and smiling at Dylan and then accelerating to walk away from him.

Brad Sanders was the second generation of an experiment in creating better men. His father, Monty Sanders, had a moniker that was usually suspected of being an honorific of WWII's General Montgomery, if not for Monty Python. Rather, his full name Montgomery was a reference to the city in Alabama, as was his sister's name Selma. His younger brother Malcolm had been named after the black activist of that name was assassinated, or he might otherwise have ended up named Birmingham. Monty Sanders' father was an FBI agent who had been traumatized by the racial strife he had seen firsthand in Alabama. A true Kennedy-Catholic from New England, E.F. Sanders had gone down into the burning south and reemerged with a fervor to make things right. Foremost among these things was "creating a new man," and so, as his children were born, he made it his mission to ensure that they were to be apostles to the nations.

E.F. Sanders made certain that his children got a good Jesuit education, and so they did, swaddled amongst the children of other agents and the Washington, DC, elite, exposed to the classics, to formation, and grounded in the life of *mens sana in corpore sano*: the sound mind in the sound body. The four-square man.

Monty Sanders went off to Georgetown for his undergraduate degree and stayed through his PhD. He chose sociology because it was there that he could best fulfill his mission of rooting out the tumors of man and cauterizing them with his wit.

At a meeting of the Democratic Socialists of America, he discovered Myra Phillips, a cute young woman with a small, upturned nose and straight blonde hair who wore flower-patterned dresses cinched around her small waist. The broad swimmer's shoulders of Monty Sanders caught her attention, and as they entered more and more into a political alliance, she let her other dalliances slip away, and the two were married. A civil marriage, Myra insisted, none of this religious nonsense. Knowing Monty's background, from then on it was always "your church," "your believers," and "your Jesus," though Sanders neither attended church nor spoke often of religion.

Monty secured his post-doctorate at Maryland U., and Myra followed along shortly after, earning a position in women's studies. The two were a well-recognized power couple at M.U. and ultimately had a little orbit of like minds. They rode the tide of the Clinton years in a sort of triumphalism, and when Myra found herself pregnant for the third time, instead of scheduling another abortion, she told Monty that they would keep this one.

Thus, Brad Sanders came into the world as an object of curiosity for his mother and an object of mission for his father. They played classical music in his nursery, used neutral colors to ensure no gender biasing, and sent him to a progressive and diverse preschool to enculturate him early. His parents were so careful not to imprint him with their own embedded and inherent toxicity that they did exactly that. Brad grew up intelligent but acerbic. Convinced of a certain superiority and with a messiah complex coupled with disdain for those he would save.

Brad's arrival marked a change in his parents as well. Monty became more and more focused on reaching tenure, devoting himself to this goal with constant socializing and cultivation of his erudition. Myra, on the other hand, didn't see the point of losing the baby weight and seemed to be deliberately rejecting conventions of beauty. Myra wasn't vegan, which disconcerted her friends, but she sympathized and affirmed their veganism in a way that said "perfectly alright for you, but I am above that." A vegan diet was insufficient to maintain her carefully developed physique. Endometriosis had led to an early hysterectomy, and Myra had welcomed the resultant changes to her body with a sense of relief, feeling a new liberation. When one of the few childhood friends with whom she maintained contact had suggested hormone replacement therapy, Myra had surgically removed the woman from her life like a condemned heretic. *Anathema sit!*

The first Christmas after Brad was born, Myra gifted her husband with a selection of toys for his pleasure, letting him know that he was to take care of his own needs. She gifted herself a strap-on dildo. On those occasions in which she became enraged at the patriarchy, she would leave the dildo on the bed as a sign to her husband to prepare himself to receive what he and other men were so used to giving.

By the time that Brad was in high school, Myra Phillips-Sanders had become a grim-faced woman with steel-grey hair, wearing a perpetual expression of haughtiness. Her slit eyes glared from behind thick, round glasses, clearly indicating to the world that she could do all of this better, if only the fools would let her.

Her staccato voice was full of a patronizing tone that overpronounced words to help the listener's limited comprehension approach (but never attain, for how could it?) the meaning she was painfully attempting to impart. This was invariable no matter how educated or uneducated her listener might be, but it was part of the forcefulness of her character that was prized by her colleagues. They might think that she was a bitch, but she was *their* bitch and the kind of woman you wanted by your side in a fight.

Myra dressed in frumpy, draped clothes—beige kaftans over long autumn-patterned tunics—and with her thin, straight grey hair, and the corners of her mouth lined in a perpetual scowl, it gave the distinct impression that everything about her was flowing downward.

Brad grew up in between these two forces of nature: the dreamy but cynical father hell-bent on his career and building a lever long enough to move the world, and the intense and disdainful mother consciously sapping the roots of the very institution that she inhabited. All in all, once he reached adolescence, he was acknowledged, accepted, and ignored by the two. The only thing he had ever done that had seemed to be rewarded with pride was to tell his parents that he was gay. His mother beamed at him and promptly started a new chapter of PFLAG—Parents & Friends of Lesbians & Gays—when she found that the existing chapter at M.U. was too heteronormative. His father patted himself on the back for raising a son who seemed to have no fear in coming out. Monty and Myra inserted the key into the back of their little windup toy, turned it, and then released their son to do their work. They were indeed building a new world.

Another Friday night, the mid-October chill bringing out letterman jackets and sweaters, the SAHS parents huddled under blankets while the senior boys (the ones in the stands at any rate) showed their toughness by remaining shirtless with their painted-on S A I N T S letters. Cheerleaders were now wearing long sleeves and nylons. Fr. Dixon stood on the sideline with a black peacoat over his cassock and a black biretta on his head, hands clasped behind his back. The Saints rolled on, the game being effectively over at the half. Dylan Norris extracted his pounds of flesh from the opposition. Freshman quarterback McDowell continued to impress. Janus Norris got his bits of playing time in the fourth quarter, but they didn't let him throw: just handoff after handoff and a couple designed quarterback runs.

The next afternoon South Carolina came to town and rolled into Seely Stadium as a four-point favorite. The odds had been tightening as the sportsbooks adjusted to the Rangers' upset win over Tennessee the week before. Dane made his appearance at Henry Cox's luxury box, completing the trifecta of Cox brothers. Anne and the kids stayed home, but Dylan went along and was the highlight of the day for the expectant fans in Henry Cox's orbit. And the Rangers went on to clip the Gamecocks with a field goal in the fourth, improving to four-and-three overall and two-and-one in the SEC.

Later that evening, Dylan's SUV rolled into the Cox Foods parking lot and up next to Brad's Honda. Dylan rolled the window down, and Brad did as well.

"Wanna get in?" Dylan asked.

"How 'bout you get in my car?" Brad said.

"Come on . . . yours is a piece of shit."

"Hey, you were the one who wanted to talk."

"Okay, okay," Dylan relented, rolling up his window, getting out of the Yukon and locking it, and then settling himself into the passenger seat in Brad's Honda. The interior was glossy leather, recently wiped down with some astringent cleaner. An air freshener hung from the rearview mirror. Dylan felt under the seat for the release and pushed it way back so he could fit in the car.

"Okay, so you wanna drive, bro?" Dylan asked.

Brad pulled out of the lot and onto the road in front of Cox Foods and started driving.

"So, what is it? Another quarter bag?"

"Yeah, that too," Dylan replied. "Here's the thing. About what happened . . ."

"I thought we were both going to forget about it," Brad interrupted.

"That's it. I can't. I, uh . . . I keep thinking about it. At first I was pissed. Like, I wanted to fucking kill you."

"And?" Brad asked, not looking at Dylan, but rather straight ahead at the road.

"I don't know. I just. Fuck man, I don't know. I guess I just wanted to talk to you."

"Falling in love with me, Dylan?" Brad asked, and the big football player just snorted.

"Fuck you. No. Nothing like that."

"Just want me to blow you again? Is that it?"

Dylan was silent. Brad remained so too, for a while.

"Listen, Dylan. I don't mind hooking up, but I'm nobody's fuckboy. Let me ask you this. Do you want to kiss me? That whole night, you never kissed me."

Dylan said nothing.

"That's kind of what I thought. I think you just want to fuck me. And that's cool. You're hot, and I like being fucked. But I'm not going to be a hookup for you. If you want something to happen, you're going to have to decide what you are and be ready for the consequences. Then, if things work out between us, then . . . cool. Like I said, you're pretty hot. But you're also an asshole."

Brad drove around a while longer and then circled back to the Cox Foods parking lot. He reached over Dylan's lap and opened the glove compartment and took out the quarter bag of weed. Dylan peeled off four twenty-dollar bills and handed them to Brad, and pocketing the quarter bag, got out of the Honda.

Billy Mullins crumpled his beer can and threw it at the storm door in the front of his trailer. Little sudsy droplets of beer flew from it and sprayed the room. A couple of drops landed on the LED screen, and in a moment, Billy was up and wiping them off.

On the screen, the Crimson Tide celebrated in the end zone. The Rangers, in their khaki "buckskin" colored jerseys, walked desultory toward their sideline. That play had clinched it. Biltmore College had played Alabama tough, in Tuscaloosa no less. But in the end it just wasn't enough, and the Tide rolled to another win.

"Fuckin' 'Bama," Mullins grumbled. He watched the kickoff and the Hail Mary play, but Alabama knocked it away, and it was nowhere near the end zone anyway. Bang Dixon didn't have the arm for it.

Rather than watch the end of the game and the commentators drooling over the damned Tide the way they always did, Billy angrily punched the "off" button on his remote and then dropped it onto the confused pile of junk on his end table.

The lights were low, but not too low, and the ratio of parents and teachers to middle-school students was about one to two in the St. James gymnasium. Inoffensive pop music played from the DJ's table in the corner, the list of songs having been carefully vetted in advance. Orange and black streamers hung from the high ceiling, and smiling jack-o-lanterns peeked from the walls. A bowl of red punch, gallons of sweet tea, donuts, and cupcake tins full of carrots and celery sat atop a long table. Colored spotlights circled on the dance floor, which was mostly empty. A knot of sixth-grade boys stood awkwardly in black trousers and white shirts and ties. A knot of sixth-grade girls stood a dozen yards away, laughing and complimenting each other and breaking into dances where they stood. The pattern was repeated for the seventh graders, but amongst the eighth graders there were the "couples" holding hands and dancing. Those whose bodies got too close received a tap on the shoulder by a chaperone.

The St. James Middle School Dance was in full swing, and Anne was there with Emilia, while Dane had traveled to watch Janus and Dylan play in Hickory, about an hour away. Emilia, taller than her classmates, and taller than any of the boys in sixth grade, stood conspicuously aside with her friend Emma. Anne remembered those days. Not the dances because of course her mother never countenanced such a thing, but watching her friends enter into little innocent relationships and feeling undesired because she was so much taller than the boys she knew.

Anne stood with some of the other room mothers near the refreshments, watching the funny little play on the dance floor. Then the DJ mumbled something unintelligible into the microphone, and Michael Jackson's "Thriller" began. Someone nudged her shoulder. She turned and saw Tim Fletcher.

"Hey, I know this one!" he said, his face brighter than she had seen in a while.

"Hi, Tim. I thought Hannah was chaperoning tonight," Anne said pleasantly.

"No, she had to work late. Since she's gone to full time, she's always working."

"That's terrible. I hope they don't make her work this weekend."

"No, she's off for Halloween. We'll be taking Emma around the neighborhood. You and Dane are welcome if you want to bring Emilia over. I bet there's not a lot of trick-or-treaters way out on your farm."

Anne laughed, "No, no there aren't. Thanks for the invitation, but Emilia is going to spend the night at Jennifer's and go trick-or-treating with her."

"Okay then. Well, I know Hannah would have loved to see you. Care to dance?" And with that, he struck one of the "Thriller poses" like a zombie—head looking up, his hands shaped like crazy claws, and taking a couple of steps forward and back.

Anne laughed again.

Janus and Dylan climbed up onto the white St. Ambrose Sports bus, waving goodbye to their father who made his way to his pickup in the parking lot. The Hickory High School campus lot was clearing out quickly, the home team having been demolished by the Saints. The few folks hanging around were cleaning up, making sure there were no stragglers in the stadium, as the SAHS team got on the buses for the drive home.

"Hey! Dane Norris! Loved watching you play at BC!"

"Thanks. It was an honor to do so," Dane said, as the stranger approached.

"Could I get you to sign this football?"

"Sure thing. What do you want it to say?"

"It's for my son, Tank."

Dane signed and handed the football back, shook hands, and made it the rest of the way to his truck without further interruption. He climbed stiffly into the seat, removed the cap from the bottle of water in the console cupholder, and took a swig to wash down a pain pill. Then he started the big diesel engine and roared off toward I-40. He was tired.

Anne gazed through the windows over the pool, now closed and covered for the winter. Beyond the cast-iron fence on the other side of the "infinity" drop-off, she could see Janus, Dylan, and Dane standing around the side-by-side. Dane's truck was parked nearby, a canvas tarp in the back on which three rifles sat, their bolts pulled out. She watched as Janus got into the side-by-side with paper targets and a walkie talkie. Dylan reached for one of the rifles and she could hear Dane yelling at him, muffled through the glass but still distinct:

"... not to fucking touch that while Janus is downrange!"

Dylan backed away quickly from the rifles, his father's booming voice still terrifying after all.

Dane directed Janus out to place the fifty-yard target, then a hundred, and two hundred—three white targets on little metal holders, placed in a staggered line slightly downhill from the truck and back-stopped by the hill rising up to the high pasture. The horses were all in the barn, but Dane would drive around the pasture just to make sure there was nothing within range before he let the boys start firing.

An annual routine: Sighting in for deer season. The boys all pulling out their camouflage and bags of hunt-scent and getting ready to trundle off to what was, to Anne's mind, a glorified shooting gallery with pre-selected blinds and stands, a nice warm lodge, and whatever other manly pursuits went on up there. There was a time when Anne would have been invited and a time when she would have happily gone along. But that time was past, during her "wild days" in Kansas City. By the time that Dane had returned to Asheville, and the Norris family hunts had begun again, Anne was a settled mother, and the idea of following her husband into the woods to kill Bambi did not appeal to her.

Within a year of moving to North Carolina, she had gotten that awful call that her mother had only days to live. Anne immediately booked a flight to Chicago and rented a car to drive down to Gary. What she found shook her profoundly. Her mother, having been diagnosed with lung cancer, had ignored her doctors and just tried to pray for a miracle. The cancer had spread rapidly, and Anne's last sight of her was a gray-skinned, shrunken mess covered with tubes and surrounded by blinking lights.

There had been nothing beyond the few cold exchanges in the years between Anne's engagement and Maria's death. Cold exchanges at Christmas, cold exchanges upon the birth of children. Always referring to Dane as "that football player," and never, never retracting that horrible word: whore.

Within two days of Anne's arrival, her mother was dead and spoke not a word in those last hours. Anne was there as she received viaticum, barely able to take the tiny fragment of God pressed between her dry lips. With the exception of Anne's eldest sister, all the others seemed to have inherited her mother's coldness toward her. All were present and efficient and paraded their children through the room. Anne's father Janus—a quiet wreck of a man in the early stages of dementia—just blinked and nodded and watched as the star that he orbited flickered away into nothing.

Dane arrived with the kids, and the adolescent Maryanne became the center of preening amidst her aunts, as the brothers-in-law stood quietly in the corners of rooms, teasing football stories out of Dane. Nieces and nephews, familiar with the haunts of the old Gary house, found little corners to hide in and games to play. Anne stood in the gloom of rooms full of Polish icons, the Black Madonna everywhere, with the faded old smells of the rotting house washing her in memories.

The Anne that emerged from Gary, Indiana, was not the same Anne who had arrived days before. Her mother's death had punctured an old abscess of guilt that had been slowly brewing since she had left for Biltmore College twenty years earlier, and the bile and pus flooded through her. By the time Anne returned to Asheville, her mother buried in a razor-wire guarded cemetery filled with the corpses of generations of Poles and surrounded by decaying houses and murder, she had begun to reconstruct a little guilt-ridden version of herself, echoing her mother's piety and copying her devotions. She turned toward a rigid God and toward a faith that had been practiced coldly, precisely. As she did so, and as her oldest daughter grew into a young woman, the cycle repeated. Anne was shocked the first time that she thought of Maryanne as "that little whore." She had a moment of clarity, but it passed, and determined that Maryanne would not fall from the narrow path, Anne made it narrower. But of course, that was exactly the wrong thing to do, and as the war raged between her and her daughter, the rest of the family stood by, unable to stop it.

And then Maryanne's sudden departure marked another change. Looking agape at the wreckage, Anne suddenly understood. If only Maryanne's rebellion had been as innocent as her own. And now she was wracked by a double-guilt, trapped between her mother and her daughter, and her will broke. She turned to God now in helplessness and submission, and His peace began to wash over her. She became gentle, timid with Dylan, who carried the banner for his departed sister. Quiet with Dane, letting him have his way with the children, since, after all, he had been right about Maryanne. But resenting him for his calm approach to it all. She shed her tears and hoped and prayed for Maryanne and promised herself that, should her daughter return, she would never hear harsh words.

"BOOM!"

The first shot went off. As Anne came out of her reverie, she saw Dane resting his rifle on a stick stand, a wisp of smoke rising from the barrel, as Dylan looked through a spotting scope at the fifty-yard target. Dane pulled the bolt back and chambered another round.

The stadium lights cast their weird multidirectional shadows on the players who still stood on the field and who had traveled all the way to St. Francis High School of Charlotte to take on their archrival. Dylan Norris had the night of his life. He was unstoppable, and the Saints won their first-round playoff game.

Dylan high-fived Janus, pumped his fist in the air, and roared. This was what it meant, to stand victorious on the field of battle. The fans who had traveled were in the stands, singing and laughing. He could see his parents sitting with Emilia huddled under a shared blanket. He roared again.

No one foresaw the outcome of the Rangers' game, except perhaps for Coach Carter, who watched the seconds tick away and the Georgia Bulldogs go down to defeat. All around him, the Rangers' players leaped and jumped as if they'd just won the National Championship. For the first time in years, BC had beaten a top-ten team. Carter smiled.

Dylan: Got someplace we can go?

Sanders: Been thinking about our last convo?

Dylan: Yeah.

Sanders: Yeah. I've got a place.

The Yukon pulled into the Jiffy Stop, and the door opened. Brad jumped out and headed inside, his breath steaming in the cold mountain air. Saturday night at the Jiffy Stop was normally not much different from any night. But on this evening, Billy Mullins stood by the counter, and he could swear that, in the dome light of the big black SUV, he could see Dylan Norris in the driver's seat.

"Shit, Ronnie," Billy said. "I think that's the Norris kid out there."

Ronnie Turbell, the Jiffy Stop's usual night clerk, peered through the front window.

"Shit, I don't know how you know all them football players anyhow, Billy. They all look like one another to me."

"Ronnie, when you spend as much time as I do on the boards, you know every damn recruit. Course tellin' some of them black kids apart is a chore."

And that set Ronnie to laughing. Billy smiled at his own wit and lit a cigarette.

Ronnie settled down a bit and said, "You know you ain't supposed to do that here Billy."

"Fuck old Renfroe. He ain't gotta know. And besides, we're celebrating. Ain't every day you beat the 'Dogs."

Brad emerged from the bathroom hallway, and the two men stopped talking and just watched him as he rummaged about and came back with some chips, nuts, and water. Brad paid with cash, took his change, and left. The little bell rang as the door closed.

"That kid looked like a faggot . . . " Billy said, and that set Ronnie to laughing again.

Inside the SUV, the door closed, and Dylan backed out onto SR401.

"I think they recognized you in there, Dylan," Brad said.

"Huh?"

"Heard them while I was in the bathroom. Couple of racist fuckers joking about it."

"Well, fuck 'em," Dylan said, wheeling down the road toward Lake Juniper and the peninsula that held the Sanders' lake house.

Anne lay in bed alone. Dane had fallen asleep on the sofa downstairs after watching the Rangers pull off the incredible upset over Georgia. A bottle of bourbon and pain pills and there he was now, snoring away with his head on a green throw pillow and one leg off of the couch. She knew he would come and thump into bed later, waking her up and rolling to one side, letting the cold air of the house spill beneath the comforter.

Anne had not forgotten the admonition from Fr. MacMahon, and shortly after that confession had tried to "do something nice" for Dane, giving him a back rub as he watched the football game. He had said "that's nice," put one hand over hers, and had gone on with his eyes on the screen. There was this big wall between them now. Anne admitted to herself that it was pride in not initiating anything more physical from him. She wanted him to look at her now as he had when they were younger, wanted him to want her. She had never had to initiate sex and didn't really know how. But even if she had, she wouldn't.

There had been years when she was happy for the slow decay in their sex life. As her religious feelings and guilt surged in the wake of her mother's death, so her desire had lessened, and her concept of sex started to turn dirty around the edges. She took to heart the prohibition against contraception and had her implant removed, and when Dane went and got a vasectomy because he didn't "want any more kids," it seemed a slap in the face to her own compliance to the law. Maryanne's departure had put an end to what little love-making that they had done. By then, Dane didn't seem to mind. The booze, pills, and pain numbed him, and he went about jovially celibate as Anne breathed her sighs of relief.

And then the strange perimenopausal reawakening of her sexual self birthed this awful resentment of Dane. *If only*, she thought, *he just understood how hurtful the distance between us is.*

Dylan: Hey bro. We just beat Ridge. Going to the Semis next week.

Sanders: Congrats.

Dylan: Meet up tomorrow? Same place?

Sanders: I'm down.

Another Saturday night. Not as big a thrill, but now Kentucky was in the Rangers' rearview mirror, and they stood at six and four, four and two in the SEC, with only the chumps of Southern Tennessee State and Vanderbilt remaining. An 8-4 season, a bowl game, and momentum heading into the next year. A great recruiting class coming in. Hell, that Norris kid was an early grad, so he'd be able to get in on the bowl practices. With Richardson and the rest coming in the spring, it couldn't get much better for BC.

Billy was just getting in his pickup and turning on WBCT radio when he saw a big black Yukon rumble past the Jiffy Stop. Instinctively, he pulled out onto the road and followed it. He got close enough to see the big St. Ambrose fleur-de-lis logo on the back of the window before dropping away. He followed at a distance as SR401 began its long curve around the lake, splitting off little roads out to the various coves and ridges along the shoreline. Coming around a curve, Billy almost missed the Yukon's taillights as they disappeared along a gravel road, winking between the bare trunks and branches.

Billy knew just about every road here, and he knew the lake houses that were down that way. The big one on the end must be the Norris place. Still curious, Billy waited a few moments, then turned around and limped up the gravel road with just his fog lights on. Most everyone out here would have closed down for the season. There were always a few folks coming and going, but for the most part the summer people just relied on burglar alarms and the occasional daytime visit to ensure that their property was safe.

Billy came to the beginning of the paved driveway of the Norris house and eased down the hill. He stopped when he could see the driveway vacant and the house dark and reversed back up the hill. Making a turn in the dirt off of the gravel, he went back until he found the first drive down toward the lake. He got out of the truck and trotted down the hill until he could see the house. Nothing there. No cars, no lights.

Back up the hill, panting and out of breath. Why was he doing this? Well, because he was the World's Greatest Rangers Fan, and here was a future Ranger, and Billy wanted to know more. So back in the truck to the next driveway. Out of the door and down by the side of the gravel, and there it was, lights winking ahead, and the big black Yukon parked in front.

Wonder what that kid's doin' in there, he thought to himself.

But he had noticed the little camera under the eaves and had a new little nugget of information about Norris, and that was enough. So he toiled back up the hill and into his battered truck and slowly made his way back home.

There was no question that Dylan Norris was ready to move up to the next level. As the Saints rolled over Green Military Academy to secure a spot in the State Championship game, Dylan was unstoppable. Even his propensity for penalties seemed to have faded, and Coach Williams patted himself on the back for the dressing down he'd given Norris after the Madison County game. The kid was finally playing up to his potential.

Southern Tennessee State University was well paid to play the Rangers in Asheville, and it was the only good thing they took away from the game. Dominated in every aspect, the Rivermen of STSU never got on the board and gave up fifty-six points. With one game left, against historic rival Vanderbilt, the Rangers were announcing to the world that they were a program on the rise.

Dane, Dylan, and Janus had said goodbye to Anne first thing on Saturday morning and driven off to Deer Camp. Up along the winding Blue Ridge Parkway, Dane's big Ford climbed and climbed, Janus beside him and Dylan leaning at an angle in the backseat. The truck's big gooseneck bed was filled with the watertight bags of guns and gear.

They stopped at a diner where they met Dane's brother Roger and Roger's sons George and Rick. His daughter Carolyn had never liked hunting, and that would have spoiled the "boys trip" anyway.

Football season always interfered with hunting. They would have gotten their start on Friday night, but of course, the semifinal game took precedence, so Dylan and Janus wearily climbed into the truck and tried to rest aching muscles on the long drive.

In another couple of years, there would be a new generation coming along on the Norris hunt, as George's and Rick's kids grew to the age to handle a rifle. But for now, Janus was "the baby," and as they crowded around the diner's table, he was the subject of perpetual teasing and unwelcome advice. This year, they would make sure he would get his buck.

The diner food exhausted, Roger and his boys climbed into their own vehicle and Dane and his boys back in the Ford, and they took their little convoy off of the Blue Ridge and up the hills to the Hackman Private Preserve.

Anne's characterization of the land as a shooting gallery was not far off the mark. The Norrises had long given up hunting on public land and instead took the expedient course of reserving their annual weekend with Hackman. The Private Preserve had over a thousand acres of land that abutted to public lands and ensured a steady supply of both meat and trophy game.

The little convoy rolled through a big wooden ranch gate with "Hackman" spelled out over the top and drove up to a long log building with a forest green metal roof and stone chimneys projecting out here and there. The day had turned cold and foggy, and the orange lights of the lodge were warm and inviting. The Norrises' trucks pulled up in front of the lodge.

Dane and Roger got out and went to check in, and their sons began unloading luggage and carrying them in under the broad porch roof, then off to the lodge rooms. Janus and Dylan, George and Rick were paired up in bunk rooms, while Dane and Roger each had a big king bedroom. They stowed away clothes and made sure they were ready for the evening hunt, then returned to the lobby to wait for lunch.

Hackman himself made his appearance soon after. With a bald, pink head and a long flat mouth under heavily lidded eyes, he looked very little like a hunter or a rancher. In actuality, he looked a great deal like a pig. He was jolly and shrewd and very rich, and he graced his visitors with a brief appearance as a sort of regal honor bestowed upon them.

"Dane, Roger, so happy you could make it this year!"

The two brothers stood and went forward to greet him.

"Great to see you, Marty."

"Gonna have great hunts for you this year. Deer are lively. Got a hundred different stand locations and more video than you can believe. Only reason you won't get one is if you can't shoot straight."

"Sounds great. You having better luck evenings or mornings?"

"Season's only a day old. Don't know yet but typically early season evenings are better. Now, y'all get a good lunch and then we'll start runnin' you out to your stands."

"Great, Marty. Thanks."

With that, Hackman returned back through a door behind the reception desk, not to be seen again, at least by this set of guests. The Norrises had the run of the lodge, having bought it out for the weekend at twenty-five thousand dollars. The staff, used to serving and positioning a larger number of guests, was solicitous, and after a hearty lunch, the Norris family returned to their rooms, dressed in their blaze-orange camouflage, and congregated with rifles and backpacks outside the lodge.

Six UTVs pulled up, and the Norris men took their passenger seats and were whisked away toward their tree stands. The drivers split up, taking trails in all directions before stopping and pointing their passengers to the little tracks leading to the stands. Each guest was handed a walkie-talkie to contact the lodge for pickup. And then off into the trees by himself went Dylan with his 30-06 and binoculars. It didn't take him long to reach the tree stand. Up he went to settle himself in and wait for evening. He listened and watched, looking for any movement, peering upwind along the track. He was at the edge of a nice clearing, and everything was good except that his aching muscles made him shift around more than he would have liked.

The cool mist settled on his jacket and restricted the range he could see, and he sat watching as the sun sank lower. From far away to his left, he heard the crack of a gunshot. From far away to his right, another. Then another. He sat and waited, but no target presented itself, and as the sun sank out of sight, he pulled out his walkie talkie and called the lodge.

"Baby" Janus had his deer, a nice eight-point buck that he had killed cleanly. He posed with his father and the deer outside the lodge, finally taking a selfie with a big smile next to the deer's vacant eyes.

Dylan stomped by him.

"Nice little doe, Jane."

"Fuck you!" Janus replied, laughing.

Dane, Roger, George, and Rick settled into the lodge with bourbons and took their cigar breaks out under the eaves. It had been a good evening for George and Janus. The rest of the family would have to be up before dawn to try their luck in the morning hunt. Dylan went to his bunk and toggled his phone on and then browsed through texts and DMs and TikTok and Snapchat and Reddit. Finally he set his phone down and turned out the light.

Now, from a different stand, Dylan watched the sun coming up, breaking through a distant line of bare trees atop the ridge and shining down into the little valley. Light hit the field, and across from him, cautiously, does started emerging from the tree line and making their way toward him. His breathing was steady, the steam of his breath diffusing in his balaclava. He eased his rifle toward his shoulder moving smoothly and slowly. The does crept across the field, stopping here and there. He could hear their little grunting noises now.

A few moments more and there he was. The buck watched as the does came close to the tree line where the stand awaited.

Dylan held the scope to his eye. The buck took a step forward.

"BOOM!" The 30-06 split the air and echoed down the valley. The big buck jumped and spun and darted back into the far tree line.

"Fuck!" Dylan said. He was sure he'd gotten off a good shot.

He ejected the cartridge, ignoring the brass as it fell from the stand. Unhooking himself and shouldering his rifle with the bolt back and the chamber empty, he climbed down from the stand. At the base of the tree, he inserted another shell, slid the bolt in place, and checked to make sure that the safety was off. Then he started across the field with the rifle held ready and his finger on the trigger.

He reached the spot where the buck had turned and saw the spray of blood in the grass. Stepping forward slowly, Dylan couldn't miss the blood trail, and only ten feet into the trees, he saw the buck lying on its side.

Dylan approached slowly, his rifle ready, but the deer was dead. He stood over it, looking at its glossy black eyes.

"Didn't see that coming, did you fucker?" he said to the deer. And then he pulled out his walkie talkie and called the lodge.

Chapter 15

THE WAY IS WIDE AND EASY

Emilia was spending the night with Jennifer again, so Anne had the house all to herself. With the high school in-service holiday on the following morning, and the boys off hunting, it was a rare opportunity for Anne to think about nothing but herself. After Mass she had lounged about her home, enjoying the solitude.

Now at the end of the evening, she sat back on the leather sofa, her fourth glass of wine by her side, the empty bottle on the end table, reading glasses at the ready, and a Liane Moriarty book half finished. Her long pajamas were covered by a fleece blanket. The snap of late-November cold that was surely chilling her boys out in the woods was making its way into the poorly defended Norris house as well.

She had just removed the little Thanksgiving bookmark that Emilia had made her, settled the book in her lap, and was preparing to crack it open when Buddy and Jingles began barking and ran to the front of the house. She heard a car coming up the drive and stopping in the circle.

Who could it be at this hour? she thought to herself, but it was only eight o-clock. The change of time and the early-setting sun, along with the bottle of wine, confused her. For a brief second a voice said "Maryanne!" but then it was silent. She got up and walked to the door and looked out through the big glass pane at its side. There was a Honda Pilot lit up by the floodlights and a man getting out. The dogs had stopped barking, but their bodies wagged, and their claws skittered on the rug.

Anne opened the door, surprised, as the dogs rushed out to meet Tim Fletcher.

"Tim? What are you doing here?" Anne asked, suspiciously.

"I hope you don't mind. I had to get out of the house for a while and drove around. I saw the road up here and thought I'd come by and see you all."

"It's just me tonight," Anne said from the doorway, hearing the slur in her own voice. "The boys are out hunting."

Tim turned to go back to his car, saying "Okay, then," but his head was hung down, depressed. Then he stopped and said, "Can I come in anyway, just to sit for a while? I'm pretty low."

Anne hesitated a long moment, and then finally said "Sure" and opened the door wider. Tim walked in, and the dogs bounded after him.

He stood uneasily in the foyer, looking around.

"Haven't been here in a while. Since your party last year."

"Can I get you something to drink?"

"Just water. I'll be going soon, and I don't want to risk it. Last thing I need now is a DUI."

"Okay. Any particular water you like? We've got Perrier, San Pellegrino, Aqua Panna . . . "

"Just regular water is fine." They walked into the big living room where Anne's book was open on the end table, and she passed through to the butler's pantry and got a bottle out of the refrigerator. Tim was still standing in the living room. She walked over and handed him the bottle. As she did so, she became aware of her nipples, erect and pushing through the front of her silk pajama top. She looked up and saw that Tim had seen them as well. She blushed, handed him the bottle, and turned away as he lowered his head.

"Anne," he said, and hearing her own name suddenly felt different. His voice was low. Anne felt a tightness in her stomach and said "You better go" without turning around. She felt him move closer to her.

Saint Michael the Archangel, defend us in battle, be our defense . . . her inner voice began, but the well-remembered prayer was fumbled, and she began again. *Saint Michael the Archangel . .*

.

And then his hand was around her waist, rubbing over her stomach. An electric thrill ran through her. If she just didn't turn around . . .

Saint Michael the Archangel . . .

Tim's hands gently turned her to face him. He looked at her, his eyes wide and hurting. They moved downward to look at her lips. Her own eyes lowered to look at his.

And then they were kissing, passionately. His arms wrapped around her, hers around him. He released her lips to kiss her neck, one hand suddenly in the back of her hair. Hands on his back, rubbing, hands on her hips, hands moving up and down each other's bodies.

Oh God! This isn't happening. Saint Michael . . . but then he was sliding her top off and the cool air of the Norris house was on her breasts. He dropped his jacket on the floor, and her hands fumbled at his waist and lifted up his polo over his head, revealing the flat stomach with just the beginning of a belly.

He dropped to his knees, kissing between her breasts, down to her navel, and then his own hands found the waistband of her pajamas, hooked into her panties, and pulled them both down and off of her. She collapsed onto the couch, one hand feebly pushing his head away even as she opened her legs.

"Tim . . . Tim . . . " she panted, relaxing her hand from his hair as his tongue touched her.

One hand clutched the leather couch, her fingernails leaving traces in the soft leather. Her other hand rested on the inside of her own thigh. Her back arched. She threw her head back and finally moaned her release, her body shuddered and shaking. Tim raised his head up and looked at her, but her eyes were closed. They remained closed as she reached for his belt.

"I want you inside me," she said, fumbling with his belt until he undid it himself and dropped his pants. Her eyes still shut as he moved on top of her. His mouth closed over hers, and she returned the kiss passionately.

Her eyes remained closed as she felt him pushing against her and until she felt their infidelity slide in to press against her walls. Once, twice, three times he thrust. Her hands found his buttocks and grabbed them, attempting to pull him in further. And then he let out a guttural moan and collapsed onto her. Her legs wrapped around him. Her own body sinewed for a few moments longer, and then stilled. Her arms wrapped around his back until her hands met, and then they joined. In a detached way, her fingers felt her wedding and engagement bands. He stayed there panting on top of her. Finally, his weight became a burden. As he shrunk back out of her, she pushed him upward. Her eyes were unfocused, and the wine was suddenly too much. Her head swam.

Tim sat and sank into the leather couch as Anne jumped up, grabbed her pajama pants, and ran for the bathroom. Through the door of the guest toilet, he could hear her throwing up, then heard a great sob, silence, and vomiting again. He stayed listening to the cycle repeat. Finally he pulled his trousers up from where they were still around his ankles. He had never even removed his shoes. He found his polo shirt and pulled it back on. Then he went to the bathroom door and tapped.

He could hear Anne inside sobbing.

"Anne?" he said, his faced pressed up next to the door. "Are you okay?"

No response, except the sobbing.

He knocked twice more and said her name. But she did not reply.

"Uh . . . I guess I'm gonna go," he said. And when there was still no answer, he found his jacket, pulled it on, and leaned down to pick up the water bottle that had fallen to the floor next to a book and the little bookmark with a row of orange pumpkins and the word "THANKS." As he rose up, he caught the eyes of Buddy and Jingles sitting on their haunches with their tails wagging, bidding him goodbye. He walked past them, patting their heads, and slipped out the door to his SUV.

The spinning stopped, and Anne rested her cheek against the toilet seat. She was still breathing heavily. She spit into the toilet, then flushed it, lifting up her head. She rose until she was sitting on the toilet, her elbows on her knees, leaning over with her hands over her face. She peed into the bowl, wiped herself and got unsteadily to her feet. Grabbing her pajama pants and her top, she ran through the butler's pantry, kitchen, and to her bathroom. She threw the shower's lever, the "rainforest" shower heads erupting from all around the tiled expanse, the tankless water heater activating and then the shower filling the room with steam. She harshly pulled her wedding and engagement rings from her finger and entered the glass walls. Anne lay in the center of the tile, the water coursing over her from all angles. Then she was scrubbing herself, shampooing, scrubbing again, standing under the showerheads, lying on the shower floor. Her tears mingled with the water running down the drain. Both dogs came and lay down on the bathmat in front of the shower door.

Whore! her mother's voice echoed in her head.

Finally, red-eyed, she shut the water off and stepped out. Around her were the little pampering luxuries of her bath. A heated rack where her towel and bathrobe waited. A cushioned seat before her vanity. Shining bucket for her makeup brushes. Hand towels monogramed with an "N" for Norris.

These were the luxuries of a faithfully married woman. They were not hers. She walked to the sink, carefully picked up her wedding ring, and slipped it over her finger. Then the same with her engagement ring. She toweled herself off, feeling the coolness of the house air for the first time. Then she strode out of the bathroom into Dane's closet. She pulled one of his leather belts from its hook, went back to her bathroom, and sat on the little cushioned stool, looking at herself in the vanity mirror.

"Oh my God, I am heartily sorry . . . "

[WHACK!] The leather belt flew across her shoulder and slapped against her back. The stinging pain was intense.

". . . for having offended you . . . "

[WHACK!]

". . . and I detest all my sins. . . "

[WHACK!]

". . . because of your just punishment . . . "

[WHACK!]

". . . but most of all because they offend You O Lord. . . "

[WHACK!]

She repositioned herself on the stool, opening her legs up and exposing her inner thighs.

". . . who is all good . . . "

[WHACK!] The leather belt slapped her thigh, as close as she could get to her vagina without hitting it. A red welt was immediately raised.

". . . and worthy of all my love . . . . " As she said this, the sobbing started again.

[WHACK!]

"I firmly resolve . . . "

[WHACK!]

". . . with the help of your grace . . . "

[WHACK!]

". . . to sin no more . . ."

[WHACK!]

". . . and to avoid all near occasion of sin."

[WHACK!]

"Amen."

And she slid off of the stool and lay on the tile. Her back ached and stung. Her inner thigh ached and stung.

Panic set in a little later. She dressed in the roughest pajamas she could and dashed about the house, trying to undo what she had done. She wiped the little sticky puddle from the couch and then found the cleaner and shined the cushions, trying to cover the thin gouges her fingernails had made on the front of one. She picked up her book and thrust the bookmark in between two random pages and placed it on her nightstand. The wine bottle was discarded, the wine glass placed in the sink. Then Anne went downstairs to the security closet and made sure that the cameras hadn't been recording inside or outside. Sure enough, all the screens were off. Back upstairs to throw her pajamas and panties and fleece blanket into the washer and start the cycle.

But she continued rushing from one room to another, looking for evidence and trying to delay that moment of stillness when it would all rush back on her.

Whore!

Finally she could delay no longer. She lay down in her bed, the sting of her inner thigh still unable to take away the feeling of another man inside her.

It was time-honored tradition for Asheville's high schools to have an in-service day on the Monday following the opening of deer season, and St. Ambrose High School of course followed suit. Generations of North Carolina gentlemen took to the woods and took their leisure on their way back, but this privilege was denied to the unfortunate teachers and administrators who were bound to their desks.

Vice Principal Angela Barstowe opened her email inbox. She scanned through the first few messages, deleting and flagging for reply. Then she got to a message with a subject line that said "Video of Last Week's Saints." The sender was a string of numbers at an unrecognized domain, and though Barstowe was usually pretty cautious about opening attachments, she simply thought this was more footage of the SAHS semifinal win, and she clicked to open the link.

A grayscale image filled the screen. No sound. Fisheye footage from a nanny-cam. Dylan Norris' bare chest. Closer to the camera, Brad Sanders' face.

"Oh dear Lord!" Angela said, placing a hand over her mouth and mousing to the pause button as quickly as she could. She closed the video window and saw in her inbox that the next several messages were all from the same email address. She sat there for a moment, breathing heavily. Then she got up and walked to the office next to her.

"Hubert," she said, and Principal Rollins looked up. "You, uh . . . you're going to have to see this."

Rollins stood up and followed Angela into her office, then behind her desk. She clicked on the attachment. He blinked and looked at the screen and said: "Close it. Has anyone else seen this? Who did it come from?"

"I don't know the address. I probably shouldn't have opened it. There are several more. I haven't looked at them."

"Shit."

"What do we do?" she asked, as he walked back from her desk and closed the glass door to her office, then sat down in the chair across from her and rubbed his palms over his eyebrows and up his forehead.

"Angela, I just don't know. I would say call our counsel, but that's Roger Norris."

"We have multiple problems here," she said. "I guess we need to get IT in here to figure out where these came from. Or is that a police matter? How old are Dylan and Brad?"

"I think they're both eighteen," Rollins answered.

"Well thank God we don't have some sort of underage thing going on here. But I think we need to get the police involved. I don't like even having this on my computer."

"You're right. Need to do everything above board, but we can't let this get out at all. Whoever sent it to us obviously wants us to react. There are privacy issues, maybe blackmail. Shit, I don't know. Call the police. Then call the diocese and find out if they have any other lawyers to refer to us."

Dane's big Ford pulled around the house, and he pushed the button to open the garage door. It rolled up and he rolled in, putting it in park. Beside him, Janus opened his door and jumped out, while Dylan did the same behind him. Dane swung his legs to the side and creakily exited the truck and stretched his tired shoulders. Outside the endless drizzle drifted down, and little puddles of water formed under the truck.

"Get all the stuff, won't you boys?" he asked, and started walking toward the door into the rec room. Anne's Land Rover was gone, but that was not a surprise. She would probably be picking up Emilia about this time.

Inside the house was quiet. He made his way over to the bar and poured a bourbon over ice, reached into his pocket, grabbed the pill bottle, shook a pill into his hand, and washed it down with the bourbon. Then he stretched himself out on the couch and closed his eyes. Dylan and Janus bustled by, lugging their duffels and Dane's up the stairs, then coming back for more until all the suitcases were upstairs and the guns and gear were piled by the truck in the garage.

"Gonna take mine to the range this week, Dad," Dylan said. "I think I need to sight it in again."

"Okay," Dane said, hearing Dylan heading out and the garage door closing.

Anne waited in the pickup line, her windshield wipers going back and forth. Two cars ahead was the Honda Pilot. Anne stared ahead, looking at nothing. Her hands moved along the little beads on the back of her steering wheel.

"Hail Mary, full of grace . . . . Hail Mary, full of grace . . . ."

She couldn't concentrate, but she repeated the prayer over and over. Her throat was tight. Then the line moved forward, and she was under the porte-cochere. The door opened, and Emilia jumped in, happy and smiling, letting her backpack slide to the floor as she closed the door behind her. As Anne began pulling away, Emilia looked at her and said: "Mommy! What's wrong!?"

Anne pulled to the side, into a fire lane, and put the SUV in park. She covered her eyes with her hands and cried. Emilia flung off her seat belt and wrapped her arms around her mother, saying "What's wrong, what's wrong?"

Her daughter's panic steadied her, and she pulled her hands down, wiping her eyes as she did.

"I'm sorry, honey. I'm sorry for scaring you. I just . . . had a bad night. I'm really emotional lately. It's something that happens when you get older."

Emilia looked back at her unconvinced.

"No, really. I'm fine. Everybody's fine. Nothing happened to anyone. I'm just not feeling well, and I'm very tired. Now, tell me about your sleepover. Did you have fun?" and she put the Land Rover in gear and pulled away.

Anne pulled into the garage and saw Dane's truck standing in a puddle of rainwater. She shut the garage door behind her, closed her eyes, and silently prayed:

Jesus, help me.

Beside her, Emilia tumbled out of the Land Rover with her overstuffed backpack and went hurtling into the house. Anne gathered herself together, grabbed her purse, and made her way in.

Thank you! She thought, as she saw Dane stretched out asleep on the couch. Upstairs, Emilia was off to her room and her shining screen, Dylan was gone, who knows where. Janus came bursting out of his room, full of excitement over his first buck. His disappointment was evident when he saw the lack of enthusiasm in his mother.

"That's great, honey. And I can't wait to see the deer head when you've had it stuffed. But I've got a terrible headache, and I just need to lie down."

She made her way to her bedroom, took off her shoes, and climbed under the covers. Outside the rain dripped off of the eaves and ran down the chains to the stone gutters below. Emilia came in sometime later and asked about supper.

"Can you make it for your dad and brother? I'm really tired, and I just want to rest."

"Okay, Mom."

Sometime in the night Dane came in and lay with his back to her and began snoring almost immediately.

She lay there awake, feeling trapped. She had nowhere to go. She had no family in town. She had betrayed one of her best friends, and when the others found out, she would be outcast. Her house was cold and an affront, a constant reminder.

She knew where she should go. The next morning she should drop off Emilia and walk right into St. James and ask to see Fr. MacMahon, and she should unburden her soul of this mortal sin. But the same voice that yelled *whore!* now whispered:

You, with your praying and kneeling and rosaries and confessions. Look at you. Hypocrite! Betrayer! You aren't worthy of God's mercy. It's all been an act with you. How is another confession going to be any different than the hundreds you've been to before? Always sinning again until your sins get bigger and bigger. There is no forgiveness for you. You liked it! And you would do it again if you had the chance. You will do it again. Confession would be a lie.

No! she thought, and the tears slipped from her eyes. But she knew that tomorrow she would drive away from St. James and find somewhere to go so that she didn't have to go home.

Dane was awakened by his mobile phone ringing on the bedstand charger beside him. He opened his eyes and looked around. Yesterday's gloomy day was replaced by a bright sunny morning that shone through the windows onto the bed. Anne was already gone.

Dane picked up the phone and looked at the screen: ROGER NORRIS, it said. He pushed the little button and held the phone up to his ear.

"What's going on, Rog?"

"I'm not sure yet, Dane. Maybe nothing serious, but I think there may be trouble for either Janus or Dylan."

That got Dane's attention, and he sat up in bed.

"Okay, what's happening?"

"I got into the office this morning and found out that Rollins over at St. Ambrose had called in Arnold Hathaway to consult on something. Hathaway's a lawyer that the diocese has used before, but I'm on retainer at St. Ambrose, so I called in and asked why they hadn't contacted me. All they would give me is that it's a conflict of interest. So I think we can safely assume that it has something to do with one of your boys."

"Okay, okay. Well they were fine yesterday. Maybe . . . maybe someone was making threats or something."

"Doesn't seem likely to me. My read is that one of them is in some kind of trouble. Can't think of any other reason they wouldn't want me involved."

"So what should I do?"

"Just hold tight. I didn't want you to get blindsided later. I'll keep working on it and see what I can find out."

Dylan walked into the little conference room to find Principal Rollins, Vice Principal Barstowe, Fr. Dixon, and another suited man that he did not recognize. Their expressions were stern.

"What did I do?" Dylan joked, a big smile on his face as he sat down in the chair that Rollins pointed to. The suited man closed the door to the conference room.

"Dylan, I'm sorry to tell you that you are suspended as of now from both the school and any school-related activities. And yes, this includes football." Principal Rollins was firm.

Dylan's mouth dropped open.

"What? Why? What?"

"You signed a code of conduct when you enrolled here, Dylan, and signed it again each year," Barstowe said. "We have become aware that you have engaged in intercourse with another student. We have evidence. Video evidence."

"How'd you get a video?" Dylan asked, stunned, and realized his mistake, but also realized that it didn't matter. The serious faces across from him were not bluffing. He spun back through his encounters.

Could it be Wendy? What about Melanie, she lived on her phone. It couldn't be . . . OH FUCK.

Dylan sat stunned, and then the implications started.

"But . . . Friday . . . it's the State Championship! Tell me I'm not suspended for that. It's just this week, right? I mean, just until Thanksgiving."

"I'm afraid, Dylan, that it is at least through this week, and possibly longer. And, no, you won't be playing in the State Championship."

Dylan took the blow, closed his eyes, and when he opened them said: "You're going to regret that, you know. But whatever. Can I go now?"

"Don't make threats, Dylan," Principal Rollins said.

"I'm not making threats. I'm done with this place. You needed me more than I needed you. Later."

He walked out, pushing through the doors angrily, and headed to the back entrance toward his SUV.

When he got home, his mother was gone, and his father was watching TV in the rec room. Dane looked up as his son came in through the patio doors.

"Dylan? What's going on? Why are you home?"

"Dad . . . shit. I got suspended."

"Suspended! What did you do? Did you use drugs? Did they catch you in a drug test? How could you be so fucking stupid!?"

"It wasn't drugs, okay."

Dane calmed down and looked at his son.

"Then . . . what?"

"They . . . uh . . . caught me having sex. It's against the fucking code of conduct, and so they suspended me."

Dane breathed a great sigh of relief and laughed aloud.

"Ha! Oh shit! Ha! You had me worried. Hold on . . . what about State?"

"No State. They're not gonna let me play."

"Well, that's bullshit. We'll see about that. You know how much money I give to that fucking school? Suspend you before State?!" Dane surged up from the sofa and looked around for his phone.

"Let it go, Dad. I don't want to play anyway."

Dane stopped and looked suspiciously at his son.

"What!?"

"I'm serious. I'm done. Even if they would let me play, I'm not gonna do it. In another month I'll be in college. If they don't want me because of some stupid thing that everybody does, then so be it. I'll finish out my classes and move on."

"I'm calling Roger," Dane said, as Dylan walked up the stairs.

Anne sat at the coffee shop in the corner and looked at the bright blue sky behind the last few red and orange leaves, a brisk wind tossing them about and fluttering one from the tree every now and then. She drank water and tea and tried to shut out the world. Then her phone buzzed and there was "DANE" on the screen. Her heart sank. She considered skipping the call but reached out and answered.

"Hello?" she said.

"Hi honey. Listen, where are you? Can you come home?"

Oh God! A chill ran through her. *Oh God not one of her children!* The cumulative weight of worry from the long summer of death fell upon her in an awful sense of foreboding.

"Dane, what is it? What is it?" she gasped, and a couple of other customers looked over at her.

"It's okay. It's okay. Everyone is fine. Just something serious we need to talk about."

Anne searched his voice to see if he . . . knew. But it wasn't that. She could feel it.

"Okay. I'm just getting coffee. I'll be there in a half hour."

She hung up, left a tip on the table, and walked out to her car.

"Suspended!" Anne gasped, looking across the kitchen table at Dane and Dylan, who sat next to each other. The same suspicions that had gripped Dane gripped her as well, and her anger rose, submerging her guilt and pain immediately.

"Suspended! Was it drugs?" her face was hard.

"No, Mom. It wasn't drugs."

"It was sex, honey. They caught him having sex." Dane's voice was steady.

"Sex? Sex? With whom?"

"It doesn't matter, honey," Dane said. "The point is, he's going to have a suspension, miss the State game, but that's it. He can graduate, and this will just be a bad memory."

"What! A bad memory? Who are you having sex with, Dylan?"

"It doesn't matter. You don't know her."

"Try me. I bet I know the little whore," and with that statement, Anne was suddenly called back to her own sins. And her hand went to her mouth, and she bowed her head.

"Honey, this is embarrassing. No kid wants to talk about this with their mother. Dylan's a young man. He's gonna be off in college soon. He's going to stay out of trouble until he graduates. Aren't you?"

"Sure. I won't see her again. I'm on the straight and narrow."

Anne whimpered: "Go to confession, Dylan. Please? For me."

Dylan looked for a moment like he was going to refuse but then said "okay," and he pushed his chair out and made his way out of the room. Dane sat looking at his wife, who wouldn't look up.

"It's okay, honey," and he got up and went around the table and put his arms around his wife. Anne remained seated, and her tears spilled out as she sobbed.

"I know you're thinking of Maryanne," Dane said, and this elicited another sob. "It's not the same. So Dylan had sex. We have to know they're doing it. It's not like we were virgins when we got married. Just try to cut him some slack, okay? And don't take it so hard."

Anne nodded her head as if she understood, and he released his arms and stood up.

Monty Sanders and Myra Phillips-Sanders drove together to campus on most days. They lived on Sunset Mountain in a dark brick cottage crowded on the steep side of a hill with just barely enough space for their three cars but with a beautiful view of the valley from the upstairs bedroom windows, and a deep, peaceful stillness that came from this old neighborhood. As Monty and Myra walked in through the front door, throwing their satchels on the hall table, they saw Brad standing with his hands in his pockets, wearing his St. Ambrose uniform.

"How are you, Brad?" his father asked. "You look like you're waiting for us."

"I am."

"Okay, out with it," Myra said.

"I got suspended today."

"What for?"

"For being gay."

"What!?" both of his parents exclaimed, their bile rising immediately.

"Well, technically it's for a violation of the code of conduct. They caught me having sex with another guy."

Monty spoke calmly and precisely.

"Explain to me how they caught you having sex."

"That I don't know, except they've got a video. I don't know from where or when."

"That's illegal. Monty, call our lawyer. We'll see about this."

Principal Rollins and Arnold Hathaway, Esq. sat across the table from Monty, Myra, and their lawyer, Donald Meese.

"I can assure you, Dr. Sanders . . . "

"It's PHILLIPS-SANDERS, Mr. Hathaway."

"Yes, I'm sorry Dr. Phillips-Sanders. I apologize. I assure you, though, that from the moment the video was emailed to the school, this case has been treated with discretion and appropriate legal actions."

"You should have notified us right away. It's our right."

"You have to understand, Dr. Phillips-Sanders, that it appeared to be two consenting legal adults. The circumstances in which the video was sent to the school were of concern, and so the appropriate action was to involve the authorities."

"So you sent a video of our son having sex to the police."

"It is important to determine, if possible, whether there is any criminal action involved in the video itself. From what little the school saw of it, it does not appear that the participants were aware they were being filmed."

"Where was it filmed?"

Principal Rollins answered, glancing over at Hathaway.

"We don't know. It appeared to be at a home. Dr. Phillips-Sanders, I think it would be appropriate if your attorney were to contact the police, as you, or your son, may be of assistance in identifying the location. Then perhaps you can help determine who would want to send this video and why."

Monty Sanders spoke up: "You can be assured that we will do so, Mr. Rollins. Now, as to the matter of the suspension. It is absurd that you would stigmatize our son, just because he is gay. There is no question at all that teenagers regularly engage in sex, even at St. Ambrose, and it's also clear that you are treating him differently because of his orientation."

"That is not at all the case, Dr. Sanders. The code of conduct is very clear, and the same suspension would be handed down regardless of the, uh, orientation of the participants."

"Well, we would like to see evidence of that. We would appreciate it if you could produce records showing similar suspensions for students engaging in heterosexual activity."

"We are, of course, not at liberty to disclose such private matters," Hathaway answered.

"We'll see about that," Monty replied, and stood up. "We will speak to the police now, and then we'll see about the suspension."

There was a knock at Dylan's door. "It's Jane," said a voice from the other side. It was late. Dane had picked up Janus from practice and must certainly have told him that Dylan was suspended.

He got up and opened the door. Janus pushed through. Dylan sat back down on the bed.

"What the fuck, Dylan?"

"You know it. I'm sure Dad told you."

"Yeah, but not what for."

"I got caught on video fucking a girl."

"Shit!" Janus laughed, "Who?"

"That's the thing, I don't know which one."

"Aw, Dylan!" his brother grinned.

"Now get out of here you little pussy, and don't get caught like I did. When you ever do fuck somebody . . ."

Janus grinned and was closing the door when Dylan stopped him, "Hey . . . uh . . . did you notice anyone else that wasn't there in the afternoon?"

"Nah, bro. Didn't notice anyone else."

The Madison County sheriffs rolled up to the front of the Sanders' lake house. The place was a ruin. Not a large house to begin with, but they could see from the gravel drive that the damage was extensive. The front door was wide open. Wires hung from under the eaves where a camera had once been. The AC unit on the side of the house was partially dismantled, the coil ripped out. The deputies proceeded cautiously, two into the front of the house while another two circled to the back to where stairs descended from a deck that covered a little storage area on the bottom story built into the hill. The doors were open here, too.

Inside, the television was gone. The refrigerator was opened and had been visited by animals. Drawers had been emptied onto the floor, cushions tossed aside, and more loose wires showed where cameras had been ripped down. In a little closet, the rack that had once held the security system was empty.

Dane walked into his bedroom and saw the bed empty. It was late. Anne was usually in bed much earlier. He walked around the house, peeking through doors, and finally saw Maryanne's door open. Inside, his wife was curled up under Maryanne's comforter. He pulled the door closed and went back to their room.

Thanksgiving was cold and brisk, and though it started out with sunny, clear skies, a front was moving through from the mountains, bringing rain, and the evening turned cloudy.

For Anne and Dane, it was a cheerless Thanksgiving spent at Roger Norris' house, crammed in among all the nieces and nephews and wives and cousins. Anne was quiet and withdrawn, despite her sister-in-law Sarah's best efforts to draw her out. Dane had too much bourbon. Dylan was overly boisterous. Roger looked concerned but did not explain why. Janus relived his deer hunting glories with his cousins George and Richard. Emilia laughed and giggled and stared at glowing screens with her second cousins, who were closer to her age, and won one of the wishbones after dinner. Football was watched by some and ignored by others. Finally the turkeys were revealed, and the buffet line formed and the twenty-odd people found seats where they could.

Dane and Anne sat at the big dining room table, Sarah giving Roger a side-eyed glance as Anne poured her third glass of wine and Dane returned to the table with yet another bourbon on the rocks. George and Richard and Carolyn made up the rest of the table with their spouses, and all felt the strange chill.

At the end of the evening, Dane, Anne, and their kids piled back in the Escalade for the drive to the farm. At Roger's insistence, Anne handed the keys to Dylan, and then Roger and Sarah watched as the Cadillac's taillights vanished down the driveway.

Transcript: The *Hopper & Howe Show*

Hopper: Hi, welcome back to the Hopper & Howe Show, *coming to you live from the Cox Convenience Studios. We hope you had a great Thanksgiving.*

Howe: I certainly did, Jason. The old tryptophan did its work on me.

Hopper: A little too much turkey for me too, Mark. During the break, we were talking about stuffing recipes.

Howe: Cornbread does not belong in stuffing.

Hopper: That's where you are so very, very wrong, Mark. Anyway, I'm sure the listening audience has more things on their mind, like tonight's matchup between the St. Ambrose Saints and the Yellowjackets of Gastonia.

Howe: This should be a great contest, Jason. Willy Williams of St. Ambrose has got his team firing on all cylinders. They've just been a juggernaut, and all season long no one has figured out how to stop them.

Hopper: Okay, well, let's take some calls. As always, or almost always, we've got Ranger Bill on the line. Morning Ranger Bill. Get enough turkey?

Ranger Bill: I'm gonna just get right to it, Hopper. I just found out that Dylan Norris has been suspended. He ain't gonna play tonight.

Hopper: Hmmm . . . that's . . . interesting news, Ranger Bill. I haven't heard anything about that.

Howe: Me neither, Ranger Bill. We'll check into it though. As you know, there isn't really a roster report for high school. I'd imagine we'd have heard about it though if Norris wasn't going to play.

Ranger Bill: Well, you heard it from me. You can count on it. Norris is out.

Chapter 16

SINS OF THE FATHERS

Dane Norris made the long, long drive to Raleigh himself. Janus was on the team bus, of course. Dylan had refused to go, and when Anne had said that she didn't want to go if Dylan wasn't playing, Emilia had said she was staying as well. He suspected that his wife was remaining at home to keep an eye on Dylan, which he had to admit was not a bad idea.

So he rumbled along alone, driving the Mercedes instead of the big Ford, taking the route through Hickory on I-40. He had to stop fairly frequently to ease the stiffness out of his legs and shoulders, take a pain pill, and walk around. He was a little resentful at his wife; if she had driven, then he could have been more liberal with the pills. She was really overdoing the Dylan suspension, too, but he supposed it was her way of dealing with it. She just expected too much from their kids, and particularly their kids nowadays. The world was changing, and if any of them were able to cling to just being decent people, he'd be happy with it.

But not Anne. It was all more real to her. The salvation thing.

Dane pulled into a Cracker Barrel for a late lunch or early dinner and enjoyed the anonymity of being in the middle of the state, where the Saints shirt peeking out from under his coat didn't elicit the same recognition, and he was just another large overweight man shuffling around.

Back on the road through traffic so light that it implied all the drivers were home sleeping off their turkey and then into the madness of Raleigh itself. He followed his GPS to the Hilton close to the stadium, pulled up to the valet, and got his overnight bag out of the trunk. Checked in and with an hour to spare, he had a couple of drinks in the lobby bar before hailing a cab and riding to the stadium.

He found his seat a little apart from the other Saints fans who had made the long drive on the day after Thanksgiving. He didn't want to answer questions when Dylan wasn't on the field, but he couldn't avoid it. After repeating "It's a private matter" for the fifth time, he got up and loitered around the concession stand until the game started.

The Saints almost pulled it off, even without their star player. But they gave up a late touchdown in the fourth quarter and were unable to move the ball at the end. The Gastonia Yellowjackets celebrated on the field and hoisted the big trophy, while the Saints walked, dejected, back to their sideline. Janus had not gotten any playing time. He stood with his clean, fresh uniform among his teammates, and suddenly Dane was embarrassed by Dylan, embarrassed that his son had so callously turned his back on his team. He waited to say a few words to Janus, who would go to stay at his team's hotel, and then Dane took a cab back to the Hilton and found his way back to the bar.

Dane woke up late, requested a delayed checkout, lounged about taking his time, and finally got on the road in the afternoon. He flipped through the satellite radio channels until he found the broadcast of the Biltmore/Vanderbilt game. The last game of the season, and the exclamation point on the Rangers' return to providence. Dane smiled as he headed back west under the looming clouds, the Mercedes spitting up mist from its tires and the windshield wipers making him drowsy. He had to stop more often and took a few more chances with his pills than he would have liked, but the Rangers woke him up with a dominating first half. Vanderbilt couldn't figure out the offense and couldn't move on the defense.

At halftime, Dane stopped for dinner at another Cracker Barrel. He ate a long, relaxed meal and made it out to his car as the sun sank below the cloud bank, casting a red gleam across the slick roads. Before he reached the interstate on-ramp, he knew of the sudden shift in fortunes. Vanderbilt had run back the opening kick for a touchdown. On the ensuing kickoff, Biltmore had fumbled, and the Commodores recovered in the end zone for another touchdown. Then a "pick six" on the Rangers' next drive, and the game was knotted at twenty-one all.

Bang Dixon suddenly couldn't hit a receiver. Vanderbilt stacked the line and got the ball back with great field position. They exchanged punts with the Rangers. Back and forth the ball went, neither team able to get in the end zone. And then, with no time left on the clock, the Vanderbilt Commodores kicked a game-winning field goal from fifty-four yards. The hated rivals had done it again.

His blood pressure up, and his knees aching, Dane reached into the center console and found his pill bottle and shook a couple into his mouth. Holding the steering wheel with his leg, he closed the pill bottle and dropped it back into the console, and as he did so, the Mercedes drifted out of its lane. Dane looked up and saw what was happening and quickly corrected, but a moment later he saw blue lights fire up behind him.

Shit, he thought, as he pulled onto the shoulder.

It was an eternity before the state trooper exited his cruiser and ambled toward the driver's window. Dane had his license, registration, and insurance in his hand. The trooper stopped just behind the driver's window.

"License and registration," he asked. Dane handed them out.

"Do you know why I stopped you?" the trooper asked, looking down at the license.

"Yes, Officer," Dane replied. "I swerved out of my lane."

Coming forward, the trooper leaned down and looked closely at Dane, before saying: "Dane Norris. I was at that Georgia game. Hell of day."

"It sure was, Officer."

"Where are you coming from, Mr. Norris?"

"Raleigh. I was there for the high school playoff. My son's on the team."

"Yeah. How did they do?"

"Lost."

"Sorry to hear that. You a little tired from staying up late?"

"A little bit. But I just took my eyes off the road for a minute, Officer."

The trooper was silent for a minute, looked down at the license again, and then handed it back to Dane along with the insurance and registration.

"If you get too tired, you better pull off and get some rest. I'd hate to have to pull Dane Norris out of a wreck. Have a good day," and he turned to walk back to his cruiser.

"Thanks!" Dane said out the window, and breathed a sigh of relief as he put the insurance and registration back in the glovebox and his license back in his wallet. The cruiser sat behind him until he pulled away, and he watched the flashing lights fade behind him as he got back on the road.

Dane drove along in silence, his eyes glued to the highway. By the time he reached his garage, the sun was down. He pulled in and made his way through the rec room, stopping at the bar for a drink and a pill. He could hear Janus and Dylan yelling from the video room, taking out their frustrations regarding both the Saints' and the Rangers' losses by burying themselves in a shoot-em-up game. He made his way upstairs to find Emilia in her room looking at her tablet. The big king bed in his bedroom was empty, and the door to Maryanne's room was closed.

Dane awoke and rubbed his eyes. It was late. He could hear someone in the kitchen banging pots and pans around, and when he padded in, there was Emilia cooking her scrambled eggs. The little basket on the counter indicated that they were fresh from the coop.

"Morning, Daddy," Emilia said.

"Where's your mom?"

"She said she wanted to go to early Mass and that we should all go in at noon."

"Huh. Okay, well, better start getting ready then."

Anne drove around for a while before making her way to the coffee shop. She hadn't gone to confession yesterday and couldn't bring herself to go to Mass today. But she also couldn't bear the questions from her family. So here she was, in a corner of the shop, eyes far away.

GoRangers Message Board

SNAKEBIT

RangerBill. Sunday, 10:24 AM

Theirs no excuse for losing to Vanderbilt. None at all. This one has to get blamed squarely on Carter. Questions:

1. How does a team leading by 21 at the half unable to put up points in the second half.
2. How does a team that can't score in the first half able to win in the second?

Answers:

1. Because they didnt change the gameplan and the Commodes were able to figure out what they did in the first and make adjustments.
2. Because the Commodes capitalized on mistakes.

The Rangers gave them that game. Were still 7-5 and going to a bowl but now Vandy can claim another win.

Billy Mullins hit the button and posted. Then he logged out of his RangerBill account and logged back in as "GoRngers1988," liked the post, commented favorably. Then he logged out of GoRngers1988 and logged in as "RangerDeRanger4," liked and commented, logged out, and logged back in as RangerBill to comment on his own comments. Satisfied at his morning's labor, he sat back and contemplated adding another username. But that would mean another fifteen bucks on top of the forty-five he was already spending. So he put that idea away.

Dane's phone rang, again waking him up. And again it was Roger.

"Morning Rog. Got any more great news for me?"

"Well, no. Not really. I found out a little more about Dylan's . . . situation. You want to come in town to my office?"

Dane was silent for a moment.

"You sound serious, Rog. I think you'd better just tell me now."

"Okay . . . well . . . they do have a video of the . . . intercourse. Dane, it's with another guy."

"The fuck it is!" Dane blurted.

"I think we'd better prepare for this, Dane. We need to think about implications."

"Where'd the fucking video come from? Who's doing this?"

"Well, that's in the police's hands, but what I know right now is that it was security camera footage that was stolen from the other kid's house. Here's another strange thing. They had a lake house right by yours, just up the road from you."

"Alright. Hold tight Roger. I'll come into your office. Give me an hour or so."

He hung up, and suddenly a memory surfaced, one that he had long forgotten.

In the late 1970s, St. James Catholic School didn't have enough kids to field a football team, so the talented Catholic boys instead went to their zoned public school to develop their skills, and for Dane Norris, that was Asheville Central Junior High. It had taken Dane a long time to convince his father to join him in opposition to his mother, who was firmly against the idea. But in the end Dane wore him down, and his mother couldn't withstand the constant pressure.

Dane entered public school for the first time since kindergarten, and with his affable nature and athletic prowess he quickly made friends. And, of course, moving from JV to Varsity happened naturally, and his football camaraderie carried over into the middle-school halls, thronged with kids where St. James had been a little class of only 25 children. Among the kids that Dane had taken up with were Mark Howe, Brian Perkins, and Leroy King. Mark was the ringleader of their little gang and prompted most of their juvenile pranks. But Mark also had a mean streak.

In their eighth-grade year, one afternoon when gym was over, the four friends sat wrapped in their dirty-white towels on the benches of the boys' locker room. The gym coaches were gone, having done their job ensuring that the odorous middle-school boys at least ran through the big communal shower. As they sat laughing, they heard a locker close from the other side of a partition.

Mark crept around and turned, putting a finger to his lips. Then he lunged across the partition. They heard a little shriek, quickly muffled, and then Mark emerged holding the struggling Jason Watt. The boy's towel had fallen, revealing his skinny body. Though an eighth grader as well, Watt was slow to develop and was routinely pushed around by the bigger boys.

"Hey, look who I've got!" Mark said, and the others laughed. "What should we do with him?"

"Indian burn!" Leroy said.

"I've got a better idea," Mark said, and pressed Jason down onto the floor, where he lay whimpering. "Now, you stay still and don't make any noise," Mark said, and then calmly inserted his thumb into Jason's anus.

"Oh Shit!" Brian said, laughing.

"You next," Mark said, pointing to Brian. Jason started crying, as Brian came over and repeated it.

"Bet you like that, you little faggot!" Brian said, and stood up, gesturing for Leroy. But Leroy just shook his head. Mark looked at Dane, who laughed and said: "Maybe he's not the only faggot here."

"Now get the fuck out of here," Mark said, throwing the towel at Jason. The little kid grabbed the towel and ran around the partition to his locker, where they heard him sobbing as he pulled his clothes on and ran from the room.

"Shit, Mark, you're crazy," Leroy said.

And for the next couple of weeks, every time they saw Jason Watt in the halls of Asheville Central Junior High, they would sniff their thumbs and watch his face turn pale. It was great fun, and then one day Jason Watt wasn't at school anymore.

Until this moment, hanging up the phone and reflecting on the news that his son was on videotape having sex with another boy, it had never occurred to Dane to wonder what had happened to Jason Watt.

The middle-aged Dane Norris, looking back on his teenage self, suddenly felt the shame that he should have felt all those years ago. The shame of not defending the little kid. The shame of laughing with his friends. The shame of continuing to mock him afterward.

But along with the shame rose another, more powerful feeling: the possibility that Dylan had just been part of the same sort of thing. Surely that was it. Surely he was just doing the same sort of thing that bigger boys had always done to the little ones. All he needed to confirm this new, reassuring thought was some evidence.

But that evidence was not forthcoming. In fact, quite the opposite. As legal counsel for his brother and nephew, Roger Norris obtained a copy of the video. And there was nothing left for Dane Norris to do but to weigh the two things against each other. The brutal bullying of little Jason Watt against the depravity of his oldest son. And though not a bad man, in his own opinion, Dane knew quite well which he thought was worse.

TRANSCRIPT – *HOPPER & HOWE SHOW*

Hopper: We'll take our next caller. Brett, you're on the line. What's on your mind today?

Brett: Hi Jason, Hi Mark. Hey, it was a shame about the St. Ambrose game the other night. Thought they might bring home State.

Hopper: Well, we certainly knew they would have challenges without their star player. They were in it right up to the end though. I thought it was impressive how Willy Williams kept going to his bag of tricks.

Howe: They almost pulled it off, Jason. In the end it was the defense more than the offense.

Hopper: You're right about that Mark. McDowell had a very impressive game. They'll have to look out for him next year. Hard to believe he's just a freshman. Anything else Brett?

Brett: Yeah, just wondering if you had heard any more on why the Norris kid was suspended.

Hopper: Well, in cases like this it's probably best that we don't discuss it. He is just a high school kid after all.

Brett: I heard there's a video involved.

Hopper: I've heard the same thing, Brett. But let's give the kid a break, okay? Probably just a school discipline issue. Hopefully nothing that will interfere with his recruitment. Thanks for the call, Brett. Now on to our next caller, Greg. Greg, what's on your mind?

Dane heard Emilia's feet running up the stairs, and she burst out into the foyer, ran into the kitchen, looking around, and then yelled: "Janus!"

"He's not back from school yet," Dane said from the living room, where he sat staring at the fireplace, a glass of bourbon on the end table beside him.

"Oh. Look at what I made!" Emilia ran over to him and handed him a cardboard rectangle. Actually, two pieces of cardboard taped together. The front was decorated with a hand-drawn sketch of a Christmas tree, and it was punctuated into twenty-four little squares that had been hand cut. Emilia had made an Advent calendar.

"It's great," Dane said.

"I'm giving it to Janus. I already know what pictures are there for each day, but it'll be a surprise for him."

"I'm sure he'll love it."

Emilia beamed and ran to where she had dropped her backpack, then scurried off to her room.

A few moments later, Anne came up the stairs. She had rings under her eyes as if she hadn't slept very well, and she was draped in warm clothes to keep out the chill, the cold air outside being enough to turn off the Norris house A/C unit for the first time.

"We need to talk about Dylan, honey," Dane said. She looked at him in a foggy sort of way.

"What about?" she asked, and then: "Can we talk in the kitchen?"

Dane shrugged and got up, following Anne to the kitchen where she waited for him to take a seat, and then sat opposite from him at the table.

Dane reached out to take her hand, but she kept her arms folded across her chest.

"Uh . . . I've been to see Roger."

"And?"

"I've seen the video they have of Dylan. It's . . . uh . . . worse than we thought."

"Worse? How?"

"He's . . . not with a girl."

"What do you mean?"

"He's with a guy. He's having sex with a guy."

Anne sat silent and closed her eyes. She hugged herself more tightly. Dane watched her forehead wrinkle and her eyes squint.

"Where is he?" she finally asked.

"Still downstairs. I haven't talked to him. He's been playing video games."

"Let's go down there. I want to talk to him before Janus gets home."

She got up and headed for the stairs down to the rec room. Dane followed her down the stairs and up the hallway to the darkened room where gunshots and explosions roared from surround-sound speakers, and red and orange lights strobed across the features of their son.

"Dylan . . . " she said, softly.

"Not now," her son answered.

Dane flipped the light switch on, and Dylan looked up. Seeing the expression on his dad's face, he paused the game and set down the controller, then stood up. He was as tall as his father and slightly taller than his mother, and a sort of fierce energy coiled around him.

"What?" he said.

"Dylan, your father saw the video. We know about the other boy."

A chill shot down from his cranium, through his spine and into his gut, and then rebounded as a confused hot flash that settled behind his eyes. His breath came rapidly.

"What?" he said again.

"We'll . . . we'll . . . " Anne began, and then after a pause, "I just want you to know that we love you and we'll get through this."

And somehow, for Dylan, that was the cruelest thing she could say.

"There's no WE in this. It's none of your fucking BUSINESS!" he roared.

And then his father's finger was jabbing into his chest and Dane was yelling.

"YOU WATCH HOW YOU TALK TO YOUR MOTHER! YOU UNGRATEFUL LITTLE FUCKER! EVERYTHING WE'VE DONE FOR YOU AND YOU HAVE TO GO AND FUCK IT ALL UP!"

Dane stood panting, enraged.

Dylan was terrified. His own rage and pride were, for the moment, unable to drive out the stinging disappointment he saw in his father's eyes.

"Now," Dane seethed, "you apologize to your mother for what you're putting her through. And you better be GODDAMN thankful she's put up with all your shit. But it ends now. You sit down here or in your room and think about what you can do to make this right. And that starts with staying in this fucking house until we figure out how to handle this. Give me your keys. Both sets. You get your truck back when we get this under control."

"Yes sir," Dylan replied, then shut off the video game controller and brushed past his parents on the way up to his room.

Anne walked over to the bar and pulled a bottle of wine from the cooler, unscrewed the top, pulled a clean glass from the rack under the cabinet, poured it full, and drained it. Dane walked over to the bar and sat in one of the stools.

"Honey . . . " he began.

"I don't want to talk," she said, quietly, refilling the glass. "I just need to be alone right now. Can you let me be alone?"

Dane, hurt, shrugged and headed upstairs, leaving Anne to finish her wine in the big rec room, while he returned to the living room couch and his bourbon.

"Holy shit!"

"What is it, Terry?" Jason Hopper asked, going to look over his producer's shoulder at the screen.

"Oh . . . my. . . . Now we know why the kid was suspended. Where did you get this?"

"Came in on the *Hopper & Howe* email address," Terry answered.

"Holy fuck," Hopper replied. "You better get Broome involved in this."

Thirty minutes later Jason Hopper, Mark Howe, Terry Medovich, and Ken Broome, the general manager of WBCT radio, sat at the conference room table.

"Does anyone else have this?" Broome asked.

"We don't know," Terry answered, in the high-pitched whining voice that universally annoyed the SportsBeast's listeners on the rare occasions he spoke on radio.

"We can't run this," Hopper said. "This is . . . private. Maybe we can refer to it?"

"I don't see the problem with running with it, Jason," Howe replied. "This is news. Dylan Norris is a public figure."

"What about the other kid?" Hopper asked.

"We don't have to say anything about the other kid. Hell, this is radio. You don't have to give a play by play. We can just break the news. The important thing is to do it first."

"You have a point, Mark," Broome replied. "But we better get an opinion from legal first. And, Terry, try to find out who sent it, and if anyone else has this. If we get the clear with legal, then I say we run with it tomorrow on your show, unless of course someone else has it. Then we run with it as soon as legal clears it. Okay?"

"Still think it's a bad idea, Ken, but it's your call," Hopper said, flatly.

But as the WBCT staff sat in the conference room debating, links began to appear on the message boards. Links to YouTube, Daily-Motion, and a dozen other sites. The downloads started, the video was chopped, compressed, and converted to a GIF. All across Asheville phones buzzed, and little clips of Dylan and Brad flew through the ether.

The offices of Mick Haynes, athletic director of Biltmore College, were located directly above those of his football coach Trey Carter. Appropriately so, Haynes thought. But in other respects, the offices were identical. The same woodwork, the same chairs, and the same big window. Haynes sat at his desk, his slick-backed black hair, tanned skin, sharp nose, and tailored suit giving an air of all business.

His phone rang.

"Mr. Cox on the line," his secretary said.

"Which one?"

"Line one."

"No. Which Cox?"

"Oh . . . sorry Mr. Haynes. It's Clyde Cox Jr."

"Thanks," Mick replied, and his phone clicked and then the booming voice came across.

"Mick! How are you?"

"Good. How are you, Clyde?"

"Blessed. Always blessed."

"What can I do for you?"

"Oh nothing in particular. I just called up to give you a little opinion about something."

Here goes, Mick thought. Cox would call on a thousand different topics, from stadium expansion to AstroTurf to alternate uniforms.

"Okay. Shoot."

"It's this Norris kid. Dylan Norris. I don't think he has . . . Biltmore values. I think y'all ought to rethink that scholarship offer."

Haynes was taken aback.

"And, is there a reason for your . . . sudden change of heart?"

"Why, yes there is. And you'll see why shortly, I imagine. And when you do, you'll know my opinion on the matter."

Haynes was silent for a moment before replying.

"Very well. Is there anything else? No? Alright then, Clyde. Nice talking to you."

"Always a pleasure, Mick."

TRANSCRIPT – *HOPPER & HOWE SHOW*

Hopper: Welcome back to the Hopper & Howe Show. *A good Thursday morning to our listening audience. But, I have to say, probably not a good morning over at Biltmore, eh Mark?*

Howe: Definitely not, Jason. Taevon Richardson was a good get for the Rangers. To lose his commitment right before the early signing period is a real blow for Coach Carter. They worked real hard to get him.

Hopper: Well, his recruitment was a pretty tough affair right from the start. I thought his commitment was a real surprise. I really thought he was going to let it go down to the wire in February. So when he committed to the Rangers, I was just very surprised.

Howe: I was too, Jason.

Hopper: As we discussed last hour, Taevon Richardson, the big defensive lineman from Madison County, has opened up his recruiting and now tells AllSports that Alabama and Texas are his leading schools. Let's open up the phones and hear your thoughts. We've got Ranger Bill on the line. How are you this morning, Ranger Bill?

Ranger Bill: Hopper, I'm mad as hell. No question that Richardson dropped his commit 'cause of that Norris kid.

Hopper: Now, hold on Ranger Bill. Richardson as much as said that wasn't a factor.

Ranger Bill: I ain't buyin' it for a minute. You know I follow Mad County football. Richardson's mamma is a God-fearin' woman, and there's no way she'd let her son be playing with a homo.

Hopper: Thanks for the call, Ranger Bill. Let's go to our next caller . . .

--

Ranger Bill: What? Why'd he cut me off?

Producer: You've gotta watch what you say on the air.

Ranger Bill: What? I can't say homo? It's not like I said faggot or something like that.

Producer: You've just got to be a little more respectful.

"Good morning, Professor," Trey Carter said, extending his hand to Monty Sanders.

"Good morning, Coach Carter. Same seats?" he asked, gesturing toward the leather chairs. Carter nodded and they sat.

"Well, here we are. First time since our last meeting in . . . June? I have to say, Coach Carter, that I was pleasantly surprised at the way you have handled the academic aspect of your players. I felt that after our last talk, we had a good understanding."

"I felt that way too. Has something happened to change your mind?"

"No, not at all. This is a different matter. Academics do not come into it. Not yet anyway."

"Well, speak your mind, Professor."

"It's the Norris boy," Monty said, and then looked closely at the coach for a reaction. But he was disappointed, and continued.

"Yes. The Norris boy. Your prized recruit, up until this week. Just as I came preemptively before, I'm coming again now. I wanted you to know that I, and many of my fellow professors, are very committed to equity and diversity at Biltmore College, and that extends to the student-athletes. I expect that many people in your profession are not quite so . . . tolerant."

"You might be surprised, Professor."

"I don't think so. In any case, I wanted to let you know that I, and many of my colleagues, would be extremely disappointed to find that a prized recruit was not so prized anymore once his sexual orientation became known."

"And this opinion has nothing to do with your son, Monty?"

Sanders was unphased.

"Nothing at all. I'm proud of my son, and he has done nothing wrong. Nor has Dylan Norris. I just wanted you to know, personally, that he has many friends at Biltmore College, no matter what the athletic department might think."

"I believe I understand you, Professor."

"Good. Glad we could have this time to talk." And with that, Sanders rose and extended his hand. Carter took it with slightly more force than was necessary and shook it for slightly less time than was polite, as he ushered the professor to the door.

Outside of Seely Stadium, over Gate 1, was a giant lime-green panel with the Biltmore College "B" displayed in white. On Friday morning, the sun rose to reveal a spray-painted penis next to the logo, and it didn't take much imagination to see that someone saw the "B" as a pair of buttocks.

The logo was quickly covered up, but not before pictures of it began circulating on the Internet with the hashtag: #RumpRangers.

"I'm tellin' you Tommy, Richardson ain't the last one that's gonna drop, long as they have that faggot committed. You mark my words."

"Shit, Billy. This ain't the eighties. There've already been gay football players. College campuses are full of 'em."

"There's only been one that I heard of. And he was graduating. Ain't never been one that was bein' recruited. Course all of 'em gotta say they don't have a problem with it. Get run out on a rail if they don't. But that don't mean they like it. Bet you ten bucks there are more kids that drop the Rangers 'cause of this. Hell, if that fuckin' Norris kid gave two shits about the Rangers, he'd drop his commit himself. But that fucker's gonna sit back while the whole damn class falls apart around him."

"I still think you're wrong, Billy. You just watch. They love them homos nowadays."

"You see that shit on campus today? Rump Rangers! Fuckin' pisses me off. We're gonna be the laughingstock of the SEC."

"It's about the reputation of the Biltmore College Rangers, Lee," insisted Clyde Cox Jr.

The three Cox brothers sat at the conference room table along with Mick Haynes, Lee Adams, Ronald Phillips, and Jennifer Salisbury. Mick Haynes had spent the morning on the phone with each of them and had finally had enough of the back and forth that he requested an afternoon meeting, which had quickly devolved into the anti-Dylan camp, consisting of the two older Cox brothers and Ronald Phillips; the vacillating middle, consisting of Lee Adams; and the pro-Dylan camp, consisting of Jennifer Salisbury and, to his brothers' annoyance, Hank Cox.

"We should be just as worried about the reputation of Biltmore College as the Rangers, Clyde," Jennifer interrupted. "This isn't your daddy's world anymore. You can't go pulling a scholarship because of sexual orientation."

"Now hold on there. I never said nothing of the sort. I don't give a damn where that kid sticks his pecker. But it's out there in public now, and it's having a detrimental effect on the program."

"Just because one kid chooses not to go here does not mean there's a detrimental effect," Jennifer countered.

"It's the canary in the mineshaft," Claude Cox added. "You just wait. There'll be more."

Claude's older brother joined back in: "You see, Jennifer, it isn't about what you or I or Jesus Christ thinks. It's about what those other kids think. If you leave Dylan Norris on that offer list, you're pickin' that one kid ahead of all of the others, and the program to boot."

"I think that's bullshit, Clyde."

"Please, please," Haynes interrupted. "Let's keep this civil. We've still got a couple of weeks until the early signing period starts. Why can't we see if this thing cools down?"

"And what if it doesn't, Mick?" Clyde asked. "You gonna commit to pulling his scholarship offer if any more kids drop?"

"Oh, Mick! You're not seriously considering that?" Jennifer asked, incredulous.

"I'm not committing to anything, either way. This is an . . . unusual situation."

"You're pussing out on us, Mick."

"Don't like the language, Clyde."

"Don't care, Jennifer."

"Please . . . " Mick said, raising his hands in a calming gesture, "we don't need to do this now. I'm asking you all just to let this play out a little more. It's not going to do any good to go rattling the cage at this juncture. I asked you all to come here so that you could see the different opinions that we're dealing with, just among the six of you. Imagine all the other different opinions. On campus. In the press. Just think about it."

"All right, Mick. We'll see how this plays out." Clyde stood,

Claude following shortly after, and the two brothers, united in something for the first time in a long while, left the room.

Back in his office, Mick Haynes took the call from Midge Jacoby, president of Biltmore College.

"Yes, Midge. The six biggest anyway. . . . No, they hate each other. Makes them easier to deal with. . . . Yes, they're settled down for now. . . . I understand. I understand. We're not going to take any actions right now. . . . No. Not without consulting with you. I'll keep Carter calmed down too. He's the one we've got to watch since he's the one talking to the press. . . . No, I don't think that's called for. We can do a presser later if there's a need. . . . Okay. Thanks Midge."

Chapter 17

FROST

Sunday morning, and the frost lay brilliantly across the fields of the Norris farm. The rising sun struck across the little frozen blades of grass and glittered on the roofs of the barns and sheds. Already the frost was retreating from the sun, remaining stubbornly in the shadows cast by the trees along the fence lines.

Dane was awakened again by Emilia banging pots and pans, and again received from her the news that his wife had gone to the early Mass by herself.

Dane walked over to Janus' door and banged on it.

"Get up Jane. Get ready for church."

Dylan lay in bed, wide awake, staring at the ceiling. In the corner of the room, wrapped in plastic, was the stuffed head of the buck that he had killed. Mounted on a plaque and leaning up against the wall, he, like Dylan, stared at the ceiling.

His phone was on the charger. Buzzing. He rarely even looked at the texts anymore. It seemed everybody had his number. The occasional messages of support from his teammates and friends were mingled with constant forwards of the GIFs from numbers he didn't recognize. And then there was the silence. The teammates and friends that hadn't texted or called. That hurt him the most. But what concerned him more was the silence from Biltmore College.

So he lurked there in his room, and from time to time in the gym downstairs, or in the game room. But all the while, avoiding his family as much as he could. He microwaved frozen meals and ate them alone. His mother would come tapping at his door from time to time, but she didn't press him, and he didn't open up.

He would have to leave the room eventually. He would have to go out in public. He would have to walk onto the practice field at Biltmore with the eyes of every person on him. He was steeling himself for a fight and rehearsing lines of bravado:

Sure I fucked him. I'll fuck anything that moves.

Fuck a hundred pussies and nobody cares. But stick your dick in one asshole . . .

You wanna call me a faggot again, motherfucker?

And along with the lines came images of rage in which he imagined pummeling his oppressors.

I'll use this, he thought, *I'll use this and fucking destroy people. And they won't dare give me shit.*

And in the rare moments when the rage was far from him, he wondered how Brad was dealing with this. But he didn't dare contact him to ask.

Inside St. James' Church, the second purple candle was blown out, and a smoke tendril drifted up lazily. Outside, Dane in his suit with his stomach bulging out, an overcoat draped over his broad shoulders, Janus in a thick jacket and khakis, and Emilia in her faux-fur coat descended the front steps of St. James. The Christmas tree awaited its lighting at the edge of the steps, but red bows already made it festive.

Fr. MacMahon greeted the departing parishioners. As Dane

approached him, the priest reached out and shook his hand, asking: "How's Anne? Is everything okay?"

Dane was a little taken aback, but answered: "She's just been coming to the eight-o-clock the last couple of weeks. Must be an Advent thing with her."

"That's a relief. I was worried about her when I didn't see her. Perhaps she went to the deacon at Communion. And your son Dylan. Is he alright? I don't see him here either."

"He's okay. But you could say a prayer for him, I suppose."

Anne awoke feeling disoriented and nauseated. She had been dreaming about Dylan, with confused thoughts running around crazy scenarios where he was arrested and tortured. She sat up in bed, in Maryanne's bed, and let the swirling in her head subside. The alarm was going off. Monday. Emilia to school.

She rose and walked through the kitchen to the bedroom where Dane lay snoring. Quietly she went into the bathroom, closed the door, and started the shower. In the past two weeks, the welt marks had vanished from her back and inner thighs, so she was no longer afraid for Dane to see her. But she was ashamed nonetheless, and so she showered quickly, toweled off and put on slacks and a baggy sweater, and crept back through the room to wake up Emilia. SAHS started an hour later than St. James, and Dane would drive Janus in, now that he could no longer ride along with his brother, but Anne had been getting up earlier than necessary so that she could be out the door while Dane still slept.

On the drive into school, Emilia asked: "Mom, why haven't we put any Christmas decorations up?"

"We will, honey. I just haven't felt up to it."

"Are you having a fight with Dad? Why don't you sleep in your room anymore?"

"It's complicated, honey. Sometimes I get sad and miss Maryanne, and it helps me to sleep in her room."

"I wish she'd come back."

"Me too."

They rode in silence, and then suddenly: "You and Daddy should go to marriage counseling."

The little girl said it so seriously, so precociously, and it struck Anne as so odd that she laughed. It was the first time Emilia had heard her mother laugh in weeks, and it filled her with joy, and then the two of them were erupting in giggles.

Dane sat across from his brother in Roger's office after dropping off Janus at school.

"So, there's been a lot going on that you should know about," Roger began. "First, the video. No progress on its source. The police know, of course, that it was from the security cameras at the Sanders' place. Apparently, they were installed by the previous owners, but the Sanders never had the system monitored. It just rolled along recording everything and buffering the contents. This is interesting because it was an older system and there was only space for about two weeks of video. It might just be a coincidence that the boys were caught on the video at all, or it might not. In any case, the tack they're trying now is to follow the source of the emails and the Internet postings, but so far no luck."

"Okay. Cat's out of the bag on that stuff, but once they find the fucker I'll sue him into oblivion."

"Yeah, well, let's hope they can trace it to the source. Second issue is troubling, but might come to nothing. Looks like there was a meeting between Haynes and some boosters at Biltmore last week. The discussion centered around pulling the scholarship offer."

"What!? They can't do that!"

"Well, they can if they choose to. Happens all the time, as you well know. Most of the time to kids when a better player becomes available for their slot. But they can use any reason. Looks like, for now, they're not going to do anything. But we should keep an eye on it, and frankly, I would encourage Dylan to open up his recruiting."

"Wait, open up his recruiting? You mean, not go to Biltmore?"

"That's exactly what I mean. Dane, you need to look at facts here. I think you've been so focused on Dylan following in your footsteps that you don't see how big of a deal this is. Imagine walking on campus when everyone there, and everyone in the stands at Seely Stadium, has seen a video of you having sex with another man."

Dane was silent for a moment.

"I'll talk to Dylan about it and see what he wants."

"Good. I think that's for the best. If he decides to open up his recruiting, it's probably better to do it earlier rather than later. Of course, you've got until February. It's just the early signing period to worry about. Anyway, enough about football. The real issue is his graduation. As you know, he's still officially suspended, but that's only because the admins over at St. Ambrose, and frankly myself for that matter, think it's hard to imagine him going back to class, either in terms of his own well-being or that of the school. If you think about him walking onto Biltmore, where half the student body wears Pride pins, just imagine him walking into St. Ambrose where, nominally at least, it's considered a sin."

"I get it. What do we do, though? How does he graduate?"

"He's going to have to catch up on some coursework from home and take his finals at a proctored exam site. The school is being fairly accommodating. They certainly don't want any more trouble, especially with all the flak that the Sanders folks are raising."

"Okay, well, I guess that's good news."

Anne had just gotten home when her phone rang. It was SAHS calling. Janus had been in a fight, and they needed her to come pick him up. Back into Asheville she drove, alone with her thoughts. Her fingers made their way around the rosary bumps on the steering wheel, but the Hail Mary didn't come to mind.

TRANSCRIPT – *HOPPER & HOWE SHOW*

Hopper: It's Ranger Bill again. How are you, Ranger Bill?

Ranger Bill: Hi there, Hopper. Hey, I just heard something interesting about Dylan Norris.

Hopper: Okay Ranger Bill, but let's keep this respectful.

Ranger Bill: Sure, sure. This is about football, nothing to do with the video or anything like that.

Hopper: Okay, what's on your mind?

Ranger Bill: Yeah . . . the Norris kid . . . he's gone from tight end to wide receiver . . .

Hopper: And that's enough of Ranger Bill, folks. I apologize for that.

The following morning, Anne was pulling up to St. James, and as Emilia got out she said: "I'll see you at Mass, Mom."

"I'm sorry; I'm not going to Mass today."

"But it's the Immaculate Conception Feast. You have to."

"Oh, yes. I plan to go later." Anne had forgotten the holy day.

As she drove away from the school, she asked herself if it were possible that she could walk back into St. James. She knew she could not present herself for Communion. All the faces of those saints, the light reaching upward, and the light reaching outward . . . she couldn't bear it. And here she was compounding her sins with lies to her family. But she needed to be stronger. Once things settled down with Dylan, then she could face her contrition. But not yet.

Then, unbidden, rather than the rosary, the prophecy of St. Simeon came to her mind: *Sorrow as sharp as a sword shall pierce her heart.*

But, Anne thought, the Virgin Mary hadn't brought that sorrow upon herself.

"Can you at least let me know what's prompting this decision? You seemed excited to come to Biltmore."

"You see, Coach Carter, I really appreciate everything you and Coach Sampson have done for me. But, just, as it got closer to signing, I realized I've got to do what's best for me. I guess my heart just wasn't at Biltmore. I'm just gonna stay closer to home."

"I appreciate that, Lester, I really do. It's a big step to move across country. Can I at least ask you to leave your commitment open? Give us until February to change your mind. See if we can get that bowl win?"

"No coach, I'm decided. I'm staying home at ASU. I really wish you guys luck. I really do."

"Okay, Lester. Well, best of luck to you too."

Coach Carter hung up the phone.

Shit. That was the third lost commit of the day. After losing Ja'Kwan Duffy and Trent Nolan, the package deal, now to see the five-star Kitchings drop.

"Sarah, get all my coaches together in the conference room," he yelled to his secretary.

Every one of his staff was going to make whatever calls necessary and contact whoever they could to lock down the rest of this class.

Transcript, WULC *Morning Show*

Burroughs: Annnnd . . . a good Wednesday morning to you, Kelly. What have you got for us today?

Briar: Good morning to you, too, Tad. It's been a busy morning already. There are disturbing reports coming out of Biltmore College today that paint a picture of sports boosters using their influence to pull a scholarship from a gay football player.

Anonymous sources tell us that a high-level meeting between powerful boosters and the athletic department occurred last week, and that some boosters demanded that the football player in question, the son of famed Biltmore College and Kansas City Chiefs player Dane Norris, be stripped of his offer.

We caught up with well-known booster Jennifer Salisbury to get her thoughts. Salisbury denied that Biltmore was planning to rescind an offer and said the meeting was to discuss diversity issues and the direction of the program, but another source indicated that it was Clyde Cox Jr. who led the charge to pull the offer..

Burroughs: Thanks Kelly. Has there been any response from the college itself?

Briar: No, Tad. The athletic department issued a brief statement that indicated that there are many changes in scholarship offers when signing period draws near, but they were not currently planning to rescind any offers.

Burroughs: Well, it sounds like this story is developing quickly. Thanks Kelly. Annnd . . . we've just received word that Professor Monty Sanders of Biltmore College is holding a press conference later today. Should be very interesting. We'll bring you more news on this developing story at five-o-clock.

The little table in the humanities building had a few microphones and a few recorders, and in the rows of chairs in front of the table were a few people. Reporters, hopefully. Myra sat far to the back, unobtrusively. She knew when it was time for her glib husband and time for her own more acerbic force, and this was definitely a time for the former. Best to stay in the background. The clock ticked, the fluorescent lights blinked, and Monty looked at his watch, wishing there were more reporters present but beginning anyway.

"Thank you all for coming. As you know, I am Professor Montgomery Sanders, a sociology professor here at Biltmore College, and also the chair of the Academic Integrity Committee.

"As you are no doubt aware, I am also the proud father of a young gay man who has experienced some discrimination recently. But that is not why I have called this conference today. Rather, I am here to address what can only be described as an egregious affront to the integrity of not only the academic function of this institution but also the ancillary student athletics. I speak, of course, of the effort to rescind a scholarship offer to a young man based solely on that young man's sexual orientation.

"We, as scholars and educators here at Biltmore College, are committed to equality, diversity, and a welcoming environment, and we will fight strongly against whatever forces are arrayed against those pursuits, no matter how well funded or influential they might be.

"At this time, it is important for not only us—the scholars and educators of Biltmore College—to take a stand, but for all the community to do so. Therefore, we have scheduled a rally in support of nondiscrimination of LGBTQ persons here on campus for tomorrow at two PM, and I will be delivering this list of demands to our president upon the conclusion of this press conference.

"Are there any questions?" Monty looked expectantly at the thinly populated room.

"Yes, you," he said, pointing toward a balding man in a checked jacket in the middle of the room.

"Tom Rolf, NewzRadio," the man said, and then continued in a voice that attempted to be tentative and soothing: "To clarify, is it your son in the video with Dylan Norris?"

"It is, and we will bring full legal action against the perpetrators of the distribution of that video, which was made surreptitiously and obtained illegally."

He waited, but there were no more raised hands.

"Thank you for your time," he said, and rose, disappointed. The few attendees came forward and picked up their recorders and microphones. There had been no television crew.

"Mr. Norris? Monty Sanders. I'm a professor at Biltmore and . . . Brad's father."

"Okay. What do you want?"

"We're having a rally on campus tomorrow, and I really hope that Dylan can be there. He doesn't need to make a speech or do anything onerous. He could just come and wave. I think it would be encouraging for him, and it would humanize him for the media."

"What the fuck are you talking about? No."

"We're doing it for him. Surely you must agree that we can't let them bully him just because of his sexual orientation."

"Listen, Sanders. Dylan's not gay. I don't know what was going on with him and your son, but just stay away from him and leave him alone. We didn't ask for this. Stay the fuck out of it."

"I see." Sanders said, his voice flat. "So that's it. Can I speak with Dylan?"

"He's not talking to anyone. So . . . no."

"Well then. I hope you change your mind, but I don't expect it. I will just give you a word of advice that you should give your son the space to be honest with you. You might be surprised."

"I don't need your fucking advice."

Brad: My dad wants you to be at a rally tomorrow for you at BC.

Brad: I told him I would text you. Asking for him not for me.

Brad: Figured you'd call me if you wanted to talk. Thought I'd leave you alone.

Dylan: You were right.

The TV cameras that had been absent at Sanders' press conference were there in full force for the rally. An impromptu stage, arches of bright balloons, a PRIDE sign, rainbow flags under a cloudless sky. Bare branches of trees in front of cold brick buildings. Steaming breath in the air. The tinny voices amplified across the square. Students and locals in coats of all types and colors gathered in front of the stage. A procession of speakers. PFLAG and GLAD representatives spoke, as did the Biltmore College chapter of the Gay Student Athlete Association, hoping to add Dylan Norris as its third member. A stirring speech was given by McKenzie Grayson, nee Michael Grayson, who was seeking to be the first transgendered woman to enter Phi Beta Nu Sorority and suing for the right to do so. Then, President Midge Jacoby, lending her full support to the rally, and pledging that Biltmore College would forever be known as a place of welcome and inclusion.

In all, a few hundred people braved the cold. A far cry from the tens of thousands who would pack into Seely Stadium on a Saturday. But a good start, and it wouldn't be much longer before the rainbow flag waved above the Biltmore Rangers as they ran onto the field.

At the end, everyone was at the rally except for its star attraction. Though it was rumored that he would appear, Dylan Norris, it seemed, was otherwise occupied and unable to hear the words shouted on his behalf.

"Yeah, it's not good, Mr. Cox."

Clyde Cox Jr. stared at the weaselly young man in front of him, with his unbuttoned shirt and unkempt hair.

"Explain."

"Well, for starters, on Twitter the hashtag #CoxHomophobe is seriously trending. Not nationally, but locally. That's followed by hashtags 'BoycottCoxMarket,' 'BoycottCoxFoods,' et cetera. You get the picture."

"So what?"

"Well, it's pretty bad press. You have what's called a 'Twitter Mob' after you."

"Okay. Doesn't sound bad. What else?"

"Well, this is a bit more serious because it comes from your own ranks, but you have a bunch of employees planning a walkout in protest of your . . . perceived homophobia."

"Let 'em walk. This is a right-to-work state. I'll fire the lot of them."

"At this point, you'll be firing an awful lot of people, some of whom are in key positions."

"What else?"

"Well, you're lucky that Cox, Inc. is not a public corporation, or you'd be getting killed in the market. The upshot of all of this is that you've got a ton of bad press and disgruntled employees."

"It'll blow over."

"Maybe. Or we can get in front of it. Establish a diversity program, that sort of thing."

"Son. Fuck those bastards. I run this company."

"You do, but you can't do it without employees and customers."

But Cox was distracted.

"How much do we spend in ads over at WULC? They're the bastards who tied my name to this shit."

"We're on the order of two million a year."

"How much of their revenue is that?"

The young man ran his hand through his hair, puffed out his cheeks and blew through them before answering: "Probably about ten or twenty percent."

"Okay, then. Pull all our ads from WULC. Shut our campaign down. Fuckers want to point fingers at me? And double our ad spending on the other networks. I'll show 'em what happens."

Coach Carter sat in the leather chair across from Mick Haynes.

"We're fucked," Carter said, dejected.

"How many now?"

"Had another four today. All told, that's eight recruits lost so far. And they were rock-solid. We can still have a decent class, but we're talking about going from maybe one or two in the country to . . . somewhere in the bottom of the top twenty-five. And God knows if any more of them are going to drop."

"Is it all just this Norris kid?"

"Who knows. There's a momentum to this. You see it every year. These kids, they all talk to each other. Not one of them will come out and say it's Norris. Maybe they just don't want to be at a program with a cloud over it. Maybe they just don't like the Rump Ranger jokes or the dicks drawn on the Biltmore B."

"What are you going to do?"

"There's only one thing I can do at this point."

"We can't pull his offer. You've seen the shitstorm."

"Then there's nothing we can do. I mean, maybe we could swing for the fences, come out as the gayest football club in the USA. Something like that."

"How do you think that would play with our fan base?"

"Like a lead balloon. So we're back to zero options. I hope you remember that when we struggle through next season."

"I brought you in here to win, not to make excuses."

Carter rubbed a hand across his forehead, looked down for a moment, and then up at Haynes, whose cold eyes regarded him.

"Get any great ideas, let me know," he said, rising and walking to the door. It had been a long, long day.

A tap at Dylan's door. He ignored it. Then it repeated. It was early—too early to be up. He heard his mother's voice: "Dylan. Please open up."

He lay in bed hoping she would go away, but she tapped again, and finally he got up and went to the door, opening it a crack.

"Can I come in?"

"What for?"

"I just want to talk to you for a second. I've got to take Emilia to school so it won't be long."

"Okay, whatever." He went back and sat on his bed. His mother walked into the room, tentatively, looking around like she hadn't seen it in ages.

"Dylan, I just want to say that I'm sorry. Sorry for Maryanne, sorry for being too strict, or too motherly, or too religious, or whatever it is. I know you don't like me. Right now, I don't like me either. And maybe you're not scared about what's happening and not scared for the future, and that's okay. But if you are scared, just remember that I love you. I'm not asking you to love me back. I just want you to know that no matter what you do I will love you. And I'm sorry if that makes it worse."

Anne stood there waiting for him to say something in return, and when he did not, she quietly left the room and closed the door behind her.

"Dane, I've got some good news for a change."

"What is it, Roger?" Dane replied, no expectation or hope in his voice.

"Just heard from Ambrose. Dylan is, of course, still registered as an athlete there. Got an offer this morning from Oregon, and about fifteen minutes later from UCLA. Then another offer from Stanford. Those schools must have great spies," he laughed.

"I'll let Dylan know," Dane said.

"Listen, Dane. This could be the best thing for him. PAC-10, all the way on the other side of the country. And these schools are . . . progressive. I don't know what's going on with Dylan, but it sure would make life a lot easier for him. Give you guys time to figure things out without so much pressure."

"Roger, I really appreciate that. I really do. I'll let Dylan know, and of course if that's what he wants. But I'm a little surprised at you. Sounds like you want him to run into the arms of this thing. If he goes out to one of those . . . progressive schools, they're just going to encourage him. I would think you, of all people, would be opposed to that."

"Dane, like I said, I don't know what's going on with him. And I have been praying daily that this was just a fluke and that Dylan turns out normal. He's my nephew after all, and I do care for him. But no matter what else happens, you've got to see that Biltmore is just ruined for him. It's too close to everything, and now he's turning into a political football."

South of SR 401 in the unwanted scrub land facing away from Lake Juniper, Penny Wilson's parents had a little tow-behind trailer that sat, immobile, on a cozy patch of land. Penny was the third of their children to make the trailer their own, and she and her small group of friends inhabited it on weekends and "cut days," filling it with music and marijuana and anger. Penny and Wendy had skipped school that Friday and had come out to the trailer instead, along with Richard Gwin, a plump, pimply classmate of Penny's from Central High, and Becky Gallaher, equally pimply but emaciated. The four were dressed in black, with cultivated pale faces. They rejected the labels "emo" and "goth," though those labels were applied nevertheless.

As the afternoon wore on, the group gathered their trash, put the bongs back in cupboards, straightened up the cramped interior, and made their way to Penny's sticker-covered Nissan pickup. The four crammed in and were rolling merrily down 401 when Wendy, who hated peeing outside at the trailer, said: "I gotta go. Stop at the next place."

The next place was the Jiffy Stop, and the little Nissan crammed full of goths pulled in beside a green Ford Ranger pickup with a tattered lime-green "B" flag.

Wendy pushed the seat forward, climbed over Richard, jumped out, and ran into the Jiffy Stop, past Billy Mullins and Tommy Hess. Billy watched her run past, turning his head conspicuously the whole way before turning back to Tommy and laughing.

"What the fuck was that? Shit."

"Gettin' weirder all the time, Billy."

A few minutes later, Wendy ran past them again and out the door, and as she did so, Tommy yelled: "Thanks for your business!"

Back in the car, Wendy pulled out her phone and texted:

Need to see you ASAP. Meet me at home?

In his room, Dylan lay in bed, the TV playing but ignored. His eyes fixed on his ceiling again. He heard a buzz from the nightstand and looked over at his phone. He was about to swipe to delete the message when he saw the name: Wendy.

Wendy: Need to see you ASAP. Meet me at home?

Dylan: BRT

He fished around in his dresser drawer and found the valet keys that he had stashed away. They would open and drive the Yukon but wouldn't open the glove compartment, and that's where his weed was stashed. Well, he'd figure that out. He dressed for the cold night, then cracked his door open and looked out. Emilia's and Janus' doors were open. He guessed they were downstairs playing video games. No one in the kitchen, no one in the living room. He walked out the front door and closed it softly behind, then moved quietly through the cold around the front of the house and down toward the barn where his SUV had sat abandoned during his quarantine.

Dylan pulled his Yukon up in front of Wendy's house. There was barely enough space along the curb in front of her mother's vinyl-sided home to accommodate the length of the SUV. It was only a moment before he saw the front door crack open, and Wendy rushed down the concrete steps to pull at the handle. Dylan pushed the unlock button, and she tugged at it again, opening the door and jumping in.

"Wendy," he said once she was in. "You're my only friend left."

Wendy was dressed in black, as always, her eyes dark and shadowed behind her mop of hair. Without preamble, she began speaking.

"I heard them from the bathroom. Dylan, they're planning to ambush you tonight at the Party Field."

Dylan was taken aback. He hadn't been expecting anything but a romp with Wendy.

"What? What bathroom? Slow down."

"I was at the Jiffy Stop on 401 and went into the bathroom. You can hear everything they're saying at the counter. There were two men there, a little short guy in a Rangers hat and the tall guy behind the counter. The little guy said they were going to jump you at the Party Field, said they knew how to get you to go up there and they would take care of you for fucking up the recruiting class."

"What!?" Dylan exclaimed. "What the fuck?" A chill went down his spine. But he hadn't been planning to go there. There was no way he was going to see Brad or anyone else. And then in the midst of his confusion, a warm feeling started in his stomach. He looked over at Wendy who, in many ways, had started all this and who now cared enough to warn him away from these dumbass rednecks. The depravity they had shared together before Brad now suddenly seemed clean, and normal, and something that belonged to the Dylan . . . before.

As he had done so many times before, he reached over and put his hand on the back of her head and started pushing it down toward his lap. But this time, Wendy violently pushed her head back up and slapped his hand away.

"What the fuck, Wendy, I . . . "

"There's no way I'm sucking that dick, Dylan. You know where it's been." And then she laughed.

Dylan's hands and feet tingled, and sharp pin pricks raced up his legs and arms to meet in his chest. A white rage exploded in his head, and before he knew what was happening, he slammed his fist into the side of Wendy's face. Her head whipped back and smacked the glass of the passenger window. Her hands flew to her face. Blood poured from her nose and lips through her hands, and she slumped backward toward the passenger door.

The rage was spent. Dylan gaped at what he had done.

"Wendy?" he said.

"FUCK YOU, DYLAN!" she yelled, spitting blood over the cab of the Yukon. "FUCK YOU!" she screamed, and jerked the door open and was out of the SUV before he could think to lock the door, which now hung open. She backed up the stairs that she had run down only moments before. "FUCK YOU!" she screamed again and again, and Dylan saw lights come on in her mother's house, saw a face look out the upstairs window, saw neighbors' doors opening.

He floored the gas pedal and tore away from the street, the open door clipping a parked car on the way, but slamming closed in the process.

Fuck! Fuck! Fuck! He thought to himself, and very little more than that. He drove madly, madly through this run-down neighborhood and back to the interstate. Oblivious of traffic at first, his mind whirled over the events of the last few weeks. Jaws were snapping at him on all sides—coaches, boosters, mother, father, priests, professors, Brad, Wendy. He whirled around seeing no escape. It was crashing, crashing.

Then his cell phone chimed. Still driving, he looked down and read the message:

Unknown Caller: Meet me at the place off 401. We need to talk. Brad.

And then his heart seemed to slow, and though suppressed by fear at what he had done to Wendy, by his own action adding to his already intolerable burdens, the rage built back up and found a new target. *Those assholes at the gas station. Planning an ambush. They'd get an ambush all right.*

Dylan was dressed in jeans, boots, a BC Rangers T-shirt, and his St. Ambrose letterman jacket. The jacket was festooned with three big fabric "A" letters from his first three years at SAHS. There was space for the fourth, which had been a certainty until the last month. The Norris name blazed across the shoulders, his number 88 on both sleeves and the back, and all surrounded by MVP patches, all-star patches, and a big "C" for captain. The jacket was warm and warmer than usual with Dylan's excited anger. He was, in fact, sweating.

He pushed the seat cooler button and dropped the temperature to 68, which reduced the heat being pumped out of the dash and floor vents. As the seat cooler began to make its presence felt, he shut off the stereo and calmly exited the interstate and re-entered in the opposite direction. Toward Party Field.

As he drove, he turned off his iPhone. *No location tracking tonight, Mom*, he thought as he did so. Coolly he made his way north, moved onto side roads, then back roads, and then to the gravel drive with its gate-pole lying useless in the grass, lit up against the black forest by his high beams.

Dylan cut the lights. There was enough moonlight to see the open road in front of him. He drove slowly, but the crunch of the gravel seemed incredibly loud. Knowing a small pull off before the road reached the Party Field, Dylan eased the Yukon off the gravel drive and into the grass. He climbed out, shut the door behind him, and made his way to the hatchback of the SUV, pressing the button on its underside to engage the lift motors. White LEDs in the hatch shone down on him and made a circle of light in the grass. The dome lights inside the SUV lit up the jumble of pads, workout bags, cleats, helmet, sleeping bag, tent and camping gear, and his range bag. On top of his range bag was the padded case for his deer rifle, still in the back of his SUV, ready to be sighted in again after Deer Camp. Dylan opened the range bag and grabbed a handful of shells

—more than he thought he would need. He pocketed them in his jacket.

As he did this, his breath shot into the cold night like smoke from a dragon's mouth. He was breathing fast and shallowly. He unzipped the rifle bag, reached in, and grabbed the rifle, overhand, by the muzzle.

The barrel pointed toward him.

The trigger caught on the padlock hanging from the zipper.

A bright flash, a night-splitting crack, and a 30-06 bullet penetrated his heart.

His heart. That noble muscle that had come down to him through generations of sturdy Norris men; that tremorous muscle that fled from its own deeds; that bitter muscle that had held goodness in contempt; that great muscle that had pumped blood through his body and driven him up and down the football field; that cold muscle that had taken pleasure in others' pain; that diseased muscle that had thrilled only in the exertion of power; that rigid muscle that could not give back love. It was gone in an instant. Liquified and sent shooting out through the exit wound in his back, Dylan's heart was sprayed across the grass. He was aware of only an instant, and then he was gone. His mortal body however, carried on, propelled backward by the force, his hand wrapped around the rifle sling and jerking it out and away from his body. What remained of Dylan Norris fell heavily to the ground, arms splayed wide, torso immobile but steaming from the wreck of his chest, his eyes staring and mouth gaping.

Stillness for a long moment.

His corpse lay in the circle of light still shining down from the open hatch. Then the cold night began its work, slowly sucking out his body's heat and dissipating it in the air, frosting the scattered remains of his heart tissue, frosting the rifle, frosting his eyelashes, frosting his tousled hair and beard. Frosting his eyes and lips. Frosting the wound in his chest, and finally frosting his jeans, shirt, and letterman jacket.

Chapter 18

THE OLD ORDER HAS PASSED AWAY

At the Hackman Private Preserve, deer season had ended. The lodge sat quietly, steam from one of the water pipes rising lazily into the air as the cleaning crew prepared to ready the lodge for the winter. Other game could indeed be hunted there, but Hackman's was a deer preserve, and when the season ended, the season ended. The row of UTVs sat outside, ready to be driven off to the barn. The trails vanished peacefully into the pines, and here and there, deer nosed about, unmolested, and aware, somehow, that they could begin to ignore the two-legged predators and concentrate on eluding the natural ones.

Wendy lay in a hospital bed, the left side of her face a mass of bruises, her lips swollen and stitched, and her tongue coming back from time to time to the gaps where her teeth had been. She had been wildly incoherent when the police and the EMTs arrived, but she had told them it was Dylan Norris who had done it and, no, she didn't know where he might be. So the police began to look.

A cruiser rolled up the gravel driveway to the Norris farm and pulled in front of the house. Anne and Dane were awakened from their separate bedrooms by the dogs barking and the doorbell ringing, and Anne, in shock at the sight of the policemen, sank to the floor in horror.

Learning that they were looking for Dylan, discovering that his room was empty and his SUV was gone, she allowed Dane to conduct her to the living room, where she sat in one of the easy chairs in shock. Dane spoke with the police. No, he didn't know where his son might be. No, his phone wasn't showing up on the tracker; its last location was on I-26N. Yes, they would call the police immediately if they heard from their son. Yes, they understood that this was serious but that it was better for the boy to come forward. Yes, he should contact his lawyer.

The call made to Roger. Sit tight. Do you think Dylan would do something stupid? Check the gun cabinet. His rifle is missing. He was going to sight it in and never put it back in the cabinet.

Wendy was interviewed at the hospital where she was admitted; her mother sat in a chair in the corner of the room making threats about Dylan Norris. Wendy remembered the Jiffy Stop, the two rednecks and their threats. *Where's Party Field? Oh that place. We know that place. Contact the Madison County Sheriff's Office and have them send someone up to check it out.*

The dogs barking again as the sun began to rise. The officers back at the door. The police chaplain, a graying Anglican with kind eyes. Anne didn't rise from her chair. She knew.

Dane in disbelief. *What happened? We don't know yet, but he was shot. Where is he? Probably still at the field. I want to go there. I want to see him. You can't go there. It's an active crime scene. They'll take him to the Madison County morgue. They'll want you to identify him there . . . if he's in a condition where you can do so.*

Janus and Emilia awake now and curled up beside their mother while the chaplain speaks works of comfort. *Is there anybody you'd like us to contact? No. I'll do it. Roger. They found him. He's been shot. He's dead.*

Transcript, WULC *Saturday Morning Show*

Burroughs: We go to Kelly Briar with some breaking news this morning. Kelly . . .

Briar: Good morning, Tad. A shocking development in the story that we've been covering over the last week. I'm standing here in Madison County off of State Route 401, where this morning sheriff's deputies discovered the body of Dylan Norris, the St. Ambrose High School football player who has been at the center of controversy since he was outed as gay. The sheriff's department is not saying how he died, but sources say that it was a gunshot wound and that he is the only victim. My sources ALSO say that Norris was involved in a domestic dispute last night and assaulted a teenage girl before hitting several parked cars as he fled the scene.

Burroughs: A very disturbing turn of events, Kelly. Do the police have any suspects?

Briar: Not at this time, Tad, but we will of course be following this story.

It did not take the Asheville Police and the Madison County Sheriff's Department long to make the connection to Billy Mullins, and he was awakened on that Saturday morning with the door kicked in and himself flung to the ground and handcuffed. Billy shouted and screamed and yelled for his friend Kenny Watkins, but Kenny wasn't there.

Hauled off to the county jail, he screamed that he knew his rights. A public defender came to see him. *Charged with murder! Shit, he never murdered no one. Aw, fuck. That was just some bullshit talk. He never went up to that field. I'm your defender, Billy, you've got to tell me the truth so I can help you. Yeah, I talked about it, and I might have sent him a text. But I was just fuckin' with him. I never went up there and I never meant to.*

The stolen contents of the Sanders' lake house were still "cooling down" in Billy's brother's old trailer. Billy denied having anything to do with it. Denied breaking into the lake house. Denied posting the videos or sending the emails. Denied, denied, denied. *Shit, all I was guilty of was mouthin' off about that faggot ruining the Rangers' season. You gotta get me out of here in time for the bowl game.*

To the end of his life, Billy decried the injustice of his incarceration, his ban from the message boards, and the refusal of the SportsBeast to take his calls. After all, he had done more than anyone else to make sure that homo didn't ruin the Rangers' recruiting class. Not his fault that it had happened anyway. He was the World's Greatest Rangers Fan.

"Dane . . . "

"Hi Roger."

"Listen, I'll come out there in a little while but for now it's easier if I follow things from downtown. How are you and Anne holding up? How are the kids?"

"We're . . . we're . . . what do you know, Roger?"

"They'll let you see him today. I'm sending a car to drive you."

"Can Anne see him? Is he . . . okay to see?"

"From what I understand, yes. But that's up to the two of you. It can be traumatic."

"She'll want to see him."

"There's more, Dane. From what I gather, the police think it was an accident. Of course, the medical examiner will be part of any final determination, but right now they think that his trigger caught on something as he was pulling his rifle out of the car. Do you understand me, Dane? An accident. Not suicide. Not murder."

Dane took a deep breath.

"Why was he pulling his rifle out of the car?"

"The girl that he allegedly assaulted. She indicated that someone was trying to lure him up there. My guess is that Dylan was trying to turn the tables, but we might never know."

The third week of Advent and the rose candle joins the two purple, which have already decreased as they burned. Gaudete Sunday: The parishioners of St. James rejoice in their cold stone castle.

O Come, O Come Emmanuel, and ransom captive Israel!

The pew where the Norrises usually find themselves is empty. Most of the parishioners know why. But the joyful hymns remain the same, and only the addition of the Norris family to the Mass intentions makes a ripple in the liturgical stream.

Monday afternoon. Anne lies on Maryanne's bed, her eyes red and puffy. Outside in the kitchen she can hear Janus and Emilia arguing. So stupid. Arguing over a video game while their brother lies cold and dead.

She hears the dogs barking. Either they've seen their own reflection in the front door glass, or there was a visitor. She didn't want a visitor. The doorbell rang and she heard the argument cease, and then heard Emilia scream: "Maryanne! Maryanne!"

Anne sat up in her bed in disbelief. And then she heard her oldest daughter's voice: "Emilia, you little punk. Jane."

She heard a bag fall to the floor, and as she turned the corner, there she was, Maryanne engulfed in Emilia's arms, Janus hugging them both. She wanted to rush forward, wanted to join them, but a voice in her head said: *You'll drive her away again.*

So she kept her distance and said: "Maryanne. Oh thank you! Thank you for coming home."

Maryanne looked up at her, tears making the dark eyeliner streak down her face. Her eyes cooled as she looked at her mother, and she simply said: "Mom, I had to come."

Maryanne was tall and dark-haired like her mother, with the same refined features and the smooth figure that had made Anne so attractive. But Maryanne's body was cultivated and emphasized, and there was a look in her eyes that spoke of carnal knowledge, of a hard, cold secret. Her long, dreadlocked hair hung down into a fur-lined, hooded coat slung over a low-cut tank-top and jeans. Her midriff was exposed, and a gold pendent hung just above her cleavage.

"Daddy! Daddy!" Emilia yelled down the stairs. "Maryanne's here!"

Dane and Maryanne spent a long time together. Maryanne vague about where she had come from and what she had been doing, pressing instead for answers about Dylan. The two had emerged upstairs where Anne and Emilia made a spaghetti dinner—Maryanne's favorite—and the family ate in silence under the oppression of the empty place at the table.

Anne had cleared out of Maryanne's room and had made the bed for her daughter, and as she sat on the comforter trying to decide where she would spend the night, Maryanne walked in. Anne looked up at her.

"I'm sorry; I was just finishing up in here."

"Emilia says this is where you've been sleeping."

"Yes."

"Going to sleep in Dylan's room now?" Maryanne asked, and the words came like a blow. *How could she be so cruel?*

"You know, I almost didn't come home because of you," Maryanne continued, and Anne sunk her head, waiting for the words. "I hope for your sake that you were better to Dylan."

Anne was quiet for a moment, and then a sort of resolve took her, and she looked up at Maryanne, blinking away the tears that had started to form.

"I hope I was too, honey. I tried to be . . . different than I was with you. I hope that was right. It may make you happy to know that Dylan carried on your fight. He was never the same with me after you left. He loved you, and he let me know in a thousand ways that he blamed me that you were gone."

Maryanne just stood there, looking at her mother, waiting for some reproach, some recrimination. But it didn't come.

"Maryanne, I'm . . . sorry. You can't know how sorry I am. I was just trying to be somebody that I'm just not good enough to be. I wanted you to be that person too. I wanted it so badly. But we're not that different, in the end. I hope you'll accept my apology. I hope you'll come home."

Maryanne looked at her suspiciously.

"And, Maryanne . . . can I stay in here with you tonight?" Anne asked, breaking down into sobs. "I'm so lonely. I'm so alone."

"Why? Why are you alone, Mom?" Maryanne asked, her voice still cold.

Anne looked up at her.

"I've done something terrible."

"What did you do?"

"I can't sleep with him. I cheated on him. I destroyed our marriage. I'm a whore."

Maryanne's head jerked as if she had been slapped. She stood back and closed the door behind her, then knelt to the floor where she could look up into Anne's face. She saw the incredible pain there, the intense sorrow for her lost son, the crushing burden of guilt, and sympathy began to well up.

"Mom, it's going to be okay. That happens, a lot. I never expected it from you. I never thought you would be one to do it."

"There's . . . there's more."

Maryanne waited.

"I think I might be pregnant. It's not . . . it's not your father's."

Like a dam bursting inside her, Maryanne was overcome with compassion and a desire to help this woman she had so recently reviled. She took her mother by the shoulders.

"Mom, Mom. Look at me. Look at me. You're going to come with me. I'll tell them I'm pregnant. You come and live with me and when the baby comes, it will be mine. It will be mine. He never has to know. We can do this. I will do this for you."

And then Maryanne's tears were falling as well, and she fell into her mother, the two of them clinging together as their agony joined and rose and fell. And much later, as they lay under her comforter, Emilia crept into the room and lay in her sister's arms as well.

Coach Carter reclined back in a chair in the war room watching his assistants wipe names from the dry-erase boards as they waited for the fax machine to start spitting pages. The first day of early signing period. The day when everything really happened. High school athletes had until Friday to commit early, but they almost always did it right away. The news feed on the LED screen showed other colleges posting their new signees, garbed in their college uniforms, striking poses. The mood in the room was subdued.

"Any word on Emerson?" Carter asked of no one specifically.

"Nothing yet," Coach Holloway answered.

"What about Beal?"

"Says he's still committed but not signing until February," Coach Quincy replied.

Carter looked across the room at the silent fax machine and then rubbed his eyes.

Monty Sanders sat across from President Jacoby and smiled.

"Tragic, tragic, of course. But also fortunate. Hearing about what he did to that poor girl. Of course, such a violent outburst might be explained by the pressure he was under. Terrible to put that young man in such a position. But no excuse, of course. No excuse. All in all, perhaps we saw his character. I, of course, have to think of my own son. I can't help but tell you that I feel as if we dodged a bullet. Imagine if their relationship had turned violent?

"But it's an ill wind that blows no one any good, and I think we made some real progress here on campus. We shouldn't lose the momentum that we gained. It would be awkward to do some sort of memorial, seeing what happened to the girl, but I think we should use this time to emphasize the consequences of bullying on all marginalized students—make it into a campus-wide event, maybe a week against violence. Not just physical violence but the social violence that makes people feel like they aren't welcome.

"Also, I'm happy to spearhead this thing, but you really need to make this part of an official office here. I'm just the chair of a non-sanctioned, independent committee. And I should also let you know that while I'll obviously help out as long as I can, I have been contacted recently by some other schools, and I'm strongly considering that interest. It might be better for my son to be away from Asheville at this time, and of course, I am not tenured here . . ."

The weaselly young man was there again, profaning the vast office of Clyde Cox Jr.

"It's going from bad to worse. They associate you now with the kid's death."

"Like hell they do. I had nothing to do with it."

"But beforehand, you became the face of the . . . opposition to the scholarship."

"But, I mean, shit. He sent a girl to the hospital. He's nobody's hero. They should see now that I was right. Bad character."

"It doesn't work like that. The public isn't rational. They can believe both that you are somehow responsible for his death and that he was a rotten kid who beat up girls. The difference is, you're here and he's not."

"Is this just more of your social media crap? I mean, do any REAL people think this shit?"

"We've had four more instances of vandalism at your stores.

And some of your numbers are dropping. Unusual for the week before Christmas."

"Yeah, I know. I already saw the numbers. I don't think they're related."

"Well, you better hope not. Or give some more thought to getting ahead of this. You've got to make some changes. This isn't your dad's world anymore."

"People keep saying that. Now get out."

Transcript, WULC *Saturday Morning Show*

Burroughs: And now over to Kelly Briar for more on the ongoing controversy at Biltmore College. Kelly . . .

Briar: Good morning, Tad. There's more trouble for beleaguered booster Clyde Cox Jr., as this morning he faces accusations of harassment. Two women, students at Biltmore College, are stating that the billionaire and his guests showed a pattern of harassment at their elite luxury box at Seely Stadium. The women, who are remaining anonymous, were students at Biltmore College at the time that they allege the harassment to have occurred. We've reached out to Cox, Inc. and to Clyde Cox Jr. for comment. A lawyer for Mr. Cox indicated that they denied all charges and looked forward to clearing the billionaire's name. In the meantime, the women's advocacy group "ListenNow!" is asking for any other students or employees at Seely Stadium who might have experienced harassment to come forward.

Burroughs: A very disturbing turn of events, Kelly. Does the university have any comment?

Briar: A spokesperson for Biltmore College said that they are looking into these allegations seriously and that they have always strived to maintain a safe and respectful environment for the students and staff who are employed at Seely Stadium's Club Level.

Chapter 19

FIVE PENITENTS

He waited for the crying to stop, and then gently asked, "Is there anything else?"

There was silence, punctuated by a couple more sobs. Then Anne's voice became steadier.

"Yes, Father." More silence.

"About three weeks before . . . about a month ago, before . . . before my son died, I had relations with a man who was not my husband. I committed adultery."

Fr. Dixon was silent for a moment. Strange, he thought, how language in the confessional suddenly became so strict and precise. The confessional was home to all the formal vocabulary of sin, never the vernacular. Instead of "I fucked someone else," it was "I had relations with another man." Never "I gave it to him up the ass," but rather "I committed the sin of Sodom." A thousand "impure thoughts" for every "I wanted to get naked." People he never would have expected it of suddenly spoke of *concupiscence* and *custody of the eyes* like they were lawyers poring over the catechism and looking for the cleanest way to make their sins more remote. Perhaps he should blame the little "examination of conscience" booklets, or perhaps it was just that people laying their sins before an almighty God put away the language they used with each other. It was, after all, the language of their sins.

"And you have stopped coming to confession until now. Have you taken the Eucharist in that time?"

"No, Father."

"Good. Then you have not compounded your sin. Does your husband know?"

"Not yet."

"You plan to tell him?"

"I can't . . . now. But he'll know. I think I might be pregnant."

"And it can't be your husband's?"

"We haven't had relations in a while. He'll know it's not his. He had a vasectomy. I told him not to. I told him it was wrong."

"Oh, Anne. Oh, dear Anne," Fr. Dixon was quiet as he considered this poor woman.

"I know. I know . . . " she whispered. "I'm damned."

"You are not, Anne. Listen carefully now. You are bearing terrible, terrible burdens. Some of your own making, and others that were thrust upon you. Your road to peace will be long, and some of it, the pain of losing your child, will never depart from you. You understand that?"

On the other side of the screen, Anne nodded her head. She understood it far better than the priest.

"But you are not damned, Anne. There is no sin so great that it cannot be forgiven. It is God's place to forgive, and He does. The only thing you can do, the only way you can truly be damned, is to reject that forgiveness."

"I . . . don't want to."

"The devil, Anne, is both consoler and accuser. Before the sin, he whispers 'It's okay. You deserve this.' But once you have sinned, he becomes the accuser, and tells you 'You are worthless; you cannot be redeemed.'"

"I have heard that voice," Anne said quietly.

"Then you must surely know that the devil always lies. Reject him, Anne, not the mercy of God. You can walk out of this confessional today with the sin removed, if not the burden of it on your heart. You can walk out with your soul intact, prepared to amend your wrongs and accept the life where God leads you. Do you reject Satan?"

A whisper: "I do."

"And all his evil works, and all his empty promises?"

"I do."

"For your penance, I will ask you to observe the Novena to Divine Mercy, beginning this Friday. You know it, I assume? Now, pray your Act, Anne."

Anne's voice was broken. She went from word to word taking in great gasps of air, and as she recited the prayer, her shoulders sagged and her head came forward until the mantilla over her hair touched the screen.

"O my God, I am heartily sorry for having offended Thee, and I detest all my sins because of Thy just punishments, but most of all because they offend Thee, my God, who is all good and worthy of all my love. I firmly resolve, with the help of Thy grace, to sin no more, and to avoid all occasion of sin. Amen."

Fr. Dixon intoned slowly and with emphasis on every word:

"God the Father of mercies

through the death and resurrection of His Son

has reconciled the world to Himself

and sent the Holy Spirit among us for the forgiveness of sins;

through the ministry of the Church may God give you pardon and peace,

and I absolve you from your sins

in the name of the Father,

and of the Son,

and of the Holy Spirit."

Anne exited the confessional and walked down the aisle of St. James, then out the front door to the parking lot, where Maryanne and Emilia waited in the Land Rover.

Thursday morning, and the confessional door opened. He was there by appointment, and so, of course, there were no illusions about anonymity. But Dane had insisted on the confessional, even after they had spent the weary half hour together selecting the hymns and readings for the funeral Mass.

"In the name of the Father, the Son, and the Holy Spirit. Bless me Father, for I have sinned. It has been about nine months since my last confession. I came before Easter, last Lent. My wife makes me do that. I haven't honestly wanted to go to confession . . . probably ever. We didn't, for years, when we were first married . . . "

Fr. Dixon prepared himself for what was likely a long, rambling account. But he knew the sorrow this man was bearing, and he knew more than that.

". . . and then, well . . . I've been here at Mass almost every Sunday. I've done all the things I'm supposed to do. But I'm just going through the motions. I drink too much, I eat too much, I take pills. And I have lost two children. One might come back. But the other, my son. My oldest son. He is gone. I didn't see him going. He was so strong, so like me. Nothing could hurt him. I wouldn't let my wife hurt him, wouldn't let her drive him away. I didn't blame her; I wasn't angry at what happened to Maryanne. But I wouldn't let her do it to Dylan. And she didn't try. She changed too. And maybe that was wrong. Maybe if I had listened to her, made sure he was going to church more . . . I don't know."

"Is there something specific weighing on your conscience?"

"No, Father. But when I close my eyes, and when I sleep, I see my son's face. I see him in agony. He wasn't . . . he wasn't doing good things when he died. All my life I haven't thought much about heaven or hell. I've had a pretty good life, and I think I've been a pretty good person. Sure, I did some stuff to excess but I never really hurt anybody. But Dylan . . . Dylan died and never had a chance to redeem himself. Why? Why was he taken in the middle of his sins?"

"Do you know the Bible verse concerning the tower of Siloam?"

"No, no I don't."

"It's strange. Not many people do. It is one of those neglected parts of the Gospel of Luke. Let me read it to you." Dane could hear him thumbing through pages.

"Now on the same occasion there were some present who reported to Him about the Galileans whose blood Pilate had mixed with their sacrifices. And Jesus said to them, 'Do you suppose that these Galileans were greater sinners than all other Galileans because they suffered this fate? I tell you, no, but unless you repent, you will all likewise perish. Or do you suppose that those eighteen on whom the tower in Siloam fell and killed them were worse culprits than all the men who live in Jerusalem? I tell you, no, but unless you repent, you will all likewise perish.'"

"What do you think Jesus is telling us?"

"I . . . I don't know."

"It is human nature to equate death with sin. We point at people who sin and suffer and say they deserve it, and we point at people who sin and don't suffer and feel cheated. But what Christ says here is that death falls upon men as part of the nature of the world and not as a temporal consequence of sin. That is why we are always to be watchful, for none of us knows the hour of our death, and we can neither earn it nor forestall it by our evil or goodness."

"I understand, but what about Dylan? I can't bear it . . . if there is a hell . . . that my son is condemned . . . that he will suffer eternally."

Fr. Dixon's voice became calmer.

"Dane, our God is merciful. No one knows a man's heart but God. We in the world may know of sin, may look at a great sinner and say 'that man cannot be redeemed,' but we don't know. What we do know is that our God loved us so much that He sent His own Son to suffer and die on our behalf, to save us from our sins. Do you think such a God would fail to have mercy on your own son?"

"Then what is the point? What is the point of all of this? Why would we have to do all of this if at the end, God will just say 'here I am'?"

"Dane, I am sure, in your many games, that you have won at the end by what is called a 'Hail Mary.'"

"Yes, a few times."

"Was that ever your game plan? Did you ever go into a game and say 'We're going to win this by a last-second pass'?"

"Of course not."

"Nor should you do so with your salvation. Those who live their life loving God do His will and love Him. And though we sometimes sin, He is always there waiting. Those who live their life apart from Him, who become farther and farther away, it becomes harder for them to return, harder to love Him. In some respects, those who are taken from us when they are young . . . I believe they are closer to God, for the world has had less time to draw them away. But even if they are apart from Him, God is merciful."

Dane was silent.

"Hope, Dane. Hope. Reflect on God's mercy. And more, remember that God, in His mercy, sent his Son to us, who redeemed us. Let your mercy redeem your son. Look for it, Dane. God will show you how, and when it comes, be merciful. Is there anything else?"

"No, Father."

"For your penance, pray the rosary with the intention of the salvation of your son. Do you know your Act of Contrition?"

"Yes."

The Saturday before Christmas. The following day the last candle of Advent would be lit, and the waning sun would begin to wax as the light returned. But this morning, St. James was somber. The wrecked body of Dylan Norris lay under the pall, and the small congregation of the Norris family stood in the pews, black clad, as the words were read and the hymns sung.

Two members of the Knights of Columbus stood at the doors, saying quietly "This is a private service" to the one or two people who entered the vestibule. St. James had been accommodating to the family's request to keep the funeral from the public, and only one "stranger" sat in the back of the church, quiet and unobserved, watching as the family, with the exception of Maryanne, shuffled from their pews to join with the body of Christ.

Dane, Roger, Janus, Richard, George, and Randy Thompson walked beside the coffin, lifted it down the stairs, and watched as it entered the back of the hearse. Then the small procession of SUVs followed along through the narrow streets to the old Catholic Cemetery. To the Norris family graves, crowded together. The older graves with their weeping angels and tree stumps. The newer graves were simply stones or plaques embedded in the ground. The fresh-broken earth where Dylan's body would rest, a scar on the earth in the cold air. The family huddled together as the holy water was sprinkled and watched as the casket was lowered into the ground. Then they turned and made their way back to the Norris farm.

As the day waned, the extended family drifted away, and on the cold Saturday night, Dane and Anne found themselves alone, upstairs in the house. Maryanne, Janus, and Emilia were downstairs, huddled together. Anne sat in the kitchen, looking vacantly out the window.

"Are you going to sleep in the guest room tonight?" Dane asked, quietly.

Anne was silent, still looking out at the darkness. And then finally spoke.

"I . . . have something to tell you. But I can't bear it now. Not on the day that we . . . buried him."

"I have something to tell you as well. I would rather do it now than go on like this. Anne, I can't do this alone. I can't."

She looked at him with pain in her eyes.

"Come here. I want to show you something," he said, and then walked into the living room.

She sat in one of the easy chairs, and Dane pressed the power button on the remote, then fumbled on his phone to cast something to the screen. Anne felt a sudden premonition, and then there it was in grayscale.

For some reason, Anne's eyes kept going back to the little time counter in the corner. There were the dogs, rushing to the door, barking. There she was, putting her book on the end table, Emilia's bookmark next to it. Twenty seconds in, she's cracked the door and speaking through it. A minute later, she's handing Tim the bottle of water. Details assaulted her. At the three-minute mark, there's her hand scratching the couch, her other hand on his back, the sudden, brief glimmer of the diamond on her engagement ring. For the next thirty seconds he lies on top of her. The dogs lie on the floor, heads up, watching. The little pumpkin bookmark slips off the end table and flutters to the rug. Then he sits up and she runs for the bathroom. Less than four minutes from the time she heard the car until she was throwing up in the bathroom. Less than four minutes to destroy her marriage. Less than four minutes to create an unwanted, terrifying life. Four minutes that had gone by so quickly that night, now excruciatingly slow with her husband standing with his back to her. His phone was in his hand; he could stop it at any time.

Anne's mouth was agape, her eyes wide.

"You might think I made you watch that to torture you. I didn't. After Dylan died, I went to see if the cameras were on. The monitors were off, but the system was still recording. I found the video and saw Dylan leaving. And then I found this. I don't show this to you to make you hurt. I showed this to you to tell you that I know what happened. I saw the empty bottle. I saw my wife. Lonely. Alone. I saw how quickly it happened, and I saw you run away. I saw him leave and I saw you crushed, and crying."

Her head was bowed. She couldn't look at him.

"Anne, I'm sorry. I didn't know. I should have known. I haven't been a good husband to you. I didn't know you needed this. I am as much to blame . . . more than you. I forgive you. Please let me."

Anne kept her head down, and then raised it.

"You're a good man. I never wanted to hurt you. I love you,

Dane. But there's something else you have to know. I'm pregnant. I took the test yesterday."

She saw the words hit him. Saw his eyes harden for a moment, saw comprehension before he closed them. Saw his fists ball up and his broad shoulders tense, his head draw upward and a breath pull in.

Behind Dane's clenched eyes, he clung to Fr. Dixon's words and pleaded: *Mercy. Mercy. Mercy. Dear God. Dear God! Have mercy on me. Have mercy on Dylan. Mercy. Mercy. Mercy.*

He let his breath out slowly and opened his eyes as tears rolled down his cheeks. He walked slowly to Anne, sank to his knees, and took his wife in his arms.

The January sky was steel gray, and a cold drizzle of rain came in staccato waves against the tall roof of St. James.

The door opened, and someone sat down. They were still, just breathing for a long time. Finally Fr. Dixon asked, through the screen, "May I help you?"

A voice came back from the other side.

"Uh, I'm not sure how to do this."

"Is this your first confession?"

"Yeah."

"Are you Catholic?"

"No."

"Have you been baptized? Are you a Christian?"

"No, Father."

"Then why are you here?"

"This is the place I can come and tell you anything, right? You have to keep it secret?"

"No, no, I'm sorry. You misunderstand. Confession is a sacrament, and the seal of the confessional applies to that sacrament. I cannot let you think that that seal is binding upon me as a priest if it is not in the context of the sacrament, and I cannot minister in the sacrament unless you are properly disposed to receive it."

"Oh." There was a deep disappointment in the voice.

"But I can make you a promise as a man," Fr. Dixon said, "that I will hold confidential anything you care to unburden yourself of, so long as I do not violate my civic or legal duty by withholding it. Do you understand this?"

"I guess. I mean, you know who I am, right?"

"Yes. It's a voice I know and love."

"Love? What do you mean love? If you know who I am . . . "

"Brad, I love all my students, but you in particular."

"What? Why? I'm the thorn in your side."

"Why? Because of all my students, you are the closest to God."

There was a snort from behind the screen.

"Father, you know that's not true. I fight against everything you say."

"You don't fight with me. You wrestle with God. You wrestle with great intellect and strength. But you wrestle. And you cannot do that without being close to Him. And you cannot win. For many others who you might think pious, God is in the distance, accepted and ignored. But for you, He seems to be the central fact of your life."

There was silence, then Fr. Dixon said: "Brad, do you still want to confess? I understand if you do not."

"Well, Father, if you won't say anything to anyone, mostly my parents . . . "

"I promise."

"How do I become . . . Catholic?"

"I don't understand, Brad. Do you mean, how can you be received into the Church?"

"Yeah, I guess so."

"Well, at your age, and since you have not been baptized, there is a process called Rite of Christian Initiation for Adults, or RCIA."

"What is that all about?"

"You take classes and meet with a group of others who are also discerning, and then if you are still desirous, you are baptized and confirmed. Usually at Easter."

"Do I have to do that? What if I just want to be baptized?"

"Is it an emergency? Do you have to be baptized immediately? Are you in grave danger?"

"No, no. Nothing like that. I'd rather just do it quietly and then see if it does anything."

"If I know you at all, Brad, you have read about this already. What is motivating this?"

"Baptism washes away our sins, right?"

"Yes."

"So I want to try that. I want to see what it's like. I want to feel not having any sins."

"But you don't want your parents to know?"

"No."

"So you want to come to Christ in secret and see what He can do for you."

"You say it in a crass way, Father. But I'm not afraid. That's exactly right."

"You want to put a slug in the vending machine and see if a Coke pops out."

"Okay, even more crass. But still correct."

"It won't. *Thou shalt not put the Lord thy God to the test . . .* "

"Yes, I remember that, Father. From when the devil tempts Jesus in the desert, and Jesus quotes scripture at him. But what you're saying is that baptism, which is supposed to be the Holy Spirit descending on someone and wiping away their sins, depends not on the omnipotence of the Holy Spirit but on the miserable person and whether they really, really want it. What about babies, then? They can't even put a slug in the vending machine. Someone else puts it in for them."

"Well, Brad, you have your own crass way of putting things, but clearly you see the difference between a reasoning person and a baby. Your vaunted free will, which we have discussed so much, is the key to that problem. You can reflect on this, but in the meantime, if you are really serious, then you can enter into the RCIA process, and I can help you do it . . . surreptitiously, although I don't recommend that. If you are unwilling to let your parents know, then I suspect that there is a little more than just a test of God that is behind this. Why be embarrassed before your parents if this is nothing more than another way to show the silliness of the Church? If you emerge unchanged by grace, then can't you stand up and say 'see I told you so'?"

Brad was silent.

"You know I'm gay, right?"

"Of course. You have been the center of a very public . . . uh . . . outing."

"Yes, Father, but I'm really gay. I mean, it wasn't just gay sex. I don't know if you know this, but there are a lot of guys that have gay sex, but it's . . . perversion? That is, there are guys who can have sex with a man but aren't really able to love another man. Does that make sense?"

"Yes it does, Brad."

"Well, I'm really gay. I am not attracted to women. I'm attracted to men, and I want to love them and be loved by them."

"And?"

"And so, knowing that, could you baptize me? Could you wash away my sins knowing that I'd just keep being gay?"

"Being gay is not a sin, Brad."

"Yeah, yeah, I know. It's the act, not the orientation. But I'd know. I'd know that I'd always feel that."

"Brad, the Church recognizes as grave sin not only sodomy and other carnal acts between men, but carnal acts between men and women, or between women, outside of marriage. There is indeed a different burden on gays because the Church cannot recognize a valid marriage between them, and thus carnal acts are always sinful, but no more so than for a bachelor, or a woman who never marries. Marriage is, for Catholics, a special way of giving yourself to God, not a license to have sex. Not everyone is called to that vocation.

Others are called to be single. Still others are called to have their fraternal fellowship in the priesthood."

"But without sex."

"You speak of sex as if it is the fulfillment. And I understand. That is the doctrine of this world. But sex is far from the fulfillment. There is a deep biological urge to procreate, and it drives us all, even when our orientation means that procreation is not possible."

"OUR orientation?"

Fr. Dixon continued without responding.

"But procreation, while it may be biological fulfillment, is not spiritual fulfillment. When you picture a life without sex, you may picture yourself growing old and lonely while the pleasures of the body remain untouched for some esoteric reason. That is what the world whispers in your ear: You have one life. Don't waste it. Do the thing that feels good. You may never have another chance."

"And what if it's right?"

"Then why become baptized? Both the world and Christ cannot be right. You should know that from logic, Brad. The principle of noncontradiction. You know your Aristotle."

"So, Father. If I'm willing to go through your RCIA, and I'm willing to tell my parents that I'm doing it not just as a test, but because something is really calling to me, and I get up and put on a white robe and you pour water on my head, and I wake up the next day and still ache for love . . . "

"Brad, I cannot promise you that you will feel Christ's love enfolding you for the rest of your life, that you will wake up after baptism like you would wake up on the morning of a honeymoon, that you will never feel lonely, never feel disappointment or let down, or never wish you felt physical arms around you. I can promise you this, though. That if you truly open your heart to Christ, if you give yourself to Him completely, that the consolations in both this life and in the next will rank beside the most perfect marriage or the saintliest priesthood."

Brad was quiet. Finally he said: "Father, thank you for your time. You've given me a lot to think about, and I will. If I decide to do the RCIA, I'd like to do it here at St. James, with you."

"I would be honored, Brad. Now, do you mind if I say a prayer for you?"

"No."

O Glorious patriarch St. Joseph, I urgently recommend to you the soul of Brad Sanders, which Jesus redeemed at the price of His Precious Blood.

Thou knowest how deplorable is the state and how unhappy the life of those who have banished this loving Savior from their hearts, and how greatly they are exposed to the danger of losing Him eternally.

Permit not, I beseech thee, that a soul so dear to me should continue any longer in its evil ways; preserve it from the danger that threatens it; touch the heart and mind of the prodigal child and conduct him back to the bosom of the merciful Father.

Abandon him not, I implore thee, till thou hast opened to him the gates of heaven, where he will praise and bless thee throughout eternity for the happiness which he will owe to thy intercession. Amen.

"Thank you, Father," Brad said, rising from the kneeler.

He opened the door and stepped out, and the little light above the door flashed to green.

THE END of Book One

About the Author

JT Dwyer lives near Asheville with his wife Elizabeth, three-quarters of his children, two dogs, and an ever-growing number of chickens. JT is southern born and bred, a graduate of the University of Dayton with a degree in history, and is a big fan of mercy, being so often in need of it.

Made in the USA
Monee, IL
20 October 2022

be80a347-e6b5-4789-bf39-22e7d3730da6R01